All in a Day's Work

The daily graft of a detective inspector

By Ron Larby

The names and identities of the characters have been changed.

therefore:

The events depicted do not relate to any person living or dead but, if a retired detective feels it might be he or she well......................think hard about your criminal misdeeds!

Read on.........................

Published by New Generation Publishing in 2014

Copyright © Ron Larby 2014

First Edition

The author asserts the moral right under the Copyright, Designs and Patents Act 1988 to be identified as the author of this work.

All Rights reserved. No part of this publication may be reproduced, stored in a retrieval system or transmitted, in any form or by any means without the prior consent of the author, nor be otherwise circulated in any form of binding or cover other than that in which it is published and without a similar condition being imposed on the subsequent purchaser.

www.newgeneration-publishing.com

New Generation Publishing

To Vivi, my darling wife, without whose patience, tolerance and input this story would never have been written.

Chapter one

The dawn temperature was barely above freezing as Don Masters, huddled in his anorak, pulled his Jaguar over and killed the engine. He and the thickset younger man beside him hunched round to stare down the long shingled driveway to snow-dusted farm buildings a couple of hundred yards away.

'Remember, Andy, it must be out of sight'. Masters said quietly. 'Behind the one on the right will do it'.

Nodding and staring, Andy asked 'Whose drum is it?'.

'Not your concern. Carry out your instructions and if it goes right there's a monkey in it'.

'When's it to be?'.

Masters looked sideways at the lounging man who was fishing out a cigarette and fumbling for a lighter. Mention of five hundred pounds hadn't apparently registered. 'Got a deal have we?'

Andy Knowles let a grin crease his face. 'Sounds about right, Don'.

Masters, satisfied, nodded. 'Tomorrow at 8.15 am be in The Green Welly café. I'll be there to give you the nod'. He handed over two keys on a ring. 'Use these - and wear gloves', he added with a smile at the easily overlooked detail.

'Naturally. How do I get back?'.

'Lay on a mate to pick you up - but not on the premises. The finger mustn't see you leaving'.

'D'you want these back?'.Knowles jangled the keys.

'Masters nodded. 'We'll have a meet tomorrow evening in the Green Welly. Seen enough?'.

Knowles nodded and slid down in his seat. 'Piece of cake, Don'.

*

24 years old Dianne Flaxman's to date unsolved murder was uppermost in Master's thoughts when he arrived at the lorry park to meet up with Andy Knowles. Her body had been discovered two weeks before on the 15th of November. She had been a pretty thing, three years into her marriage to Kevin, by all accounts a loving husband. Her raped and naked body had been found on a freezing cold morning by two youngsters scavenging for golf balls in the out of bounds wide stream between the 10th fairway of the local golf course, and a road fronting a row of terraced council houses. The lads, Douglas and Francis Scott, 10 and 12 years old, lived in one of them. Her nightmarish end was captured in mottled features of strangulation, confirmed by the inch wide weal around her neck. Pasapula, the pathologist, had pointed out a pattern of what he thought was a a belt buckle because, he conjectured, a central abrasion was probably caused by a securing metal clip that had puckered her flesh. 'If we can find the belt, the pattern, hopefully', he gave Masters a quick glance, ' could be matched with its buckle'. He traced the indent in the woman's neck. 'Quite deep, Don. A very determined killer'.

Parking in the gravelled area of the café, his mind still on the enquiry which two weeks on had hit the buffers, he climbed out of his Jaguar and glanced across at Knowles, who was wearing an old pair of overalls for the occasion, clambering out of an oldish Consul. He smiled. Nice touch Andy. Ambling towards the café he inclined his head to the lorry. He went in first and bought a coffee and newspaper. Glancing around he spotted the target driver filling his face and inclined his head to Knowles, who had drifted beside him and was paying for a cup of tea. Each man went to separate tables. Masters sipped his coffee and looked over at Andy who had his cup in his hand and was peering at a newspaper he'd found on his table. After a few minutes Masters was satisfied the driver was concentrating on his breakfast and caught Knowles' eye and nodded in the direction of the lorry park. Knowles put down the cup, left the paper, and walked out. Masters watched him through a window make his way to the articulated container lorry, unlock it and climb in. When it had trundled out of the lorry park he glanced at the unsuspecting driver, who was by then downing his tea and burying his nose in a newspaper.

Smiling his satisfaction, he told himself a few minutes later when he dropped into his car. 'So far, Don. Sweet as a nut".

5am the next morning, tired. burly, detective sergeant Dusty Miller, no tie as usual and this time unshaven, settled himself beside detective inspector Masters in his Jaguar and grumbled at the early start. 'What's so urgent, Don?, he asked as he slid down. He'd spent an hour the previous evening on Betty, his tasty bit from the flying squad typist's pool; and then given Valerie, his unsuspecting wife, her share. He fidgeted with his crotch and shot a glance at the DI, who hadn't answered. 'What we into here then, Don? Why so early?'.

The DI smiled and looked across at his friend. 'Nice little earner, Dusty'. He started the engine and moved off. 'My snout has done us proud'.

'Used him before?' Miller queried after he'd lit up.

Masters nodded while he overtook a lorry. 'Couple of times'. He flicked a smile at his friend. 'He shopped the firm pulling the Hatton Garden blag'.

Miller nodded disinterestedly and opened a bag on the dashboard and peered at the sliced contents. 'Jean make these?'.

When Masters nodded he pushed the bag away. He settled back and stared down the road, his thoughts jumbling the past with the present, momentarily reliving Dianne Flaxman's murder, the image of her strangled, naked body hardening his penis. Beautiful. A right turn on. Sorting his crotch out and dragging his mind back he glanced at his friend while he finally sorted out his discomfort. 'How's Jean? Been a while since we had a night out. Val keeps on about it. Love a natter don't they'.

Masters smiled and eased the car into the flow along the A13 and picked up speed. 'Got a problem down there!'. He shot a quick smile at the sergeant before concentrating on the road ahead. 'How are things now between you two?'.

Miller pulled his unbuttoned coat tight, shut his eyes and yawned. 'About the same. Arguing most of the time. Frankly, Don, I've had it up to here'.

Masters nodded and said nothing. Jean had said Val was unhappy more than once. 'I'll have a word with Jean', he said 'Maybe they can get together'.

Miller opened his eyes and pulled the bag of sandwiches onto his lap and peeked disinterestedly at the curled bacon. 'Hundred per cent this one, Don?', he muttered as he pulled out a sandwich.

'Had a meet last night', Masters told him. 'Like I said, he's done us proud. It's there. Not far now. Pass me one of those'. Taking the sandwich he nudged the sergeant and nodded at two police cars in a lay by ahead. 'Essex coppers'.

He eased the car over and stopped beside the first one. Getting out, he thrust out a hand to the detective in the front seat. 'Masters', he said with a smile. 'You've been briefed?'.

'Yes, guv. Follow you do we?'.

Masters nodded. 'Should be interesting. When we

get there I'll spin off to a barn on the right of the drive. You go ahead to the only other barn. If I'm right you'll have a busy day. We'll do the nicking'.

Fifteen minutes later the three cars crunched down the unlit shingled drive, Masters easing his to the right and behind the asbestos-sheeted barn he'd pointed out to Knowles. The Essex cars went straight ahead to the other large barn which, if Masters' information was right, housed the evidence of a successful run-in.

Andy had carried out his instructions perfectly: Until he'd turned the corner there was no sign of the lorry: but it was there, with the back end facing him. Masters clambered out, crossed to it and pulled on the lock securing the two hinged doors. Fishing the keys Andy had returned from a pocket he opened the doors and smiled at his expectant pay day stacked neatly on pallets in front of him. Giving Miller a thumbs up he closed and locked the doors. Dropping into his car he grinned at Miller, who was climbing beside him. Reversing and three pointing, he drove ahead and manoeuvred his car beside one of the police cars outside the second barn. Staring up at the nearest detective he said, 'Good hunting there. Don't wait for us: bust in'.

Easing the car into gear he trundled to the house. Handing the lorry keys to Miller he pointed to a detached building beside the house. 'Let's have a shufty - my snout says its used as an office'. Masters eased a partly open side window further open and noticed the desk his snout had told him about. The DI angled his head at the window to Miller. 'In the desk'll do it'. Miller climbed in and placed the keys in a drawer of the desk.

Five minutes later Joyce Woodhall, the farmer's wife, draped in a dog-eared dressing gown and hair bedraggled, opened the door to Masters' insistent ring and was pushed to one side by Miller. With the DI close behind, he ran up the stairs and went into the lit bedroom and grabbed Woodall, wearing Y fronts, on the point of getting up from the bed, his face a picture of angry surprise. His wife had recovered her composure and followed them up. Standing in the open doorway she stared at the goings on and let rip a tirade of foul-mouthed abuse. Miller ignored her and turned her husband face down and pinned his arms, gesturing impatiently to Masters to snap the cuffs on. Ignoring angry pillow-muffled cursing and the wife's ranting, Miller dragged him from the bed.

'You're nicked, me old son', Masters told him. 'Grab his gear from that chair, Dusty. We'll take him as he is'.

'What's going on! Who are you? What's this all about?' Woodall shouted as he was propelled down the stairs.

'You're coming with us, so can it mate', Miller told him.

Hauled out of the house struggling and swearing he felt the pain of Miller's hand yanking his hair and the shingles stabbing at his bare feet before he was pushed into the Jaguar.

'Sit tight mate, and shut it'. Miller threw the man's clothing in and leaned against the car and shook out a cigarette. Lighting it, he enjoyed the sensation of smoke ruining his lungs, as Val, in one of her more convivial moods, warned him it would.

Masters meanwhile had crossed to the other barn and stood beside the group of officers standing and staring at cut up cabs and lorry engines on the concreted floor.

'My Christ, sir', one officer said. This bastard's been well at it'.

'Well -get on with it then', he told him brusquely. 'We're not here for a bloody picnic'.

*

Later that morning the lorry was back at it's base and detective chief superintendent George Makepeace, unusually good humoured, stood beside the transport manager, who had finished supervising the unloading of the palletized cigarettes onto his loading dock.

'All there?' he asked anxiously as he stared at the outcome of yet another Masters' caper.

The clearly relieved manager nodded and turned to shake Masters' and Miller's hands. 'Well done inspector...sergeant. Eighty thousand pounds that lot. I don't mind telling you I thought my driver was in it up to his bloody neck'.

Masters smiled with practised modesty. The man was right but it was another driver who'd taken the bung for the duplicate keys. 'All in a day's work, sir. I'll need the delivery notes, and a valuation statement from the shipper'.

Makepeace had heard it all before from the two officers. Look at them, he thought, butter wouldn't melt. Masters was smiling when the manager pushed the documents into his hand; and Miller was his usual arrogant self, lolling against wrapped palletized cigarettes and, unknown to him, contemplating what he would do with his cut.

'Well done Inspector', he said grudgingly. 'Full report on my desk in the morning'.

*

Woodall had been dumped in a cell, his clothes chucked at him and left to ponder a shaky future for two hours before Miller stood smiling in the opened doorway, beckoning. 'On your feet Woodall. Time for a chat'.

Half an hour later, with Masters' accusation of

receiving giving his stomach the gyp, Woodall's indignant claim of innocence was being met with natural amusement. Detective constable Barton, who had earlier been dispatched with a team of constables to the farm and had searched the office, as directed, and found the lorry keys sat, watched and learned, as Masters had told him to. He smiled at the way his guvnor was going at the prisoner.

'Bit pat that mate' Masters answered coldly to the last of Woodall's hoarse, useless, denials. Like Miller he was experiencing the effects of the early start and feeling a wee bit grumpy. But with Barton as a witness the performance was necessary. 'Give me his name. Give me a description I can go on. I'm not wearing that someone walks down your drive and asks if he can leave his lorry overnight. A right load of bollocks. Try again'.

Barton was impressed with his guvnor. Catching his eye he gave an approving thumbs up.

'But it's the truth. I swear it! Youngish man - thirtyish - well built. He told me the lorry was playing up. Sounded like it: grating gears down my drive. Like a fool....... yeh, I know', he said to clearly disbelieving detectives. ' I said he could leave it overnight'.

'Give me a name'.

'I don't know his name! I'd never seen him before. I told him he could use my phone'.

'Did he?'.

'I don't know for Christ's sake He told me he'd stay in the cab until a mechanic turned up in the morning'.

'So where was he when we turned up?'.

'How do I know. I've told you the truth. I swear it'.

'Bollocks. What about the keys?'.

'What frigging keys?'.

'The ones in your office'.

'What you going on about?

'Very careless Woodall'. Masters stared over Woodall's head at Miller, and then at Barton, who was grinning, and inclined his head at the prisoner 'Load of crap?'.

'Definitely, guv' Miller answered with a satisfied smile as he exhaled. Valerie might be right, but the smoke was doing its stuff.

Barton was enjoying the interrogation. His guvnor was on top form.

The DI transferred his gaze to the burly unshaven Woodall. 'I'm not satisfied with your statement of innocence. The charge, Woodall, is receiving a lorry load of cigarettes, knowing it had been stolen. Bang him up again, Dusty. We'll sort him out later'.

*

An hour later both detectives were tucking into fry ups in the canteen. Downing the last bit of bacon Masters sat back, yawned and stared at a lonely egg on a now greasy plate. 'Jesus, Dusty, I'm knackered. You don't look any better'. Sliding his fork under the cold egg yolk he paused and reflected on what had developed the previous day. 'Judging by the cut up cabs and engines he's been at it for some time'. He balanced the egg and squirted it with tomato sauce and downed it whole, his thought shifting to the murdered young woman. 'Can we be sure Dianne's hubby's in the clear?'.

Miller nodded. 'His alibi's a hundred per cent'.

'Sure of that?'.

'Can't be off it, Don. Works for Aldriges, you know, the furniture outfit on Elizabeth Way. Knocked off work at 5.30pm the day she went missing. Nipped home for his darts. Workmates back him up from eight until ten. They were in the Dog and Partridge, works dart match against Woolards, engineering outfit next to

Aldriges'. Several drinkers saw him. They've all made statements'.

Masters digested the information. With his wife last seen at Gym's Place around 9pm and disappearing the chances were his alibi was a hundred percent. 'Was she a tom?'. Masters downed the egg and studied his friend, who seemed suddenly disinterested.

Shrugging, Miller said 'There's no evidence of it. Her old man went potty when I put that to him. All we've got is she left work that evening to go to a keep fit class at Gym's Place. Complete dead end'.

'Dorothy Perkins wasn't it? Who covered that end?'.

'Did it myself, Don. Been there with Val a couple of times. Seen her. Val chatted to her as I recall. Worked there four years apparently. Nice girl everyone reckons. Left work that evening around 5.30pm. Reappeared at Gym's Place around 7.30pm. I work out there myself: never seen her there'.

Masters took a sip from his cup and showed his surprise. 'Didn't know you were into that stuff?'.

Miller shrugged. 'Need to keep fit. The job don't help'.

Masters put his empty cup down. 'Fancy another one?'.

Miller nodded. Loading his fork he changed the subject. 'Miss the Yard, Don?'. he studied the result. 'Crap this'.

'Mine was alright. No, glad to be away, really. Malcolm nearly sank the bloody ship back then. If he'd. done what I told him he wouldn't be doing a five stretch'.

Dusty knew all about detective sergeant Malcolm Sneed who had been in Masters' squad. 'What really happened that day, Don?'.

Masters shrugged at a memory. 'Bit like today's caper. I'd organised the robbery but Malc couldn't keep it buttoned when the rubber heels got round to him'.

'How much does Jean know?'.

'Nothing - and I want to keep it that way. I'll get the coffees'.

Don Masters' wife was a beautiful slim blonde who, from time to time during his stint at the Yard, had told him how unhappy she was living in a crime-ridden area of Leytonstone. Her mother's mantra: "if you're born here you'll die here", borne out of resignation at her own lot in life, so many times clouded her day when she struggled to come to terms with her unhappiness. Even his promises of a better life if he was eventually transferred from the Yard rarely lifted her spirit because they had no substance. When she pleaded to be told where they would eventually live he had no answer.

Leytonstone was, Don admitted to himself, definitely the pits. Recidivist scum seemed to migrate there. His promise came alive when he was transferred from the Yard to Walthamstead and bought the four bedroomed house designed by his architect friend David Saunders. Dragging his thoughts back he said. 'She loves her new home. Getting out and about more has changed her. Her job has helped'.

'Estate agent's isn't it?'.

Masters nodded and reached for his cigarettes. 'How about Valerie: don't mention her much do you?'.

'She's fine. You know we have our ups and downs. She can be a handful at times'. He smiled at Masters. 'Like I said she misses female company. Have a word with Jean, maybe we could manage an evening out together. How's Kay these days -still seeing her?'.

Masters sighed. Addicted to sex with blondes, Masters found Kay irresistible. She was beautiful and slim like Jean. She was five feet three inches of seductive charm needing instant gratification. His balls tingled at a recent memory.

Miller looked sympathetically at his friend. 'No regrets, Don?'.

Masters grimaced. 'Some, Dusty. Some'.

The start up had been a chance encounter in a shop in Walthamstead High Street on the run up to Jean's birthday. He had been doing his best to choose a suitable jumper for her when he became aware that Kay was beside him, smiling, shaking her head and pointing to another one, which she removed and handed to him with an alluring smile. Taking it, their hands touched and she squeezed his while gazing up into his eyes, her own offering a promise he couldn't resist.

The sergeant didn't know that two evenings a week, more if work permitted, during the six months that followed, they lay together in her bed, his hands caressing her silky smooth body while her hand was, as usual, urgently caressing his hardening penis. With his old man fit for purpose and her hand guiding, he did as he always did: easing her on top and let her guide it in and start her routine, her eyes closed as she thrust against him.

'Slowly', she always whispered. 'slow.....*leee..*'.

And then, only two nights before, he had held her waist as she moved against his gentle thrusting while he gazed up at the lip-biting expression he knew so well, knowing she was going yet again. With the tension suddenly gone from her body she had leaned forward to kiss him briefly and eased away from his slackening penis to lay beside him, her steady gaze, as had happened before, suddenly devoid of romantic feeling, boring into his half closed eyes. 'When?, she had icily demanded.

Of late, the 'when' and the unexpected sudden coldness was occurring more frequently. Masters had eased himself up against the headboard and cuddled her against his chest, saying nothing but hoping his silence and caresses would deflect her from the demand he wasn't going to give in to. 'Soon, sweetheart', he had whispered after a while. He'd heard the question many times and always managed to duck the straight answer she wanted. Easing out of bed he had dressed quickly while Kay, her tussled blonde hair framing a beautiful face, bedclothes pulled against her chest, watched.

'You never take your socks off do you?'.

He had given her a quick smile. 'Hard to find in the dark'.

'You'll ring me?'.

I will. You know I will'.

Dressed , he had grabbed his radios, leaned over, and kissed her forehead.

'Is that all I get?' she had demanded.

No, sweetheart, it isn't'. He saw himself leaning down again and kissing her unresponsive lips.

He was at the bedroom door when he recalled her cold challenge. 'Fuck her tonight will you?'

Her change of attitude wasn't unexpected but was becoming more demanding and dangerous.

*

The news from Essex had confirmed his snout's information: Woodall's run-down farm had been an active run-in for stolen lorries for some time. With several more receiving charges coming his way, telling unsympathetic villains in Brixton he'd been set up by a crooked copper got the usual derisory laughs.

"Join the club" was a universal response.

*

Chubby police constable Joe Jardine was glad Geoff Tims, his late turn shift sergeant, had detailed him for the front office that afternoon. The odd snow flake had drifted down when he cycled to work and the thought of freezing his balls off on A beat was a pisser. He took the call that bleak winter day from a woman who said she'd seen the body floating in the same stream where Dianne Flaxman's body had been found. Being a golfer, he knew from her description it was beside the 9th fairway.

Jotting down her her name and address, he asked, 'Are you alone?'.

'My little girl's with me. It was very distressing for her. She's crying'.

'I understand. Take her home now. And thank you for letting me know'. Making a note in the front office occurrence book he belled the CID.

*

Masters, with the help of detective constable John Barton, took the dead woman's hands and pulled her onto the grass. A quick scan of her body for injuries revealed what had been clear from the start: her suffused face and the weal around her neck telling their story.

Masters shrugged deep into his anorak and pointed. 'From her soggy state, John, it's a fair bet she'd been tipped into the water some time ago. Get on the radio. Organise a tent to cover her until we're finished here'.

Masters took his hands out of warm pockets and fished out a cigarette packet. Lighting one he stared around at the the golfing gawkers who'd gathered on the far side of the stream.. He pointed to a suited man with a small holdall in his hand walking their way.

'Met Chandra?' . He gestured.

Mystified, Barton asked 'Who's he, guv?'.

'He, John, is our pathologist. You're going to attend

his post mortem'.

Chandra Pasapula greeted the officers with a flicked smile and knelt beside the body. After a few moments he looked up at the detectives, grimaced and said quietly, pointing to the woman's neck. 'You don't need me to tell you how she probably met her end Don. Like the other one. When I've got her on the slab I'll be a better position to guestimate when, and most likely confirm how. The freezing conditions of the last week'll make it difficult to be precise but off hand, from the nature of her body, I'd say she's been in the water for days'.

*

'So who was she?' Masters asked rhetorically of the assembled detectives in the smoke laden room. 'It's three weeks since Flaxman's body was found. Looks a lot like her. We've got her dabs and dental details. As you can see she was another blonde, and at five feet three inches the same height as Dianne. Sergeant Miller has ruled out Flaxman's hubby for the job. No brothers, or any evidence she was overside with men'. Like his colleagues, he was looking at the enlarged photos of the dead women pinned to the wall board. 'I'm waiting for a report that'll hopefully indicate approximately when she was dumped in the water. Once we know that we can widen the enquiry'.

'Naked, guv?'

'Yeh. Both. Same MO: garrotted using a belt most likely. The DCS is laying on press coverage'. He smiled briefly. 'The camera's kinder to him'.

*

The telephone's insistent ring eventually roused

detective inspector Masters, who earlier had spent the best part of an hour with Kay. He listened to the brief message while he was sliding out of bed for the second time that evening. "I'm on my way', he told the caller from his station, shivering as he reached for his clothes. With the handset balanced on a shoulder and jammed against his ear he told the caller what he wanted done, adding, 'Ring him back. Let him know I'm coming'. Putting the receiver back on its cradle he hurriedly finished dressing and looked across at Jean, who had woken up and was sleepily watching him dress.

'What is it, darling?'. She inched up the bed. yawning as she pulled the covers up to her chin.

'David's in a spot of bother, sweetheart' he told her. 'He's been burgled. I'm nipping over there. Go back to sleep'.

Now fully dressed he bent over and kissed her. 'He had a set to with a burglar apparently. Snuggle down and keep warm'. He flicked off the light and ruffled her hair as he straightened and turned away.

David Saunders was standing in the open doorway as the detective's Jaguar pulled into the drive and shook his hand once they were in the hall. 'I'm glad it's you, Don'. He said quietly. 'Betty is beside herself. She's in the living room. The man's upstairs'.

'How did it happen, Dave?'. Masters opened his top coat while he studied his friend's distraught face for a clue.

'Follow me, Don'.

He led the way upstairs and stood to one side to let his friend see a dead man sprawled on the carpet.

'Betty didn't see any of it, Don. Sound asleep - she'd taken a pill - suffering with her legs lately', he explained as he watched the detective scanning the room. ' I heard him downstairs'.

'Sorry?'.

'I heard him moving about'

When was that?'

'Seems like years ago. About an hour and a half ago in fact. He must have made a noise when he got in through a window. I didn't know that when I woke up but I do now. When I got to the bedroom door I saw his torch light bobbing up the stairs. I was very frightened, believe me, Don'.

'Have you checked? Did he get in through the window?'.

'I've looked outside, Don. There are muddy footprints on the living room carpet under the window. -we leave its fanlight widow on the catch. You can see where he scrambled to get in. His coat is out there. He must have opened it and climbed in. I don't know how he managed to climb through the small gap, but. there's no other way he could have done it'.

Masters nodded and knelt beside the dead man who had a bone handle of a knife protruding from his back.. He pointed at the open drawers of the dresser.

'Going through them?'.

'He was shining a torch in them'.

The DI stood up. 'What happened next?'.

'I crept up behind him and......well, stabbed him............'.

Masters bent down and peered at the knife. 'It's a carving knife isn't it? Do you keep it up here?'

Saunders nodded but could see his friend was concerned. 'I was scared, Don. I didn't think. I just did it on the spur of the moment'..

Did he threaten you?'

Saunders shook his head. 'Is that important, Don?'.

'Definitely. Did Betty see what happened?'.

'Like I said, she was asleep'.

'But she made the call?'.

'Have a word with her. She'll explain. Apparently I

was in a dead faint lying beside him'.

Masters nodded and searched the dead man's trouser pockets, taking out a fold-over wallet and scanning its contents. A driving licence identified him as Albert Fraser. Pursing his lips as he scanned the room once more, he determined to keep his friend from a certain murder charge. Gesturing to the open drawers he told his friend to close them. He pointed to a framed picture on the wall. 'Put it on the floor and stamp on the glass'. Seeing a puzzled expression he said quietly 'Its important, David. And your face - it must be scratched, we'll do that now. Get down beside him. Take off his gloves - I'll put them by the bed. And when my team arrive you're coming with me to the station to make a statement'.

*

Later that afternoon, beefy, florid-faced Makepeace put Masters' report on the killing to one side and leaned back in his swivel chair, giving the lean detective his hard, disbelieving stare. 'Can you feel it?' he asked.

'You've lost me there, sir?'.

'The wind'.

For once in his life Masters was lost for words at the change of direction. 'Wind sir?'.

'It's right up you're arse. You're sailing so close to it it's a wonder your farts aren't clogging your nostrils as we speak'. He leaned forward to study Masters puzzled expression. 'The Pitsea run in? I'm not convinced. Not at all. Woodall's shedding buckets of tears in Brixton, reckons he's been set up. Now it's this one. From the top, inspector', he demanded, 'this is brief to say the least. I can't say I accept your conclusion'.

Masters had expected that response and had decided to go half-way to agreeing with the scepticism. 'I know where you're coming from, sir. I felt the same after I'd seen the scene. Open and shut I thought – until I heard the full story from Mr. Saunders and his wife. The dead man got his comeuppance with a vengeance, the poor sod. He was up to no good with Mrs. Saunders. If it was down to me I'd strike a medal for her old man'.

Makepeace picked up the report again and paraphrased it to Masters. 'The dead man broke into Mr. Saunders home through a ground floor window, went upstairs where Saunders saw him attempting to rape his wife and stabbed him.. That's about it isn't it?'

'In a nutshell, yes, sir. His wife slept through it all'

'While she was being raped!'.

'She wasn't being raped. Fraser had eased the bedclothes off her. Saunders thought the worst was about to happen'.

'Heavy sleeper the wife?'

'As it turned out sir, yes, took a sleeping pill. Saunders grabbed him at that point'.

The DCS steadied his disbelieving stare at Masters.

'For God's sake, inspector! You expect me to believe this man was going to rape her with her husband in the room, watching the goings on!'.

Masters stared back and kept to his script. 'Saunders makes it clear in his statement Fraser didn't know he was in the room. The fact is the man was a burglar and a possible rapist and he's dead because of it. I can't change the facts'.

Makepeace was shaking his head.

'Didn't know he was in the room! They're husband and wife, for God's sake! Where was Saunders while the man was yanking at the bedclothes?'.

'Hiding behind the bedroom door, sir. Petrified'.

Makepeace was listening with one ear while edging his finger down the report.

'Keeps a carving knife in the bedroom?'. His

sarcasm was obvious.

'As I've said, I can only present the facts as I found them. Might seem odd to you, sir, but it's as well he did. That's roughly how it went: and the bit about the creaks'.

'Creaks.................?'. The DCS's finger stopped
He heard the creaks'.

The finger moved searchingly. 'What creaked?'.

'The stairs, sir. They creaked. Its in his statement'.

The DCS stared sharply in disbelief. Shaking his head he eased Saunders' statement from the thin file.

Masters waited until the statement was being read. 'These did, sir. Saunders has lived in his house long enough to recognise the creaks'

'So........according to you, Saunders had time to pick up the knife and put on his slippers before they had a fight in the bedroom?'. Makepeace had spotted an apparent weakness in his account and was staring hard, a cynical smile curling his top lip.

'Its in his statement about the knife, sir. He stated he always kept it on the bedside cabinet. And you've forgotten the window and the creaks sir. That's what disturbed him in the first place. He makes it clear in his statement he intended to go downstairs. The knife was in his hand at that point'.

The DCS leaned forward to make a point. 'So. Our dead man conveniently ends up pushing Saunders against a wall'. He broke off to fix Masters with an unblinking stare. 'Back against a wall, eh? Up on case law is he!'.

The detective inspector raised an eyebrow and responded indignantly: 'The man was fighting to prevent his wife from being raped. The dead man could easily have done for him as well'.

'Stabbed in the back'. The DCS's disbelief had moved on to anger. 'He managed that with his back against the wall?, he said with heavy sarcasm.

Masters bottled a smile but adopted a serious expression. 'They were face to face, obviously. These things happen fast, sir. We're talking split seconds here. Our dead man scratched Saunders' face. He must have swung his arm around the back of Fraser. The tussle must have moved across the room. The pathologist has confirmed the wound could well have been caused in a face-to-face struggle'.

'What has Saunders' wife said about all this?'

'She was against keeping the knife in the bedroom but is thankful now that it was, in view of what has happened'.

'Anything found in the dead man's bedsit?', Makepeace asked after a lull while he grappled with his disbelief.

Masters shook his head. 'Albert Fraser travelled light, sir. One suitcase, a couple of shirts, underwear - dirty, the usual. In the town two weeks. Been out of nick four months. According to his CRO file he had an odd perversion: he got off climbing in through fanlight windows!'.

*

'So now we know', Masters told the assembled detectives. 'Our second victim is Amanda Price. Thirty-two. Married. Husband's Paul Price, no cons, a lorry driver for Bowker Transport. Run from an industrial site outside town. Refrigerated haulage. He's being treated as suspect No.1 for the murders until we get a clearer picture of his recent whereabouts. Right now he's in Northampton with his lorry and is expected back sometime later today. His boss will let us know when he gets back. Ds. Miller will go there today and get a bigger picture'. He looked across at the sergeant, 'We need his time sheet for the days leading up to Dianne's murder and his wife's'. Turning back to the expectant detectives he brought them up to date. 'Dianne didn't, so far as we can say, but Amanda may have had, a double life. She worked for a solicitor in town and may have got involved with a couple of villains. This is speculation at this point but John'.....................he smiled towards detective constable Barton.......'will be following up a phone conversation I've had with a senior partner where she worked, which hinted at something shady going on between her and another member of the firm'. Nodding to Barton, he said ' Get onto that this afternoon John'. Returning his attention to the assembled detectives he told them a detective was parked outside the woman's house. 'I can't authorise an entry at this time. When hubby turns up he'll be nicked. We'll do it then. And I'm having his car brought in for examination. Our killer must have used a vehicle to get Dianne to the stream'. He turned his attention to an enlarged street map and indicated the road fronting the stream. 'A mile or thereabouts long. As you can see it runs beside two fairways of the golf course and a row of council houses. We have no evidence to date of sightings of anyone loitering in the area, hence every occupant of the houses must be interviewed in the meantime. Let's make a start on that'.

*

Detective constable John Barton was a well-muscled thirty year old eight years into the job, the result of strenuous training at Gyms Place. Not the brainiest type he'd managed nevertheless to scrape through his sergeant's exam the previous year. A shift inspector recognised potential and made a recommendation he be given a chance in the CID.. After his years in uniform life in plain clothes gave him the opportunity to have it off with the woman of his choice which, at that particular time, was Sheila Walters.

Now he looked impatiently at Terence Blake, the grey-haired fifty something pasty-faced solicitor, who was apparently studying documents in front of him. Finally turning his attention to the detective, he twiddled a pencil and gave Barton a flicked smile. 'Mrs. Price, as I told your inspector, hasn't been here since she left around 5.30pm last Monday. I've had calls put through to her home. Nobody appears to be there'. He leaned forward to look directly at Barton. 'Amanda Price is Mark Bateman's secretary', he explained conspiratorially as he peered intently at the detective. 'And *he* hasn't been here for days either'.

'Mind if I smoke?'. Barton, a forty a day man, was trying to concentrate, but his craving had got the better of him. On a nod from the solicitor he pulled out his packet and held it up.

'Do carry on -no thank you -I don't smoke'.

The detective, under instructions from Masters not to let the man know Amanda was dead, lit up and studied the other man before putting it bluntly. 'Do you believe harm has come to Mrs. Price?'.

He watched the other man struggle for words, before spreading his hands. 'It's a gut feeling, yes'. He handed a framed picture to the detective. 'Christmas party photo' he explained. 'But with both missing, as it were, I must admit I'm concerned for Amanda's well being'.

' Is that Bateman beside her?'

'Yes, that's Bateman'.

The detective recognised the man from his fitness evenings. 'May I have the photo?'.

'Of course'.

The detective looked up from the photo, pointing to Bateman. 'Married?'.

'Indeed, yes'.

'What do you know about Mr. Price?'.

'He's a lorry driver', he confirmed. 'From what I gathered from Mrs Price, he's away a lot'.

Barton looked quizzically at the other man. 'Tell me a bit more about Mark Bateman'.

Blake sat forward and held the detective's gaze. 'Quiet sort. From his build you wouldn't think that'. He smiled 'Athletic I believe would be the right word'.

Barton nodded in agreement. 'Lover's tiff?', he queried with a smile as he looked for an ashtray

Blake pointed to it and shook his head and smiled back. 'I wouldn't categorise their relationship the way you are suggesting'.

'So why are you concerned?'.

The solicitor reached for his phone and cradled the handset. 'I'll let John White know you want to talk to him.. He's our solicitor - he deals with criminal cases. He can explain'. He spoke briefly and nodded, replacing the handset. 'Sorry, officer. He's still in court. I'll leave a note for him to ring you'.

*

The next morning the detective returned to the building and was shown to White's office. Recognising him as a solicitor he'd seen at court on several occasions he shook the tall, slim, solicitor's hand and explained his interest. 'Fill me in: why is Mr. Blake concerned about her well being?'.

A pretty young woman in a figure-hugging dress came in at that moment with cups of coffee and gave the detective a smile as she left. His eyes followed her shapely figure. Mentally undressing her he shook his head at the image of her shapely bum and picked up his cup and turned his attention to the solicitor, who tersely explained he was genuinely worried for Mark Bateman and Amanda Price, before explaining why. 'I'm dealing with the defence of Philip Jakeson and Bill Williams. They're accused of armed robbery. The stolen money, twenty thousand pounds actually, was never recovered. Mark is my legal executive: he prepared the defence brief for me. He leaned forward. to stare meaningfully at the detective. 'And they're out on bail'.

'How on earth did they get it?'.

'Unusual, yes, I agree. I never believed bail was a possibility, frankly. The arresting officer would be in a better position to answer that question'.

'Why say that?'.Barton was intrigued at the pointed comment.

With palms towards the officer White held up his hands. 'Speak with a detective inspector Lindley. He's the flying squad officer dealing with the case. He went into the box and told the magistrates the men would answer bail'.

'Have they jumped bail?'.

'Well no -they were remanded on bail to appear at the high court for trial. The court calender hasn't yet been finalised'.

'Let's get back to the missing people. Mr. Blake seems to believe you can explain his concern for their safety. Can you?'.

'I think so. Look, I'm not making allegations but Mark told me on one occasion that Jakeson offered him money believing, apparently, he could arrange bail'.

'Did he?'.

'Of course not'.

'Did he accept money?'.

'That I don't know. But I did inform Mr. Blake'.

'Explain about their bail. I'm mystified'.

'I didn't think for a minute they'd get it'..

'And that's when DI. Lindley said his bit?'.

'Yes. I was surprised when bail was agreed'.

Barton put down his cup and lit another cigarette, holding the packet up to the other man, who shook his head. 'What have we got here? Be straight with me: do you believe money changed hands and the pair of them shot off?

White nodded 'It's possible but.......'. He searched for the right words, 'Amanda is a gem of a woman. Very sexy. Bit obvious at times. Bateman I'm not sure.........'.

Intrigued, the detective angled his head at the other man. 'What is it?', he probed. He could see the solicitor had something else on his mind.

'Bateman was always going on about money' He made up his mind to be frank. 'I did wonder if he'd tried to blackmail the men. I had a feeling he knew something more than I did...........about the inspector I mean'.

Barton studied the solicitor's worried face before he asked 'I'm not hearing all of it am I? Do you think Bateman was threatened, and possibly Amanda?'

White held the detective's questioning gaze before shrugging.

'Could Bateman have put the squeeze on them?

'Put like that, yes, I suppose its possible', he agreed.

Barton recognised White had nothing more to add so changed the subject. Does Bateman have a car?'.

'A Rover. Dark blue as I remember'.

'And Mrs Price?'.

'Not that I know. She came by bus. That's about it. Does any of this help?'. He stood and offered a hand to Barton, who got to his feet and shook it, smiling as he added 'Anything's better than nothing, John. If anything else comes to light, you'll let my station know?'.

White followed him to the door. 'I will' he confirmed.

*

It was two days since Amanda's body had been found and another bitterly cold December morning. 'Both detectives had taken the precaution of wearing heavy top coats. Masters had forgotten to put rubber boots in the car and was glumly studying his dog-fouled, snow-sodden shoes when Miller, who hadn't forgotten his, sidled beside him. The DI pointed to his own shoes.

'What a fuck up' he said irritably. 'And mind where *you* step'. He gestured at a dog, sitting beside a man crouched some distance away. 'He belled the nick from that call box'. He pointed.. 'That dog of his sniffed the stiff while it was having a crap'. He pointed to his own fouled shoes.

'Is it him?' Miller was staring down at the dead man and saw a likeness to the photo of Blakeman

'Could well be'. The DI looked towards a lay-by off the nearby dual carriageway and judged the distance. 'Might have taken two to carry the stiff', he surmised.

Miller had moved to line himself up with the body and the lay-by. 'Snow has covered any flattened grass', he observed. 'Ground'll be like concrete. Carried and dragged most likely. Might have been a one man job' he added.

'Whoever did the carrying might have got smeared with his brains'. The DI had crouched while Miller was speaking to look more closely at the man's head. ' Shot above the eyes'. He eased the body onto its side for Miller to see. 'And came out the back of his head. What a mess! Pasapula will be here soon. When he's finished get SOCO started here while I get enquiries underway'.

*

The pathologist's report of Fraser's death has settled it',

Masters was able to inform Makepeace . 'Nothing to establish murder, sir. The entrance wound of the knife does fit with the alleged struggle. We can have our suspicions but, without additional evidence, in my view it's a closed case'.

'Nothing in Fraser's CRO file points to rape, inspector' was the jaundiced response from the disbelieving DCS, who studied Masters' face for a glimmer of guilt.

'Always a first time, sir'. Masters offered, smiling when he added, 'Semen in Fraser's pants according to SOCO. It's possible he ejaculated while he was leering down at Mrs. Saunders. Or when he climbed in: it's in his file, sir - he was a weirdo who shot his lot doing that'.

*

Later that evening Masters and Jean were in Saunders' home with the detective doing his best to reassure him.

'Does that mean its all over, Don?' Unconvinced, David Saunders' face was etched with the worry of it all. He downed a glass of brandy and stared for reassurance at his friend.

Masters nodded and smiled. 'The coroner's inquest has wrapped it up, "death by misadventure". That's a definite end to it'. He sipped his own brandy and studied the other man's troubled features and reached to tap his hand. 'Believe me Dave – it really is all over. How is Betty coping?'.

'She doesn't talk about it, Don. He refilled his glass and took a sip and looked over his glass at Masters. 'Another one, Don?'.

The detective shook his head and checked his watch.

' Will there be any come backs for you, Don?'

Masters smiled and shook his head again. 'The

coroner's enquiry has put it to bed'. He raised his glass to his friend. 'Must be going'. Finishing his drink he put the glass down. 'Put it behind you, Dave'.

*

Burly detective sergeant Miller eyed Sheila Watson, a pretty young blonde with a short skirt sitting behind her desk and could have given her one there and then. He smiled when she looked across at him under dipped eyebrows and winked. 'Nice legs, love', he told her as he shifted his gaze from her ample breasts, most of which were on show from his vantage point.

He shouldn't be long', she simpered in her best imitation of Marilyn Monroe, thrilled she was being ogled by the handsome, dark-haired detective.

'That's alright miss. Worked here long have you?'. Miller had edged into the office to stand close beside her. His searching eyes on her stockinged thighs, his penis instantly hardened when his imagination got to work on what was higher up.

His lusting gaze thrilling her to bits, she fluffed her hair and squinted up at him, giving him her practised, inviting smile. 'A year and a bit'.

'And the transport manager -what's his name?'. Miller edged to peer down at her thrusting breasts.

'Not what's his name' she trilled and giggled. 'George Wiley. I don't know how long'.

'Know Paul Price?'.

She thought the detective had all but lost interest in her with his silly questions. 'Of him. I don't get to see many of the drivers'. She hitched her skirt and tried again. 'That sliding window, head and shoulders is all I see'. She broke off when a heavy set man entered the room 'This is Mr. Wiley', she explained as she adjusted her hem.

'And you are?' Miller was asked as the manager flicked an uninterested glance at him.

Miller showed his warrant card. 'Detective sergeant Miller, Mr. Wiley. Can I have a word'.

'Come through to my office', he told the detective and walked ahead to his spacious office.

Before he followed, Miller squeezed the young woman's shoulder and winked as he pouted a kiss.

Once settled Wiley studied the burly man before asking 'Your inspector has already had a word with me about Paul. 'How can I help you?'. Wiley settled himself in his swivel chair and looked with curiosity at the detective.

'Paul Price's wife hasn't been to work since Monday. I'm trying to piece together her movements since then. Has he mentioned any problems between them to anyone here?'.

Wiley shook his head. 'Wouldn't know would I? 'Hardly a CID matter, surely? Were there problems?'.

Miller smiled briefly and shrugged away the question. 'You mentioned to my DI that Mr. Price was up in the Midlands: Northampton was it?'.

Wiley nodded.

'Due back tomorrow I think you told him?'.

'That's right'.

' Was he working last Monday?'.

Wiley pulled out a work sheet. 'Three drops Left here at 5am. Back............got his tacho here.....4pm'.

'And Tuesday?'.

The manager tapped the documents in front of him. 'Got these ready for you. Tuesday...........left the depot at 5pm. First drop Hinkley......... then Manchester.........two drops there, picked up a return load, back here Wednesday. Does that help you?'.

'Hard to say, Mr. Wiley. My enquiry is routine at this stage. Does he have to clock in?'.

'Everyone does. In and out'.

'We'll need a copy of his time record for the last few weeks. Can that be arranged?'.

'Of course. Sergeant............' he broke off to lean forward and look questioningly at the officer 'What is your enquiry really about? Does it affect my firm?'.

Miller offered a disarming smile. 'Not in any way, Mr. Wiley. I can't say any more at this stage. Tuesday night. Where would he have slept?'.

In his cab. Its equipped with a sleeper behind the drivers seat. All our units have them'..

'And since Wednesday?'.

The transport manager tapped the documents. 'Out again. He refuelled and took another container: Portsmouth this time'.

'Does he always have the same lorry unit?'

'Each driver has. As it happens his unit's in the workshop He reported a brake problem when he got back yesterday. He's using a spare unit today'.

'It would be helpful to have a snout around the cab. May I do that?.

Wiley, giving the sergeant a steady, questioning, look, probed: 'Is there something you're not telling me, sergeant?'.

'No Mr. Wiley. Like I said, it's routine, covering all angles. These things have to be done, unfortunately. We'll need to have it at headquarters. Can that be arranged?'.

The transport manager got to his feet. 'Follow me'.

As they passed a smiling Sheila, Miller squeezed her shoulder again and whispered 'We'll have to have an evening out together. I'll ring you'.

With the men gone she reached for her handbag and took out a small mirror and pouted at her reflection. 'He could be the one', she whispered at the reflection.

The workshop was vast, large enough to house six units

and their trailers. 'Bert', Wiley called to an overalled man sliding out from under a cab, beckoning him over when the man stood up. 'Paul's unit - have you finished the brake job?'.

The mechanic nodded. 'Going out is it?'.

Wiley pointed to Miller. 'Give him the keys, Bert. He needs to give it the once over'.

Miller gestured to his radio. 'I can arrange for a driver to take it to headquarters. You alright with that?'.

'HGV licensed?.

'Of course'.

*

We've got an ident, Dusty'. The DI looked up from reading a report summing up the forensic enquiry regarding the dead man. 'It is Bateman.......was I should say'.

Miller nodded. 'Expecting that. A snout at the Yard put me onto a scrap yard in Bow where she reckoned his car was stashed. The car squad found his Rover. From the blood and gore somebody was shot inside it'.

'Have we got it?'

'SOCO are taking it apart as we speak'.

'This snout........how d'you get onto it so quickly?.

Miller grinned. 'Betty, the typist in the flying squad office - you know her, surely. Tasty bit'.

Masters did. 'Giving it one?'.

'Of course. Nothing serious'.

'A particular squad?'

'Lindley's'.

Masters looked sharply at the sergeant.'What have you told her?'.

'Dropped Bateman's name, Don. Mentioned I was looking for his car'.

'Will this get back to Lindley?'.

Miller was already shaking his head. 'I'll say no to that. Bit risky for her - you know how it is'.

Masters did. Typists were trusted to keep it shut- until they slept with Miller. He smiled at the thought.

'Something amusing you, Don?'.

Masters shook his head.

'Anything of help found in Price's cab?'.

'A packet of contraceptives, two pair of knickers and Amanda's fingerprints' Masters told him.

With a vivid image of Amanda's beautiful, naked body in his mind, Miller asked casually. 'What d'you reckon -he our man?'

'He might be. Did you check with Wiley: is he allowed to carry a passenger?'.

'Yep. It's no he can't, but it's a grey area he reckons. It's not enforced. I can check with his workmates'.

'Let's get him in first. Do it then'.

Miller nodded his agreement.'And the blaggers - ruling them out are we?'.

Masters shrugged. 'Nothing to tie them to her -at the moment at least. Let's see how it goes with her old man'.

Later that day with the SOCO report in, Masters drove to divisional headquarters and brought Makepeace up to speed.

'Bateman's car was the crime scene', he told him, explaining that brains and fragments of skull were splattered against the roof lining and the rear seat; and the fingerprints of Philip Jakeson and Bill Williams were found in the car. 'William's appeared to have been the driver. The bullet that killed Bateman was found in the boot- went through the rear seat assembly'.

"What are you doing about it?' demanded Makepeace.

'It's all in hand, sir. Both of our suspects are at the addresses they gave as part of their bail surety. The

Bow CID are keeping tabs on them until I give the word to lift them. Sergeant Miller's informant put us onto the Bow scrap yard, just in time as it happens - another hour or two and it'd been crushed. So far enquiries have linked them to the dead man by their fingerprints in his car: its when they got there we need to establish. On its own the legal johnies say they're not enough to lift them'.

'The dead woman, Amanda Price: Was she tied in with Jakeson and Williams?

'No evidence -but its a possibility. Mrs. Price was Bateman's secretary and may have got to know the two men. Money talks -and', he stared hard at the DCS, 'twenty grand is missing from that job: the flying squad ran the job, as you know, sir'.

The DCS's expression said it all. 'I am aware of their involvement, inspector' He was staring at Masters in his usual dismissive way. ' I approved their running that job. It was their snout and their call'.

Masters own expression didn't reveal his feelings when he asked 'Does that explain why the squad didn't bring me up to speed?'.

Makepeace stared hard at the D.I. 'What are you suggesting, inspector?'.

'Nothing, sir. A job gets pulled on my ground and from start to finish my team was out of the loop? And the two blaggers got bail? Any explanation would be nice'.

Makepeace's annoyance had hardened his face. He leaned forward, tapping his desk to emphasise his point. 'Don't question my decisions, inspector', he said coldly. ' DI. Lindley is an experienced and respected officer. I don't have to explain anything to you'. He leaned back, staring at the DI before adding pointedly, 'and don't rock the boat. You've got enough on your hands with three murders. You've got your suspects for

Bateman's: deal with them. If I believe Lindley's squad should get involved I'll let you know. And'..........He stopped and jabbed a finger.....'don't jump to conclusions you may regret'.

'Fair point, sir.' Masters changed the direction of the interview. 'Amanda Price had been missing for several days, sir. Her old man hadn't said a word about her to his workmates. I've got a strong feeling he's our man. His work record puts him in town when the Flaxman woman went missing. If I'm right he murdered her as well'.

'So. What are you doing about him?'.

'When he gets back from his present trip he'll be pulled in for questioning'.

'What has Bateman's wife got to say about her old man being shot? Can she be involved?'.

'In a state of shock when sergeant Miller interviewed her. He didn't raise the possibility of Bateman having an affair with Price's wife. Wrong time'.

Makepeace wasn't having that 'This is a murder investigation, inspector. Be thorough. Upset people. Get the answers!'.

Chapter two

'Charlie Hobbs is in a cell.................again'. Geoff Tims put down his mug on the charge desk, wiped his lips, and looked across at the DI for a reaction.

Masters, hands stuffed into anorak pockets, looked up from the occurrence book and grimaced at the sergeant. Reading the entries again, he asked. 'No mention here. What is it this time?'.

The sergeant tapped a charge sheet. 'Housebreaking again. On the ball your John -caught him red handed leaving the dead woman's drum'.

'Which one?'.

' Amanda Price's.

'I don't believe it!'.

Tims leaned on his desk and fingered the charge register. 'Believe it, Don'.

'Cash job?'.

'Fifty quid on him'.

'Wearing it?'.

'No option'.

The detective inspector knew a lot about Charlie Hobbs. Still only twentyone, Charlie was fast becoming an institution at the nick. His criminal antecedents from the age of ten were well known; but it was his winning ways that set him apart from his peer group and endeared him some members of the CID, Masters in particular. Charlie was a charmer, especially with young women. Recently it was Janet, a very beautiful young woman, who obviously loved him.

Charlie's problems, he explained to Masters at one time, always began with the wooden tops. Always the first on the scene of crimes these uniform berks, as Charlie identified them, homed in on him and his mates whenever a house got tipped over. Masters knew from

Charlie that he was at approved school when his mum and dad died, on a double decker bus, he explained. None of the passengers was aware the driver was new on that particular route. Imagine, he told the detective inspector with an impish grin, there it was, a bloody great low arched bricked Victorian bridge, coming full tilt at the bus, ripping off the top deck and doing for mum and dad. Which is how Masters got to know of Mavis, Charlie's gran who, according to Charlie's tale, the court at that time handed him into her care. However, good as Mavis was to him, Charlie was soon off to Borstal for his bit of training.

Charlie was languishing in his appointed cell pondering upon life's unfairness. He'd taken every precaution after all was said and done. He'd watched Amanda leave her house most evenings and bugger of somewhere for hours. It was a bit risky, especially since he'd spotted the detective across the road chatting to a woman but, ignoring him and sneaking around the back to do the business, he eventually nipped out the front and got collared and cuffed by the same detective.

Hearing the clank and the grind of the cell door he looked up at the familiar detective entering his cell and scrambled to his feet to stare nervously at the tallish, lean man he knew so well. 'Morning sir,' he managed after some seconds of intense perusal, wondering if he could expect a helping hand, yet again.

Masters studied Charlie when he removed the youngster's breakfast tin plate from the mattress. Flicking crumbs away he settled himself on the plastic cover, pulled his anorak tight, and patted the shiny cover. 'Sit down lad', he said. He fished out his cigarette packet, opened it and offered it to Charlie: 'Let's have a fag'.

A grateful Charlie ta'd his thanks as he took one and lit it from the detective's glowing end.

'Why that drum, Charlie?'.

'Seen the bird many times, sir. Right tasty. Spur of the moment really'.

'Have a good snout around?'.

The youngster nodded. 'I only wanted some bread, sir'.

'This little episode puts you in the middle of a murder enquiry'. When Charlie's mouth gaped Masters grinned and patted his shoulder. 'Not to worry, lad. We know you didn't do it'.

'She the one on the news?'.

Masters nodded and studied the younger man for a while. 'Charlie', he said, 'You've had a shit of a life, let's face it'. Masters was bouncing up and down on the mattress and looking critically at Charlie. He liked his winning ways and cheeky grin, but was pondering if the young man was up to joining his firm.

Charlie, meanwhile, was working on that shit of a life bit. The DI was right about that. It took a while because he had a lot of shit in his life to mull over; what with worrying about Janet's threat to bugger off if he got nicked again; and gran always giving him an earful, reckoning he should get a proper job.

The detective was a patient man and filled in the seconds blowing smoke rings at the ceiling.

After a few nervous drags Charlie nodded in agreement 'You're right about that, sir. Life's been a shit'.

'A downer, Charlie. I understand. It's Don'. Masters had drawn a folded foolscap from his pocket, which bore no relationship to Charlie's life and his on-going problems but was his usual interrogation tool. He wiggled it about. 'It's all here. Antecedents. This is what the court will hear. Your gran tried -you and I know that don't we?'.

Charlie nodded.

'You know what Charlie, the whole bloody system has let you down. Even Borstal was a complete waste of time'.

'True, sir, true', He was impressed. Finally someone understood what a pisser his life had been.

It's Don, Charlie. Now this little tickle. Do yourself a favour: Fifty quid!'.

'Forty, sir, A tenner's mine'.

The detective laughed and prodded him 'You're a cheeky sod, Charlie. Alright forty quid -until the householder gets home; but you're looking at three years'.

'Three…..!' Charlie was lost for words.

'Three Charlie. You're over 21. That's what the law has got in store for you'.

Charlie, did his best to absorb the news and stared dumbfoundedly at Masters.

'It's a possibility, Charlie. Unless we manage to scrape a deal out of this mess. What do you think?'.

The black cloud shifted a little and Charlie eagerly hunched forward 'Wot kind of deal sir?'

'Don', the DI reminded him

'Wot?'

' Don'll do, Charlie. No guarantees mind, but I believe you and me can work something out'.

'Ow d'you mean?. Charlie's eagerness to hear more had perched him on the edge of the bed.

The DI studied the expectant face and gathered his thoughts before explaining. 'There is a way you can do what you do best, Charlie, and not keep getting nicked'. He patted Charlie's shoulder and stood up to stare thoughtfully down at the young man.' I like you, Charlie. If I can work it for you I believe together we could straighten out your life'.

Charlie wasn't the brightest lamp in the cell but his present misery urgently needed the lift he thought he was hearing. 'D'you mean no bird, guv? Can you really make that happen?'.

Masters nodded and turned away. At the cell door he turned and smiled at him before abruptly leaving, slamming the heavy door, and grinning towards the uniformed officer on cell duty.

'Give him a mug of tea. He's not such a bad lad' he told him breezily.

Later that day Don had a chat with Cecil Fortescue, Charlie's probation officer. A likeable young man used to having the piss taken out of him because of that name, he had a soft spot for Charlie. The soft spot was well known to the CID officers: it wasn't only Charlie it encompassed, Cecil's charity took in most of the layabouts infesting the streets of their patch. Masters played on that sympathy for Charlie and it did the trick: Cecil was persuaded that the young man was yet again worth saving

*

Paul Price, a thick set five feet eighter, was shaking his head and staring at the fish and chips on the tin plate being offered to him by the uniformed policeman on cell duty. The sight turned his stomach. 'How much longer?' he complained. ' I've been in here two hours'.

' Not up to me'. The constable said coldly. ' Eat your dinner. The boss'll see you all in good time'. Like most of the officers on his shift he'd seen the photo of the man's wife with the weal around her neck and reckoned that the murderer of two women was staring back at him.

'What's this about? Surely you can tell me that?'. He gestured at the dinner. 'And you can take that away'.

'Up to you. It's a long time to breakfast'.

The cell door was slammed and opened again a few

minutes later. Miller, unsmiling, stood in the open doorway and beckoned to Price. 'You're wanted upstairs. Time for a chat'.

'Cuffs skip?'. The constable dangled handcuffs to Miller.

Miller weighted up Price and shook his head. 'We're not going to need them, are we mate?'. He grinned at the constable in the doorway ' His hands'll be full holding up his trousers'.

Price, by then on his feet and staring nervously from one to the other, finally stared at Miller. 'What's it all about?. Why wasn't I allowed into my own home?' And why have you taken my car away? And my bloody belt? How d'you expect me to hold up my trousers?'.

'My guvnor will tell you. Let's go -walk in front of me and go where I say'.

As they passed through the custody area officers turned to stare at killer Price disappearing upstairs and, guided by the sergeant, into Masters office.

Pointing to an armless chair opposite his desk, Masters told him to sit. 'Know why you're here?', he asked quietly.

Price looked around the sparsely furnished room before he slumped down and stared back and shook his head.

'For starters Paul, your house was burgled today. We've got the man who did it. Fifty quid on him: yours?'.

'Can't say to that. What's the other thing?'.

'Amanda. Anything to say to me?.................No?', he added, when Price said nothing.

'We know, Paul', he said quietly. ' Talk to me. You'll feel better'.

Price's anger was on display when he shook his head. 'You've got to tell me what this is all about. I'm pushed into a car, shut in a cell, get stared at by your lot. So tell me: What's going on?'.

Masters ignored the demand and glanced across to Miller, who had taken up his usual spot by the door, for his reaction.

The sergeant shrugged and spread his hands non-committedly.

'We've found Amanda, Paul'.

Price stared back into Masters grim face. 'What's going on here?'. He looked at Masters and then at the unsmiling, threatening sergeant. 'Am I missing something here? Found her? What do you mean?'.

Masters leaned forward and stared at Price, letting the pregnant silence hopefully do his work.

Price's anger subsided a bit but he was unnerved by the detective's manner. 'What has she done? Buggered off with one of her boyfriends?' He turned to give Miller a puzzled stare. 'Know you don't I?',

Miller's granite features didn't react

'It'll come to me', Price said. Turning his attention to Masters he asked, angrily: 'You going to tell me or what?'.

'Tell me about her boyfriends, Paul'.

'Ask her! She throws them in my face when she's in one of her moods. But she never lets on who they are'. He shifted his gaze again to Miller, and frowned, trying to remember..................

'Do I gather you and Amanda have rows?'.

Masters' question dragged his mind back to the present. 'You could say that. Look. I'm away a lot. I'm not a bloody fool. She's always telling me she needs company. But what can I do? I'm a driver. I spent days away from home. And I find things', he added.

'Like what?'.

'You've had a good look around my place by now. Did you find the school kid outfit? And those knickers?'.He looked from Masters to Miller, who was grinning now. 'Well she doesn't wear them when I'm at home'.

Masters nodded. 'Wondered about them, Paul. Very sexy. Knickers with a slit: new one on me'.

'Well they have nothing to do with me! Ask her what she gets up to. I have and she laughs at me'.

Masters leaned forward: 'Is that at the root of your rows?'.

Price clenched his hands into white-knuckled fists and looked away.

'We talking sex Paul?'. He put the question softly and shot a warning glance to Miller, who looked ready to land one on him.

Price looked at Miller's threatening face for a few seconds before staring at Masters 'What's this really about?', he demanded.

'Did you kill Amanda?', Masters asked quietly after a few seconds, staring hard at the man.

Price's expression froze into open-mouthed shock. 'She's dead?', he whispered.

'Now Paul, listen carefully'. Masters was hunched towards Price. 'You're not obliged to say anything but what you do say will be taken down in writing and may be given in evidence. Do you understand what I've said?'.

With tears streaming down his face Price dropped his head into his fist-clenched hands. 'I don't believe this', he mumbled. 'How? Who did it?'. He raised his head and stared through misted eyes at both detectives. 'You think I did it!'.

Masters kept a steady gaze on Price for some seconds before he answered that. 'You're a suspect for her murder. You had the opportunity and a motive'.

'Motive!' What motive?'.

Masters waggled a pointing finger at Price. 'You've told me enough to put you top of my list'.

Price stared wide eyed at Masters as the realisation of his position sank in. He shook his head. 'You've got this all wrong'.

Masters tapped a statement in front of him. 'You got back to your base at 4pm.on Monday. Uncoupled the trailer and washed down your unit. Clocked off at 5pm. where did you go?'.

'Home of course'.

'What time was that?'.

I don't know! Around 6pm'.

'Was Amanda at home?'.

'She came in, I don't know, about half an hour later. We had a row straight off -about the kinky stuff. She stormed out and that was the last time I saw her'. Price sank his head into his hands. 'I can't take any more of this...........I've nothing more to say'.

'Time will tell' Masters said coldly. 'Take him back to his cell, Dusty'.

*

'How awful, Don', Betty Saunders remarked when Masters related a brief account of his interview with Price. She glanced across at her husband who was clearly worrying about something else. 'Is it the burglary, darling?', she asked gently, recalling the repeated nightmare he told her about.

He was reaching for his glass as she spoke and nodded, but he was looking at Masters. 'He hasn't admitted killing his wife has he? You said he cried a lot. That's not an admission is it?'.

The DI shook his head. 'What can I say, Dave. Experience?'. He smiled at the women and offered the wine bottle. Both shook their heads.

'What about evidence?'. Saunders persisted, leaning towards the detective, keen to hear more.

Masters could understand his friend was troubled with the death of Fraser so was careful how he answered. ' Jealousy, David. Men will kill because of it'.

Jean understood the look she got from Saunders' wife and smiled at the men. 'Why don't you go into the living room while I clear up?'

'I'll help, Jean'. Betty gathered up her and her husband's plates and followed Jean into the kitchen.

'Put them on the drainer, Betty. Let's have a coffee and let Don talk to David'.

*

'Inspector', remarked the chairman of the bench 'We are minded to commit Hobbs to a higher court for sentence. The last paragraph of the antecedents suggests you think we should do otherwise. Can you enlighten us?'

'Yes sir'. Masters, suited and tied for the occasion, responded in his acquired courtroom attitude. 'Firstly, Hobbs' grandmother is willing to take him back under her wing and, importantly, he has a girl friend who loves him. May I add, sir, I believe Hobbs is redeemable'

'And why do you believe that?'

Masters adopted a thoughtful expression. 'I understand your natural scepticism, sir, but he is a likeable lad who I believe will benefit from one more chance. I have made enquiries at local factories. I have been advised there is a possibility he can be offered work'.

The chairman looked to left and right at his bench colleagues for the day and then back at the detective. 'Is the grandmother at court?'

'She is'.

'Is she willing to give evidence?'
'She is'.
'Let her take the stand'.

Mavis Venerables' smiled gratefully towards Masters before saying her piece, her love for her wayward grandson shining through her plea and swaying the magistrates.

Next up was Cecil, who duly confirmed Charlie's petty record and fractured life but also declared, smiling at Masters, what a redeemable young man Charlie was. Sternly told by the magistrate that he was being given a last chance, Charlie sailed out of court on a cloud to do a two year stint on probation.

*

Masters glanced at the detectives assembled for his briefing. 'Morning all. We've got three murders on our hands. You're to be split into teams. Team one - Mark Bateman. According to his wife everyone loved Mark, except the killer that is!' he added with a grim smile. 'He is, was, thirty-five', he glanced down at his rough notes. 'Worked for solicitors Blake Partnership. Legal executive . They've got an office in the town -some of you already know that. We've got two suspects for the job - their photos and ID's are up there', he gestured at the wall. 'Their dabs are all over the dead man's car but I can't establish when they were put there. Because we're missing the gun used for the job they haven't been pulled in, yet'. He smiled around. 'Complication there, but I hope to get it sorted'.

'How was it done, guv?' a detective constable asked.
'Head shot'.
Detective constable John Barton raised an arm
'John?'
'He was a member of Gyms Place in town. Does a

bit of weight training. I go there myself. Seen you there sometimes sarg', he added, smiling towards Miller.

'You've met him there?'

'Seen him, guv. well muscled bloke as I recall'.

'Anyone with him?'

'On his own, guv'.

'Seen him, Dusty?'.

'Might have done. Rings a bell'.

'Amanda - she a member?'.

'Yes, guv', Barton confirmed. 'Spends her time on the running machine'.

'And Dianne Flaxman. Seen her there?'.

'Can't be certain, guv. Mrs. Price was friendly with another young woman.........might have been her. She was blonde. Could have been I suppose'.

'Sarge?'.

Miller spread his hands. 'Can't be certain. Amanda had a friend that's true, but Dianne...............It's no good, Don. Can't say for certain'.

Masters turned his attention to the assembled detectives. 'Let's get started. What do we know about Bateman's murder? For starters, he wasn't shot where he was found. We've got a car with fragments of his head splattered inside. Dead for at least three days when found. No footprints of any use found'. Masters smiled, remembering his soiled shoes. 'A dog had a good nose around before we got there!'.

'Overboard with a woman, guv?'

The DI looked across to detective constable Read. ' Might have been Amanda Price. She also worked in Bateman's office. Right then - Bateman first: traffic's involved in this one. We know roughly when he was put there. I've arranged for an on-going road check at the lay-by. Someone knew where to dump him. We need to fill in those missing days, starting from 8am on the Tuesday he went missing. We know that's when he left home and didn't turn up for work'. He looked at the detectives detailed for the Bateman enquiry ' Get out there and fill in the picture and remember, this is a murder enquiry so be thorough. Sergeant Miller will give you your individual tasks. Background checking is most important. I'll deal with the robbery suspects for Bateman's murder. Liaise with Dc. Barton. He'll be checking Amanda's history -there may be an interesting overlap there. Right then. Bateman's team: off you go'.

With them gone Masters turned his attention to the others. Pointing to the enlarged street map on the wall, he told them 'House to house enquiries at each of the houses facing Whiley Road haven't turned up sightings of a vehicle at the material times. I need thorough background enquiries for each woman. Girlfriends, boyfriends, their interests, fantasies - if Amanda's husband is telling us the truth she had a few- and anyone that knew of them. I don't care who you upset but get detailed statements. Build a life story that gives me something to go on. I'll deal with Amanda's connection with Bateman, and her relationship with her husband. The suspicions we have so far may be leading us away from what really happened to her. All right? Any questions?'. Smiling back at shaking heads he said 'Off you go'.

As they trooped out he gestured to Miller, who had returned from his briefing. He checked his watch. 'Time for a chat'.

Chapter three

With DCI Makepeace constantly on his back about the station's arrest rate Masters turned his attention to Walthamstead's declining clear up rate for burglaries. It was not rocket science that a firm from outside the manor was outdoing the local villains. The method was the same each time: round the back, jemmy a door, tip the place upside down and nick anything not nailed down. The largely useless enquiries by his team of detectives indicated one thing: none of the local hard cases had access to a van capable of carrying away the eclectic loot.

Eight thousand pound richer from the Woodall job, Masters had bade farewell to the insurance representative and turned his attention to the outstanding eighteen housebreakings, and re-read a report from the neighbouring police area that suggested three tearaways on their patch as likely suspects: put in the frame were Fred Spence, Brian Winch and George Brothwell. Each had the usual teenage cons for theft and housebreaking and were, according to the author of the report, highly likely to be responsible for Masters' jobs. Interestingly, the report added that Fred's dad Leonard Spence had cons for armed robbery. He sat back and mulled over the best way to go about it and settled on Charlie Hobbs' indoctrination. He popped his head around the detective constables' door and beckoned to detective constable Read

'Guv?'.

'Grab a car from the pool, Ted, nip over to Romford and collect Charlie Hobbs'

*

Charlie, thin as they come, was regretting leaving his coat at home. Shirt-sleeved and freezing, he was hunched forward in the passenger seat beside Masters, hugging himself and occasionally wiping the misted screen with a grubby hand.

'Couple of miles. Soon be there. And don't do that, Charlie. It'll make it worse'.

It was already turned 4pm. Masters switched the fan to full to clear the misted screen while outside the freezing fog had reduced visibility to a bare hundred yards. Indicating, he steered the Jaguar off the dual carriageway onto the minor road he was looking for. After about a mile he pulled onto a verge, switched off the headlights and killed the engine.

"Ere are we?. Charlie rubbed his elbow against the misted door window and peered through. the fog. 'Can't see fuck all, Don. And I'm freezing'. When the detective didn't answer but started to get out he raised his voice as he too clambered out. 'Eerie me doing that dead woman's drum, Don. You got it sorted yet?'.

Masters shook his head as the younger man hugged himself and ignored the question. 'We walk from here, Charlie', he said, glancing at the shivering young man.

'Do me a favour, Don. I'm bloody freezing!', he complained to the disappearing back of the detective . 'I don't fancy this one little bit'.

'Told you you'd need a coat' Masters called back. 'There's a coat on the back seat'. He set off with a reluctant Charlie in tow, pulling on the coat as he struggled to keep up. After a short while the detective recognised the driveway lights of the house he was looking for and pulled a still shivering Charlie to one side.

Pointing to the house set well back from the road, he told him it would soon be unoccupied for two weeks. He smiled briefly at the younger man's questioning face. ' Trust me on that, Charlie. I want you to get on side with a three man firm who's been screwing my manor. Bring them here. I'll tell you when. Can you do that?'.

Still shivering, Charlie nodded and suggested they went back the way they came. 'I need to fix the route in me brain box'.

The detective smiled and ruffled Charlie's hair. ' How's Janet making out?

'She's alright. Doing a bit of hairdressing she is'.

Back in the car Charlie angled towards Masters, who had turned the car around. 'These geezers -do I know 'em, Don?'.

'Only if you get over to Leytonstone'.

Hobbs shook his head. 'The pits that place. That where we're going?'.

Masters nodded. 'I want you to go into the Greyhound pub - I'll point it out - Get on board with Fred Spence'. He fished a photo from a pocket. 'This is him'.

Charlie took the snap and studied it. 'Don't know 'im. Should I?'.

'No, Charlie. But get to know him. He's a couple of years older than you. He fancies himself as a housebreaker. He's got two blokes in tow'.

Thirty minutes later he eased the car into the kerb and killed the engine. 'Here', he pulled out some money, and handed it to Charlie. 'There's a ton there. The pub's over there. Not now. When you go in there use your wits. Get in with them. Tell them about the drum we went to'. He smiled at the younger man 'I've got confidence in you, Charlie. If you manage it bell me and we'll set it up. Can do?'.

Charlie grinned as he dotted his cigarette end. 'Piece of cake, Don. Run me home, yeh?'.

Masters nodded and slid into gear.

*

The three villains screwing the house with Charlie by then trusted his convincing way. Charlie didn't do violence: that wasn't his style. They knew that because Charlie, being engagingly persuasive, had convinced them he was a softy; but unknown to them was his cunning. So confident were they in Charlie's info that their van was parked outside the front of the house and accessed by a carriage driveway.

Don and two detective constables had been hidden up for half an hour before the break in beside the detached garage and were bitterly cold when the van arrived and the four shadowy men broke in round the back.

'Guv', whispered Read. He was pointing to the shadowy back of Charlie, the last to go in. 'That makes four'.

Masters nodded and offered a hunch-shouldered grimace by way of acknowledgement. Charlie being seen but not recognised was a gamble he had accepted.

'They'll come out the door', the DI confidently told his men, pointing to it. 'Quiet, now. Let's cover it'. With that done he whispered to the detective who had moved beside the villains' Transit, 'Let the tyres down, Brian'.

'Done it?' he queried after a lapse of hissing minutes that suddenly went quiet.

'Yes guv'.

'Let'm get on board before we nick m'. With that said Masters radioed for the stand-by support vans to block the exits from the drive.

'Check outside, Beanpole', hyped-up Fred demanded of Charlie.

Charlie moved a curtain, saw Masters, who had moved to cover the front of the house and winked. 'All clear Fred'

'Get it by the door', Fred told the others.

The nicked gear was rapidly piled near it.

'All set?'

The others, dead keen to be off, nodded in turn and the door was opened and the mis-match of stolen property hastily stuffed into the van via its' sliding side door. Charlie hung back until the others were on board and Fred was reaching for the ignition key. He saw Masters grab it and slam the door, and had it away on his toes through the hall to the back door.

Masters was staring at a bewildered Spence.. 'You're nicked lads', he said quietly at startled faces staring back at him. 'Don't do anything silly now'.

Charlie didn't hang around. Nipping out the back he legged it over a fence and settled into a steady lope to where Janet was waiting in his Viva, which she'd parked on a grass-surfaced area some distance away from the two police vans. Climbing on board he leaned across and kissed her. Pulling back he grinned and looked towards the police vehicles, which by then had their lights on. 'Let'm go first, love. Sit tight'.

Janet peered through the gloom. 'Wot 'ave you done Charlie? You never said the old bill would be prowling about?. Won't they see us?'.

'No way. They'll go the other way. Trust me. There goes one of them'. He gestured to disappearing tail lights. 'The other one's going up the drive, see?'.

'Yes, Charlie. Do they know you got away?'.

'Not a chance, love. We can go now. Nice and steady does it'.

Janet engaged the gears and looked at the love of her life. 'I love you so much, Charlie. I couldn't bear it if you got arrested'.

'Come on, love. Let's get moving. There's not a chance of getting nicked, believe me'.

*

DI. Masters, called to divisional headquarters for the usual interrogation, dropped into the chair indicated by his grumpy chief and waited while the beefy man read through his brief report, from time to time shaking his head and glancing over his glasses at Masters.

'Anything to add to this inspector?' Wary now, he leaned forward in his chair and hooked a stubby finger at the DI and demanded through the silence ' This is what, eight, or is it nine times we've had these chats? One always seems to melt away -I'm not a bloody fool, inspector'.

'Straight forward nick, guv. They've had a good run. Nineteen drums turned over'.

'Same one?'

'Sir?'

'The informant. Same one as last time?'

'As a matter of fact, no, sir. But solid as a rock'.

'Why that house?'.

'I don't get you, sir. Mind if I smoke?'.

'If you must. Inspector. It so happens the occupants are away on holiday. It's in the book for Christ's sake. Did you know that?'

'The villains did, obviously. And so did my snout'.

'And how the bloody hell would they know that!'

'One of life's mysteries, sir. These blaggards are always one up on us, aren't they?'. Masters eased forward in the chair and tapped ash into a tray on the desk.

Scowling at the DI, Makepeace picked it up and emptied it in a waste paper basket. Opening a desk drawer he took out a tissue and wiped it clean before replacing it on the desk.

Masters decided to be humble. 'My fault I suppose. The info was three would screw the house. As it turned out I was a man short for the collar. None has named him so far. Give it time. You know how these things go: one'll come clean'.

The DCS wasn't listening. 'Its the same old story, inspector. You're telling me man number four, as usual I might add, had it away from right under your bloody nose?'

'That's not how it went, sir. He must have scarpered out the back way. The dog eventually followed a trail to a road and lost it'.

'So you actually saw this other man?'

'Heard him, sir'.

'Heard him?'

'Feet sir'.

'Feet!'

Running feet, sir'.

Remembering the creaks a smile was gone so soon as it flicked across the DCS's podgy face . 'Woodall, inspector', he said, changing the subject. 'Chelmsford crown court in two weeks. The defence are digging hard. They want details of your information leading to his arrest'.

'No problem there, sir. The call was logged in the occurrence book'.

'Naturally it was you who logged it?'.

'It's a fishing expedition, sir. Not the first time I've produced that book'.

Makepeace shook his head. 'One day, inspector, your boat will slip its moorings and over you'll go. If it does I suspect you'll be swimming out of your depth'.

'Sir?'.

'On your way. Just be bloody careful'.

*

Charlie drove his clapped out Viva onto the top deck of

the multi storey car park in Walthamstead, killed the engine, doused the headlights and settling down to wait for the detective inspector. Several sets of headlights swept the area before Masters' car pulled in beside his and the detective clambered in.

'Well done, Charlie. Bloody well done, Masters told him quietly, ruffling the younger man's hair as he spoke. 'Any come back at your end?'

Charlie shook his head but asked nervously ''ave they grassed me?'

'No Charlie. We had a go at them as per normal. So far they haven't. It'll take a few more days of chat, but I know we've got the right fingers for all our jobs'.

'What's the drill if they do name me?'

'I'll have you in for questioning. You keep your mouth shut and out you go. They're at Court in the morning. Come along if you want. You'll see for yourself'.

Charlie hunched round to stare at the DI 'Come to court? D'you fink I'm mad!'

'It's a game Charlie. Your presence'll be a warning. One look at you and they'll know its time to keep their mouths shut. Do it and your street cred'll go way up. Believe me' added the detective when he saw the younger man's obvious doubt. He pulled out an envelope and handed it over. 'Hundred quid, Charlie. That do?'

'Yeh. Fanks, Don.

*

19 year old Janet West lived with Charlie in rented rooms above a fish and chip shop in Romford. Janet's upbringing was the usual deprivation. Being bright hadn't helped her into a decent job, never did where she came from. Apart from shoplifting, she was straightish,

her mum saw to that. She could have had any young man on her arm but she had picked Charlie on a visit to Borstal, where she had gone to see another wayward tea leaf. When he was out from Borstal and her mum got to know him she reckoned Charlie a total waste of space. But Janet was in love. Her attachment to him was one of life's mysteries explained if you understood how a young woman's mind ticked. She knew she was pretty, many hours spent in front of her mirror confirmed that for her, but Charlie knew she was a radiant beauty, all five feet three inches with her slender body and blonde hair and, importantly for Charlie, big tits.

Charlie to her was someone special but she never could be sure of his affection for her. He told her he loved her. In fact, every time they were panting away in bed, stuck together in sweaty endeavour, he used that word a lot. Sometimes when she was alone and in a reflective mood she did accept that he never said he loved her during daylight hours. But the real Charlie, the one she loved, the Charlie in bed, the sex god at night, was the only young man who made her feel special.

'Charlie'. She ran her fingers down his back. 'Charlie……..'.

He flopped over and looked into those lovely blue eyes, inches from his own and his old man stirred. He slid an arm under her body and pulled her on top, sliding his immediately erect penis between her legs as he caressed her beautifully shaped bum.

'Put it in Charlie', she urged.

'You do it' he likewise urgently urged.

Janet quickly got into position and did that bit and Charlie held her waist and moved gently against her slender body, his hands reaching for and firmly holding her tiny waist as she pushed against him, moaning her usual delight until their orgasms erupted in a breathless moment of shared passion.

'Easing away she rolled beside him and stroked his face. 'You do love me, don't you Charlie?'

'You know I do' he told her as he reached for his fag packet.

'Say you love me'.

'I love you'. He lit up.

'Why don't mum like you?'

'Ask *her*'. Through a smoky haze he cuddled her, and kissed her forehead.

'I do ask her, Charlie'. She pulled back to look at the love of her life. 'Many times I do. She doesn't know you like I know you. She says cruel things about you sometimes'

'Like wot?'

'I don't like to say............'.

'Tell me'. He reached for an empty pie dish and tapped.

'Well............for one fing she says you mix with a bad lot'. She hunched up to stare at Charlie, concerned he was looking even thinner lately.

He was easing himself from the bed as she was speaking and reaching for his underpants.

'Aren't you going to shower, darling?'

Charlie pulled on his jeans and shirt. 'No time love. Fings to do'. Bending down he pecked her forehead again. 'You are still taking the pill aren't you?' he asked as a worrying thought struck home.

'You know I am, Charlie. You told me that first time didn't you'

A satisfied Charlie nodded and said 'Got to fly. Oh', he added as he pulled out notes from his trouser pocket and peeled off fifty pounds 'Buy yourself something nice'. He turned at the door and looked back 'Meeting Anne today?'

Janet laid back and pulled the bedclothes up and nodded.

'Young for you. She's a bloody school kid'

'But I like her. She's good company, Charlie'.

*

'Yes, Inspector?'.

Masters got to his feet and picked up his brief. 'Your worships. My application is for a remand in custody. Many enquiries have to be completed before we can proceed with this case. The accused is the husband of the deceased woman. He has offered no corroboration of his movements for the critical period in the deceased woman's life. Enquiries in hand are such that in a week's time I hope to be in a position to proceed with this case'.

The chairman was staring at Price. 'Are you represented here today?'

John White popped up to identify himself.

'Well?'.

'I am representing Mr. Price. I am informed he loved his wife, your worships. His appearance here today is a travesty of natural justice. The police have offered no evidence that involves my client in the savage death of his wife. My application is for a remand on bail'.

The three nodding heads turned as one to each other and the chairman, looking over his spectacles at Masters said 'Inspector. It really isn't good enough to bring a defendant to court on such flimsy evidence. Are you going to produce evidence that the defendant was involved in the death of his wife?'.

Fully aware that he had charged Price on flimsy evidence in order to question him and search his house and car for likely evidence, he rose to his feet and explained his position. 'The defendant admits he and the dead woman rowed. We have only his word that she left their home on the evening of the day she was last seen alive. He alleges she had sexual partners but cannot, or will not name them'. He sat down.

The magistrates huddled for a few moments, then the chairman said firmly. 'We are prepared to grant bail on a surety with a condition of a fixed abode. It is clear to us that the defendant should not return to his home for the duration of the investigation and likely ensuing legal proceedings. Can you offer an alternative address?'.

The lawyer looked across to Price, who was nodding.

May I have a few moments with my client?'

'Of course'.

White crossed to the dock and Price leaned close and whispered to him.

'Well, Mr. White?'.

'My client's parents live in the town. He assures me he is welcome to stay with them'.

'Very well. Give the details of his parents' address to the Clerk. Once confirmed bail will be granted'.

Masters got to his feet once Price had left the dock for the cells and watched Fred and his clan escorted up from the cells to stand nervously in the dock.

'The defendants are presently charged with one count of burglary' he began, stopping to stare at Fred and his mates. ' Enquiries are ongoing into other serious offences which we have reason to believe are connected with the three defendants. My application today is for a remand to police cells for seven days to facilitate those enquiries'.

'Mr. White?'

John White hauled himself up again, looking firstly at Fred Spence's dad Len. Giving a quick smile to Masters he turned back to the magistrates and became solemn. 'There are no civilian witnesses against my clients' he stated firmly. 'No previous records of violence are recorded against any of them; and violence was not used to commit the alleged offence. In view of those facts which indicate, I submit, that these men are of no danger to the general public, my instructions are to apply for bail'.

'Inspector?'

Masters stood. 'With due respect for the defendants' lawyer, sir, many ongoing enquiries which would assist in the recovery of stolen property would be prejudiced should these men be released on bail'.

The magistrates: Bob, the butcher, a fat lump of a man; Tony, the builder with a red face and hairy tattooed arms, and George the undertaker, a weedy bloke with a pointed nose, agreed with the D.I that the men should remain incarcerated. After all, they were well aware from articles in the local press that some thieving bastards had been having a field day breaking into local houses. One, as Bob had mentioned to Tony and George before the remand hearing, was a neighbour, the captain of the local cricket team, a member of the same lodge, whose house had only the week before been turned over.

'Bail refused. Remanded to police cells for seven days'.

'Sorry about that John'. Masters smiled at the solicitor beside him gathering up his papers. 'We must have a chat soon about the brief Bateman was preparing for you. My gut feeling is there's more to it than the file says. When can we meet?'

'I've got a window tomorrow morning if that's okay for you?'.

'Your office?'

'My office at 10 say'.

Leonard Spence, a forty-eight years old recidivist

armed robber and veteran of CID interrogation, sat in the well of the court picking up on the way the remand hearing was going. No stranger to the proceedings, with many court appearances and various spells in prisons behind him, he shook his head in disbelief when his son was refused bail. He watched as the fair haired, fit-looking thirty-something Masters gathered up his papers and walked from the court and followed him.

'Have a word, guv?' he asked when he was walking beside the detective.

Masters stopped and studied the older man. 'What is it?'

'Not here, guv. I'm Fred's dad. We need to talk'.

The detective started to walk on but Spence gripped his arm 'It's worth your while to listen to what I've got to say', he urged. 'There's a transport caff a mile out of town. Let's have a meet there'. With that said he walked ahead and Masters followed him to the car park and watched him climb into a newish looking Zephyr. As he drove away he glanced towards Masters and raised a thumb.

The DI, memorising the car's number, fished a scrap of paper from a pocket and scribbled it down before walking to his own car.

Several artics were backed into a corner of the gravelled parking area beside the 24 hour Green Welly café and cars were dotted about; but Masters was looking for the Zephyr. Spotting it he parked away from it and went in. Spence, a burly ex-docker, his personality displayed on tattooed muscled arms under rolled up shirt sleeves, had picked a table away from the other drivers, slung his coat over the back of his chair, and was tucking into a fry up.

The detective took his mug of tea and plopped into a chair opposite and waited.

Spence looked up at Masters a couple of times and studied him between mouthfuls. 'What're his chances?' he asked as he wiped a slice of bread around the greasy plate.

Masters said nothing and sipped.

Spence devoured the slice, wiped his mouth and took a swig from his mug of tea, all the time staring at Masters, trying to read him. 'What d'you reckon?' he asked quietly.

'Not good'.

Spence frowned.

The D.I leaned forward. 'Fred's in the frame for eighteen other jobs. Lots of gear nicked. Now.......if I could lay my hands on most of that stuff things might brighten up'.

Len nodded. 'I get the picture. Is he bang to rights for these other jobs?'

'He is', the detective lied easily.

'Can I have a visit?'

'How will that help?'. Masters pulled out his cigarette packet and looked at it. 'Should really pack this in', he said, as he put the packet away.

Digesting Masters question, Len sat back, taking the opportunity to think carefully. He knew how to handle the filth at his local nick but Masters was unreadable. Finally he sat forward, pushed his plate away to place his elbows on the table and stare intently at the D.I, before quietly suggesting: 'I might be able to put something your way. Interested?'

'What are we talking about here?' Masters held the other man's gaze.

'A blagging firm'. Spence sat back and waited for Masters response.

'Where does Fred fit into this?'

Spence was shaking his head 'He doesn't. But his mum will do her nut if he gets banged up. He needs a leg up. If I give you that firm will you give me Fred?'

'What about the other two?'

'Let me have a word with them and I'll sort that for you. Their dads are mates of mine. You'll get your other jobs'.

Masters was digesting the offer while the man was speaking and now he nodded 'Okay. Put the firm up and you can see Fred and his mates. But I must get gear back and the tic's guaranteed, otherwise the deal's off.'

*

Chapter four

Doubling work with pleasure that evening, John Barton grabbed a vacant rowing machine in Gyms Place and worked out for a while. From where he was he could see Melvyn Arrowsmith, a fleshy man he guessed to be in his thirties, heaving at weight training apparatus. Word doing the rounds was he was an odd ball. Someone had spread a story that he hung around girls' school playing fields. Had a camera apparently. Miller was working out beside him. He moved across and settled himself in the apparatus the near side of Arrowsmith, giving the sweating man a grin before heaving at the weights 'Seen Amanda lately?, he asked several minutes later when Arrowsmith let go of the apparatus and leaned back, breathing hard.

'Not this week' Arrowsmith panted, his eyes half-closed at the effort he'd put into lifting.

Barton lowered his weights and glanced at Arrowsmith. 'Good looker............you reckon?'.

'Definitely. A charming young woman', he agreed, opening his eyes and glancing at Barton, who was tentatively raising weights again.

'Do much of this?' Barton asked as he heaved.

Melvyn patted his stomach. 'Trying to get this down'. He smiled at Barton. 'That's enough for me. It's a coffee and home. Got things to do'.

'I'll join you'. Barton looked across to Miller. 'Fancy a cuppa sarg?', he called

Miller shook his head and carried on heaving.

Over coffee Arrowsmith opened up about Amanda. Nudged on by Barton he reckoned others saw her as a trophy to be won. It became clear after a few more minutes he was jealous of Barry Lakey. Barton recognised the name from his enquiries. 'He works out here doesn't he?'

'He does. Amanda told me about him. She didn't say what but she did things with him. Mentioned your colleague once - seemed to like him'.

'Dusty Miller?'.

'Yes'.

'Teasing you was she?'.

'Could have been I suppose -she *was* smiling'.

'Seen Mark Bateman lately?'

'Not this week. Does weights like us. Keeps himself to himself".

'What about Dianne................get on with her?'.

Arrowsmith shrugged the question away and sipped his coffee. 'Bit rude I thought' he explained. 'Had that air about her, you know, on the look out for a man. That's what I thought anyway'.

'Not your type then?'.

'Definitely not. Your colleague fancied her........I could tell'.

Surprised, over the rim of his cup Barton asked, 'What makes you think so?'.

'Something about him. I think he knows I liked Amanda. He's crude. He's always making suggestive remarks'.

'Such as?'.

Arrowsmith twirled his cup in it's saucer and looked over Barton's head. '"Amanda needs a real man"' - he said that more than once. That's not a nice thing to say, is it?'. He transferred his gaze to Barton. 'It's not is it?'.

Barton saw the man was clearly hurt by his sergeant's comment. 'No, Melvyn, it's not. Don't take it to heart. Dusty can be arrogant sometimes'.

*

A CRO search on all the male club members turned up only Arrowsmith and Lakey as weirdos of interest. Arrowsmith's predilection for young girls came to light when he was nineteen and placed on probation for exposing himself to a girls' hockey team on sports day. Apparently their ball came his way and he retrieved it, giving it back to a panting girl with his cock hanging out. Since then he'd been done for indecent assault and handed a six month sentence the first time and twelve months the second. He'd been clean for three years. Lakey was a different kettle of fish: still single, he was down as a violent sod who got off inflicting pain on women who chanced his way. His cons were for three indecent assaults, each with a nasty edge involving the use of sadistic weapons up vaginas. The details on his CRO file were sparse but sufficient for Barton to form a realistic picture of a kinky man likely to seriously hurt a woman.

The enquiries by the team of detectives trawling Amanda's past had revealed she had been seen going into Barry Lakey's home of an evening. Sheila Ashwood, a nosey spinster with a pair of binoculars, lived opposite Lakey's. Shown the photos of Dianne and Amanda she was sure she had seen Amanda use a key to go into Lakey's semi-detached house around 8pm on the Monday that Price has stated she left their home. When pushed she said she might have seen Dianne Flaxman going in and out of Lakey's house.

'You've done a good job' Masters told Barton when he related what he'd been able to find out at the fitness club. Dianne *had* also been a club member; and Mrs. Ashwood's sharp eyes appeared to have pushed Amanda's husband out of the frame. With nothing to lose Masters turned his attention to Arrowsmith and Lakey, who had been brought in for questioning.

'Lakey seems favourite, but we'll have Arrowsmith first. Get him up here, John'.

Brought up from his cell and pushed onto a chair opposite Masters, Melvyn Arrowsmith went in denial mode, staring back wordlessly at the detective.

'One more time, Melvyn. She was a good shag. That's about the strength of it isn't it?'.

Melvyn was horrified. 'How dare you! Amanda wasn't like that!'.

'Why did you kill her?'.

'Kill Amanda! I loved her!'. He looked at Masters and then at Miller, who was in his usual spot by the door, grinning and hunching forward, this time in a chair; and at Barton, who was in a chair behind him, also grinning. 'I didn't kill her!'.

'Let's see shall we. You're a dirty bastard who's into flashing it about. What did you get up to with her?'.

Reduced to a trembling wreck Arrowsmith stared through misted eyes at the detective, whose steely gaze was frightening him. 'We.................'. His voice trailed away.

'Yes?'.

'My wife...............' Arrowsmith looked from one officer to the other. 'She doesn't have to be told about Amanda does she?'.

Masters leaned forward and stared into the frightened man's face. 'That's down the road. Tell me what you got up to'.

'I never got undressed. I didn't. You must believe that'.

Mystified, Masters demanded, 'Just tell me'.

'Well...............she.............I mean I...........I pulled my zip down and she............'. He broke off amidst a welter of tears.

'For Christ's sake, Melvyn. Just spit it out'.

Head down and staring at the floor he mumbled

through tears. 'I pulled my penis out out and she.....she....... sucked it'.

The detective's looked from one to the other disbelievingly. Then, recalling that the search had discovered the school girl outfit, Masters, desperately trying not to smile, asked. 'Was she wearing a school skirt and blouse at the time?'.

The tearful, broken, man nodded.

'Is that it, Melvyn? You were with a very beautiful woman and all that happened was she sucked your cock! I don't believe you'.

'It's true. I swear it'.

'Did all this take place in her home?'

He nodded again and looked from one to the other. 'Does my wife have to know?'.

'Depends. You'll be staying with us for a while. We've got a lot of checking to do, and that includes searching your house. So tell me: when was the last time you did it with Amanda?'.

'Oh my God!' Arrowsmith whispered. His nightmare was taking on a terrifying reality. The end of his marriage loomed large. His frigid wife Joyce abhorred any talk of sex and would switch off the TV when any subject got close to discussing it. She had a rule, her mantra went: sex was a once a month joyless get together done because, she would tell him coldly, on the run up to the moment she laid back and opened her legs, it was something a man wanted and a woman had to endure. Now he was looking at Masters through misted eyes.

'Met hubby?'. Masters' tone was dispassionate

'God no!. What a nightmare!'.

Half an hour later he looked at the steel door with its small grill and knew the punishment for sexual transgression his wife often proclaimed, awaited him in the world on the other side of that door.

*

Barry Lakey, brought up from his cell by John Barton, sat in the chair opposite Masters and stared, shaking his head at the accusation. 'No way. You've got the wrong man'. He switched his gaze to Barton and Miller, who was his usual threatening self, and back to stony-faced Masters.

Masters leaned forward and stared back.'Try again shall we?'.

'Try all you like but it wasn't me'.

'Alright, Barry. Tell me this: you had it off with Amanda in her home. Is that right?'.

'No comment'.

'In your home?'.

'No comment'.

Masters stared at Lakey for some seconds and then at statements in front of him. Looking up he studied Lakey, who stared back unflinchingly. 'So when I tell you we know Mrs Price was seen entering your house on the evening of the day she was last seen alive I'm wrong am I?'.

'No comment', Lakey muttered, dragging his gaze away from the detective's accusing eyes.

Masters nodded. 'Got you in one, Barry. Prove it, yes?'.

Lakey shrugged.

Watching him carefully Masters said 'Same goes for Dianne.........yes?'.

Lakey clenched hands into white-knuckled fists and stared away from the detective. 'No comment', he muttered.

Masters got to his feet and stared dispassionately at him. 'Take him back to his cell, John'.

With them gone Masters studied Miller, who had remained impassive throughout the interviews. 'Never told me you knew the dead women, Dusty. How well?'.

Miller shrugged the question away and got to his feet. 'Just two more attractive birds, Don. You know me -chat 'em up. Always a chance!'.

Masters did know. It was common knowledge the sergeant was always on the lookout for a bit of crumpet. 'Let me have a statement, Dusty. Your involvement is bound to crop up'.

'Will do, Don. All done for now?'.

'All done'.

*

'Yes, inspector?'.

Masters got to his feet and looked at Lakey in the dock before returning his attention to the bench. 'It is my intention, at a later date, to offer evidence the defendant had sexual relations with Amanda Price. The prosecution can prove the dead woman had been in his house. A fact he has chosen to deny. In fact, he has denied knowing Mrs. Price. Faced with his denial I am applying for a remand in custody to enable further enquiries to to be completed'.

'And Mr. Price?'.

'The charge will be formally withdrawn when this hearing is over'.

The chairman nodded and turned his attention to the defending solicitor. 'Mr. White?'.

The solicitor got to his feet and glanced back at Lakey. 'The inspector has advised me of Paul Price's position. The defendant is applying for bail'.

The three heads closed up and the chairman nodded and looked over his spectacles to White.

'Denied. Remanded in custody for one month'.

*

Masters' telephoned enquiry at the Yard revealed they had a line on a firm associated with Leonard Spence, but nothing to positively connect him with known blags. According to C.11, the criminal intelligence section, they could put five blags down to the firm. Sawn off shotguns and automatics were used on each job. "They're getting bolder and a frigging sight more dangerous" stated an officer in that office. "They shot the driver on their last job. No need to do that. The finger had his arms in the air".

'Dead?'

'No. Easily could have been'.

It was distinctly possible, Masters thought, they were the firm Spence was talking about. He pulled their records from the criminal records office, CRO, revealing that Leonard Spence was a known associate of Richard Silver, one of the sussed blagging firm. The others were James Pollard, Reginald Cook, and Edmund Burke. From their mug shots Masters knew he was possibly about to deal with a right nasty bunch of villains. "Time will tell" he thought.

*

Len Spence was keeping in mind his wife's warning that morning before he set out. "He's the old bill, Len. Don't trust 'im". Good girl my Jane. Usually right. He cast an eye at the uniformed constable with his back to the cell door and thumbed him 'Does he have to be here?' he asked Masters.

The DI gestured for the officer to leave the cell. When the door had been slammed he concentrated his gaze, firstly at Len and then at his son. 'I've got no time to muck around' he told them. 'Either Fred goes for the lot or we find a solution. You've got ten minutes'.

Outside he pacified the cell block officer 'Take their shit and forget it son. Their world and ours are poles apart. When the bell rings call me'.

Ten minutes later Masters was staring back at Len Spence, who wasn't looking too sure of himself. His gangly son had picked his nose and was staring at the result on a fingertip. 'So what have we got?' he queried.

Fred's dad was in a quandary. Come out straight away with a bung was the option he favoured. With his wife's warning in his head he decided to play it by ear. 'You got kids?' he asked the unreadably-faced Masters.

A shaking head answered that.

'Mum alive?'.

'Very much so. Why are we into this?'

'Family, inspector. It's about family. How would your mother feel if your collar was felt. It could be you, and your mum out of her mind with worry. His mum wants him home'.

'And how am I to achieve that miracle?'

Len Spence placed a large envelope on the bed.'It's in there. Take a look and let me know if we can come to an arrangement. Let me have a visit with the other two, they know the drill. Work my son out of it and I'll keep to what we agreed'.

Masters scooped up the envelope, pocketed it, stood, and stared down at the pair of them. Gesturing to Len Spence he said 'We need to have a meet about another matter. Might do you a bit of good. In the meanwhile you can have your chat with Fred's mates. I'll lay that on'.

It took an hour but Brian Winch and Ginger Brothwell had listened to Len's persuasions and reluctantly agreed to take the t.i.c's and leave Fred out of it, on a promise their birds were looked after for at least a year.

'That's the best I can do', he told them. ' I'll put the

word out. You're stars, lads'.

They weren't daft. Prison was a cert, parole down the road a possibility, and the offer was better than they could have expected. Masters' half of the deal was they would identify the drums they had burgled and Masters, knowing once the houses had been identified, was guaranteed they couldn't back away from the t.i.c's at court.

It was later that day they were sitting across from detective sergeant Miller and DI Masters, who was in a good mood and smiling when he asked them: 'where's the gear?'

The two youths shot glances at each other and then back at the detectives.

'Well?', Miller asked

'All over the place, guv' George said cagily

'Recoverable?' Masters asked stonily.

'Some, guv. Some'.

'How much is some?', queried the sergeant, crunching knuckles.

'Depends on who knocks on what door, guv' Winch offered, reckless considering who he was talking to.

'Listen you prats' said Miller, an ex boxer, the short tempered one with a penchant for violent solutions. 'Who gives a fuck who knocks on what door. If I knocked on the bloody doors, what happens?'

'For you guv, fuck all. But we could do it'.

George Brothwell meanwhile apparently saw something hilarious in the on-going chit chat. Restraining the sergeant Masters warned Brothwell: 'Don't get cocky, son. You're in deep shit and you're fucking up your way out. Either we get the gear back or you two get five years each. And that's a promise I can keep'.

'If we help with the gear nobody else gets nicked, right?' Brian said as he stared at Masters.

'My word, son'.

*

As it turned out the stolen property went mostly south of the Thames. It took several trips with Brian and George in tow to recover around eighty per cent of the stolen property. It was enough to satisfy the DI, who kept his word not to nick the jittery receivers.

DCS Makepeace popped into the nick when the last van was off-loaded, finding time while he was
there to grudgingly congratulate Masters and Miller on a job well done.

*

'Frederick Spence. You have pleaded guilty to a charge of housebreaking and have indicated you want the case heard before this court. Very well. Having heard the evidence of detective inspector Masters, and mindful of the circumstances of your family life, for which we are grateful to the detective inspector', Bob acknowledged the DI with a slight dip of his head, 'we are prepared to consider probation. Is the probation officer in the court'. Considering the magistrates knew Cecil, who was sitting in the well of the court, the question was rhetoric.

'I am your worships', he responded eagerly.

'Have you prepared a report on this man?'.

'I have'.

He listened to Cecil read out from his copy of his report which lay before him and turned his attention to Fred, who was leaning nonchalantly against the rail of the dock. 'Listen to me Spence', he said coldly. 'In view of what has been said on your behalf I am considering a period on probation. Do you understand what that will mean?'.

White stood up 'My client agrees to a period of probation, your worships', he said hurriedly..

'Two years probation it is'. Chairman Bob leaned forward and pointed at Fred 'Step out of line and you will be brought back before this court and go to prison'.

With Fred gone his accomplices were ushered up the steps to the court and faced the Magistrates. The eighteen t.i.c's were a likely problem: their trust was in Masters who had straight-faced assured them the magistrates could deal with their housebreakings. It was a lie, naturally. Because each t.i.c. had been pulled at night housebreaking technically became burglaries, dealt with at a higher court. Sure enough, Bob the butcher, whose next door neighbour in the same lodge had been done over, didn't hang around and brusquely remanded them upstairs for trial and sentence.

*

Jane Spence, the same age as Len, was starting to fill out. Anxious to find a size 14 to fit she shopped wisely and spent a lot of dosh in the better class shops whose sizes were generous. 'It's the menopause' she always responded to those saucy enough to tell her she was putting on the pounds. 'Mind you' she always added 'When your thyroid packs it in you haven't much chance of being the apple of hubby's eye, have you?'. Naturally proud, when she studied her profile in the hall mirror she pulled her tummy in a bit and told herself 'There now. You're not so bad'.

She and Len had grown up together. Same school, same everything, except prison. "My Len", she always referred to him that way, "hasn't put on the pounds". It annoyed her sometimes but she had to admit she was proud of him. Keeping fit was a necessary way of life in his game. A true professional, she reckoned him. Blagging kept him slimmish, he reckoned. Half-inching stuff out of Boots was the most she'd ever done: and managed to get away with. He was in Wandsworth nick when he proposed on one of her regular visits. She was a right raver back in those days. Mindful of the occasion she always put on a show on visits. Plenty of leg and tits for his mates to ogle at.

Since his last incarceration Len had never been short of a bob or two. He was more careful these days; Jane saw to that, insisting his sawn off shot gun and blagging kit weren't kept in the house but in the garage that couldn't be traced to them. But Fred was the apple of her eye; and right then she sat and watched him tuck into the big fry up she had laid on for him.

'Alright son?'

'Lovely mum. Ta'.

'Your dad and me can't understand why you got nicked. You're so careful usually'.

'Me too, mum. At least Charlie did a runner', he added as he loaded his fork. 'This is smashing'. He gave his mum a thank-you smile. After another mouthful he pointed his fork at her and told her Charlie had turned up in court. 'Got to hand it to him. Took bottle that'.

'Never met Charlie 'ave I? You sure he's alright?'

Fred nodded and pushed the empty plate away and took a swig of tea. 'Great to be home, mum. Nah. Charlie's alright. How did dad work it?'

'Bunged the copper a grand'.

'Where is dad?'

'Having a meet with that detective. Bit of business'.

'The usual?'

'I expect so, son. He never says much does he'. She patted Fred's hand 'Going round Pat's? She's been worried sick'.

Fred hauled himself up and stretched. 'Jesus, I'm stiff. That bloody cell –like an icebox it was. Yeh.

I'll nip round and see her'.

*

With Len driving his Zephyr, he and Masters were casing the factory the DI had put up for a blagging. From past knowledge the DI knew that on the day he had in mind for the robbery the opposition was down to three wage clerks. He was guiding Len, pointing out the roads in and out of the area he had selected for the getaway and change over of cars. On the way he told him thirty thousand pounds was up for grabs and Len whistled his surprise.

'Stop here', Masters told him. He pointed to a house set back from the corner of the tee junction ahead of them. 'I'll have a bloke in there on the day. Put a change-over car there when the robbery's a definite'.He gestured to a low wall fronted by a deep lay by in front of that house. 'You sort it but the two who go to that car get nicked. You and the other finger will get a clear run in the blagging car. My men will be too busy nicking the others to chase after you. It's down to you to be sure the changeover car is left when the blag is on. The timing is important. The driver is to walk away and bugger off. If he follows orders he's out of it'.

Len didn't like the uncertainty of his escape 'Where will I dump the car?'

Masters understood Spence's concern. 'Drive on', he told him. 'I'll put you in the picture'.

The DI directed him to a cul-de-sac half a mile away, back to back with another one with a foot way between them. 'Have a car put in that turning area the other side of the footpath', he pointed to it. 'Same arrangement: only when the job's on. Dump the Jag and drive to the railway station car park - it's half full that time of day'.

'How you going to do the nicking?'

'That's not your concern. Keep to our plan and you'll be in the clear'.

Len was satisfied. 'I'll bring the team down here and recce the place. I'll bell you when we're ready'.

'Remember, Len. Split the cash before you reach the lay-by. You get to keep your cut so long as the blaggers we nick have the rest. And leave Ronnie Silver out of the team, the Yard's got a line on him that ties him to you'.

Spence studied Masters, remembering their earlier conversation. 'What's the other matter you mentioned back at the nick?'

'Let's get away from here and I'll tell you. Park up in town. We can have a bite to eat while I fill you in'.

They drove in silence and eventually the detective told Spence to pull into a lay by. 'There's a café just up the road', he explained.

With each deep in his own thoughts the meal was eaten in silence until Masters pushed his plate away, picked up his mug and leaned across the table to speak quietly. 'Read about Mark Bateman's murder?'.

Spence was instantly intrigued and nodded.

'You've read he worked for the brief you hired for Fred?'.

The other man nodded. 'What's it to do with me?'

Masters smiled and patted the other man's hand reassuringly. 'Nothing. But we believe there's a background to his murder tying it to an armed robbery that went down on my patch. The sweeney nicked two blaggers. Bateman's firm represented them at the initial court hearing'.

'What's their names?'.

'Phil Jakeson and Bill Williams. Both have form for robbery. Live out at Bow, near the tunnel. Know them?'.

Spence shook his head but he said, 'Heard of them. Which squad handled it?'.

'DI. Lindley's'.

Spence nodded. Lindley he'd heard of.

The detective leaned across the table to speak quietly. 'I think its likely they've killed Bateman. See if you can come up with anything. I'm looking for the gun'.

Spence nodded. 'I'll put the word out and get back to you if I hear anything on the grapevine'.

*

Makepeace chaired the hastily arranged meeting at divisional headquarters and introduced Masters to the assembled detectives.. 'The inspector will explain what is going to happen and what has to be done. He turned to Masters. 'Inspector?'.

Masters crossed to the blackboard, faced the detectives, and ran through what was to occur, giving them details of his plan to set an ambush. He indicated the get-away route from the blag to the lay-by he had agreed with Spence. 'My snout knows a car will be put there for the change over. It's a three man firm. ' he explained. 'Two will be armed. On the day I shall inform the company's boss that we've had a tip off'. He gestured at Ted, 'He'll be in there when the blag goes off.'

Turning, he said to Read. 'One of the girls is being pulled. You'll replace her. Make sure the two birds understand we don't want any heroics'.

Ted grimaced at the the news and waved away comments from two other detective constables who reckoned he was a lucky bastard and why can't they have that job.

'Whatever the villains say, they are to do,Ted', the DI told him. ' The slags'll be ambushed away from the factory'. He turned to Makepeace. 'I shall need armed support on this one, sir. Will you arrange for it - it may be at short notice'.

Makepeace had been studying Masters while he was speaking and his concern had hardened. 'Can your informant come up with names?', he asked guardedly while he decided on an answer.

'No, sir. I've been down that road. The information is one hundred per cent reliable. The job will go down. When, I'll know nearer the time'.

'What do you need?' The DCS asked after a while.

Masters told him what was needed and how he wanted the ambush to go off, adding, 'if it goes pear shaped at the change over I want cars with armed officers here and here'. He was indicating routes out of the town well away from Spence's run to the change over spot.

*

Len and his fellow blaggers watched from a hundred yards away as the security van pulled away from the building and drove off.

'Let's do it' Len muttered as he pulled his balaclava down over his face. 'Frigging thing this.....can barely breath'. Nudging Ted he said impatiently, 'Start the bloody thing then!'. He swung round 'Cover you faces for gawds sake!' he hissed to the two in the back. . What 's it with you! It's not a bloody picnic! And get that bleeding shotgun away from my head!'.

Trundling to the entrance Ted kept the engine running, watching Len smash a sledge hammer through the flimsy locked door and disappear inside with Pollard and Cook in tow.

Detective constable Ted Read heard before he saw the blaggers. Jimmy Pollard was a scary sight waving his sawn off shot gun around, frightening the life out of him.

'Get on the floor! Stay down!' he heard Spence shout.

Pollard fired a barrel into the ceiling while Len scooped up the still unopened bag on the table and they were off, racing to the waiting Ted with his foot hovering over the accelerator and the engine in gear.

'Let's go!' Len bawled as he slung the bag in the car.

Ted went with screeching wheels and spurted through the open gates, hurtling the car towards the prepared change over spot half a mile away. Spence had the bag open, grabbing handfuls of notes and stuffing them into his own holdall. Reaching over he handed the company's bag to Cook and spotted the lay-by ahead. 'Get ready for the off', he said quietly to the psyched up men in the back.

Meanwhile detective constable Read was enjoying cuddling one of the scared young women with one arm and managed to reach his radio with the other. 'They've done it, guv!' he shouted excitedly. 'They've bloody well done it!'

John Barton, in the bedroom overlooking the lay-by had just seen a Rover pull in and watched the tall thin driver walk away. 'Guv' he radioed Masters 'A car's just been left where you said. The driver's walked off'.

'Keep an eye on it'. Masters told him. He radioed the armed officers hiding behind the low wall beyond the lay-by. 'It's coming you way' he warned them. 'Let the blaggers get on board. Shoot the tyres. Surround the car and smash the windows and wave your guns around. Frighten the shit out them'.

The Jaguar screeched to a halt, Jimmie and Reggie piled out, and the Jag was off with tyres smoking. Still encased in boiler suits and balaclava hoods, gloves still on, shotguns in hand and a bag of dosh, they sprinted to their waiting car and dived on board. Jimmie turned the waiting key and that was it: the explosions were loud, the car sank and they saw geezers shoving guns in their faces and all Jimmie could say was, 'where the fuck d'you lot come from!'.

John, watching from his vantage point radioed to the DI. 'Two men have been nicked, guv. But two more have had it away in a red Jag'.

Meanwhile, Len and Ted, boiler suits discarded in the Jaguar and the changeover car dumped in the railway station car park, the gloves, balaclavas, Len's shotgun and the swag in holdalls gripped tightly in their hands, strolled onto the railway platform, waited and, within ten minutes as planned, were on their way home.

Yet another member of Masters growing firm, he muttered to Ted. 'Know what mate. That was a dead easy tickle. The filth played a blinder on this one!'.

*

Hard case Jimmy and thuggish Reggie had been hauled back to the nick and were banged up in cells well apart from each other. Upstairs, the swag was being carefully counted under the ever watchful eye of Makepeace.

'Well?' he asked impatiently, a question hovering: had a Masters' job finally been one hundred per cent successful?

Nineteen thousand five hundred and fifty pounds, sir', he was told.

"Oh my bloody God", he thought despairingly, "here we go again"! 'Absolutely certain of that?'

'Absolutely, sir'.
'Then get Detective Inspector Masters here. Now!'.

*

Chapter five

Detective sergeant Miller was curious. His CRO check on the two villains in the cells revealed that his DI had drawn their files, along with three others, a week before. 'Have a word, Don' he said quietly to Masters. 'In the canteen?'.

Untouched coffee mug in front of him the DI was studying the other man.

' What's the score?' Miller was peering at his DI over the rim of his cup.

'Meaning?'

'The prisoners. You drew five files on blaggers a week ago. Two of them are in the cells. What's the SP?'

'What are you getting at?' Masters sipped his coffee and stared at the sergeant and waited.

'Is there anything I should know?'.

Masters sighed and leaned back to think.'This firm, Dusty', he explained, 'have been well at it. One finger has been shot to date'. He sat forward and cradled his fingers and kept his steady gaze on the sergeant 'You know by now it was a six man firm. I'll be straight with you. One was a snout. One was his mate. But the two we've captured are blaggers with form. Men number five and six were on wages. The whole idea was to capture those two'.

'I can understand that Don'. Miller finished his coffee and gave the DI a quick smile. 'And the rest of the money?'.

Masters studied his friend's smiling face and nodded his understanding. 'We're on an insurance earner down the road. Interested?'.

The sergeant smiled 'Always interested'.

Masters stood up and at the doorway reassured him, 'When the dust has settled we'll get it sorted'. adding with a half-smile, 'Boss wants me!'.

Makepeace's five minute grilling was getting nothing from Masters' bland expression. 'Ten thousand pounds, inspector. Ten thousand four hundred and fifty pounds to be precise! Where the bloody hell is it?'

'I've got teams at the homes of associates as we speak, sir. We may get lucky', Masters nonchalant response was accompanied by a reassuring smile.

'Lucky! Inspector you'll need more than luck to get out of this one'.

The DI saw that the DCS was at boiling point and changed tack 'Out of it, sir? I don't understand . I've got the blaggers in the cells'.

Makepeace was furious. Glaring into the inspector's serene face he shouted, 'Every time!', he levelled a shaking finger, 'Every bloody time something goes wrong with your jobs! Why for God's sake did it have to happen today?'.

'No one's perfect, sir'. Masters eased himself forward in the chair, ignoring the accusing finger, and stared back at his boss while he fished out a cigarette. 'I played it straight down the line. My snout can't be expected to have the entire SP. Look. sir' he said with beguiling sincerity. 'We could have had blood splattered around today but we didn't, did we? By my reckoning we had a bloody good result'. He lit the cigarette and settled back in the chair and offered a smile.

'Informant up for an earner?' Makepeace's temper had subsided but suspicion clouded his voice.

'Naturally, sir' Masters responded. 'He might get a few quid from the firm's insurance company as well if he's lucky', he added breezily

'Is he the one who fingered Woodall?'.

'Can't say to that, sir. Anonymous if you recall'.

The DCI was doing his best to stop his blood boiling

but he nevertheless shook a finger at the DI and warned him. 'This is not funny. When it gets to court I trust you will have all', he leaned forward and thrush his head at Masters, '*all* the answers because, believe me, the Yard won't support you if pear-shaped becomes the order of the day'.

*

'You're in the newspaper again, darling'. Jean Masters walked into the kitchen, reading the front page of the Daily Mail. 'Did you have a gun..........? It says armed police shot the tyres of the robbers' car'.

Masters smiled as she settled in a chair, her soft contoured face expressing her concern. 'No, sweetheart. I wasn't armed'. Popping the last piece of toast into his mouth he pushed his plate away and got up, still chewing. Stroking her hair he leaned down to peck her cheek. 'Might be a late one today. Lots to do. Paperwork mostly. I'll ring you at your office and let you know when I can get away'.

They walked to the front door and Jean, still concerned, pulled Don to her and kissed him tenderly. 'Be careful, darling', she said quietly, her mind still on the article she had just read.

He cupped her face in his hands and kissed her again. 'I'm always careful, sweetheart' he said. 'My work's not as dangerous as the newspapers say. They spice up stories to sell papers'.

'Are we having a tree this year? Jean looked at him. 'Hasn't crossed your mind, has it?', she asked impishly, recognising his surprised expression.

'Can I leave it to you to get one, sweetheart?. Get one like the one you got last year. The way my work's going you'll be decorating it as well, as usual!'.

Jean held onto his hand to be certain he was

listening. 'And you agreed my parents are spending Christmas with us?'.

'I did and I'm glad they're coming, sweetheart. Now.........I really must dash'.

While his wife hugged herself in the coldness of the open doorway he dropped into his car and looked back at her and thought of Kay and, for the minute it took for him to exit the driveway, guilt swept over him but, once on the road, he couldn't get her image from his mind. Lustful for her seductive body to be against his he drove to his usual spot near her flat.

When she opened the door she was wearing her usual silk dressing gown and, he knew from experience, nothing underneath. His old man stirred just looking at her beautiful face and her lovely body and, experiencing the familiar ache in his groin, he wordlessly scooped her up, held her tightly to him, and started up the stairs, whispering his desire for her.

His words must have got lost in the ether because once he'd lowered her onto her bed, she started on him. 'Where were you last night?' she asked nastily

'Kay, love. I have to work'. He sat down beside her prone body……………..

'You could have rung me!'

'I know, sweetheart, but I was up to here with work. Anyway'…………….he was running his hands slowly up her thighs and reached the looped belt and was slowly tweaking the ends apart…………..

'Why didn't you call me?' Her voice was icy.

'Sweetheart. It's been a really heavy time'…………..he was slowly opening the dressing gown, relating as he did so a brief account of the previous day's robbery. He bent forward to kiss her, half expecting her to jerk away but she melted into his arms. Well practised, he kept the kiss going while easing her out of the dressing gown. He sat back and gazed down at her beauty and undressed quickly, She reached up and Don slid inside her arms to lie beside her and run a hand down her body, over a breast, down her stomach and................she opened her legs for him. With practised grace he was quickly on top and inside her and holding her to him and enjoying her cries of pleasure when he drove home his lust for her.

'They laid together for a few minutes before she said 'Will I see you this evening?'

Most definitely not he thought. His libido assuaged he said quietly, 'Difficult that, Kay. Work's going to tie me up all evening'. He hunched onto an elbow and kissed her. 'I really must dash'.

'You'll ring me?'

'I promise'.

*

Because Makepeace had made it clear that each witness statement was to be processed through him Masters was concerned at the direction the robbery enquiry was heading. Len Spence and Ted Burke had not been described in any of those statements, albeit witnesses saw the Jaguar being dumped in the cul-de-sac and the men run away to another car and, possibly the same two men, minus boiler suits, were seen by a woman walking her dog, running along the footpath to the other car, which was driven off to the main road. In each case descriptions were vague. Nobody saw the car before it was found dumped in the railway station car park. Without a definite link Masters was satisfied Len Spence had got clean away.

Like the other two cars, it's arrival in town was a total blank. Nicked in North London and fitted with plates identifying similar models, like them it turned up nothing. The car whose tyres had been shot out had been stolen in Leyton, east London, from a lock up garage. A union card, in the name of David Davenport, was unearthed tucked at the back of the driver's seat. It wasn't the name of the registered owner nor, enquiries established, anyone of that name having access to the car, but it was sufficiently important to have Makepeace hopping around, insisting something be done about it.

Masters, handed the union card by Makepeace, passed it to Miller to follow up. 'Check it out with the victim, Dusty. If there's some kind of connection find it for God's sake. The boss wants it done'.

*

Miller arrived back at the nick with a thin six footer in tow who he'd dumped in an interview room before bringing the DI up to date. 'He's the holder at that union card', he explained.

Masters gestured Miller to a seat opposite. 'What's the score?'.

'Unfortunately, it looks bad. The car owner has never heard of Davenport, and he, like a pratt, more or less chucked his hand in. I didn't mention his union card. I told him I was investigating the theft of a car and he rolled over'.

The DI crossed to the interview room, opened the door, and glanced at Davenport, dipping his head in acknowledgement as the man stared back. He closed the door and gestured to Miller to follow him back to his office. He settled back in his swing chair and stared at the sergeant 'From the top. How did the nick go?'

'You might say he was expecting a pull'.

'Wife there?'

'Yep. Like a mouse. Pretty though. I could have given it one'.

'So tell me. Who said what, etc, etc'

'Like I said. I told him I was investigating the theft of a car dumped on our ground and he caved in'.

'To what?'.

Miller shrugged. 'Not his exact words, but he said he'd been expecting a pull'.

'Checked him with CRO?'

'Yep. A few nickings. Sentenced to eighteen months for violence was his last'.

'Drawn his file?'

'No time yet, guv, but I'll get onto it'.

Masters stood and paced the room. The arrest of Davenport was not what he had wanted or expected. He stopped pacing and turned his attention to Miller. 'He knows the snout Dusty. The whole bloody thing could easily unravel with him in custody'. He went back to his desk and slumped in the chair and stared hard at Miller. 'What a fuck up. Somehow he's got to be convinced we want to help him. He mustn't get dragged into this one.. What a frigging nightmare! Be interesting finding out how the hell he came to lose his union card in that car'.

*

Jane Spence was doing her best to calm down Dave Davenport's wife. 'Len'll be back in a mo, Betty. He'll know what to do'.

Betty was a pretty thing, around thirty-five, and very, very worried. Her Dave had been out of trouble for three years since his last bit of bird for grievous bodily harm, and being nicked was clearly the end of her tidy world.

'Why, Jane. Why Dave? What has he done? He's a good man, my Dave. You know what he's like. Stand his corner in a punch up, that's my Dave, but the detective said something about a robbery. My Dave on a robbery?' She started to cry.

'Did the dick actually mention a robbery?'.

Betty's tears were on a roll by then. 'Dave did. I said to him: "David", I said "tell me the truth now. What's it all about".

'And?'.

'Well, the dick was having a piss upstairs like and Dave said, all conspiratorially like, that he thought he was going to get banged up for robbery'.

'Calm down Bet'. Jane came over all motherly. 'We'll see what Len reckons'.

Len Spence let himself in at that moment and took in Betty's upset right away. 'What's wrong Bet?' he asked as he sat beside her.

'Dave's been nicked. That's what's wrong' she managed to say through a welter of tears.

'Nicked for what?'

'Robbery, that's what!' Betty sobbed

Len sat back and looked at Jane and tilted his head towards the kitchen. Following her in he eased the door to and quizzed her. 'She's in a state right now. Has she said anything else?'

Instead of answering, she sat down at the table and gestured for him to do the same 'Len'. Jane said quietly. 'Tell me the truth now. Was Dave in on the job'?

'He ran one of the cars down for us. That was all. He's in the clear'.

'What do we tell Betty? We can't leave her like this. She has to know something'.

'I'll tell her something that'll satisfy her. But you've got to make sure she keeps her mouth shut'.

*

Miller saw the DI's wink and knew he was confident Pollard was not going to name names but waited until Masters gave him the nod before whacking the man again.

Pollard hauled himself up again and ignored the smirking sergeant as he righted his chair. He stared at Masters, before shifting his gaze to the ceiling. 'No comment. How many times do you want me to say that?'

The DI spoke through the incident 'Grass the slags is my advice. Which of us do you really want to deal with?'.

Pollard was staring at Masters' smiling face when he told him how his criminal code worked. 'I'm no grass and I don't give a fuck. No comment'.

Later that afternoon Reggie Cooke stared anywhere but at the questioning detectives and eventually hunched forward to make it clear to them. 'I'm no grass' he too said firmly. 'I'm in here and they're out there. I'm not doing your job for you'.

With the man back in his cell the satisfied detectives headed for their favourite pub to sink a couple of pints, tick a few boxes, and decide how best to deal with Davenport who, Masters knew, if push came to shove, could identify Spence.

'We can't let that happen, Dusty. And if Makepeace decides to take over the interview we're in lumber. We need to close the thing down in case that happens'.

The sergeant took a long draught of his beer and wiped his lips, nodding in agreement. 'What's the next move then?'.

'First thing in the morning we chat with Davenport. He's got to be convinced he's down for conspiracy and a bung will square it. If I can get John on board I believe I can swing it, otherwise I can see trouble down the road'.

'Do we need John?'. Miller held up his empty glass. 'Another one?'.

'No more for me, Dusty. I think we do'. Masters stood and looked thoughtfully at the sergeant before telling him about the ID parades he'd arranged. 'Three people claim to have seen Davenport leaving the car in the lay-by. Only one is likely to identify him. I've had a chat with her'...........he broke off and winked at Miller. 'I fed her the line we couldn't guarantee her safety if friends of the man decided to get at her. Might work......we'll see soon enough'.

'Why John then?'.

'I need someone I can trust to do the right thing. Davenport's got to believe he's down for robbery and a bung'll square him. I'll have John in on the interrogation'.

The sergeant's doubt was all over his face. 'If John'll square the circle Spence is in the clear. Is that the idea?'.

'Precisely. I don't need a statement from John. Just his word he'll go along with my line at the interview. Get him in here'.

With Barton sitting in his office Masters explained how the enquiry stood. 'We've got the bastard's union card from the car, John. God knows how he came to drop it but he did. I've got a witness linking him to the car. She's attending the parades like you. All I'm asking is that you identify him'.

John glanced away from Masters hard stare for a moment before looking back. 'Guv. I only saw his back, you know that'.

Masters spread his hands. 'I know John. But we know he was part of the job. And the guvnor knows it. That's why he wanted Davenport pulled in and charged with conspiracy to rob. As it stands, John, the case is very weak. He could walk away from this one. All I'm asking is that you strengthen the case. The boss would expect that'.

For some seconds Barton stared back at the DI, amazed that his governor was asking him to tell lies.

'You reckon he would?. You're sure it'll be alright?'

'Dead sure, John. Come on, let's nip down to the cell block'.

Later, after his peep as a reminder through the cell flap at Davenport and, an hour later at a nod from the uniformed constable outside the identification room, he attended the parade to be told by the uniformed inspector to point to the man who'd put the car in the lay by.

Nervously John did his bit and walked straight past Davenport but came back and pointed to him.

The woman was next to stare at the line up. She walked along the line and back again to stand in front of Davenport. He stared at the ceiling. After a couple of seconds she shook her head.

Escorted from the parade to Masters office, it was clear to the detectives his confidence had been shaken by Barton's pointing finger.

'Cuppa?' Masters queried. His friendly manner relaxed Davenport.

' I could do with a fag, guv'.

'Of course. Sorry. Here. Have one'. He offered a packet.

'Thanks'.

The DI held his lighter up and waited for the man to take a few deep puffs. 'Better?'.

'Yeh. Thanks'.

Masters lit up and studied the man. 'You know the drill, Dave. You were identified on the ID parade as the man who placed a car for the blaggers................'

'Hey. Hang on a minute!' Dave broke in. 'Where's

all this coming from. What was all that about in the line ups? The copper told me they were to do with a car being dumped somewhere on your manor. He never mentioned a bleeding blagging!'

The detective ignored the remark 'What d'you do for a living?' He scanned the man's CRO record while he waited.

'Electrician'.

'Self employed?'

Davenport shook his head. 'You know all this don't you? I work for Howard's in Enfield'.

'You're in a union then?'

'I don't know what the frigging heck it has to do with anything but, yes. I'm in a union'.

Masters opened his desk drawer and took out the union card and pushed it across to Davenport 'That yours?'.

Davenport leaned forward, looked at it and sat back. 'Yeh. That's mine'.

Masters nodded and put the card back in his drawer. 'Dave', he hunched forward and placed his clasped hands under his chin, 'I've got a problem. That card was not in your gear'.

'Then how come you've got it?'

'That's the problem, Dave. Somehow you managed to lose it in the car you brought to town'.

Davenport had started to get to his feet to protest, but was shoved down by Dusty.

'I'm being fitted up here!' he shouted. 'I want a solicitor!'

'All in good time, Dave. All in good time. My boss reckons that card says you were part of the firm that pulled the blag'.

Davenport sat and glowered back, his mind racing back to Len's assurances since he'd been taken to the lock up in Leyton and shown the nicked Rover. A dead cert, Len had said. He'd driven him to where he had to dump the car. Leave the key in the ignition. Walk away. Get a bus to the railway station and go home. The detective's expression was telling him the situation was anything but as sweet as the nut Spence reckoned. He hunched towards the inspector and pointed a finger. 'I delivered a car for a mate' he declared angrily, 'and you can't prove I didn't'.

Masters looked across to Miller, whose raised eyebrows and relieved smile said it all.

'We can word a statement how we like, Dave', Masters told Davenport. ' Helpful or hard. Which is it to be?'.

'How helpful is helpful?'. Suspicious, he looked at Masters and then spun round to stare at Miller.

'Dave, look at me. That's better. Want another fag?'. He did and Masters lit it for him. 'We've got the firm for the job. We know the score. This is how I see it. Your brief may well turn it your way. It's if he can't you've got a problem'.

Davenport nodded 'Is this the helpful bit?'.

'You could say that. But a statement under caution saying you did someone a favour would smooth the water.. You don't have to put up a name -you're no grass, Dave, we know that. I'll settle for that providing, that is, we come to an arrangement'. He broke off to study the other man drawing on his cigarette.

'Providing? We talking money here?'.

Masters smiled 'Well. That's down to you. You're going back in your cell. Think it over. Bell the missus if you want to -I'll square that with the custody sergeant'.

Indecision shaping his face, Davenport dotted his fag in Masters' ashtray and rubbed his hands together, looking from Miller to Masters. 'Do that do we?', he said, his confidence partly restored at the way things were shaping up.

'When our bit of business is squared away, then we'll do it'.

'So what happens now?'.

Masters got to his feet and gestured to Miller. 'Like I said: It's back to your cell for a while'.

Chapter six

Charlie Hobbs was back in a cell and truly pissed off. He'd been banged up all evening because detective constable John Barton had seen him, yet again, leaving a house he'd just burgled. Ignoring the presents under the tree he had nipped upstairs and did his usual business. He wasn't to know it but the house was owned by a friend of the detective; and it was his wife the detective was having an affair with. Unfortunately for Charlie the randy detective had called by on the off-chance she'd got in earlier than usual. Seeing Charlie leaving, his understandable jealousy turned to anger when he recognised Charlie coming out.

With the eighty quid he'd nicked in one of his socks he once again sat on the plastic covered bed and stared despondently at the walls and thought of Janet. His head dropped and for once in his life he felt truly sorry for himself. The pisser of a life Masters had gone on about was back again.

Heavy-sounding metal on metal made him look up at Masters standing in the open doorway, shaking his head.

'Charlie! What the fuck have you gone and done!' The detective crossed to the bed and dropped onto it and stared quizzically at the young man beside him, waiting for a response.

'Sorry Don', Charlie managed to mumble without looking up. 'I was short of a few bob. Can you 'elp?'. He raised his head and stared earnestly at the DI, the worker of miracles, whose annoyance that the newest member of his firm had gone solo was on show. Charlie wilted, and stared at the floor.

Masters didn't muck about.'You're on probation, Charlie. This could mean bird'.

Totally dejected, Hobbs hung his head. 'Can't you 'ave a word with the detective wot nicked me, Don?', he pleaded'.

Masters knew he had a problem. Stitching up a villain on an ID parade was normal police work, but with DS. Fountain newly on the team Masters knew care had to be the watch word. To help Charlie meant Barton's assistance was needed.................again.

'Don?'

'Sorry Charlie. Thinking'. He absently studied Charlie while sorting out how best to handle the youngster ' Are you up for a few more jobs?' he asked finally.

Charlie, dead keen to ingratiate himself with Masters, sat upright. 'Anything Don!' he said eagerly.

Masters nodded but he was seriously studying the young man. "No more of this solo nonsense?'

'No, Don. I promise'.

'Then I'll see what can be done' he told him.

*

'Oh!............Oh!.......John................*Johhhnnnn!* Sheila had thrown her head back in the ecstasy of the moment ....oh!..........OH! *John*! Don't stop! Faster!. Faster!.............*oooh*' she was all but screaming now and John was getting very concerned. His old man had done its job and was shrinking fast.

'Honey'. He never called her Sheila because he always called his wife Honey. 'Honey…..I've got to go. Job on tonight. Honey................?'.

Sheila held onto him, loving him and loving to hold his strong, lean body tightly to hers. 'When are we going to get it together? She pleaded with her head on his chest.

'Soon' Barton unwisely answered. 'Soon'.

*

'John. A word'

John Barton shoved an overdue case file to one side, stood up and stared at the DI in the open doorway, and then down at his muddled desk and decided life was definitely way off track, mainly due to Sheila. What to do was something that escaped his imagination.

'John. Spare a minute?' This time the DI was insistent

The disconsolate detective followed Masters into his office and sat in the chair a finger pointed at and stared across at Masters, who had perched his elbows on his desk and was smiling.

'Spill it out, John'.

'What guv?'

'Need I mention Sheila?'

'How............why mention her?'

'John. You can't do anything without I know about it. Is she going to be a problem?'

The detective constable was flooded with the relief he could unburden himself.. 'How long have you known, guv?'

'That's not the issue, John. What affects your work is. How serious is this affair?'

'Nothing I can't knock off' the detective said with more confidence than he felt.

'Sure? No come back?'

'It's possible, guv. She's hot on me but...' he shrugged at his boast but knew it wasn't the truth when he added. 'I can handle it'.

'That's good, John. Good. Right now I want to discuss Hobbs. What's your take on him?'

'Layabout. Petty thieving. Bit of housebreaking. That's about it'.

'Sheila. Her drum was it?'

The detective constable's stomach tightened. 'Yes it is, was. Is there a problem with that, guv?'

Masters leaned back in his chair and placed his clasped hands behind his neck. 'Possibly John. 'The slag broke into her house. What we don't want, John, is any comebacks on you and the force do we?'

'That's considerate of you, guv. Can you see nicking Hobbs leading to that?'

The DI could see that the younger man was being nudged in the right direction. 'I'm thinking of your career, John. Women have been the downfall of many men and coppers are no exception. The only way out that I can see it is to let Hobbs go this time'.

Barton's puzzled stare cued Masters to add 'Can't see any other way to keep you in the clear'.

The detective constable was impressed with his guvnor's consideration. 'Can we really do that, guv?'. A bloody great weight shifted at the thought.

Masters, frowning, had pursed his lips but allowed himself to apparently brighten up. Leaning forward, he asked 'Are you on good terms with Sheila's husband?'

'Is that important?

'He's the key to this, John. Come up with something believable. Tell him Hobbs is helping us with other serious matters. Play that line. See how it goes?' Masters stood up and smiled at the younger man 'Give it a try, eh? Women!'. Recognising the younger man's relief as he left the office his thoughts switched to Miller, who Barton had casually mentioned might have known the two dead women. He mulled over the little he knew about Miller's affairs. One was a certainty: Betty, the typist in Lindley's squad. Were there others? He shook his head at the troubling thought that swirled in his head, offering no foundation, no solution................

*

With his many enquiries going along nicely Masters was up for another session with Kay and struck lucky. Unusually, she was in one of her rare good moods. The moment he was in the hall she had arms around his neck and smothered him with kisses. While he was busy sliding hands under her dressing gown and caressing her lovely, firm, sensuous body he was unaware she was rubbing her heavily scented wrists against the collar of his coat as he carried her upstairs to lay her gently on her bed. Undressing quickly he eased himself onto the bed beside her, sliding an arm under her to gently turned her to face him. He freed his hand and cupped her face and kissed her passionately. Kay reached between them and fondled his erect penis and urged him to make love. Easing on top to straddle her, she reached down and took hold of his engorged penis and expertly guided it home. Within seconds he forgot his wife and the other worries his job piled onto him. In that instant, being with her and making love, pushed all of that to the back of his mind. Kay's fingernails were digging urgently into his back as they got closer and closer to her climax which, when it came, thrust her body at his with a series of violent jerks to which Masters gentlemanly responded.

'Kay, darling', he panted, ' you're magnificent!. He rolled off and lay beside her, looking sideways into her lovely face.

'What are you thinking, Don?'

'You know what I'm thinking'.

She studied his face 'I don't. Are you like this with her?'

Masters frowned and propped himself on an elbow. 'Why do you do that? You knew I was married when we met. How's hubby?' he added defensively.

Mention of her husband who was four years into a seven stretch for armed robbery was sufficient for loving Kay to switch to the nasty one he dreaded. In an instant she slid to the edge of the bed with her back to him. 'I want you to go!' she told him icily.

*

That evening Jean Masters pecked Don on the lips as he wandered into the kitchen. 'Let me take your coat' she said firmly, deciding that he was going to sit down and eat properly for once. 'I've got a stew almost ready. Dumplings are made, when the stew is hot enough I'll put them in'. She caught a waft of scent as she hung up his coat. She had noticed it before and it wasn't hers. The earlier buried worry briefly surfaced.

Don, sitting at the table scanning a newspaper, smiled up at her as she came into the room and returned his gaze to the paper.

Jean decided not to question him. Instead she put the dumplings in the stew and busied herself setting the table, glancing at her husband from time to time, trying to imagine him with another woman

Don was deep in thought throughout the meal, unaware she was interpreting his silence in her own terms, her imagination dragging up past conversations, looking for the odd word or change in behaviour. For his part, like any man in a similar situation, his relationship with Kay hadn't diminished his love for his wife. He was fully aware that lust was his feeling for Kay but love, of that he had no doubt at all, was his feeling for his beloved wife.

*

'You're a lucky man, Charlie. First thing, son. Hand

over the eighty quid'. He pointed to the young man's socks.

Crestfallen, Charlie took off a sock and pulled out the money.

'Right, get your bits and pieces from the station sergeant and you can go'.

Charlie hauled his stiff frame from the bed with alacrity. 'Wot –no charge?'

'No charge, Charlie. I've managed to square the finger you screwed but this is the last time. Next time if you step out of line it's prison'.

Charlie was on his feet in a flash. 'Fanks, Don. I really mean that. Janet finks you're a star. So do I'.

Masters nodded and waved the praise away. 'Just keep that clean from now on', he said, pointing at Charlie's nose.

'I promise, Don'.

*

Chapter seven

That same evening Len Spence and Ted Burke were round at Dave Davenport's pacifying Betty. Jane was there -she'd stayed the night because Betty was in a state.

'You've got to do something!' Betty wailed to Len, not for the first time because the men didn't understand she needed her Dave back home. 'He wants you to help him out'.

Spence edged a glance at Burke and then at Betty. 'Did he say what he wants me to do, Bet?'.

By now she was in tears and Jane did her best to comfort her, giving her husband a mean look at the same time.

'What am I going to tell the kids, Jane? Their dad's locked up at Christmas? It aint right. It just aint right', she sobbed between her anguished words.

With her arm around Betty's shoulders Jane was giving her husband another hard, demanding, look.

'And he asked me to ask Len for some cash for the copper. He did Jane. He really did!'.

Spence got the point and did his best to pacify Betty. 'I've already told you I'll have a word in the right quarter. If it comes to that I'll sort it'. He was sorry for Betty but, until he'd belled Masters and got the down on what the situation really was, there was nothing he could do.

Jane was trying to calm her. 'Bet, love. Try to be patient. Everyone's on your side. Look, I'll stay with you for a few more days until the boys have sorted it.' She gave her husband the nod to get going and hugged Betty 'Let's go shopping, love. Cheer ourselves up!'.

Len bunged her a wad of notes. 'Buy Bet something nice, Jane'. With a quick grin he and Ted were off.

*

The men were sipping brandy when Jean Masters nudged her husband's knee, caught his eye, her's turning to face Valerie Miller, who was clearly upset. Masters squeezed his wife's hand under the table. He didn't need telling that something was wrong: throughout the meal at their favoured Indian restaurant Dusty hadn't said a word to his wife. Instead, their conversation had hovered around police work, which Jean told them should be left at the police station. He watched Valerie rummage in her handbag and take out a pack of tissues, and dab at her downcast eyes. Dusty appeared to be ignoring her distress.

'So, Dusty', he said brightly, 'You do weight training'.

'A bit'. Miller shook out a cigarette and offered the pack up to Masters, who shook his head.

'John goes to your gym. But you'll know that. In your younger days - what weight did you box at?'.

'Light heavyweight' he replied, giving the DI a hard, questioning stare.

'Have many fights?'.

'Dozen or so'. Miller relaxed and grinned at recalled memories. 'Only lost two. On points, mind you. Won the rest on knock-outs'. He downed the remainder of his brandy and jiggled his glass in Masters direction. 'Another?'.

'Thanks, Dusty. A small one - driving'.

On Miller's way to the bar, Jean took the opportunity to give her husband a quick glance and looked across at Miller's wife, who was again dabbing her eyes. When he nodded she caught Valerie's eye and suggested freshening up. She stood and waited for her to stand and again glanced at her husband, who inclined his head, guessing what was in her mind.

Miller spotted the women winding through the occupied tables and eased into his chair, pushing a brandy across to Masters. 'Cheers', he said with a quick smile. He raised his glass and sipped.

'What's it all about, Dusty'. Masters held his glass and looked intently at his friend.

'Meaning?'.

'You and Val. You haven't said a word to her all evening'. When his friend didn't answer he tried again. 'Jean's spotted it, Dusty. You know what women are like. If it's a row I'll understand.'. When Miller didn't answer, he suggested. 'Can we help? Can Jean help - you know, have a chat with Val. What d'you think?'.

The sergeant downed the brandy and put his elbows on the table and looked closely at his friend. After a few seconds he spread his hands on the table, and explained. 'Val's got it into her head that I've been overboard. That's it in a nutshell'. He grinned. 'Not exactly, but almost, caught with my trousers down'.

'Is that all!'.

'That's it, Don. Watch your back or it could be you!', he added with a fleeting smile.

*

A phone call got Masters out to the now brightly decked Green Welly transport café to meet with a troubled Len Spence. Ever careful, he noted the cars and clocked the number of people when he went in. Coffee bought, he sat in a corner. Grabbing a newspaper from the empty table beside him he went through the motions of reading it until, over it, he spotted Len with Ted Burke in tow coming in and gestured. Coffees bought they drifted over and sat down in front of the DI. Spence picked up his mug and stared at the detective and got straight to the point. 'Can you do anything for Dave?'

The DI sat back and swirled his coffee in his cup before answering 'Like what?' he asked when he looked intently at the other man.

Has he admitted anything?'.

Masters smiled. 'No need to worry, Len. Its going to be sorted. Dave's prepared to make a statement keeping himself in the clear. You're Fred he met in a pub. Did him a favour and ran it down'

'So what happens now -his wife is doing my nut in'.

Masters nudged Spence's hand resting on the table. 'Ted in on all this is he?'.

Spence nodded.

'This is all about keeping you and Ted here in the clear. Dave believes he has to bribe me to clear himself and not grass anyone. Can you arrange it so he believes that happened without putting yourself in the frame?'.

Spence leaned back and locked his fingers behind his neck and smiled at Masters.'Why are we into this, Don. Don't you blokes normally sort it?'.

'You're missing the point, Len. My boss is running the job now. He'll be charged with conspiracy to rob and get banged up. In my view there's not enough evidence for a conviction. It's down to Jimmie and Reggie. Are they likely to drag him in? If you want Dave out of the frame they've got to be squared'.

'I'll have words with them. Don't concern yourself with that line'.

'Can Ted leave us, Len? We need to talk over a few things'.

Hearing that, Burke nodded at Masters and was on his feet and off without Spence asking him to go.

'I've no beef with you keeping the cash. I've got another proposition. You put yourself up front with the insurance people as the informant and sign for the two grand reward money. I'll settle for that as my cut from the job. Agreed?'

'Seems fair enough'.

*

Two weeks after Bateman's body had been discovered Pasapula and Masters were looking at the naked body of another blonde young woman. She had been discovered by a woman who, calling for her dog that had run off, stumbled on the body beside the same stream beside Whiley Road where Dianne Flaxman's and Amanda Price's bodies had been found.

'Same method, Chandra?. Masters stared down at the body lying on the grassy bank.

'Similar. Not a belt though. The bruising around the neck could have been caused by a thin rope'.

'Has she been raped?'.

Pasapula nodded. ' Do you have a name for her?'.

'Early days yet. Can you estimate when she died?'.

The pathologist shook his head. 'As we can see she's almost frozen, which will have slowed deterioration. Your lads might help with soil samples from under her body'.

*

A week week later Davenport was first up the steps. Donald Swift, the brief from the prosecuting solicitors' office looked over his shoulder at the tall thin man before facing the bench. 'If it pleases your worships, this hearing is an application for a remand in custody. The defendant is accused of conspiracy to rob. His alleged involvement was that he brought a car to the town, knowing its' subsequent use was to facilitate the escape from apprehension two of the men who, with others, carried out an audacious armed robbery in this town. It is my intention to subsequently place evidence before this court to that effect'.

'Mr. McDonald?'

He hauled himself up. 'Your worships. My client has given a full explanation for his action on the day in question. My application is he be released on bail'.

'Hmmm. Mr. Swift?'

The solicitor respond firmly. 'Should the defendant be released, sir, ongoing enquiries to apprehend other men who so far have escaped the reach of this court will be jeopardised'.

'Hmmm'. The chairman, once more Bob the butcher, leaned in turn towards each of the other two magistrates and listened and then returned his attention to the lawyers. 'Remanded in custody for seven days'.

Jimmie and Reggie never stood a chance either. The neighbour, the one in the same lodge as Bob, who was by then pissed off with all dastardly law breakers, had shoved in his pennyworth and got the chairman on side. All three were back in the cells within an hour of court proceedings starting.

Masters was a happy man: his earner was guaranteed and now he had the blaggers within his reach for a few more days.

'Get Pollard out of the cell and up to my office, John', he told Barton.

Fifteen minutes later he was sitting across from a subdued man who, if it went right, was likely to be useful. 'Afternoon Jimmie' was his opener 'Fag?'

Pollard took a cigarette from the proffered packet and the light but said nothing. He sat and drew on the cigarette and blew out, mainly in the direction of the detective.

'Life's a shit, Jimmie' the DI declared after he had lit up himself.

Pollard kept his counsel.

'I see from your file, Jimmie, you've got two grown up girls. Still at home?'

Pollard shook his head.

'The missus. How's she going to take this?'

Pollard let his burning anger out. 'Just get on with the frigging routine!'

'Your choice, Jimmie but............I might be able to help you'.

Pollard had stopped his defiant slouch and was leaning forward but still saying nothing.

Masters piled on sincerity. 'Five other blaggings, Jimmie. I know you were on them but..................' he was spreading his hands expressively, 'A word here and there.........'.

'In words I frigging understand!'. Jimmie was quite rightly at boiling point with coppers trying to fit him up. Bang to rights was bad enough but all this chat and Masters sitting there smiling was eating into his self confidence. What did the bastard know? What frigging cock up had they made? 'All right' he said at last. What's all this about a word here and there? More bullshit you arseholes are good at?'

'No, Jimmie. No bull shit. I'm not from the Yard. Forget them. It's you and me. You, me and Reggie if you prefer. A blagging's a blagging.. You're not the only team at it'.

'Where are we going with this?'

'Shifting responsibility, Jimmie'

For the first time Jimmie clearly saw the wind was not blowing up his arse. Flo, the missus, the apple of his life, would expect him to do the right thing by her and the girls. It hit him hard that she was back there worrying herself sick about him, tucked up as he was in a cell. Guiltily, he admitted to himself that his own preservation had nipped in front of his obligation for his family. The DI was still rabbiting on..................

'Do yourself a favour, Jimmie' he was hearing., ' Think of your family'

Copping five after his last nicking was a bleak chapter in his life. Flo had warned him so many times since his release three years ago. " Just be careful Jimmie" she told him each time he was preparing to go on a blag. "I don't take chances do I" she had told him after the last blag. A well trusted receiver herself, she wouldn't have their kit in the house. A lock up garage had been rented to stash their holdalls with their blagging kit. Each time he'd duly done that on their way back from a job. Think of the family! He'd done nothing but that since being nicked. 'What have you got in mind?' he queried finally of a patient detective.

'I'll give you a name, Jimmie. When you're back in your cell work out whether he should be put in the frame for those other robberies, or whether you and Reggie should go down for them'.

Pollard leaned towards the detective and, with more confidence than he felt, said, 'You've got nothing on me for these other jobs you're going on about'.

'Jimmie –are you prepared to gamble you're in the clear? My proposition is a once only offer'

'What's the name of the finger?'

Ron Silver………..Put him up; give me something to nail him on and I promise to put in a word for you at court'.

'And these other jobs you keep on about?'

'I'll lose the evidence against you and Reggie for other jobs'. He watched the changing expression and shifting body language and could see his gamble might be producing a result. With no evidence whatsoever against any of the firm he had nothing to lose by the gambit.

'I'll tell you what I'll do' said Jimmie after a thinking spell 'I'll have a word with the missus and we'll go from there. Will you lay on a visit for her?'.

Masters agreed and rang down for the station sergeant to have Pollard taken back to his cell.

*

Flo Pollard came to the police station with Reg's wife Tina in tow. The front office constable alerted the DI and was told to put Mrs. Cook in a waiting room and bring Flo to his room.

'Detective Inspector Masters', he said as he held out his hand which she took for a very brief two-finger clasp.

She constructed a smile and followed his hand directing her to the chair opposite his desk.

'Mrs. Pollard I've arranged for your visit for a couple of reasons............smoke if you want to'. He offered his packet. 'One of these? Embassy?'.

A forty a day smoker, Embassy especially, and dying for one, Flo naturally refused the offer from the filth.

Masters outlined the scenario facing her husband. Nicked red handed on the run from an armed robbery. In possession of a sawn off shot gun 'That makes it a prohibited weapon' he added gravely

Flo was keeping her counsel. She'd been down the same road a few times in the past and never trusted a copper. She smiled at Masters and kept shtum.

'Mrs Pollard. Jimmie is going to have a chat with you about his future. If you want to see me, tell the sergeant at the counter. I'll take you down. He'll arrange your visit'.

*

Tina Cook was in her middle forties. Lovely, according

to her old man, but when the filth came calling she was a hard woman to confront Her experiences had reshaped her face: gone were those soft contours of unspoilt youth that promised so much. Her first husband was Alfie, from society's dregs as she subsequently found out. He shagged her when she was seventeen and not yet in the bloom of womanhood. Alfie wasn't bothered about all that bloom malarkey. Tina was a right turn on and his old man was a beanstalk looking for a home. Thankfully for Tina, either Alfie couldn't chuck in the right stuff or she was going through a negative time of month. Anyway, her Reggie, soon to be her second husband, shattered his jaw as a starter. A few solid kicks to his head and Alfie lost his memory. To this day, those still willing, and there weren't many of late, to push his wheelchair, believed what his shamed mum said about it all: "it was those fucking stairs! If we'd lived in a bungalow you wouldn't be doing the pushing"

Tina you didn't muck about with. Totally unlike Betty and Flo, bullshit, or what she rapidly perceived to be bullshit, was out the window. Coppers were the villains. Her Reggie was a straight up member of society. Down the local, home to most of his friends, Reggie and Tina were the stars. They were looked up to. And why not? Reggie supported the local club for disabled kids, chucking in a few bob: well, in reality Tina would reluctantly admit to close friends, several hundred nicker which he didn't want bandied about. Who else did that? Did the filth? Did they frigging hell. More interested in scrounging for their own kids' Christmas do. Frigging police. Scum of the earth. She waited. When the counter coppers eyed her she gave them a one finger salute. And why not? Like Jimmie Pollard, Reggie had had his fair share of bird. Is there any wonder she knew the filth were total bastards. Up went the finger again only this time it was the sergeant advancing on her to take her to the cell block.

*

Flo and Tina, in their present state of mind, were a formidable team to come up against. Villains' wives certainly, but as you would expect, thoroughly decent women. The usual chit chat of their daily doings put them streets ahead of the Mets' intelligence gathering network. If it happened they knew about it first. It was one of those things: word gets about, info is taken on board, lips are sealed and money flows in. It was the way things were. Their husbands were good providers and the women knew how to look after their men. If the filth came knocking if was piss off time.

Jimmie and Reggie never strayed from their nests. Love was a word that never got a look in but, if asked, you knew, cornered in a pub with the blokes banging on about other birds, out it would come. It was slag off time because our two heroes wouldn't stand for such immorality. Straight up family men. Salt of the earth. Wouldn't hurt a fly.

Flo and Tina knew their men were fiercely loyal to them but love? "Of course they love us!". Flo was heard to say that to Tina on a recent occasion down the boozer when the other women in their group were winding up about their bastard straying husbands who didn't know the meaning of love.

However, family coming first, Jimmie had told her to have a word with Len and Ted. 'Don't show out, love. The Old Bill might be staking out there drums. 'Len might give you a handle on the firm Ron Silver's running with'.

Ron Silver had a drum only a few streets away. Flo knew he'd done two blags with her husband but was currently in with another firm. She also knew Silver was an arrogant sod –that's why he'd been outed from their firm. "He's a fucking liability" Jimmie had told Flo. "He shot a geezer on the last job".

Flo drove the family Cortina past Len Spence's drum. The road was awash with parked cars but she felt sure the filth wasn't about. She skirted the area without stopping and came back from the opposite direction. Satisfied, she drove on and found a gap in the line of parked cars and jiggled in.

'Time we did something to help the boys' she said quietly to Tina who had wanted to come along. 'Let's give it a few minutes. See of anyone's about'.

They gave it fifteen and on a nod from Flo they got out and walked back to Len Spence's house.

Jane was surprised to see them but ushered them in quickly. 'Feel bad for you Flo, Tina. Come and sit down. Tell me what's happening'.

Flo leaned forward and patted Jane's hand reassuringly. 'Len'll be alright. Jimmie and Reggie know the score. I'm here for another reason, Jane. I know Len'll want to give Jimmie and Reggie a leg up.'

Jane nodded quickly.

'Have a word with Len. .Let us know if he's up for putting Silver in the frame'

Jane's astonishment was there on her face.. 'We talking about the old bill here?'

Flo and Tina exchanged a glance. They'd mulled over the best way to put it to Len Spence but, seeing Jane first might be the best way forward. She knew her old man better than anybody; but turning someone in? The shock was on her face.

'Len must know that Ron's a loose cannon. The man's a nutter according to Jimmie. That's right aint it Tina?'

'That's right Flo' Tina agreed hurriedly.

Jane was cocking an ear. 'That's Len now'. She left the two women and when the old man was in the hall brought him up to speed.

'Hello girls' Len said as soon as he saw the two. He crossed the room to plant kisses on their foreheads before dropping into a leather armchair with a heavy sigh. 'That's better!'. He was smiling back and forth at the women. 'So, come on. Fill me in' He gestured to his wife who was hovering, waiting. 'Bring us a beer, Love'.

*

'The adjourned hearing's at Chelmsford Crown court today, Dusty'. Masters flapped the message. 'Woodall's not wearing our caper'. He was smiling at Miller who had popped his head around his office door. 'Should be interesting'.

'Pleading guilty to the rest?'.

'So Essex have told me. Six receiving charges. They're well chuffed. Makepeace is coming, as usual.

'Why this time?'.

Masters shrugged. 'Because my name's not Lindley at a guess'.

'Not flavour of the month then?'.

Precisely. Anyway, must get going: mustn't impede the wheels of justice'.

'When is Lakey's trial coming up?', Miller called after him.

Masters turned in the doorway. 'Not in this month's calender. Should be soon'.

Later that afternoon, his examination in chief finished, Masters turned his attention to Woodall's barrister, who was busying himself arranging notes he'd taken while Masters was giving evidence. Nodding to the prosecution counsel he rose to his feet, shrugged his gown, fussed with his wig, smiled to the judge and turned to look at Masters, smiling disarmingly. 'Acting on information received, inspector. That is what you have testified to isn't it?'.

'It is, sir'.

Counsel nodded. 'You have produced a book in evidence that purports to verify the origin of your information. That is so isn't it?'.

'It is'.

'Inspector, exhibit one, the occurrence book: refresh my memory, where is it kept?'

'In the CID general office'.

'Who has access to it?'.

'All members of the station's CID'.

'What, er, occurrences are recorded in it?'.

'They're in the book, sir..........'.

'Thank you, inspector. Just tell the jury what occurrences are entered in it'.

'Not so much as occurrences, sir. Information of use to all detectives'.

'Thank you, inspector. The underlined entry on page eighty .... He sat down while Masters glanced at the relevant page. Standing again and staring at the detective, he asked 'Is that your handwriting?'.

Masters nodded. 'It is'.

'Why?'.

'Why sir?'.

'You were in the office, obviously'...............he smiled. 'Why write a message that was intended for yourself?'.

Masters handed back the book to the court clerk before answering. Staring into the suspicious eyes of the barrister he said, 'I happened to be the one who picked up the phone'.

The barrister saw the winning post galloping

towards him. Adopting a disarming smile again, he said. 'Then you are able to tell the court the name of the informant?'.

Masters killed the smile that anticipated the question. 'Jesus Wept, sir'.

Woodall's barrister shifted his annoyed gaze to the jury before returning it to Masters. 'I will put my question again: are you able to tell the court the informant's name?'.

'It's a code, sir. Nobody knows his real name'. He glanced around the court and smiled at a giggling woman on the front row of the jury, and then at the ruffled lawyer. 'He's usually on the ball, sir. Very reliable we find his information'. As he was saying that he glanced at Woodall, who was white-knuckling the dock rail.

*

Back at the station Masters bumped into Miller and gave him the down on the result. 'Eight years. Dusty. Majority verdict on our job'.

'Makepeace have a word?'.

'Not so far. It'll come'.

*

Chapter nine

'Sit down, inspector'. Without giving Masters a glance Makepeace gestured to the chair opposite his desk. He leaned forward and placed his elbows on the desk, crossed hands under his chin, and stared. 'So now it's three murders', he said, studying Masters' expression and failing to find a chink of concern that enquiries into Watson's murder had hit the buffers.

The DI shrugged and settled into his anorak and glanced critically at his boss, whose expression said it all: his watertight case against Lakey was leaking sieve-like. 'Lakey was charged on the evidence available at that time, sir. Sheila Watson's murder may be copy cat. It's been known'. He spoke with a confidence he didn't really feel.

'Copy cat! For God's sake, inspector. Get into the real world. You cocked it up. You've got a man locked up for murders he in all probability didn't commit!'. His beady, angry eyes were boring into Masters'. 'What are you doing about it, tell me that'.

Masters fingered an evidence file he'd brought along and explained. 'Miss Watson worked for Bowker Transport -Price's employer. She was secretary to the transport manager. Sergeant Miller met her there..........on one occasion'. He rifled and pulled out Miller's brief statement. 'Just the once. He saw her there when he was checking out Price's movements', he added after scanning Miller's statement to refresh his memory. 'Single. 21. Lived with her parents. They own a house in Trinity Street which, as you probably know, sir, is in that estate that backs onto the council estate beside Whiley Road. No steady boyfriend. That's about it'.

'So what do we know of her movements for her last

day?'.

Masters shuffled statements and slid one to the top. 'Detective constable Barton's sir. He saw her at Gym's Place - 9pm he believes -that's a fitness centre in the town centre. Didn't see her leave. Nobody else recalled seeing her, hence Barton's evidence is important. The gym closes at 10pm. We've traced all the members who were there that evening -detective sergeant Miller was there, sir, as it happens. He can't recall seeing her. Nobody saw her leave -alone or with anyone else. She doesn't run a car so her trail died in that club'.

'What about Lakey?'.

'He stays where he is, sir. He's there on evidence that the legal johnies approved at the committal'.

Makepeace's thoughts had raced ahead and he was shaking his head. 'If Lakey is innocent God help you'. He waved a dismissing hand. 'Get out there and sort it'.

*

The three man firm were tooled up and edgedly waiting for the security van to leave. Ron Silver had cased the factory on Fridays for two weeks and knew it took four minutes from the van's arrival to leaving. He had driven the route from the blag and knew backwards the fastest escape route.

Ron's info was, of course, gold plated. Daisy, a lively, lovely piece of skirt was Ron's present shagging partner who worked in the wages office of the factory. The pillow info from a rampant Daisy was it never varied. Always on time; always around eighty grand, allowing for a bit of overtime here and there.

Daisy and Ron were wearing themselves out. His temper was under control when he was on Daisy. Wriggle and squirm! Ron thought she was an Olympic champion at the sex game, but he had awarded himself a gold medal for providing but..........it was the providing bit that was becoming his problem. The way he was feeling he wouldn't get a bronze.

'Give it a rest, sweetheart!' he had said only the night before. He'd rolled off her athletic beautiful body totally knackered! Twice! A record? It bloody well was! Ron had to admit she was becoming too much for him. Providing was harder than........... , watching the van he compared himself with the rampant sod he'd been in the years not that long ago…………………. But that was the night before and this was now and Ron, bleary-eyed and sexually fulfilled with admittedly an aching groin because, even then, he was remembering last night, a fatal misunderstanding because of what was about to unfold. He watched the empty security van trundle from the premises. And there was Daisy, divine Daisy, waving to the driver and disappearing back into the office.

But Len had already belled Don. 'The job's on.' Address and exact time of the upcoming blag passed over. Masters, and his team of detectives expecting their earner, had the ambush in place. This time all members of the firm were getting nicked and all the money recovered. All eighty grand of it. At ten per cent the shared earner was not being sneezed at.

But back to the blag: +

'Let's do it!' shouted excited Brian.

They did it.

Three minutes flat. It was that easy. Lots of shouting. An exploding shotgun and away we go. Oh no. Not quite. Shouts of armed police hollering 'lay down on the ground you thieving bastards'; and from another bloke waving a pistol about ranting 'you thieving bastards are nicked'. There probably was much more but Ron had long since accepted, what with all the shouting. and his aching groin, that it was all over.

Strangely, bearing in mind the criminal code, it never occurred to Ron he'd been grassed up.

The following morning, the present excitement pushing the unsolved murders from his immediate memory, Makepeace was in his own surreal heaven. He looked across at the seated Masters and told him, for once admiringly, 'Inspector. What can I say? Bloody marvellous! And…and...we've got all the money back! It's…it's…'. Words failed him. 'Sit down and tell me how the bloody hell you did that!'

'Not much to tell, sir. Useful snout. Routine mostly', the DI said with his usual constructed modestly.

' Bateman and the Watson woman: how are we getting on there?'.

'Progressing, sir'.

Makepeace shook his head. 'That's not an answer. It's not good enough, inspector. Lakey's QC has informed out legal team he's going for no case to answer when he comes up at the Old Bailey. Get your finger out on this one. Find something to prove you've got the right man. Can you *do* that?'.

Standing now, Masters responded confidently. 'He's our man. I'm confident the judge will let the trial go ahead'.

'It's your head if he doesn't', the DCS warned him.

*

Detective inspector Brian Lindley, waiting for Masters' car to edge to the kerb, dropped into the seat beside him and shook the proffered hand. He said nothing until the car was underway. Masters, meanwhile, was working on the best way to approach the other detective. As casually as he could manage he said while he kept his eyes on the road. ' We need to talk about Bateman's murder. You most likely know we've got Jakeson's and Williams' prints in Bateman's car'.

'So?'.

The DI kept the pace of the line of traffic ahead and wasn't looking at Lindley when he told him what he knew, adding 'He was killed in in his own car, Brian'. He shot a glance at the other man, trying to gauge his reaction. ' We've got the bullet that did it'.

Lindley angled himself to look directly at Masters. 'What's that got to do with me?'.

'The guns used on your job- what's the score there?'.

'Only William's figures in the case file'. Lindsey gazed unblinkingly at Masters, leaving it for Masters to get the point.

' You did a deal with Jakeson?'.

The other detective nodded. 'He bunged me two grand to forget his gun and arrange bail for the pair of them'.

'How did you manage that, for Christ's sake ?'.

Lindley shot a quick glance at the unsmiling detective beside him.'Wheels within wheels, Don'.

Immediately concerned Masters asked, 'are we talking commander level here?'

'Leave it where it is, Don'. Lindley came back with. 'Let's have a brew, That café over there'll do'.

Masters angled the car into a slot and they entered the café.

Cup in hand, Masters followed Lindley to a table and took in his smiling face over the rim of his cup. 'Where does Bateman fit in?', he asked quietly.

Lindley shrugged. 'He got greedy. According to Jakeson he found out about our deal and wanted a cut from the robbery'.

'What became of the money?'.

Lindley pointedly ignored the question. 'Where's all this going? Look, if Jakeson topped Bateman it's nothing to do with me'.

Masters shot a glance at the squad DI and smiled. 'Of course not Brian'.

Lindley sipped his coffee and was the first to break the silence. 'He's overboard with a bit of skirt, Don. She lives at Leytonstone'.

'Where does she fit in?'.

Lindley put down his mug and spread his hands. "ID her and you'll get your hands on Jakeson's gun'.

'If I get the gun and prove it's the murder weapon, is he going to spill the beans about the bung?'.

Lindley's unflickering gaze didn't change when he said, 'It won't get to that, Don. He knows the score'.

Masters pushed his empty cup away and stood. ' Sure you can you cover it?'.

Lindley got up and nodded. 'No problem. Like I said, his gun didn't figure in the arrest. You understand where I'm coming from, Don?'

'I think so. You can prove armed robbery without his gun?'.

'No trouble'.

'Jakeson's revolver wasn't logged as an exhibit?"

'No'.

'What's the strength of your case?'.

'Hundred per cent. Got to be a guilty plea. So far as I'm concerned he's just another snout who pushed the boat out too far. He took liberties. Drop me back at the Yard'.

*

The next morning Don had Ron Silver sitting opposite in the low chair Miller had scouted around to find. 'Bang to rights Ron. Lovely that', he offered for starters.

'Fuck you'.

'And fuck you Ron. Thing is, you're going down for a long time. Three cheers for that'.

'Fuck you'.

'Charming. It doesn't sadden me to say this; you're a piece of shit well past its use by date. But....? He left the words hanging in the air while he stared at the angry thug.

'What's with the frigging but?'

'It could be your salvation'. Masters held the other man's eyes and offered a smile but waited to see if the bullet had been bitten. A change of expression suggested he was on a winner.

'Fuck you', Silver said finally, but the earlier arrogance was missing: he seemed to be mulling over the DI's but. Staring questioningly at Masters he asked bluntly. 'Where we going with this but business?'.

Masters bluntly told him 'Get something down on paper, Ron. Look after number one. You reckon that?'.

Silver's long association with bent coppers was doing wonders for his state of mind. 'Need to think things over' he said after he'd digested what he had heard.

*

With Silver back in his cell it was Brian Fellows' turn to face Masters.

'You're a frigging wanker', he muttered when the inspector banged on about blaggings.

'Try again shall we Brian?'

'Wanker'.

'Quite. These robberies, for which I have a bucket full of evidence, are going to put you and your wanker mates away for very many years. Lovely that'.

'Bollocks'.

'Nicely put Brian. Very articulate that'.

'Fuck you'.

'Let's see shall we. In your garage you cleverly stashed the empty bags from four robberies. Then there are the three automatics. As I speak they are being examined by our firearm experts. You know what they are going to find?' Masters grinned. He was enjoying himself. 'Remember the geezer your firm shot? Well, we've recovered the bullet and our firearm chappie's got it along with the gun'. Still grinning into the hate contorted face opposite he added 'His evidence is going to put you away for attempted murder. Nice one that'

'Never shot the stupid geezer. Ron did................'.Brian broke off. 'Just fuck off'.

'Masters was still grinning. ''Ron'll be pleased to know you've stuck him up for attempted murder.

Take him back to his cell, Dusty. Bring Jones up'.

Fred Jones took a different line. The certainty of a long stretch had already honed his crafty intelligence, and the honing reckoned the detective opposite might............he was staring hard at Masters, not really taking in all the crap about other robberies........

'Guv', he broke into the DI's flow.

'Yes Fred?'

'Been thinking. If I help a bit....I mean.........if you and me can do a deal. Will it help me at court?'

'What kind of deal, Fred?'

Fred was chewing his lip and clenching and unclenching hands. It was obvious to Masters and the watching Miller that the man was sifting through his limited lexicon for the right words. 'Murder, guv. Two of 'em' he finally managed.

The DI exchanged a startled stare with Miller. After a few seconds digesting the unexpected outburst, Miller asked 'Which ones?'

Fred was by then very edgy and worrying about

trusting the detectives. He was dealing with the filth after all, and naturally had good reason not to trust them. He knew from past experiences, and his mates, who reckoned that one word in the wrong ear and he was a dead man.

'Fred? Masters urged.

'Guv. Not easy this one. Him and his mate, right dangerous nutters. I want a guarantee you'll keep me name out of the frame'.

'You've got that Fred. Who are the nutters and who was killed?'

Fred Jones told him about Gardner and Peel. According to him they were a pair of nutters from the East End who were very territorial. Anything going on south of the Thames was for frigging juveniles. Their mantra was East End villains were men. Masters and Miller already knew of the two killings. Not on their manor but interesting chit chat in the canteen. Two different East End pubs within days of each other. "Crowded they were", he told them. "They walked in. Sorted out the blokes they were after and one shot them in the back of the head. There were twenty or so men in each pub at the time', he added.

'And the gun?'

'Searched Brian's garage yet?'

'Yes'

'Then you've got it, guv'

Pardon?'

'One of the automatics Brian's looking after'.

'Tell you what, Fred. Let's get this in writing shall we'.

'Do me a favour, Guv! I thought I could trust you!', Jones protested.

'Insurance, Fred. That's all. You do me a favour and I'll return the compliment. Know what I mean?'

With his statement under caution added to the

thickening file, Miller hauled Jones to his cell

*

The dead men were Charlie Swain and Bert George, well known well-connected villains from South London who made the terminal mistake of crossing the Thames to do a bit of business. Gardner and Peel were well aware that face was being fronted by the bastards. They were pissed off at the sheer bloody arrogance. Anyway, that was the word on the street fed to the detectives on the jobs following the shootings. No witnesses. There never were in the East End. A few villains took earners from their Met paymasters, pissing them about a bit, you know how these things go, but their fingers pointed in the wrong direction, as always.

*

Makepeace was in his element. Masters and Miller were enhancing his profile at the Yard no end. A string of clear ups, dangerous men under lock and key; and two murders about to be solved! And, best of all, one of the guns was the gun what did it!. Bloody marvellous!

'Gardner', he was reading his CRO file and the C11 intelligence file. 'Never been arrested for violence, inspector. I see from C11's file he is suspected of gangland connections, in particular to a Len Spence. Do we know this man?'

Masters was shaking his head, his bland expression adding nothing.

'The other man: Leslie Peel. I see he gets a mention in the C11 file. Believed to be running with Gardner'.

'We know of him, sir. It's all in hand. If you'll lay on to have armed officers on standby, we'll

organise two teams to nick 'em.

*

Melvyn Gardner's house was in Chigwell. The seedy streets of East London where his mum and dad still lived and where he was honed were long forgotten. He'd offered to buy them a house at Haverhill down the road a bit. Nice area that, he argued, but no. "Born and bred here son. The family's down there in the graveyard. Why would we want to move?".

Les Peel's house was in Barking. Nothing posh; just a typical Edwardian end of terrace job. He had no mum and dad to think about. They'd died in a motor accident two years back. From what he'd picked up he knew it was a revenge attack for what he had done- they died not knowing what that was. Stupid it was. Les had cuffed two South London youngsters for swearing in front of his missus. That's all it took. On the day of the accident Les had let his dad use his car to nip down to the Labour Party do. The filth reckoned their demise was down to a robbery that went pear shaped and filed it under 'no chance of a clear up'. Les's info said otherwise. South London figured high on his vengeance scale.

*

The detectives had crept into positions at 5.30am. Front and back were covered with marksmen in strategic spots keyed up for a killing shot. Other armed officers, equally hyped up, were ready to pounce when the doors were broken down. Unarmed detectives were there as back up for the entries. The coordinated 6am start time came and officers wielding sledge hammers had the doors open in double quick time and armed officers were racing up stairs, guns at the ready, fingers on triggers ready to blast a hole at the slightest sign of resistance, not in evidence when arms shot ceilingwards when guns were nudged to heads. Carted off in handcuffs Gardner and Peel, still in underpants, had plenty of time to ponder what had gone pear-shaped.

The swearing, snarling, cockney voice of Mel's wife Gloria soon filled the air once the full realisation of the goings on hit home. Shoved out of the way by the detectives, which included Dusty Miller, John Barton and Ted Read, her house was searched and she was dumped in a hurry up wagon and driven away. Les's wife Kathy shouted a bit but soon calmed down. However, she too was carted off to enable the search to get under way.

Masters lingered in Gardner's house. When the coast was clear, under the watchful eye of Miller, he tipped two bullets from a small bag he'd kept back from the killing gun recovered from Fellow's lock up into a kitchen drawer. 'John' Masters called when he drifted into the living room.. 'When scenes of crime have finished here, get them in the kitchen'

The detective constable acknowledged that. 'Will do, guv'

'Tell the lads to be thorough'.

Minutes later Masters was called back to the kitchen 'What's up?.

The officer pointed to a drawer 'In there, guv. Two bullets'.

Masters peered into the drawer and turned to look at the officer 'Have you photographed them?'

'Done that, guv. I'll bag them shall I?'

'Do that'.

*

Len Spence's relationship with his bent detective at his local nick revealed that Doris Dorkin, living in a flat above a bookmaker's in Leytonstone High St, was Phil Jakeson's lover and a regular punter at the shop. Nipping over there Len mingled with the usual drop outs infesting the betting establishment and dropped Jakeson's name. His: "He's a mate who owes me a few bob -seen him lately?" worked after a while. He'd been seen going through the door two down from the betting shop two days before Mark Bateman's body was found. His information had Masters and Miller in her flat the very next day and the murder weapon recovered. Two teams of detectives were sent to bring in Jakeson and Williams.

Chapter ten

The two detectives working with Miller trawling unmarried Lakey's background had located his Ford Consul in one of a block of six lock-up rented garages at the side of a row of shops two streets from his house. Enquiries revealed he had a rolling rent, minimum two months. Miller chose to rummage under the front seats. Opening his top coat he pulled out a leather belt from his jacket pocket and held it up to his colleagues. 'Got the bastard!', he called, grinning up at Barton, who had popped his head into the car.

'Where was it, sarge?.

'Here..........under the bloody seat'.

Ted Read wasn't as confident.'Just a belt, sarg. Don't prove he's our man'.

"I've got twenty quid that says he is. Give me a bag. Get the SOCO lads here and fingerprint the bloody car and the garage'.

*

The next day Masters reviewed the case against Lakey. Amanda Price's fingerprints were found on the window winder beside the front passenger seat. and Dianne Flaxman's on the ashtray. With Amanda's prints found in Lakey's house on the front door, the stair handrail, the inside of a bedroom door; and on the vanity lid of the toilet in the bathroom beside the bedroom, Masters felt confident he had his man. Some of the women's clothing found in a wardrobe was identified by Price as similar to his wife's. In view of Lakey's denial Amanda had ever been in his house Masters was confident Lakey would go down. The third body had yet to be identified but in view of the different MO he was confident it was a copy cat murder. The legal department agreed and, on the strength of the additional evidence, authorised Lakey be charged with the second murder.

Late that afternoon, Fresh from charging Lakey in his prison cell, Masters returned to the police station and nipped upstairs to have words with an angry Jakeson who, with Williams, had been pulled in earlier that morning. With Dorkin's statement fingering him in front if him, he leaned forward and stared into Jakeson's challenging eyes. 'I've had words with Doris', he said quietly. 'Face reality.........you're on your own on this one'.

The heavy set recidivist thug stared back, determined to see it through. The grapevine had fed him the news that the murder of Bateman was pushing his relationship with Lindley too far. Word was he was on his own. Jakeson was digesting that reminder as he looked across the desk at the DI, who had looked up from the file of evidence in front of him and was staring again. 'So?' he said at last.

'You're bang to rights for the hit, Jakeson. Why d'you do it?'

'No comment'.

'Will Bill go down that road?'

'No comment'.

Masters nodded. 'Not much more to say is there? I've got enough evidence to put you away for life. Still no comment?'

'No comment'.

The robbery, Phil? This is the gun you used. Have a look at it'. He opening his desk drawer and eased out a revolver, laying it on the desk between them..

'I didn't have a gun'.

Masters nudged the gun towards Jakeson. 'Your dabs are on it'.

'So it's my gun. So?' he said to the smiling detective.

'It's the murder gun, Phil. It proves you shot Bateman'.

Jakeson stared at the unsmiling DI. 'This is a fit up' he said at last. 'I want my brief here'.

'Your privilege Phil'. Masters lit a cigarette and inhaled contentedly. 'You know, Phil, I can trace your gun from the robbery to your bit of skirt at Leytonstone and back to you'. He stopped to stare at Jakeson. 'Doris', your ever faithful Doris, has dropped you right in it. She's made a statement. Want me to read it to you?'.

Instead of answering him Jakeson spoke to the ceiling. 'Had words with Lindley?'.

'That'll be the DI you bunged a couple of grand to? Yes, Phil, I have. How do you suppose I got onto Doris?', he suggested.

'I've nothing more to say'.

Masters stood up and gestured to Miller standing by the door. 'Bung him in his cell, Dusty, and fetch Williams up'. When Miller and Jakeman were at the door he added 'You're playing with fire, Phil. Do you honestly believe DI Lindley's left the door open to be nicked?'.

Masters, coffee ordered down the phone, was downing it when Miller reappeared with Williams. Offering his cigarette packet he waited for him to take one and light up from his own

'This is the score, Bill', he told him bluntly. 'Phil is down for Bateman's murder. We've got him bang to rights'...............He held up a hand when Williams was about to speak 'I can imagine a way for you to walk clear of a murder charge. Let's not bullshit each other, Bill. You were part of the hit and I can put you in the car where the shooting took place. However.............', he stared earnestly at the other man ' You could have been in the car for some other reason. What d'you think?'.

'I'm listening'.

"So, Bill, if you make a statement today along that line we can say what Phil did came out of the blue?'.

'And if I do?'.

'You'll be in the clear but', he leaned towards the other man 'You become a prosecution witness'.

'And then?'.

'You get our protection'.

'Guaranteed?'. Williams was understandably sceptical that the filth wanted to help him.

'Guaranteed', Masters glibly reassured him.

Williams, grinning as he did it, shook another cigarette out of Masters packet and lit up from his own stub and digested the way the interview was going, nodding at his own train of thought. Pointing his fag at the detective he made a point that was troubling him 'Do I get banged up in the meantime?'.

'Fair point, Bill. Once I've got your statement yes, you get banged up and remanded in custody. In your own interest once you're inside say nothing. Down the road, when the prosecution file has to be served on Phil's legal team, we get you out on bail and into a protection scheme until the trial. How does that sound?'.

Williams dotted his butt and held out a hand to Masters. 'You've got as deal'.

*

Chapter eleven

Shown up to Masters office, Gavin Snodgrass, a slim, nervous-looking young man, clad as he was in a bespoke suit, looked the real thing. His card said he represented Bent Insurance Company of London and New York. Settled in the chair that Masters indicated he told the detectives his company was obliged to pay the widow of Charlie Swain, who was shot dead in the Hare and Hound public house in Whitechapel Road, London, the sum of £50,000. There were, he explained, clauses that could nullify the policy.

Masters and Miller perked up. 'Clauses?'.

Snodgrass nodded and donned spectacles. Peering at his copy of the policy he read out: "In the event the policy holder brought about his own death by suicide or deliberate involvement in a criminal act, the policy is null and void". 'I'm here, inspector..........', he broke off and smiled, 'hoping you will be able to clarify a few points raised by our legal department'.

Masters, sniffing an earner, was already working on the deliberate involvement angle and put the obvious question. 'How do you define deliberate involvement in a criminal act?'.

Bespoke, encouraged by the question, repeated the clause 'Did he bring about his own death by his own voluntary but criminal act?'

Masters looked at Miller, on hand when an earner was in the offing, before looking back at the rep. 'This deliberate involvement clause. Is that further defined?'

It appeared the man was bemused by the question. 'I realise you are trying to be helpful' he said without fully understanding what lay behind the question. 'I have read the coroner's summary –murder by person or persons unknown. Have you anything you can add to that which would help me?'

It had been a long day and the detectives needed a break. Masters suggested to the other man they break for a meal or a drink. Bespoke agreed and they went to the restaurant a few blocks down from the nick.

Over curry Masters told the suit that Charlie Swain was a villain. 'Several years since his last incarceration, mind you, but a villain nevertheless. How that does square with deliberate act?'

'A person's life style is not always crucial. Dangerous sports…..that sort of thing, yes, of course. But…….I'm reasonably confident I can say that being a villain, as you put it, is not relevant in this instance'.

'So…….see if I've got this right. Swain, by traipsing across a bridge from south to east, is not seen as performing a deliberate act causing his death?'

'Did he do that?'

'Well, yes. But it was only on the evening of his death the poor sod.'

'On the basis of what you've told me' the suit stated 'I must advise my principals of their obligation to fulfil on the policy. It seems to me that Mrs. Swain is the rightful person to claim against the policy'.

The future was getting rosier and rosier. First thing, though, was to keep the suit from banging on Gladys Swain's door. Masters moved up a gear and the suit was duly impressed

'I can help you I believe' he said earnestly. 'Let me have a word around. It might just be, you never know with villains, that Mr. Swain was into something that could prejudice his wife's claim against your company. How do we stand on this?

'I am not at all sure I understand your point?'

Masters put it bluntly 'would your principals consider a ten per cent reward to the team of detectives I could put on the enquiry?' He added 'Of course, should you wish, you could be part of that team and be suitably rewarded'. Masters and Miller were smiling genially at the young man and saw that the penny had landed

'Oh. I see! Well, yes. I believe my principals would readily agree to a reward if the policy was proven, by diligent enquiry of course, to be null and void'

Meals finished Masters and the sergeant got to their feet and offered their hands to the suit and bade him goodbye, knowing they needed to get to Gladys before bespoke paid her a visit.

Half an hour later they stood at her front door and smiled at the frowning, apron-clad woman who was eyeing them suspiciously.

'Mrs. Swain?', Masters asked.

Gladys nodded. 'Who wants to know?'

Masters offered up his warrant card and thumbed towards Miller behind him. 'This is detective sergeant Miller. Might we come in?'

'What's it about? My Charlie's a gonna' she said nastily because they were the filth, 'and all I get from you lot is questions'.

Masters had already stepped into the hall and the woman was backing away. 'You might as well come in' she said reluctantly. Turning her back on the officers she walked into her kitchen. 'So. What did my Charlie do that brings you round here?'

'Put the kettle on, love' Miller suggested

Masters meanwhile was scanning the typical council house room, with its small walk in larder, vinyl floor covering and a bricked-in copper in the corner with the hand pump. The whole atmosphere was of relevant poverty. But an East End villain in poverty didn't ring any bells with the detectives.

'Look,' began Masters 'I know we're the filth around here but some of us have a heart. Charlie going like that was a right downer. That's right, isn't it love?' When she just stared back Masters threw in 'We might have turned up something'.

Gladys welled up, even though her old man had been dead for four months.

The detectives didn't know that Gladys wasn't skint; that Charlie had always provided for her as all villainous Londoners do. No. She wasn't hard up but deeply, understandably, suspicious of the detectives. The best way of dealing with the filth, as her husband had told her so many times once he'd pulled a job, was to say nothing if the filth came calling.

She probed 'Turned up what?'. She was giving Masters her hard look her old man went on about when they had one of their regular set tos.

Mrs. Swain, Call you Gladys....alright?'

'Don't mind. I suppose you want a cup of tea seeing as how he wants the kettle on?'.

'Nice of you, Gladys'

'Sugar?'

'Two for me' Gladys, Miller acknowledged

'One for me'.

Don sipped his tea and worked on a ploy to prime Gladys that Charlie had known he was in danger if he went east that day.

Out of the blue she said 'He told me a firm on the East Side had put the word out he was marked for a beating'

'Did he put a name to to the firm, Gladys?'.

'Wouldn't do that would he'.

'So, Gladys, what d'you reckon, a brave sod your old man to go east that day?'

'Could say that'. She stared at them in turn 'You will catch them won't you?'.

'Let's get all this in writing, Gladys. You have my word we'll nick the bastard who did for your old man'.

*

Two days of routine work passed before Masters' wife, hitched onto an elbow in the bed, expressed her natural concern. 'You look tired, darling', she said with sincere feeling. 'You need some time off -can't you arrange for a few days away from police work?'.

He shrugged her concern away. 'The job, sweetheart', he said as he slipped an arm around her. 'Gets tiring sometimes'. He'd spent an hour only that evening on Kay; he'd been home an hour, it was eleven o'clock, and all he really was up for was kip. Sexually, he was knackered and totally undeserving of Jean's wandering hand. But he did his bit when she eased on top and put his old man into her already moist, expectant, vagina.

The morning daylight reinvigorated him. Two women in one night: one demanding of his sexual competence and other his sexual love. Masters felt as all men feel when the reality of true love is mangled by lust.

He was a shit and he knew it.

*

'John. Oh John darling, **hurreeeee**!'.

John Barton knew, launching himself onto Sheila's unbelievably sensuous slim body and getting down to work straight away, was taking a chance. He was supposed to be on a burglary enquiry but couldn't resist the chance to be with Sheila on her afternoon off.

'John?'. Sheila panted his name questioningly between urgent thrusts.

'Honey?' he whispered as his armed sperm prepared to started its journey............

'About the housebreaking.........' she gasped.

'Yes sweetheart?' he whispered, thrusting hard.

'The housebreaking.......oooh........ yes!.......**Don't stop!**'.

John didn't.

'David doesn't understand', she went on once her fulfilled body had collapsed on the bed, 'why...........well, why did that nasty man...... what I mean to say is ....well, why wasn't the man charged with breaking into our home?'

'I need to talk to Dave about it, Honey. Better I don't explain it to you first. He might suspect something'. He leaned across and kissed her.

'You're so caring, John. If only David...........yes, of course I understand'. She cuddled up to her white knight and sighed. 'Oh John' she whispered 'I love you so much',

His old man started to stir.

*

Chapter twelve

'Put up Lakey'.

'On your way arsehole'. The prison officer handcuffed to him tugged his arm and nudged towards the steps.

The low murmur of voices died away as expectant heads turned towards the dock at the Old Bailey. Lakey's head and shoulders appeared behind the polished wood enclosure, his black shirt, open at the neck visible. He was a different man to the one defiantly denying any involvement in murder many weeks before in Masters' office. The weeks in prison in solitary had sallowed his face and etched it with the worry of it all.

'The accused will stand', the Clerk intoned.

A hush settled over the courtroom

Urged to his feet Lakey looked around, seeing everywhere unsympathetic faces and eyes accusingly staring.

The clerk addressed himself to Lakey. 'On count one of the indictment, you are charged that, on or about 15th. November last, you did murder Dianne Flaxman, contrary to common law. How say you: guilty or not guilty?'

Lakey gripped the rail and stared at the man. 'Not guilty', he answered huskily.

'On count two of the indictment, you are further charged that on or about the 5th, December last, you did murder Amanda Price, contrary to common law. How say you - guilty or not guilty?'.

'Not guilty'.

'Be seated'.

The judge looked over his spectacles at the prosecuting QC, who nodded and rose to his feet, acknowledging the defending counsel with a dipped head. Turning to the jury he told them: 'I shall firstly outline the case for the prosecution, and then put evidence before you that will establish beyond reasonable doubt that the man in the dock was responsible for the murders charged against him in the indictment. The case against the accused begins with the savage death of Dianne Flaxman..................................'

.................outside the court, peering through the windowed door at the goings on, Masters turned away, experience telling him it was going to be a long trial. Miller, unusually for him, hadn't said a word on the journey to the court and had chosen to sit apart from the prosecution witnesses.

The morning session and the lunch break over, himself and the other prosecution witnesses gave evidence. His own evidence given, Masters had time to mull over the likely affect Sheila Watson's murder might have on the outcome of the trial. The prosecution's case was straightforward: Lakey's denial of even knowing the murdered women was strong evidence he was the murderer. The killer blow was the leather belt found in his car.............................

The judge was addressing the court............. 'I am inclined to adjourn until 10am tomorrow morning'. He smiled down at the defending counsel 'Would that be better for you?'.

Hinchcliffe, Lakey's QC, bowed his head to the judge who, incidentally, was a member of the same club as himself, and smiled briefly.

*

........................'Detective sergeant Miller - I remind you that you are still on oath - in your evidence in chief you were quite clear: you discovered exhibit ten, a belt, that belt', he gestured to the bagged exhibit, 'in the accused's car. Yes or no?'.

'I did'.

'Remind the jury -where was it?'.

'Under the front passenger seat'.

'Why look there?'.

Miller smiled at a heavy-breasted women in the front row of the jury, before staring back at counsel. 'Why not?'.

'Is that sarcasm, sergeant?'.

'No, sir. it answers your question'.

'Very well, officer. We have heard evidence from two other detectives', he studied his notes: 'Barton and Read'. He smiled disarmingly at the sergeant. 'They have testified they did not see the belt under that seat. Is that your recollection of the events that day?'.

'It is'.

'Thank you, officer. What led you to the garage?'.

'Local enquiries, sir. We got lucky, I suppose'.

'Indeed officer. Indeed you did. A fingerprint officer has given evidence that has established both Mrs. Price and Mrs. Flaxman had at some time been in the car. The defence does not dispute that'. He paused and looked at the jury for a few seconds before returning his steely gaze to Miller. 'You put the belt in the car, didn't you?'.

Miller, expecting the accusation, stared back, his expression a picture of outraged indignation. 'No, sir. I didn't'.

'You have framed my client, haven't you?'.

'No. The belt was where I said'. Miller's face had paled but his anger was under control.

'Mr. Hinchcliffe'. The judge had leaned forward to give the lawyer a hard stare. 'Are you calling a witness to corroborate that allegation?'.

'The accused, M'Lord. It is my intention to recall him'.

'Very well'.

'Sergeant', the barrister had turned back to face Miller. 'Detectives Barton and Read did not corroborate your allegation. You showed the belt to them. I put it to you again, sergeant, that the belt was not in the car that day'. He stopped to stare, and then turned to face the jury, studying their reactions.

Miller grinned. 'It was there'.

'You find this a subject for humour?'.

'With respect, sir. You have accused me of perverting the course of justice. Your accusation is outrageous'. His composure now under control he leaned forward in the box. Gripping the rail and staring at the lawyer for some seconds he transferring his gaze to the jury. 'I did not frame your client, as you put it. He was stupid to leave it there'.

Hinchcliffe looked away from Miller and studied his notes for some seconds before looking again at the detective, who was smiling towards the jury. 'A scientific examination of the belt did not conclude it was the murder weapon, did it?'.

'The scientist answered that'.

The judge leaned forward and glared at the detective 'An answer yes or no will suffice'.

'Similar type as I recall. The buckle was a clincher'.

The judge glanced between the two adversaries and asked: 'Have you any more questions for this witness, Mr. Hinchcliffe?'.

The lawyer shook his head and sat.

*

The two men paced the court foyer waiting to be called back to hear the verdict. 'You'd better hope the jury comes back with a guilty, inspector'. The trial had gone on for three days and DCS Makepeace was worried. It had attracted a nationwide media coverage and Miller was headline material. 'The Assistant Commissioner is onto this one. Is there a chance - a slim one mind you - we know what the sergeant is like - could he have planted the belt?'. He stared hopefully at Masters, who had his own concerns about Miller.

'To strengthen the case you mean?'.

'Well, yes I suppose. But he wouldn't - would he?'

'Lakey's a cold blooded killer, sir. I would, definitely'.

'And so would I, but...........times have changed, inspector. Media........shape the news don't they? Must be more careful'.

'Got your point sir. Better not to know, eh?'.

An usher popped his head around the courtroom door and beckoned, holding the door open for them. The court was crowded, expectant faces peering at the eclectic members filing back to their seats. Masters and Makepeace sat in their seats and stared over Miller's head at the elderly suited man who had stood, acknowledging he was the jury foreman.

......................'Have you reached a verdict on count one of the indictment?'.

'We have'

'How say you: guilty or not guilty?'.

'Guilty'.

'And on count two of the indictment. How say you: guilty or not guilty?'.

'Guilty'.

'And is that the verdict of you all?'.

'It is'.

'Please be seated'.

The judge stared hard at Lakey and told him the facts of life. 'You have quite properly been found guilty of the murders of two young women. I shan't waste time: you will go to prison for life on each count. It is my recommendation that you are not to be released for twentyfive years. Take him down'.

Masters leaned forward and lightly punched Miller's shoulder. Whispering, he said 'Well done'.

Chapter thirteen

Detective Sergeant Brian Fountain, married to Trisha and childless, knew four of the seven detective constables at his new station. He'd heard of Ds Miller. The grapevine had it he was a womaniser, and a violent sod who got results.

Like Masters he was thirtyfive, but had been in the job for fourteen years. Getting into CID had always been his aim and after six years he finally made it as CID aide, then to detective constable; finally to detective sergeant after 12 hard, slogging, years..

Thorough, he was seen as dour by some who knew him but, unlike Miller, he abhorred rough stuff. Keeping his nose clean and his mouth shut had kept him afloat amidst the routine criminality enjoyed by the other members of the CID at his last nick, and he was determined to keep it that way at his new one.

Around 4.45pm that afternoon he had been called to coordinate the on-going search for Karen, a missing seven years old. Headquarters had relayed her mother's story to Geoff Tims. Mrs. Franklin had gone with her to the local park around 3.30pm, taking the family Jack Russell for a run. Throwing a stick for her untiring dog she failed to notice that her daughter was nowhere to be seen. After some frantic minutes in the darkening afternoon she ran to a phone box and called the police.

Ds Fountain drove to the park and could see by the several flickering torch lights that the search was fairly widespread. He called a constable over.' What have we got so far?' he asked.

'Not a sniff, sergeant. It's a big park. Because of the darkness the inspector has concentrated our search to this area where the mother says the girl was. No witnesses to seeing the girl at all'

A uniformed constable, torch in hand, had just then disappeared into a small copse about fifty yards away.. After a short time he ran out and waved his torch. Fountain ran to the copse, where he was guided to the missing girl.

The sergeant knelt down beside her. She was unclothed from the waist down. Turning away from the sickening sight of the poor little thing he saw knickers, shoes and a skirt on the ground some yards away. It was clearly a serious sexual assault, probably rape. The girl was bleeding from her vagina and whimpering. He radioed for an ambulance.

Ten minutes later the mother, by then sitting nervously in a police car, saw the ambulance arrive and the two man crew open the rear doors, remove a stretcher, and run to the copse. An agonising five minutes passed before they started back with someone on their stretcher, with sergeant Fountain walking beside them.

Fountain opened the police car door and asked the woman to get out. 'Come with me, Mrs. Franklin', he told her gently ' We've found Karen. We'll follow the ambulance'. He helped her into his car and set off after the ambulance.

"She's hurt herself, hasn't she?. Please tell me. What has happened?'.

The sergeant reached for her hand and squeezed it, but avoided eye contact. 'She'll be okay. We'll be there soon'.

'It's serious. I know it is. I can feel it. What has she done?'

Out of the corner of an eye he saw that her hands were clasping and unclasping and tears were streaming down her face. 'She needs to be seen by a doctor, Mrs. Franklin. We'll be there in a few minutes'.

It took some minutes to find a parking slot and, by

the time he'd parked the car, Masters was waiting for them. 'Hi, guv' he said quietly 'This is Mrs Franklin. How is Karen?'

'She's been taken straight to surgery, Brian'. He turned his attention to the mother and decided not to tell her exactly what must have happened. Recognising her distress he said 'Your husband is on his way. He's been picked up from work. Mrs Franklin' He guided her to a chair. 'Karen has been sexually assaulted'. He paused to give the mother time to understand what he was telling her. 'I have been assured by the doctor that she is going to be alright. When she's been attended to she'll be taken to a side ward and you can see her'.

The sergeant had gone off and was now back with cups of coffee. 'Hold this, Mrs. Franklin'. He held the cup out to her, 'drink it if you feel up to it'.

Sipping the coffee it was minutes before she was able to ask for more details of the assault. 'Please tell me what happened to Karen'.

'She's in good hands', he said quietly as he grasped her free hand.' Try not to worry too much. As soon as she's in the recovery room I'll take you to her'.From her distressed state nothing he could say would console her, but he had to get her to understand catching the perpetrator was an urgent issue for the police. He had her clothing and samples from where the girl was found, but no witnesses. 'Mrs Franklin', he said, gazing into her distressed face, 'It's vitally important what she can tell us. When she's able to, would you get her to tell you something about her attacker?'.

'Isn't that something you should do?'. Surprised at the suggestion she stared at the detective.

'Usually, yes Mrs. Franklin, but Karen is so young. I want you to be the first person she sees when she's recovered. If she saw one of us, she would worry, wouldn't she' .

'I don't want her to be traumatised by memories of this. Does this have to be done?'

'Mrs. Franklin. It must be done. Without her assistance we've nothing to go on. Please do this for me?' The sergeant took her hand and gently squeezed it, and smiled.

Still tearful but more in control, she nodded.

'I'm sorry to keep on Mrs. Franklin' he said, determined to keep her attention. ' When you're with her, it's important Karen doesn't see your distress. If you get upset she'll get worried. She may believe she has done something wrong. Can you manage this?'.

*

The hours ticked away before, at 8pm, the girl's mother came out of the recovery room and crossed to where her husband and the sergeant were sitting. It was the first time mother and father had been together since the attack and they clung to each other for some minutes.

Fountain left them to their private moments. Eventually, with her husband's consoling arm around her shoulders, Mrs. Franklin felt able to tell the detective sergeant what she had been able to get from her daughter.

*

The assembled officers listened to Ds Fountain in silence while he described the suffering of the little girl, and her brief description of the attacker. 'CRO are in the picture', he added 'They're pulling out stops.. My gut feeling is the man is local', he told them. 'Anyone?'. He scanned the expectant faces one at a time.

'Not much to go on skip' said one detective constable. 'The age could be anyone'.

The sergeant turned to the collator 'anything from your end?'

'Any one of a dozen could fit the bill', he said worriedly. 'Far too many of these bastards roaming around'.

'Make out a list'.

Turning his attention to the other detective constables he told them 'When he's come up with it go to town on the arseholes. Search their houses; bring them in if necessary; grill the bastards'

'What about the local nut house. Reckon it sarg?' asked John.

'Good point. I'll cover that end. You come with me'.

*

It was 9pm by the time they got to the mental hospital. Ushered into the duty psychiatrist's office they looked down at a fat, seated man and introduced themselves.

'And you are?', Fountain asked, disliking the man instantly.

'Woolner. Dennis. What can I do for you?'.

The DS related what had occurred and told him: 'it's a long shot but this is what we've got. A white man, could be in his forties, around five feet seven, unshaven, smelling of tobacco, wearing either a shirt or tie that was described as pink polka dotted. Does that description mean anything to you?'.

'No it doesn't. I don't see how I can help you', he answered curtly. 'Why are you here?'.

The sergeant didn't mince words. 'The attack was violently brutal -the attacker must have been off his head to carry out such an attack. Does that answer your question?'.

The doctor, shaking his head, stood up and gestured to the door. 'I think it best you leave. The patients are in the care of the hospital. I cannot permit you to question them'. He moved around his desk and opened the door, staring at them.

Mr. Woolner, listen to me'. The sergeant moved close to the doctor and stared hard at him. 'We can resolve this enquiry quite simply. Allow me to search all lockers of informal patients. I don't believe it will be necessary to talk to any patient'.

'I can't agree to that', he answered stiffly as he moved away from the door and went back to his desk.

The officers watched him seat himself and lean back, swivelling his chair from one officer to the other and stare as he made up his mind what to allow.

'How many are informal?' Fountain asked, breaking the silence.

Woolner continued to stare, contemplating a refusal to answer. His mind made up he opened a file and ran a finger down a page. looking up he told them. 'Seven, all male'. he told them.

'Have any of your formal patients absconded today?'

' Nobody absconded'

'How many informal can go out if they want to.'

'Several'.

'How many is several?'

'Five actually'.

'Why didn't you say that straight away! Are you prepared to let me see their quarters?'

The doctor was shaking his head and getting to his feet. 'This interview is ended officer. Please leave'.

'Doctor'. Fountain was very angry. 'Let me spell out the situation you're in. We're dealing with a serious sexual assault on a little girl. If it turns out one of your patients did it, and you persist in your uncooperative attitude, I shall return and arrest you. Is that clear?'

The psychiatrist stared up at the angry sergeant and spread supplicating hands and managed an apologetic smile 'There's no need for that attitude', he said as he rose.' I'll take you. But I must ask you to be discreet'.

It didn't take long. In one of the lockers, lying on the floor, was a polka dotted pink shirt and other discarded clothing. 'Get scenes of crime down here John '. He turned to the doctor 'Whose locker is this?'.

'Frederick Jacobs'.

'Check with the ward staff. Find out where he is'.

The response was quick. Jacobs had been out that afternoon, had come back, and gone out again.

We'll wait for him' a grim-faced sergeant stated firmly.

Shortly before 11pm Masters popped his head around the sergeant's door and stuck up a thumb 'Well done Brian. Bloody well done. Has he coughed it?'

'No option guv. Made a statement. Too early for a result from forensic on the girl's and Jacob's clothing. No doubt it's him'.

'Form?' he asked as he crossed to a chair and slumped down.

'You wouldn't believe it, guv. Peeping Tom. That's all. He's a voluntary patient at the nut house. I haven't seen his medical file yet. CPS'll want to have sight of it for the remand –will you see to the court order?'

'Will do. Anyway, belated welcome, Brian. Settling in alright?'

The sergeant nodded. 'Much the same as the last nick. I know some of the lads –that helps. I read you've been hitting the headlines lately. Like old times for you'.

Masters shrugged the veiled compliment away and stayed in the open doorway, momentarily bringing his mind to bear on the unsolved murder of Sheila Watson, and something Barton had said in the canteen the day before. What the hell was it? Walking to his office he resolved to speak with the detective.

*

Chapter fourteen

Brian Winch and George Brothwell were pissed off with life on remand in Brixton. Brian's on-off girl friend, Daphne Ferret, was on a visit and didn't like what she was hearing. 'What's Fred done to piss you off?' she asked, knowing he'd clocked the screw whose face was wearing the come-on look at her. She gave the winking warder a smile and looked back at the present love of her life.

'We're in here and he's out there, alright!'

'So?' She opened her handbag and rummaged.

'What you doing?' he hissed, casting a watchful eye at the screw.

'Lipstick, Brian. A girl's got to look right ain't she?'. She shot a quick one at the warder when she'd repaired the damage to her luscious lips.

He winked back.

'Stop eyeing that bloody screw! Are you listening to me. We want Fred done'.

'Why. Fought he was a mate, like?'.

'Well we fink it's bloody obvious. His dad conned us. We took the friggin' t.i.c's and his son gets probation. We want him done over'.

Daphne was shaking her head while the words were flowing but eventually, by the end of his tirade, she could see that Brian was right. Fred's dad must have squared the copper and Fred deserved a bashing. 'What do you want me to do?' she asked, quietly now because the warder was near.

*

Len was troubled. He'd decided that Masters' insistence he stuck himself up front for the insurance payout was a non starter. 'I don't want my name on any bit of paper. You'll have to get someone else to do it', he said adamantly .

They were in that same café; it was dark, Masters had insisted on that, and he could see Spence was in a determined frame of mind. 'Has anything happened?'

Len was holding his mug and keeping a steady gaze on the detective. 'Look', he said, his voice now had a brittle edge 'I'm running with hard bastards. I've helped you and you've helped the missus, and Fred's grateful. But these things have a habit of going pear shaped'. Breaking off he watched Masters' reaction. It had sunk in over the weeks that he was at the mercy of the detective. A few words here, sly remarks there, and he was in deep shit. And the arsehole was smiling?

'No problem, Len' Masters assured him. 'I can sort out the insurance angle.. At your end though –any shit flying about?'

'That's what's worrying me'. He stared hard at the detective for a while and decided to tell him. 'Fred took a hammering a couple of days ago. He'd never seen the fingers before so what was that all about!'

'Police involved?'

'Do me a favour! I've put the word out. Won't take long to put names to faces'. He smiled, but the DI saw there was no humour in it. 'It'll get sorted', Spence assured him grimly.

It took all of two days for Len's friends to home in on Sid and Frank, Daphne's hired thugs. Waylaid coming out of their favourite boozer late that evening, they were grabbed and bundled into a Transit. On the short journey they were coshed, blind-folded and gagged. The van was driven into the service area of a group of small service units and the youths were unceremoniously dragged by their feet by four muscled thugs who ignored their pained, muffled, cries when heads scraped on the ground before legs were tied to railings and, quickly, were given the treatment and heads kicked.

In the early hours of the next morning at hospital, with legs in plaster and doctors' waiting for the result of brain scans, they had time to reflect on what happens when you mess with the Spence family.

A week after that bashing Winch and Brothwell were in the court cells waiting to be ushered up. Nudged by their handcuffed escorts, they swaggered into the dock to face their immediate future. Each knew that word in Brixton was that Len Spence was onto them. Len, and a recovering plastered Fred, his eyes still somewhat off-colour, sat in the spectators' bit and Brian spotted them and nudged George. His head momentarily turned it gave George a clear view of Len glaring at him.

'Brian Winch. George Brothwell. You pleaded guilty at a lower court to housebreaking. The committal papers indicate you accepted your responsibility for eighteen further offences. Do you wish for those offences to be taken into consideration by this court before sentence is passed?'

They listened to their brief telling the judge they did before going on about their upbringing and lack of the care and attention.

'When Winch was quite young, ten years of age in fact, his father abandoned the family; and nothing is known of him since his conviction before this court six years ago. I ask that you consider the unfavourable circumstances of his youth and spare him from prison'.

'And the second accused, Brothwell?'

' A sad case indeed. No parenting again since he was ten………..

'Why is that?'

The wig shuffled his notes again before answering

'Both parents are in prison, M'Lord'

'Why?'

The gown got shrugged about a bit while the brief worked out the best way of putting it but settled on the truth. 'Murder M'Lord, I'm afraid' he said at last.

'Both?'.

'Yes. my Lord'.

'My God'.

Brian and George stood as ordered and heard themselves described as recidivist deviants from the underclass of society which should be protected from people like them. Three years each was the end result of getting involved in one of DI. Masters little scams.

*

Chapter fifteen

'John - run it past me again. A Ford Consul..........seen in Whitney Road beside the stream beside the golf course'. He smiled at Barton as he picked up his cup. 'That sounded like the beginning of a song!'.

Barton put down his knife and fork and nodded. "Kids saw it, guv. Blue they reckoned - although it *was* by torchlight. Boot lid up'.

'When was this?'.

'Saturday evening around 6pm. Three weeks back. You remember the lads who found Flaxman's body?'.

Masters sipped his coffee thoughtfully. 'Golf balls as I recall'.

'That's right, guv. With nobody on the course of an evening nobody's going to give them a mouthful'. He smiled at an image of the lads poking about with their torches.

'What's tickled your fancy?'.

'The lads, guv. Fancy themselves as sleuths'.

'How did you get to hear about them?'.

'Cropped up on a house to house enquiry. They live at number five, you know, the council houses?. Told their mum, she told me'.

'Made statements?'.

Barton nodded. 'Before you ask, guv: no, they didn't make a note of the car's whole number -the older brother thinks there was an eight, but it might have been three'.

'Say when it was did they?'.

'Couldn't be sure, guv. It was a Saturday, but weeks ago'.

Masters gestured to Barton's plate. 'Finish that and call on their mum. Arrange an interview at the station. It's worth chatting to the lads again. You never know, out of the mouth of kids I think the saying goes. We'll do the interviews in the canteen. It's quiet around 2pm. Let me know which day is okay for their mother'.

*

Masters smiled at Angela Scott and her sons and gestured to the chairs he'd arranged around the table. Looking at the younger boy he asked 'Douglas?'

The lad shot a glance at the mother before looking at Masters and nodding.

'Francis?'. The DI was smiling at the older boy.

The older lad also nodded.

Masters turned to their mother, who was sitting opposite him. 'Mrs Scott - you probably know what lies behind the reason detective Barton has asked you to come here today. Your lads have been very helpful'. He turned his attention to the boys, who were busy scanning the large room. 'I want you to know we're grateful for your help regarding the poor woman you found in the stream. Would you like a coke, or something else?'.

'Coke'll be fine', their mother answered for them.

'John? Do you mind?'.

Masters waited until Barton was back with the drinks before turning his attention to the lads. Smiling, he explained who he was. '.I have to look into these things........if you carry on as you have you'll be inspectors too one day!', he said jokingly.

Douglas nudged Francis and he nudged back while their mother scowled at them and told them to behave.

'Detective to detective'....................Masters smiled from one lad to the other. 'Think back to the day you saw the car near the stream. In this statement, Francis, you say it was a Consul. What made you think that?'.

Mrs Scott answered before the boy could respond.

"Their father had one before he got the Victor. He's good at makes of cars'.

'That right, Francis?'.

The boy nodded.

Masters, reading from the boy's statement, asked, 'Where was the car?'

When he saw that the boys were puzzled at the question he tried again 'From your home - use it as a marker'.

'There's a lay-by nearly opposite our house. There'.

Masters glanced at Barton and gestured for him to take notes of what was being said. 'So. The boot was up. You both noticed that?'.

Looking at each other the boys turned to Masters and nodded.

The DI tapped statements and grinned. 'You haven't mentioned touching the car. I'll bet you did!'.

Their mother spotted their hesitation and spoke sharply to them. 'Tell the man the truth!'.

Francis nodded at last and, glancing at his brother, said 'We didn't steal anything. We opened the doors, that's all. There was nothing in the boot, honest'.

'Nothing. No spare wheel. No tools?'.

'Nothing, sir'.

'I'll bet you sat in the driver's seat'. Masters was smiling from one lad to the other.

Douglas nudged his brother. 'He did. I told him not to'.

Masters reached to pat the older lad's arm. 'You're not in trouble, son. These details help us. Were you wearing gloves?'.

Their mother answered for them. 'Never wear them............do you', she added, looking sharply at her sons.

Masters turned his attention to the boys again. 'Can you remember any detail of the car............dents, scratches, rust perhaps?'.

They shook their heads. Suddenly Francis looked eagerly at his brother. 'Remember........I told you about it..........there was a tear in the driver's seat. Near the front it was'.

'Big tear?'.

Francis spread his fingers. 'Like that'.

'About two inches........yes?'.

Francis nodded.

'Nothing else?'.

'Only the hub cap...........it was missing'.

'Which wheel?'.

'Front..........the driver's side'

While Francis was answering, Douglas had wandered to the windows and was staring down into the car park. 'There's one down there', he said without looking back at the detectives.

Masters gestured to Barton to follow and crossed to stand beside the lad and follow his pointing hand to Miller's car. 'Like that one? Same colour?'

Douglas had joined them at the window and spoke first. 'Yes, sir'.

'Francis?'.

'It was dark . But it looked blue -like that one, yes'.'.

'You've been a great help, lads', Masters told them. 'Thank you for coming in, Mrs. Scott. Detective Barton will run you home. We'll need to take additional statements from the lads. And take their fingerprints. John here will arrange that'. Inclining his head to Barton he said 'See to that, John'.

*

It was there. Peering through the door window Masters saw the tear, just as Francis Scott had described. And a hub cap was missing from the front wheel on the driver's side. With Miller on an enquiry he was faced with a dilemma he could not ignore: in the sergeant's interest the car would have to be transported at once to divisional headquarters for a scientific examination. He returned to his office to inform DCS Makepeace.

The DCS's worried voice said it all. 'What are we looking at here, inspector?'.

'Not the point, sir. His car was at the murder scene. Sergeant Miller's interests come first. Whiter than white, sir?'.

'I agree. See to it'.

Within the hour the car was loaded onto a flat deck trailer and driven away. Miller, who had returned to the station in time to see his car driven off, stormed into the front office and demanded to know why his car had been taken away.

'Don't have a go at me, Dusty'. Sergeant Tims responded angrily. ' The DI arranged it. Have a go at him'.

*

'Read these, Dusty'. Masters pushed copies of the youngsters' statements across his desk and studied his friend's angrily set features.

Miller picked them up but stared hard at Masters. 'What's this all about, Don?. Alright....I will' he said when, instead of explaining, Masters gestured at the statements. He read them and pushed them towards Masters. 'What's the fuss about? So they saw my car there. Why impound it?'.

Masters shook his head in despair. 'You left your bloody car very nearly at the spot where Sheila Watson's body was later found. For God's sake, Dusty. Where was your brain?'. What else could I do? I have to clear you of any suspicion. Why in God's name were you there?'.

Miller grinned and winked at the DI. 'Over side with a bird. She's married........you know.....couldn't use her place or mine, could I!'.

'The open boot?'.

'Blanket, Don. I always keep one there on the off chance'.

Masters had listened to his friend's explanation, wanting it to remove the lingering doubt that had knotted his stomach. Now, looking at him smiling back, relaxed, he wondered if he really knew him. No, he told himself firmly, he couldn't have. 'I shall need to have the name of the woman, Dusty', he explained. 'Makepeace is in on this one'.

'Need a bit of time on that, Don. Might be a problem - you know - married?'.

'A week at the most, Dusty. For your sake we'll keep this under wraps until SOCO's finished with the car. They don't know you're the owner'.

'Won't they check?'.

'Makepeace wants his steady ship - you're lucky there'.

'Why SOCO?'.

'Dusty - wake up. Your car is sitting in the middle of a murder enquiry'.

'What happens now, Don?'.

'You carry on as usual but.............', he smiled and winked at his friend, 'leave crumpet alone for a while..............at least until this murder enquiry is over and the bastard's collared'.

'Fair enough, Don'.

*

Time stood still for Reggie, Jimmie and Dave since their committal to the Central Criminal Court. Their brief had made a couple of visits 'tidying up loose ends for the trial', McDonald had told them. His gut feeling they'd been set up had hardened over the weeks, but Reggie and Jimmie were adamant they wouldn't pull Spence and Burke into the frame. McDonald knew the score and could only advise. As Jimmie told him on one of the visits 'we wouldn't see the night out in here if we grassed them up'.

Flo and Tina weren't so squeamish. Jimmie told them what the brief was going on about. For Betty, who couldn't cope with her Dave being locked up, it was all too much; and her depression was getting to them. Len Spence and Ted Burke's charmed life had been ringing bells; and because Jane had changed, becoming more distant they thought, it seemed obvious to the women their husbands had indeed been grassed; and Jane probably thought her old man had done it. Something had to be done about it before their men got weighed off.

Tina set the ball rolling. 'I think we should face Jane with this' she declared firmly. 'If she's in on this I'll.............' Her anger had narrowed her eyes to slits.

'Calm down, love'. level headed Flo interrupted. 'I don't think that'll do any good. There's another way we can find out if her old man is a grass'.

The other women listened. Betty was too worried about her Dave to take in what Flo saying but Tina, her face brightening, smiled. 'Now that is a really good idea' she said as a broad smile reshaped her face.

*

Lindley's arranged visit with Jakeson in Pentonville was likely to spread wide. The risk was there but he took it.

'In there', he was told by a surly faced warder whose

mum had been done for shoplifting only two weeks back.

Jakeson, charged with the murder of Bateman, and remanded several times, was in no mood to talk to Lindley, who sat there offering up a packet of cigarettes once he'd settled into a chair opposite him.

'So what's this about then?', he demanded. He took the offered fag and lit up from Lindley's glowing end and then stared.

'Loose ends, Phil'. The detective was studying Jakeson's expression and let his words hang in the air.

'You know what', Jakeson said angrily, 'I'm facing a lifer and you, you frigging bastard, sit there talking about loose ends! Get me out of it'. He leaned over the table and stabbed a finger at the detective ' If I go down for this I'll take you with me!'.

The detective leaned close to the stabbing finger and, equally angry, told the other man the facts of life. 'I had nothing to do with the shooting. You know why I'm here?. No?'. Then listen you arsehole. If you try to bring me down I'll have you done over as a grass. Got that?. A grass'. He stood and glared down at Jakeson. 'You're a loose cannon with a big mouth. Just try me! I promise you'll regret you ever heard of me!'.

*

'Your car's back, Dusty'. Masters jangled keys. 'Minus the blanket - SOCO's holding onto it until we've caught Sheila Watson's killer'. He smiled at the sergeant when he'd taken the keys 'Better safe than sorry'.

Miller dropped into a chair opposite the DI and looked quizzically at him. 'Am I a suspect, Don?'.

Masters looked thoughtfully at him before answering. 'Use your brain, Dusty. You parked your car near where her body was found. Stands to reason whoever dumped the body must have wrapped it in something to get it to the stream. Your blanket fits the bill so far as SOCO's concerned. It's got to be eliminated'.

'Seen Betty Wainwright?'.

Masters nodded and tapped a document on the desk. 'Her statement. Doesn't help much -been down that road with you a couple of times'. Masters chuckled at an image her statement created. 'Can't be sure of that Saturday though'.

Masters phone rang and he listened, sliding the statement into a folder with the rest. Replacing the handset he got up, checking his watch. 'It's the Old Bailey for me, Dusty. Jury's due back'.

No 5 court at the Old Bailey was unusually crowded when the clerk to the court called out for the prisoners to be put up. Reggie, Jimmie and Dave appeared from below, each handcuffed to a prison warder. While the bewigged judge's attention was on papers in front of him they looked along the spectators' seats. Reggie spotted Tina and gave her a thumbs up. Flo saw Jimmie and waved. Dave's gaze swept the seats but Betty wasn't there. It was a failed hope because Jimmie had told him after Betty's last visit that she wouldn't be able to face her Dave being sent down.

The Clerk of the court intoned 'The accused will stand'.

'Members of the jury. Have you reached your verdicts?'

The smartly dressed woman Reggie had winked at whenever he caught her attention stood up 'We have'

'On count two of the indictment, how do you find against Davenport of conspiring with others to commit armed robbery: guilty or not guilty?'

'Not guilty'.

'In regard to count four of the indictment, that of theft of a motor car. How do you find: guilty or not guilty?'

'Not guilty'

The Judge gave the woman a hard look before declaring 'The accused is free to leave the court'

Betty should have been there! The tug by a warder broke the spell. 'Let's go, Dave'.

The Clerk turned his attention to the jury forewoman. 'How do you find for the accused Cook on count one of the indictment of armed robbery: guilty or not guilty?'

'Guilty'

'And count two of the indictment: conspiracy with Pollard and others unknown to commit armed robbery, how do you find: guilty or not guilty'

'Guilty'

'And on count three of the indictment of possession of a prohibited weapon?'

'Guilty'

'How do you find for the accused Pollard on count one of the indictment of armed robbery: guilty or not guilty?'

'Guilty'.

'In regard to count two on the indictment: conspiracy with Cook and others unknown to commit armed robbery. How do you find: guilty or not guilty?'

'Guilty'.

'And on count three of the indictment of possession of a prohibited weapon?'

'Guilty'.

The Judge nodded to the Clerk and thanked the jury. Turning to the two men in the dock he said 'all options are open to me but I must tell you now that imprisonment is certain. Sentence will be decided after the lunch break. Take the prisoners down'.

*

Masters, the oath taken yet again, handed to the clerk the list of further robberies the men had admitted to. The clerk asked them if they admitted them and wanted them taken into consideration before sentence was passed.

McDonald popped up and agreed.

But the Judge's cold expression told them their blagging days were over for a long time. The note slipped to him from the prosecuting counsel in regard to Jimmie Pollard's assistance in regard to the murders had given him pause for thought, but helping the police with their enquiries didn't register high on his radar. Each man was given 10 years on each count, to run concurrently.

*

Three weeks after Cook and Pollard had been sent down Jane hopped off a bus near the Whitechapel Road hospital. It was her second visit because, at the first one, Len's face was concealed behind bandages and he couldn't make himself understood. This time the wrapping was off and his enlarged and battered face told a story.

'Where does it hurt love' she asked, perhaps naively, but in a vengeful tone he recognised.

'Every fucking where! My fucking legs are giving me whats it; I've ribs a butcher wouldn't sell for a barbecue! My fucking arms are knackered....!'

'Calm down my love' she told him as she laid a gentle hand on his outstretched plastered arm. 'Put me in the picture and I'll make bloody sure it's sorted'.

'Shut the door and listen', Len told her.

Chapter sixteen

'Ted....'

'Sarg?'

It was 7pm and Geoff Tims was holding up a hand to detective constable Ted Read who had just walked in and was heading for the stairs.

'I see.........Your name is?. Address? Right....Last night?....underwear!...............Right. Got that. We'll get someone round to you'. He turned to the detective constable and shoved the note across the desk to him. 'We've got a knicker-knocker. Nip round and see what that's all about'.

Ted drove to the address which turned out to be the end one of a terraced block of six houses. Before knocking on the door he scouted around and saw through the street lighting that the block had a footpath at the rear which fronted the rear of another block of six houses. He walked along the footpath and saw, some with hanging clothes, lines stretched down each garden. Drifting to the front of the house he was looking for he rang the bell and was fronted by a beautiful woman, in her thirties he guessed, in a dressing gown, belted at her slim waist.

'Detective constable Read miss'. He showed his warrant card. 'You rang the police station a short while ago? Clothes stolen? May I come in?'

Liking what she saw she smiled and nodded, and held the door sufficiently ajar for him to squeeze past.

Ted briefly touched her dressing gown and caught a waft of perfume as he brushed past.

'Go in there'. She was pointing to a door opposite the detective.

It was a living room kitted out with a feminine touch. Scatter cushions of different shades were on leather chairs; the carpet was cream coloured; and magazines were neatly stacked on a glass-topped coffee table. The window curtains were swagged (you and I know this description, Ted didn't) and Ted, not into aspirational female working class design, was duly impressed.

'Sit down' she offered smilingly. 'Would you like a coffee?' She was hovering close.

Ted, aware that his old man was rising, sat on a settee and looked up at her and nodded.

She walked to the door and turned to look at him, again liking what she saw. 'I won't be a minute', she told him. 'Make yourself comfortable'.

He took the opportunity to shove his old man into a comfortable position and look around the room again. He picked up a magazine and flicked the pages but couldn't get her image from his mind.

'Cream and sugar?' came from the other side of the door.

'No sugar. Thanks'.

She came back with the cups on a dainty woven cane-edged tray, offering Ted a seductive smile. Cups on the coffee table in front of the settee she sat beside him.

'Mrs Whitelaw...'.

'Miss. I'm not married'.

'Oh. Sorry'.

'Divorced', she explained into his questioning, lusting eyes.

'The clothes, miss. From your line?'

'Lucy. Call me Lucy. So much friendlier don't you think?'

'Lucy'.......... it was stirring down below again. He shifted uncomfortably while he took sips from the cup. 'The clothes. I shall need a description?'

She stood up. 'If you see some the same you'll

know what to look for?' she suggested. She leaned down to take his hand.

Ted took it and clambered up and, when she turned to lead the way, he again shoved his rigid old man, which was pulling his underpants uncomfortably into the crack of his arse, more comfortable against his stomach.. Allowing himself to be led from the room, up and into a bedroom, he watched Lucy open a dresser drawer and take out several pairs of scanty silk-looking knickers and drape them on the quilted bed.

Ted could only stare from the knickers to Lucy, who was smiling at him, and back to the knickers and back again to Lucy.

She opened her dressing gown, slowly and seductively, and he stared at her beautiful body in identical knickers.

'Marks and Spenser', she explained unnecessarily", smiling sweetly at awestruck Ted.

'Oh', he managed through dry lips. Every instinct was urging him to reach out and touch her body.

"You're a copper" he told himself. "Control yourself!".

'You must be very hot in that overcoat'. Lucy reached and started to slide it from his shoulders, her face inches from his, smiling. 'There now. That's better isn't it?'. She folded the coat and placed it on a cane chair near the window and came back to stand close in front of him, her dressing gown open and her slender body exposed to his searching gaze.

Still with that alluring smile, Lucy took a chance and reached down to trace the outline of his erect penis with caressing fingers. 'You want me, don't you? Why don't you cuddle me? That would be very nice, wouldn't it?'. Still stroking it she smiled into his eyes and didn't have long to wait for the action to start.

Ted by now was in the grip of an urge to throw her

onto the bed and get started straight away but hesitated, waiting for her to stop stroking his penis, which was close to firing both barrels.

'I'll cuddle you, shall I?'. She took her hand away and placed her arms around his neck, pulling his head forward and kissing his cheek and Ted, unable to control himself any longer, wrapped his arms around her, tingling at the sensation of holding her close while his hands were tracing her sensuous body. He pulled back and slid the gown off, letting it fall on the bed. He reached around her back, doing his best but failing to unclasp the soft, unpadded, unwired, silky bra. Lucy giggled and reached round, unclasping it herself. He pushed her back slowly onto the bed and tried to pull her knickers down, succeeding at the second attempt when the first caught on her feet. Naked now and unabashed, she pushed him away, eased herself off the bed and slowly, seductively, undressed him, caressing him as she did so. Settled on the bed she raising her arms to him. 'Make love to me', she whispered.

Ted was no novice in the bedroom department but, even so, as he placed his hand over her's on his cock and positioned himself above, he hesitated until, with her hand urgently guiding his, he experienced her moist expectancy against his hand. 'Do it now', she urged.

'You do it', he panted, waiting for her guiding hand to fire the starting pistol.

Lucy expertly located the goal and Ted eased himself into her and lay on top and thrust, slowly at first, but with more urgency when he experienced her silky smooth body thrusting back at him until, minutes later she gasped 'Oh! this is **so *beautiful*!**'. Their orgasm's came together and Ted lay still, his lustful desire sated but wanting to continue making love to her. He looked lovingly into her blue eyes and kissed her.

'Do it again', she whispered into his ear.

Ted did.

Later, over coffee, she told him about Joe Swift.

'Joe', she stated firmly, was a pest. 'Whenever I looked out of a window at night, he was out there, staring at me. It must be him who's been stealing my knickers'.

'Don't you draw the curtains?'.

'I forget sometimes', she fibbed.

'Who is Joe?'.

'Swift. Lives at the far end of the block. He's married. Got six kids. Should know better'.

Ted got to his feet and held out his hands to her, helping her up. Placing his hands to her cheeks he leaned towards her and kissed her tenderly. 'I'll see him tomorrow. I promise you he won't trouble you again'.

The following evening around the same time Ted was ringing the door bell of the house at the furthest end of the block.

'Mrs. Swift. Is Joe in?' he said to the stern-faced woman who opened the door.

'Who wants him?' she challenged, her folded arms lifting her ample bosom.

Ted had done his homework and knew Joe ran a car. He smiled reassuringly and showed his warrant card. 'To do with his car. Nothing to worry about. Is he in?'

Half turning she called 'Joe. Someone wants you' before turning back to Ted and telling him he could come in.

'I'll stay here if it's alright with you, Mrs. Swift'.

As his wife disappeared into the side room a muscled bicep-tattooed brute approached our Ted. His 'who are you?' sounded like "this had better be important or I'll break your frigging arms".

Out came the warrant card again. 'Mr. Swift. I think it would be better if you came with me to the police station. Ted motioned along the hallway and added 'Very private, this matter Joe. Best the wife is kept out if this one'.

For some seconds biceps stared at Ted and Ted stared back. 'You gonna tell me what it's about ?', he demanded.

'Knickers'.

Joe shot a quick look over his shoulder and motioned for the detective to step back. He came out and asked 'Anything to do with Lucy?'

Ted nodded

Joe stared at the detective for a few more moments before saying 'I'll get a coat'.

Word gets around quickly in a police station because knicker knockers are a breed of men with kinky, deviant, unfathomable motives. Joe was big, truly big, with huge arm muscles. 'God knows what his prick's like', Ted remarked to Tims once he'd been led to the cells. Naturally inquisitive, officers took turns to peep through the observation flap.

Ted nipped upstairs to the CID floor and telephoned Lucy to tell her Joe was nicked.

Worried because of his size, she asked 'Did he cause any trouble?'.

'His wife was in. He came quietly'.

'Has he admitted stealing my underwear?'.

'As good as, Lucy. He and me'll have our chat in a few minutes. I'll ring you later'.

*

Joe and Ted were having their amiable chat in an interview rooms when Dusty Miller, a changed man since his car had been SOCO'd, had briefly scanned the charge sheet and nipped upstairs to the interview room and thumped Joe in the chest, knocking him flying backwards off his chair. 'Tell him the truth you frigging wanker!' he ordered Joe, as he turned to leave the room.

Ted stared at Joe, who was getting to his feet. 'He's being cooperative. Tell him, Joe. Lucy's a raver isn't she?'

'Lucy's a raver' Joe said to a scowling Dusty.

'See Dusty. No problem here. Joe's in a fix. The wife. Big problem. Joe's got something going in his head about a neighbour. Problem is she doesn't want to know. You know how it is –women are choosy aren't they'. Pride washed over him as he said that, remembering........... 'Wants to know if he can square matters without going to court. What'd you reckon sarg?'

Miller and Ted exchanged knowing looks. Dusty was thinking a grand and Ted a more realistic three hundred. 'Tell you what Joe', Ted said, his mind made up, 'You say her knickers are in your garage: let's give it the once over'.

Ted drove Joe home to get a key and, as he'd admitted on the drive, the garage revealed a dozen pair of Lucy's knickers in a roll of lino. Ted folded them carefully and slid them into the glove compartment.

'Where do we go from here?'. Swift dropped into the car and stared hopefully at the detective.

'Bit embarrassing this'll be for you if it went to court'. Ted mused as he angled to size Swift up.

'Does it have to?' Joe asked hopefully.

'Should do. Kinky thieving wasn't it. You got an alternative in mind?'.

'Would a few quid sort it?'.

Ted recognised the man's desperation and nodded. 'Shall we say three hundred sobs?'.

'Done. I'll nip indoors and get it'.

Ted was surprised the man had money lying about

and said so.

'Do a bit of wheeling and dealing. Tax man don't have to know everything does he!'.

The next evening, one hundred and fifty quid richer because Miller had wanted his cut up front, Ted was back round Lucy's with the knickers. Daintily, fingertipilys, Lucy identified them and Ted's reward lasted a blissful hour upstairs.

Ted was rapidly falling in love. The painful memory of Brenda, his live-in girl friend of two years who had one day left, telling him she loved another, faded completely as his friends had told him it would. As he lay beside beautiful naked Lucy he imagined her living with him in the house he had bought for himself and Brenda. He traced her silky skin with gentle fingertips and cupped a boob and knew he was in heaven..............................

'What are you thinking?' Lucy asked

'You....................... Just you'.

She cuddled up to him. 'That's nice' she whispered.'Let's do it again'.

*

They were in the usual café and Masters was giving the man facing him a businesslike stare. Charlie, standing over by the wall, was saying nothing because that was his role that day.

'My principals are satisfied' Masters was told 'you have arrested and caused the convictions of the perpetrators of the crime and recovered two thirds of the stolen money. They agree to the usual ten per cent reward which, in this case is two thousand pounds. Is he the man responsible for helping to solve the case and, thus, for the recovery of the money?'

The DI gestured for Charlie to come forward. 'His

identity must remain unknown for his own safety', he told the man gravely. 'I have brought him here today for you to see the flesh and blood of police work. This man's life would be in jeopardy were you to reveal his identity. Sign his document', he told Charlie.

Charlie signed with a cross.

*

With Melvyn Gardner and Leslie Peel glaring at him from the dock a self-assured DI Masters was being cross examined by McDonald, who looked much more impressive in his wig and gown. 'Inspector...........' he had papers in one hand and went into the shrug routine that all barristers seemed to want to do. 'You have stated that exhibit number two....' He picked up the labelled bag of bullets and flourished it for the jury's benefit.......'was recovered from the kitchen of the accused?'

'Others have testified to that'.

'Very well. Exhibit number one: it contained bullets of exactly the same calibre?'.

'Is that a question, sir?'

McDonald gave the DI a long hard stare.' I'll rephrase that. The bullets in the gun: are they of an identical type to those you say were found in the accused's kitchen'.

It was obvious to the detective inspector that McDonald was working his way to allege the bullets and gun were planted. 'The firearm expert clarified that point, sir'.

'I believe you stated the accused Gardner had access to the garage?'

'It was rented it in his name'.

'Quite. Rented. Could others have had access to the garage?'

'Hardly likely'.

'Yes or no, please inspector'.

'No'.

'You are certain of that?'

Masters half smiled.

'Inspector. I must remind you that you under oath'.

'Would you let someone else access your garage when you had a gun stashed away there!'

A couple of teenage girls in the spectators benches giggled and the Judge warned Masters to refrain from speculation.

McDonald was hard put to keep calm. "You bastard", he thought viciously. "You bastard!" He recovered and said 'You have not produced evidence that the accused actually rented the garage. Have you inspector'

'No'.

'Why not?'

'I would prefer not to answer that question'. Masters turned to look at the Judge for guidance

'Answer the question officer', he was sternly told.

Masters looked at the jury when he answered. 'My witness has been intimidated………..'

Up popped the brief to complain. 'M'Lord. I must protest' he said as he attempted to regain the initiative.

The Judge, directing his remark to the jury said, 'I instruct you to disregard the officer's last statement'. He turned his grave features to the DI. 'Inspector. Can you produce a witness to a rental agreement for the garage?'

Masters inclined his head to the Judge. 'I can produce the name of the witness who can substantiate the rental agreement'.

McDonald sniffed a trap and studied Masters bland expression for a clue. He turned his attention to the Judge and asked 'may I be granted a short recess,

M'Lord?'

To digress. The garage in question was one of a block owned by a villain named Balls, Charlie Balls to give him his full moniker. He was on nodding terms with Gardner and Peel; and the deal was his name was kept out of it if it went pear shaped down the road. Down the road pear shaped it went when Gardner and Peel got nicked and the garage was subsequently turned over by the flying squad. Briefed by Masters, the squad DI planted the gun and four of its six bullets recovered from Brian Fellows garage in a drawer under a work bench.

With the two retained bullets in his possession Masters had, as you will recall, undertaken the search of Gardner's home. Miller, John and Ted helped in the search. Masters with Miller as an alibi witness if necessary, was not present at the search of the kitchen, hence was not implicated in the recovery of the bullets by a SOCO officer, who had produced in evidence photos of them in situ. With Gardner nicked Charlie Balls had a visit and a pasting by mates of Gardner. Villains are not up to Brain of Britain standard and Melvyn Gardner is no exception. You don't go about pasting a fellow villain and expect him always to roll over..................

The deal with Masters was quite simple. To save face, Balls would have to be subpoenaed to court if his evidence was needed.

For McDonald that moment had arrived when he cross-examined Balls. 'Can you be sure, beyond any reasonable doubt that the person who rented the garage from you that day is in this court today?'

'Yes'

'And where is that man?'

Charlie pointed to Gardner. 'That's him in the dock. The bloke on the right'.

All in all the case was wrapped up satisfactorily. The barmaids of the two pubs came forward and swore they witnessed the killings and fingered Gardner as the gunman and Peel as his accomplice. McDonald couldn't budge them.

The summing up was clinical. The Judge pointed out to the jury the damning evidence of the two bullets, bearing Gardner's fingerprint, found in his house. 'You must decide whose evidence you believe. You have heard two versions: the accused who stated' he paused to refresh his memory from his notes, before peering over the rims of his spectacles and offering a half smile "I've been fitted up by the bastard sitting over there grinning". 'You will recall he had to be restrained at that point'. Turning to his notes he referred to the evidence of DI Masters. 'Did you find him a compelling witness?' He paused again and peered over his glasses at the jury members. 'The gun in his rented garage, the bullets in his house, and the evidence of the bar women. It is for you to decide who is telling the truth'. He turned his attention to the case against Peel. 'Should you you believe the two women who gave evidence against the accused Gardner, you should also find Peel to be as guilty as Gardner. It is for you to decide. You may feel his presence gave encouragement to Gardner. You are entitled to ask yourselves why he was there on those two evenings. The two men were in the public houses for no more than three to four minutes, according to the women. They did not purchase alcohol. The allegation is that they entered the buildings for the purpose of murder and carried out those heinous crimes. However, the law states that you must be sure beyond all reasonable doubt to convict. Members of the jury. Retire now and consider your verdicts'. It took an hour to return a guilty verdict, during which time the judge had made up his mind what to do. Brought back up to the dock he gave each of them life, with a minimum term of thirty years.

Ronnie Silver and his two villainous mates got the same treatment as the killers. Masters being a glib bastard in the witness box erased any doubts the jury might have had. Silver was sent down for 15 and his mates for 10 each.

Importantly for the DI, he put Charlie on standby to collect the eight thousand pound reward from the insurance company. It was a different company but the routine was the same. When Masters and Charlie were back in the multi story car park the deal had been closed and the young man drove off contented with five hundred pounds.

*

It didn't need a member of MENSA to follow the gist of Melvyn Gardner's drift. McDonald got it straight away. He and the convicted killer were hunched across a table in a side room in Wandsworth prison and Gardner was emphasising his points with a stabbing finger. A warder was outside the door ready to dive in if our killer got nasty.

'I've been fitted up! You and me know it and I want those bastard coppers done'.

'Quite, Melvyn. Quite'. the lawyer studied his client and frowned . 'The problem we have is that the summing up was immaculately fair. No point of law there. The jury was asked by the judge to weigh your story against the police officers who found the gun and the bullets. Unanimous, you will recall'.

'Well fuck you! That gun was in Brian's garage not mine. I've paid you a mint of dosh. Do your frigging job and get me out of here. Stick an appeal in'.

'The women. What about their identification of

you?'

Gardner started stabbing again 'Forget 'em. Once I know you've set the ball rolling they and Brian'll have a visit'.

The lawyer got to his feet and Gardner, also standing by then and placing his palms down on the

table, told the lawyer coldly 'You sort the evidence. I want out of here'.

*

Brian Fellows was in Parkhurst prison on the Isle of Wight when both the grapevine firstly and a beating secondly told him Gardner was not a happy bunny. It was the gun, apparently, that the law had fitted him up with that was truly pissing him off. Prison being a dangerous place to get on the wrong side of a fellow villain no matter where he was incarcerated, he sent word back via a bent screw he'd help if he could.

Gardner's wife Gloria got the drift of what Mel wanted done. The barmaids were going to have the frighteners put on them. They'd be too scared to give evidence at the appeal, she reasoned. With that in mind she had visited both pubs and sussed out where the barmaids bedded down. Both were single and lived in rented bed sits in Whitechapel Road: one above a betting shop and the other above a greengrocer. In each case the women had a front door to the side of the shop: the first floor becoming in effect a flying freehold above each shop.

The fire brigade at first thought it was an electrical fault that set fire to the stairwell beside the betting shop. When the second stairwell caught fire the same night not far from the first a few eyebrows went up and a more thorough investigation was carried out. The two way switches in each case were faultless. There were no power sockets in the hallways. There were, however, badly scorched front doors! Yes, we know. But even fire investigators have days off. Surely, what is important here is that nobody got hurt or died?

*

The suit read Gladys Swain's statement through and turned to smile at Master and Miller. 'From what she has stated I believe our legal advice will be that the policy is null and void. Thank you for your assistance'. He looked from one officer to the other 'We are most grateful' he told them 'In due course, subject of course to a legal decision, a reward of five thousand pounds will be paid to you'. He stood up from the café table and held out his hand. 'Once again. Thank you'.

Masters shook the proffered hand and explained 'It'll have to be cash. I'm sure you understand we should not have behaved as private investigators for your company?'

'Yes of course. On behalf of my principals I again thank you for your valuable work'.

*

Chapter seventeen

'Anne', Mrs. Shepherd told munching Geoff Tims, didn't come in for tea tonight'. It was 7pm on what was likely to be a busy Friday evening and he could tell the woman standing in front of his counter twisting a handkerchief was most likely going to be one of those civilians who buggered up his routine. He pushed his sandwich under the counter and asked the obvious: 'What time should she have been home?'. A bacon remnant was stuck between his teeth while he sucked at it and stared.

'Five o'clock. Anne is a good girl.. She knows that five means five'. She started to cry softly and Tims got the attention of a women constable sitting at a desk. 'Take her to to an interview room'. He buzzed the CID and heard John Barton's voice at the other end. 'Get down here. We've a missing girl...........I know..........yes..........it's a CI......John. Just come down and speak with her'. Satisfied he retrieved his sandwich and started over.

*

Mrs. Shepherd blamed someone called Cathy, she told detective constable John Barton. It took a few more questions before Cathy turned out to be Catherine Smart who lived three doors down. 'Same age as Anne'. she explained. 'Fourteen'. He knew the area only too well: a part council estate, home to a few villains and layabouts who the authorities had sensibly quartered in one area. The Smart and Shepherd families' homes were a couple of streets away from there, far enough in that neighbourhood for inhabitants' to defend their middle class status.

'Have you spoken to Cathy?' he asked the tearful woman.

She shook her head. 'Her mum and me don't get on like'.

'She on the phone?'

She shook her head, 'We're not eever'.

'Why blame Cathy?'

'Like 'er mum. Rude she is'.

'So, she could be with Cathy?'

'No. Her bloody mum don't like Anne. Told me once Anne was a bad lot. Bloody cheek that'.

John drove her home and collected a recent photo of of the girl.

*

Cathy sat and listened to her mum going on about Anne being a bad lot. John Barton took notes and nodded as he listened to the diatribe. Eventually the woman stopped rabbiting on about Anne and her nasty mum and John took the opportunity to quiz the girl.

'You're friends, yes?'.

'Sort of'.

'Did you leave school together?'

She shook her head

'Why not?'.

'She didn't go to school today'.

*

Fork still in hand he was trying to be patient 'I'm trying to be helpful, inspector' the headmaster said, holding up a hand to his wife who was gesturing to the dinner table. 'I understand your concern, really I do. What she does after school is out of my hands. Her mother has been informed many times about her absence from school. Surely she can be of assistance?'

With the phone back in its cradle his anxious wife asked 'Who was that, dear?'

'Police. One of my girls playing truant again'.

'Oh dear. How tiresome for you, darling. Couldn't it have waited until Monday? Come on –your dinner's getting cold'.

*

Masters' concern was evident when he looked at the assembled officers. 'Let's get started.' he said firmly. ' I want everyone in the girl's street interviewed. She left home at the right time for school but didn't go there. Where did she go? Who knows her friends, other that Cathy Smart? Someone must know. There are five streets between her home and the school which, by the way is on a bus route. One of you go to the school. Got to be a lead there, surely. One of you check with the bus company - sort out who was on the route around the time she went missing. Off you go. Find anything that'll point us in the right direction'.

*

Anne had got to know Charlie's Janet months before on one of Janet's shoplifting exercises. They had met at a perfume counter in a shop in Romford. Janet had just slipped a bottle of her favourite perfume into her bag while Anne watched in open-mouthed admiration.. She had gone back with Janet to her flat and met Charlie on that one and only occasion.

Now Janet and Anne were at it again. Skipping school had become part of her miserable life, brightened by being with Janet. She had caught a bus near the school to Romford and spent the day and night with Janet. Charlie wasn't keen on her being around Janet but finally agreed she could stay the night.

Once Charlie had left to meet with his mates they walked to the High Street. Janet wanted a bottle of her favourite perfume, she told Anne. In Boots, while Janet was fussing about different brands, Anne slipped two lipsticks into her bag without paying enough attention to a woman who was applying a sample perfume to her wrist and was smiling at her disarmingly.

'Come on' Janet urged, clocking the woman.

'Alright. No rush. I want to look at the perfumes' Anne told her grumpily.

Concerned by the woman who was by then applying another sample perfume to the same wrist Janet tugged Anne's arm.

Outside they were stopped by the woman who had a stern-faced young man as back up 'I saw you take the lipsticks and the bottle of perfume' she said firmly 'You didn't pay for them so I want both of you to come back into the store'.

*

'Heard, Charlie?' said a mate in the snooker hall above Burton's in the High Street as he took his eye off the object ball.

'Heard what?'

'Janet's been nicked'

Charlie dragged on his fag and turned to his mate who was lining up his next shot. 'Nicked for what?'

'She was with anuvver bird: got pulled for shoplifting'.

''ow'd you 'ear that?'

His mate stood up from the shot and pointed to another acquaintance of Charlie's. 'He saw them at the nick as he was leaving'.

Charlie knew what the bloke had been sussed for. 'Lucky bleeder getting bail. He's a right violent sod' he said.

'Yea. Funny old life, Charlie. Mind you, you got bail on your last job remember'.

Charlie shrugged the remark away. 'I'll get down the nick and see what's going on. My shot aint it?'

'Nah. You fouled on the green. My shot. I potted that red, if you remember. I'm on the blue'. He looked at the lay of the table 'Tell you wot Charlie me old mate. A fiver says I'm gonna win this one'.

*

John Barton popped his head around a door of an interview room and looked at the two of them 'So you're our missing girl?' he said as he shifted his gaze from Janet to Anne. 'You any idea of the trouble you've caused?'. He eased into the room and stared at the girl 'Well?'. He demanded when she went into a sulk.

Anne fidgeted and glancing from him to Janet. Then she shook her head. 'Wot trouble? It's only a couple of lipsticks an' a bottle of perfume. Not wurf much is they like', she muttered defiantly.

Closing the door John shook his head. Asking Geoff Tims if they'd been charged he was told, grumpily, 'I'll get to it. Got two in the cells to sort out yet'.

John heard the door and spotted the DI coming in. 'Hello guv. Missing girl's in there'. He gestured to the interview room. 'Another bird with her. Shoplifting. The skipper's got the stuff'.

Masters opened the door slightly and recognised Janet immediately.

Slowly closing the door he asked Tims if they'd been charged.

'Too busy, Don' he grumbled..

'Don't worry yourself with this one, Geoff. I'll take it over'.

*

With time on his hands Masters was scanning a thickish file on Anne he'd retrieved from the collator. She was a regular at skipping school. The report from the local authority and the school assessment of the girl didn't mince words: a summarised covering note explaining why she went off track was clear: it was mum and dad's fault. It was nurture wot done it. Peer group pressure, socialisation, and the girl's urge to break rules were blameless.

The DI deciphered the conclusion that he reasoned so badly judged the understanding of strapped-for-cash working class life: Mum was the root of Anne's problem, albeit she lacked a proper education herself, was short of money, and didn't understand the needs of her young daughter. She didn't connect, was underlined. The girl had become isolated from her peer group by uninformed parental pressure. Education was the key. She was not encouraged at home; and her mother didn't understand the needs of a growing young woman. Masters got the subtext: being abjectly poor, the mother must be thick. "Is it any wonder", the summary concluded, "that this young girl strayed and is to be pitied? The mother should be trained to acquire mothering skills". Italicised in bold type was: ***Counsellors are available for this task who have been trained and awarded a certificate.***

Masters' intuitively had other ideas. The girl was a shit. Her mother had done her best with very limited resources to provide for the greedy little bitch. Her environment was all that the mother could provide. Her husband had deserted her. She herself had not had the opportunity of a sound education. Her father had been in prison and then shot off; her mother had handed her over to a grandparent because she had no surplus cash to provide for her. She was truly skint. She had no other situation to bring up her daughter in but what passed as her enforced poverty-stricken life style.

His conclusion was that Anne rebelled at her perceived restriction of opportunity to do as Janet was doing. A bit of thieving here and there..........so what? Anne was conditioned by her environment and her peer group to want the unattainable. His own childhood relationship with his own mother sneaked into his mind, bringing memories of her as she had undoubtedly striven hard in the working class upbringing of his youth. Memories of Dagenham and of London's dockland life dredged themselves from dark recesses and he was back as a teenager being searched at the dockland gates by the Port of London bent police officers, who always kept for themselves what they confiscated; and understanding that those who had the authority and power, even though working class, would use that power to enhance their own self image and lifestyle. There were two working classes he learned in those days: those that had it and those that didn't. His mother didn't ascribe to that duality. His mother was the beacon of his life. Whenever he thought of that earlier life of honesty and her undemanding love for him; of her strength of character that brooked no deviation from her chosen way of life, he knew guilt and sadness, but he had made his choice.

*

Even though Don and he were mates, as Charlie thought of the detective inspector, entering a nick still initiated a churning in the pit of his stomach.

'Yes?' barked Geoff from behind the counter while Charlie was trying to work out what to say.

'YES!

'No fucking need to shout!'. Charlie was on his feet and glaring back at Tims, who wagged fingers at Charlie.

'Watch your lip, sonny. What do you want?'

'Inspector Masters here?' he demanded bravely.

'And who, pray, wants detective inspector Masters?' Geoff was half a mind to turf the fuck pig right out the door. 'You taking the piss, sonny?'.As he said that he recognised Charlie as Barton's housebreaker.

'Is he here? I wanna see him'. Charlie went across to the desk and shoved his face in the face of the sergeant. 'Tell him it's Charlie wot's here!'.

Tims was fronted by the dilemma Hendon Training School had drummed into him. Never, ever, hand out a thumping if there's the slightest chance of being rumbled by the civilian populace. Tims instinctively recognised Charlie was deserving of a thumping. He resisted the temptation to straddle the counter and dish one out because of that timely training. His training was clear: only ever resort to GBH when out of the public gaze and, looking from Charlie to the front door, he accepted he could get caught bang to rights. With a forced smile the words 'I'll let him know you're here', floated across the counter to Charlie instead.

'Tell him I'll meet him this evening in the usual place', an emboldened Charlie retorted.

*

'Charlie. She's trouble. How did Anne get tied in with Janet?' They were in the usual car park sitting in Charlie's old Viva and detective inspector Masters was beginning to regret roping Charlie into his firm.

'Janet's alright. Trust her Don'.

'Not the point Charlie. She knows me. How long have you and Janet been an item?'

'Don, for Christ's sake: she's one hundred per cent. She 'ates the old bill'.

'Which, Charlie, includes me'

'No Don. No. She reckons you'.

'What does Anne know?'

Nuffink, guv............'

'Don'.

Charlie stared earnestly at the DI., 'Sorry guv....Don. 'onestly I've told her fuck all'

'So when she got the helping hand on this shoplifting escapade she thought she could do what she liked? Do me a favour Charlie!'.

Charlie didn't like the way their chat was going and wondered if Masters was cutting him adrift. 'Wot you getting at?' he asked worriedly.

'You and me have got to have a word with Janet. She's got to straighten Anne out'.

*

Anne and her mum sat across from John and the detective inspector in the police station and listened. Something about a caution the mother was hearing –or was it the court could caution Anne? The girl was in the midst of a sulk and couldn't care less. Knowing Janet had brightened her life; and Charlie was alright too. All this was for the birds.

'However,' Masters went on, 'the local authority has intimated a care and protection order might be made, Anne. Do you understand what that would mean?'

Anne was shaking her head but her mum was alarmed. 'You mean......take Anne away?' She became agitated and reached with an unsteady hand for her fag packet.

'Smoke if you want to' Masters told her. Turning to the girl he held up her school report. 'Not good Anne. Your attendance is appalling but', he paused 'that's not the issue here is it? Do you want to stay at home with mum?'

She shrugged and said nothing.

'Sweetheart' her mum said. 'Answer the policeman'.

The girl slid forward in her chair and sulked. Burying her chin on her chest she ignored her mum and Masters, who tried to imagine what the mother was going through: her daughter was demonstrating a profound ignorance of the benefit of joined up family life that was the staple joining together disparate family members. So what if her father had buggered off?. He knew there were grandparents in the wings, willing to help...............

Anne. Do you want to stay at home?' he asked pointedly.

Feet scrabbling at the carpet she sank lower in her chair, her fingernails scoring the arms of the chair, eyes cast up at the ceiling.

Both detectives were pissed off with the brat of a girl. 'Well?', Masters demanded

Mum was by then more distressed. 'Anne?' she pleaded

Wot?'

'Anything to say?' Masters demanded, breaking the girl's silence.

Anne's mum was getting very worried about mention of care and protection but what was it? Her mixed thoughts couldn't get a handle on it. She lit another fag from the burning stub and studied her nicotine-stained fingers for a while, and coughed. 'Will she have to leave home?' she asked Masters, having recovered and taken another deep drag on her fag and exhaled into the smoke-filled room.

'I hope not Mrs Shepherd. Depending on this interview my report may be helpful, but only if Anne is clear about what she wants'.

'Anne, sweetie. Tell the man. You want to stay with me don't you?' she pleaded.

'Wot's care and protection? She asked defiantly

'It means young lady you'll be taken into the care of the local authority. They have special homes for girls like you. Believe me you wouldn't want to be there with them. What's it to be?'.

*

Charlie was caressing and kissing Janet but his mind was elsewhere. Don had been blunt earlier that evening: "Janet's facing nick if she continues a friendship with Anne", he'd said bluntly. 'Women can't keep secrets, Charlie. I'm thinking of you here. If word gets out on the street you've helped me a few times your life won't be worth a light'.

The young man was grateful for that. Right good bloke was Don, he was certain of it. "No uvver geezer 'as ever 'elped me" he reflected. The problem he wouldn't tell the detective about was that Janet liked Anne. It was that girlie thing he couldn't get his head around.

*

'Darling?' Jean, suddenly awake, squeezed her husband's hand. 'What is it?'

Don's guilty thoughts, hovering in and out of his consciousness, had kept him awake for about an hour, tossing and turning. He squeezed back and reached for the light and turned towards his wife to slide an arm around her shoulders and pull her to him. 'Sorry, love. Didn't mean to wake you. It's work, that's all' he reassured her.

She nestled into his chest and looked up at him 'You've been this way for days. Won't you tell me what's wrong?'

'Nothing's wrong, darling'.

'Sure?

'I'm sure'.

'You need a holiday, darling. You spend so much time at work. Sometimes I feel we live separate lives. You do love me don't you?'

'With all my heart sweetheart!' He squeezed her shoulders reassuringly and felt a lump. Alarmed, he said 'Never felt that before'.

Jean raised her right arm and reached over her shoulder 'Where?'

Don guided her hand 'Feel it?'

Jean ran her fingers over it and turned to look at him. 'What do you think it is?'.

'You've most likely pulled a muscle. Does it hurt?'. Hunched round now he saw she was concerned. Recalling an ache that seemed to come and go she shook her head. 'No, darling. You're probably right. I've overdone it somewhere'..

*

Chapter seventeen

Sergeant Fountain was reading a teleprinter message that gave brief details of a hijack in Essex. "At 2am a rigid closed 17 tone lorry with a silver bullion cargo had been hijacked on the A12 on the outskirts of Colchester. The crew had been dragged out and bundled into a Transit van later found at Marks Tey in the car park of a public house. The attacked vehicle had left it's depot around 12.30am, travelled along the North Circular to the A.12. Its destination was Felixstowe docks. The transport firm ,Wrights Transport of Enfield, has been informed of the hijack".

Sergeant Fountain was fluttering the teleprinter message.' See this one guv?'

Masters strolled over and looked over the sergeant's shoulder. 'Nothing there to say it came this way?' suggested the DI after reading the message.

'Nothing lost by trying, guv. Want me to take it on? I've got a couple of contacts in Hatton Garden. A likely area to sell the stuff.You never know'.

'Do that Brian. While you're at it have a word with Enfield CID. Get what you can on the crew. Might be an insider job'.

*

Geoffrey Hind and Bill Gore weren't badly hurt. According to their statements a van stopped suddenly in front of their lorry. Geoff was driving and managed to brake hard and stop without crashing into it. Two men with stockings over their faces had appeared at their doors and hauled them out. Both had been coshed and, judged by the medical evidence, it was something similar to a sand-loaded sock. The cuts and bruises were superficial, possibly caused when the men were allegedly dragged from the vehicle. The skipper at Enfield CID agreed with Brian Fountain that something was a bit iffy about the circumstances.

Wrights Transport Ltd was registered at Companies House with its registered address in Enfield. The single shareholder was James Holden, who lived, it said, out at Chigwell

Ds. Fountain took a drive out there. It was in fact two miles out of that town. It was a magnificent drum set well back from the country lane fronting it. By counting the windows and a bit of guesswork he reckoned a possible five bedrooms. He took a drive into Chigwell and asked a helpful estate agent for prices of houses of that description in that area.

'Exclusive area. Not many change hands. But' the agent smiled winningly 'at an educated guess I'd say £40 to £45 grand would be a reasonable price to ask. May I put you on our mailing list, sir'?

*

Len Spence was fully recovered from his whacking and was watching the TV news item about the silver bullion hijacking. 'Got to nip out love', He told Jane. 'Something's come up'. Donning a top coat he walked to the phone box on the corner of his street and made a call to Don's station. 'Speak to DI Masters, please'.

'Who shall I say wants him'

'Tell him Jacob. He'll understand'

Spence scanned through the small panes and drummed his fingers on the coin box while he waited for the DI to come on the line. The good hiding had raised his guard and waiting for Masters to come to the phone had him peering again into the darkness.

'Detective inspector Masters here. It's Jacob, yes'.

Viney', Len added, confirming his identity. 'Its about the silver job -you got a line on it yet?'.

'Have you?'.

'I reckon, yeh. Meet at the usual tonight?'.

Masters sighed but agreed. 'An hour. yes?'.

'I'll be there'.

It was 10pm by the time Spence got to the café for the meet and Masters, who was already in a corner holding a mug between his hands watching the approaching man, transferred his gaze to the entrance. Only a few others were in the place and nobody followed Spence in. 'Fancy a tea, coffee?'

Len shook his head and dropped onto a chair apposite the detective. Leaning forward he said. 'You want Justin Swain's firm. The hijacking is right up their street'.

Not really convinced Masters sat back and spoke quietly when he made his point: 'Len, the job went off miles away from London. The hijacking was on the A12'.

'So? Swain's firm 'ave a run in at Galleywood near Chelmsford. That aint far from the A12. He don't shit on his own doorstep'.

'You got a lead on the run in?'

Spence nodded. 'I know how his firm operates. Been there a couple of times'. He grinned. 'Bought a bit of this an' that. I know the score. The gear won't move for several days. The buyer will pick it up from the run in when Justin is confident he's in the clear'. He smiled when he added 'Justin never delivers'.

'When can you take me there?'.

'Why not now?'.

*

At 11am Makepeace, accompanied by a tired Masters

and sergeant Fountain, mugs in hand, told the Chelmsford detective inspector in the New Street police canteen what they knew about the run in and the best way to go about the raid. 'Inspector Masters housed the lorry this early this morning', he said. 'It's in a barn. His informant says the load'll be shifted within days. He can identify the run in if you want to run the job'.

The Essex officer shook his head and smiled towards Masters. 'It's his call. How many men will you want?'.

'Four will do' Masters told him. - 'and two cars to block the drive once we've gone in'.

'Time?'.

'3pm here'.

*

The unkempt drive went up to the barn and a little way beyond, maybe 50 yards, but died away into a grassed area leading to a field down to sugar beet. Masters and Fountain were climbing out of the Jaguar when they heard a shouted demand: 'What the fuck do you geezers want?'.

Masters, and Fountain on a nudge, waved and strolled over to the thick necked man who had come out of the house to their left, and was walking towards them. 'Is Justin here?'., Masters asked him. Face to face by then Masters grabbed him and forced him face down on the ground. Fountain knelt on the man's back and cuffed him. Hauling him to his feet he grinned into the man's angry face and explained: 'The ingots mate. That's what we want!'.

On a wave from the DI the other officers climbed out of the other car and followed his pointing hand to a barn.

*

The lorry had been brought to Police Headquarters at Chelmsford and given the once over. With the head of Essex CID standing beside Makepeace and Masters, they stared at the palletized silver . 'What does that lot weight? queried the Essex detective.

'About three quarters of a ton' Masters told him. 'The ticket is still in the cab. Its pure point 999 fine silver. According to my enquiries the stuff is worth around £70 a troy ounce. We're looking at around £120,000'.

The Essex officer turned to Masters and held out a hand 'Well done inspector. Jolly fine work!'.

*

Thick neck turned our to be Justin Swain's cousin Bert Finch. To his mates he was a rough diamond; to those who ran up against him he is a violent sod. Nasty. Right then he had a smiling Don sitting across from him and a tensed up, ready to pounce, Miller standing immediately behind him and Fountain leaning against the wall by the door.

'Bang to rights Bert? Nice that'. Masters said cheerily.

Bert glared.

'Nothing to say to me?'

Bert managed a shrug.

'Dabs everywhere, Bert. Justin's as well. Shame that'. Masters turned his gaze to the sergeant 'What d'you reckon, Brian.. Ten years?'

'At least, guv' Fountain responded gravely.

'Just get on with it!' growled Finch.

*

I've a got a job for you, Charlie'. Masters' phone response to the younger man's earlier call was enough to get Charlie to the usual car park where Masters joined him that evening in the clapped out Viva.

'Bloody cold, Don' complained the shivering younger man.

'Two things'll get that sorted. Eat a bit more and get the bloody heater sorted Charlie'

'Cost too bloody much, Don. Need a few quid like don't I'. He angled a glance at the DI and grinned.

'That's why we're here. How d'you fancy a real job drawing wages. A few weeks, maybe more. Depending'.

'Doing what?' Charlie's anxiety for a few quid clouded his suspicion of real work.

Masters explained what he had in mind.

*

Ds. Brian Fountain was treading carefully. The Enfield detective sergeant didn't have much to offer about the haulage company except that 6 months previously one of the company's loaded lorries was stolen out of the yard overnight. Security wasn't the best at any time but that particular evening the night watchman didn't show for his shift. He was rounded up and grilled but stuck to his story. He'd been in the local pub when he was told to take the night off. "Never seen the bloke before", he said, "but the threat was obvious", With no proof of his involvement the enquiry ended there. Fountain established that Geoff Hind and Bill Gore had only been with the firm for three months up to the hijacking. A few more questions gave up Jennie's name as the front officer typist.

*

Bulky Commander Bob Stewart was looking into the angry face of Jakeson and digesting the very detailed information he was hearing that accused detective inspector Lindley of corruption and involvement in murder. 'Get all this down', he instructed detective sergeant Galloway sitting beside him. 'You realise this is a very serious accusation, Jakeson', he said as he stared at the man. 'Can any of this be proved?'.

'Prove it! That's your frigging job. The man's bent. He should be in here. Have words with Bill'.

'Who's Bill?'.

'Williams. Your frigging bent DI nicked him and me for the blagging'.

'Bang to rights, Jakeson. The evidence is all there' the commander told him.

'Fuck the evidence! Your frigging DI should've kept me out of it! Two grand I bunged him -what for? To get charged with murder! I've told him: if I go down he goes down. Got that? That's all I've got to say!'.

*

George Makepeace and Masters were in Charlie Smithery office at the Yard doing their best to persuade the deputy commissioner for crime not to suspend Miller. Smithery had Miller's personal file open in front of him; and had already read through the statements taken in the investigation of Sheila Watson's murder.

'The lads' evidence does not prove anything, sir', Masters reiterated. 'It's the blanket that says he might be our killer. But it's not enough. CPS agree'.

'Her blood group is the same as the blood stain on that blanket, inspector'. Smithery's tone told them he was clearly not impressed with Masters' stance.

'And so have possibly millions of people. It's not enough, sir'.

'And we have soil samples from beneath her body - the same as on that blanket. No, inspector, I have serious doubts about Miller'.

'Sir'. Makepeace leaned forward in his chair to look intently at Smithery. 'If you suspend Miller, Lakey's appeal will be strengthened. He's sticking to his story that the sergeant planted the belt. Suspend Miller and Lakey's on a winner'.

'And if he did plant the belt?'. Smithery looked from one to the other. 'Thoughts on that one?'.

'Miller's a good detective, sir'. Makepeace said. 'If he did, he did what a good detective should do'.

Smithery nodded. 'Fair point, George. But what if Lakey is innocent?'.

'Not a chance, sir. What do you think Don?'.

Masters was pleased the way the interview was going. 'Not a chance of that, sir. Lakey's where he belongs. Out there is our second killer. We should concentrate on finding him, not wasting time chasing Miller's alibi'.

Smithery caved in. 'Keep me posted on developments'.

*

Jennie Howell was eighteen, blonde, pretty, wearing a short tight skirt and blouse and tucking into a pizza in the café Masters' discreet enquiry had come up with. Briefed by Masters, Charlie, wearing scruffy denims and an open necked shirt and Janet, her figure enhanced by a skirt similar to Jennie's, carried their cups of tea to a table close to her.

'Let's not argue, Charlie', Jennie heard Janet plead.

'Who's arguing? Your idea this to come here'.

'If you feel like that why don't you...........' Janet's broken off threat hung over the table while Jennie caught Janet's sad eyes and spread her hands sympathetically.

Charlie was on his feet and staring down at Janet when he blurted out 'I'm off then. You know where I am if you want me'.

Jennie watched Charlie disappear and reached across and patted Janet's arm. 'I know' she said 'They're all like that. Come and sit wiv me'.

*

Charlie led Janet into the flat and sat her on the settee opposite the tele. How'd it go?' he asked as he sorted a vodka and lime for her and a lager and fag for himself.

'We chatted and you're right. She works for that transport firm. She does somefink in an office like'.

'An'?'

'Couldn't be obvious could I? I told her I might be looking for an office job like. She reckons she can get me a part time job there. Bit of typing. That sort of fing'.

'Wot did you tell her about me?'

'Love you don' I. Lovers tiff, she reckoned. Wants us to go out wiv her and her bloke. I said I'd see'.

'Did you tell her I was looking for a job?'

'Course. Reckons her boyfriend might be able to 'elp getting you a job loading the lorries'.

*

Masters read the memo from the legal department informing him that an appeal had been lodged on behalf of Gardner and Peel. A date had yet to be fixed, it advised, for the hearing to be heard at the law courts . Lakey's appeal was in the list.

'Dusty. Read this', he called across to Miller, who

had just walked in and dropped into a chair opposite Masters desk.

'Expected it really, guv' Miller said once he's read it.' They've got no chance'.

The DI nodded slowly, and then said 'I'll have a word with the legal department. We need to know which witnesses they are calling'. He pointed to the mention of Lakey 'You're in for a grilling, Dusty - stand your ground'.

'Got nothing to worry about, Don. He's a killer and bollocks to him. I don't give a fuck'.

Masters thoughts shifted to his meeting at the Yard with Makepeace and the suggestion Miller might be Sheila Watson's killer. And of the other two?

'What's on your mind, Don? Something you're not telling me?'.

Masters relaxed and smiled. The sergeant's questioning stance was normal Miller. It couldn't be; not Dusty. 'Just be very careful how you answer Lakey's brief, Dusty. Like I said - stand your ground'.

'No worries there, Don. Piece of cake'.

*

Joan Scot, 25 years and Irene Tasker, 28 years, the bar women at the Hare and Hounds and The Blind Beggar public houses where the murders occurred sat beside each other in the back of the police car Masters had sent for them. They were two very scared women. The promises of the investigating CID officers that no harm would come to them had been shattered by the arson attacks. At the station they were ushered up to the CID floor and into Masters' office. He stood up and extended a hand to each and asked them to sit in the chairs he had arranged at his desk. Smiling, he said 'You already know why you're here?'

They nodded and looked at each other.

'Try to relax. You're among friends. That's Dusty Miller behind you'.

Each swivelled to glance at the sergeant before returning worried eyes to Masters.

'What I want to explain is how the appeal system works. It's quite straight forward. Should you be called to give evidence you will be taken through the evidence you each gave at the trial and be asked if you agree that was what you said under oath at the trial. That's it in a nutshell'.

Irene looked at Joan and back to Masters 'Then it's pointless?'

The DI wiggled his head before answering 'Not really. The lawyer for the convicted men will suggest you are mistaken in your identification, that it wasn't the men they are there to represent'.

'Well I'm not. What about you Joan?' asked Irene.

'Dead right. That bugger stood there as calm as you like and pulled the trigger. I mean, bone and blood all over the bar. Right scared I was'.

'But you're positive it was the men you picked out?' Miller asked

'To my dying day I'll 'ave it in me 'ead'.

'Miss Tasker –what about you?'

'Never forget it. Never said a word 'e didn't. Just walked up shot the poor sod'.

Masters was eyeing the young women and evaluating them as witnesses. According to the trial papers they were nervous. If they were different at the appeal; if they were more confident, he knew the lawyer would suggest they had reinforced their memory of the event. He looked sympathetically at each in turn and reached across his desk to pat Irene Tasker's hand and then squeeze it. 'Just be yourselves in the box. You're bound to forget something -that's to be expected.

Anyway, between now and the appeal, officers will cruise your street on a regular basis. The idea is to make it obvious to anybody thinking of harming you they'll get nicked'. He smiled encouragingly 'Try not to worry'. He got his feet and before shaking hands said, 'Just answer questions put to you. If the questions suggest you're lying, just be yourself' He smiled again.

The women had clearly relaxed since they'd been in his office and his words and the atmosphere appeared to have pushed fear to the back of their minds.

*

Chapter eighteen

The commander gestured to Lindley to sit opposite and waited, tapping the file on the desk once the DI had settled himself. 'This', he said gravely, staring at the younger man, 'can end your career..............'. He paused and added ' or put you in the dock at the Old Bailey'.

Because he had been expecting the interview, Lindley relaxed when he noted the absence of a tape recorder: CRO had belled him on the QT the commander had drawn Jakeson's file; and C11 had belled him, putting him in the picture about the commander's visit to Pentonville. He smiled at his boss 'No caution, sir?'.

Stewart shook his head. 'Our chat is unofficial, Brian. The rubber heel boyos at A10 are not involved....yet'. He leaned forward and clasped his hands on the desk 'This is about a gun and a couple of thousand quid. Only sergeant Galloway knows about this: he took Jakeson's statement. Talk to me, Brian. Can you dig yourself out of this shit?'

'Unofficially, guv?'

'That'll do for now'.

'Mind if I smoke?'.

'No. Carry on'.

Lindley lit up and took a deep drag and studied his boss while he exhaled. 'That's the gist of it is it. The gun and the money?'.

Stewart nodded.

'It's a load of crap, guv. The finger's got arseholey because he's banged up. He's a snout on a mission, guv'.

'A mission by a man charged with murder, Brian. He's dug his heels in on this one. And the governor of the 'ville knows about the accusations. This file', he tapped it, 'has to go to A10. Are you prepared for that?'.

'No problem there, guv'.

'You know your bank accounts will be scrutinised by them?'.

Lindley smiled again 'No problem there either, guv'.

' They dig deep, Brian', the commander warned.

'Just the one, guv'.

Stewart stood up and reached for Lindley's hand. 'This chat didn't take place'.

*

Bill Gore was nervous. It was two weeks since the run in had been turned over and Bert Finch and Justin nicked. Something was up and he felt it. Because Bert had a big mouth he'd expected to be pulled by the filth. Justin was a diamond. He'd never grass anyone up. Even so he reckoned on having his collar felt soon. Geoff had been a bit off since the hijack and had taken to eating his sandwiches on a table away from his. The new bloke, Charlie, he was alright. Pulled his weight did Charlie. Lot to say for himself but alright. For a thin bloke he got stuck in.

'Wot you doing tonight, Bill' Charlie asked as he wheeled a load onto the lorry.

'Not much. Down the pub for a pint probably'.

'Mind if I join you?'

'Why not. I need a bit of company'.

*

Justin Swain couldn't get his head around the nicking. One day it's an adrenalin rush the next it's in a bloody cell. Stretched out on his cell bunk in Brixton he had time enough to work it out but couldn't. The only conclusion that meant anything hovered, flicking in and out of his consciousness until, finally, it settled. It had to be Bill Gore. But if him, why? He was on a good earner, so why balls it up? His memory relived the event from the hijack to the run in. Not a single witness out there, he was certain, could have nailed him. Then there was Jimmy Holden. Could he have gone bent? "I'll talk it over with Bert on exercise" he decided as he pulled up the blanket.

*

Ds. Brian Fountain had come up with a lead. A snout fingered a small outfit that dealt with a bullion dealer in Hatton Garden. The man was Keith Mooney who traded as a factor in general goods and worked out of a small set up in East Ham. CRO had a file on him. His only arrest was for receiving 200 TV sets in 1970. The only witness against him lost his memory on the run up to the trial and the prosecution was withdrawn at court. The sets were on a lorry stolen from a café car park in broad daylight out at Bishops Stortford.

Brian drove out to Romford and located the man's address shown on the file. A helpful neighbour reckoned Keith would get in around seven o'clock.

'Want me to tell him you called?'.

'Don't bother' Brian told him 'Bit of business. I'll catch him later'.

*

The Essex stolen car squad had carried out a thorough search of the run in at Galleywood.. Out back of the barn, accessed through a large sliding door, were three cut up artic lorry units and the cab of a fixed 17 tonner and two skips. Flogging off the missing engines might have been a profitable side line because they were missing.. When the details were checked out the squad found that one of the three artics had been stolen from a haulage firm in Enfield. The other two had been hijacked weeks apart on the A12 the same year; and the 17 tonner in 1970.

Sergeant Fountain, scanning the report on the discovery, homed in on the 17 tonner: it had been carrying 200 TV sets. Mooney's file revealed a lorry had been stopped on the A11 for a routine safety check along with several other lorries. When it was the turn of the driver to be checked he didn't have any dispatch notes for the load. He did have a phone number he was to call, he told the transport officers, when he got to a café on the A13 near Southend. Keith Mooney was right in the frame. Not being police officers, and the vehicle passing their safety checks, the lorry was allowed to proceed. Enquiries subsequent to that road check confirmed the lorry has been stolen and Mooney was pulled in.

The straightforward case of a single hi-jacking had developed legs. Masters, Fountain and a senior Essex Constabulary officer were running over the widening net. Land Registry showed the run in was owned by Justin Swain who bought it in 1968. Local enquiries had turned up sightings of lorries toing and froing since that time. No positive idents. Skips had been delivered to and removed from the run in regularly since 1969. Interviewed, the drivers recalled seeing lorries round the back in various stages of being cut up. The skips were tipped at a scrap metal yard near Dartford. That yard was a nightmare for enquiries. The usual cars, cut up cars, squashed cars, bits and pieces of cars and lorries and oil and mud were everywhere. No reliable paper work to speak of led the enquiry to a dead end.

Masters and Fountain made it clear that anything that turned on the activity of Wrights Transport at Enfield was to be filtered to them. Masters meanwhile had asked for the search results of the homes of Finch and Swain to be forwarded to him.

*

'So what have we got?' Masters had called a meeting of the CID team to run over what they knew. 'Before we start, Essex police have turned up something interesting on one of the artic cabs at the run in'. He broke off at that point and with a satisfied smile he added 'Nicked out of Wrights Transport's yard last year. £50,000 worth of fags on board. He looked around at the team 'Now it gets better. Anyway, let's run over what we know'.

John Barton opened up first. He explained 'As you know, guv, Swain banks with Barclays. 'His savings account stands at £25,000, leaving off the small numbers. I've got copies here'……..John handed them out to the others. 'Nothing regular. From £500 to £2000 at a time.. Finch banks with the Midland and has £12000 tucked away. Not bad for blokes who don't draw wages anywhere'.

'Cash deposits?'

'Mostly. On one occasion a cheque for £2500 was paid in by Swain. The manager was helpful there. He fished around in the system and established the cheque issued by K. Mooney'.

Ds Fountain tuned into that bit of information. 'That would be Keith Mooney' he told them 'runs a factor business at East Ham. It's a one room operation. No staff, just Keith. I've got a line on him into Hatton Garden'.

'What's a factor?' asked one of the detective constables.

'To you and me it's a villain. Think business agent. Our man Mooney finds buyers and sellers. He places gear. He must have been at it a long time. If I'm right he's a crafty bastard. He doesn't actually need to see the gear. He's a hi-jacker's dream. They've got the gear and he sends the buyer in to collect. He gets whatever cut he can arrange for himself. He's been renting the office for three years to date'.

'I could do with a bit of that!' said one officer

'So could I!' said another.

Masters took it in good humour and then told them 'A tap on each of their telephones is being arranged. I'll also arrange for Wrights Transport calls to be monitored. With this latest info we need to plan ahead. I'll arrange with the DCS to get a tap on James Holden's private phone. Not much to go on but I'm fairly sure he's running the transport firm as a cover'. After a pause he added 'Small point, but Holden doesn't have logos on his cabs. Doesn't make him a villain but it's what a bent firm would do'.

'What are we doing about the crew of the hi-jacked lorry, guv' Ted queried.

'I've put a snout into the firm. We'll bide out time on that end'.

*

Charlie didn't take long to get on board with Bill Gore. A good listener he had the unhappy family life of Bill soaked into his memory in no time. The wife, obviously, didn't understand him. 'It's the over nighters' Bill reckoned when Charlie came back with two more pints. 'She don't understand'. He turned to stare blearily at the younger man. 'You understand, don't you me old mate?'

Charlie was a patient listener and knew when to nod.

He nodded.

'Charlie.......you takes a frigging lorry to Scotland and....and....run out of time. I mean. I've got to sleep aint I?'.

Charlie wisely nodded because he didn't have a clue what the bloke was running on about.

'Take this last run. I mean. A doddle, yeh?' He stopped nattering to take a long swig of the beer and looked down at the waiting whisky chaser Charlie had on hand. Nodding his satisfaction he looked at the fading image of Charlie and reached out to touch his hand and missed at the first attempt but grabbed it at the next. 'You understand don't you?'.

Frankly, Charlie didn't. They moved in different worlds. Charlie's was razor edged while Bill's was blurred into his present unreality.........................

Charlie knew what Don wanted so he sipped his lager slowly. He was beginning to believe Bill had something of interest to say . With him well on his way Charlie reckoned on another whisky chaser to loosen his tongue. 'Get that down Bill' he advised when he closed Bill's hand around yet another glass. 'Cheers!'

Down it went and Bill blubbered.

'Bill? What's wrong?'.

'What's wrong? What's frigging wrong! I get a whacking and no dosh, that's what's wrong!'

Charlie patted Gore's hand. 'Wot dosh we talking about, Bill?'.

'Three hundred nicker, Charlie. It aint right that'.

*

'Oh, Charlie! Come in sweetheart'. Janet took Charlie's hand and pulled him into the flat and flung her arms around his neck. It had taken him three weeks to come up with the goods on Bill Gore. Three weeks away from the girl he loved dearly and who loved him passionately. He pulled back from her embrace and looked into her lovely blue eyes, before he pulled her to him and kissed her.

She broke away and said 'Charlie darling. I've missed you. If it wasn't for Anne the first week I don't know what I would 'ave done'.

'She been here?'

'Only the first week. They came here and took her back to the home'.

'You back working in that hairdresser place?'

'Yes Charlie. I get bored on me own, you know that'.

'Tell you what. Grab your coat. Let's go and have a meal'.

*

Lucy opened the door to Ted again and stood there in that silky dressing gown which he knew covered only knickers and bra. Her femininity overpowered him when he took her in his arms and simply held her to him in a loving embrace.

She eased away from him and smiled 'My beautiful man' she murmured. Taking his hand she led him up the stairs and into the bedroom which faintly exuded the scent of her perfume. Turning to face him she held out her arms and he moved gladly to her and they kissed, passionately. Backing away now she pulled him to the side of the bed and slowly slid out of the dressing gown. Hooking thumbs into the waist of her knickers she slowly pulled them down, all the time keeping her smiling gaze on Ted's face, watching his changing expression. Reaching behind she hooked the bra open and let it fall. For a few seconds she stood with arms beside her body until, raising them, she urged Ted to come to her. He stepped in front of her and she began the routine they enjoyed. First the coat, the tie, the shirt, the belt and trousers, which she eased down to the floor so that he could step out of them. Then she pulled down his underpants and kissed his stomach and held his erect penis which was waiting for the start whistle. Still holding it she eased back onto the bed and gently but with feminine expertise pulled him on top of her and put it in. It was the moment she had longed for all afternoon and the moment which raised Ted to heaven. The minutes passed with Ted in a cloud of ecstasy until...............................

'What was that?' Lucy asked when she heard a voice. She raised herself onto an elbow

'My radio. I must be wanted. I'll call back'.

'Does the station know you're here?'

'Course not'. He groped in his jacket, fished out the radio and called back to the station

'Return to the station John', he was instructed 'The DI wants you'.

'You said course not. Why course not?' Lucy had sat up and drawn the sheet up to cover her chest.

Ted was dressing hurriedly when he replied 'they don't need to know everything'.

'You said course not. Are you ashamed of me?'

Dressed now Ted was looking at an angry Lucy. 'Course not, darling. Course not'. He bent over to kiss her but she pulled away. 'I've got to go. I'll ring you. Bye darling'.

'Don't bother' she called after him icily.

*

As bad luck would have it Kay was angry that evening as well. Showered, perfumed and, this time in her sexiest underwear, he hadn't shown up. 'Bastard' she fumed to herself 'Who does he think he is!' She rang the police station. "He's out" she was told. Bastard! *Bastard*! She strode around the living room, plumped cushions, slung his photo in a drawer and glared at the wall paper, hating it. 'Right' she said to herself 'it's coming off'. She strode to the kitchen and filled a saucepan with hot water, strode back and slung the water over the wall and then flounced into an armchair and cried in sexual frustration.

*

Don Masters was facing the dilemma of what to do about Kay. Colleagues at the station by now were aware of her existence. Phoning. Coming in. On one occasion resorting to kicking the station door, wanting to know where he was. And word had reached him that her old man had been put in the picture and was the laughing stock of his prison. She had taken to visiting him and bragging on about how good her policeman lover was. He was heard to say he would kill the bitch when he got out. Masters was alerted by the prison authority to the threat which he felt he couldn't ignore. Taking a chance on the reception he would get he nipped round and put her in the picture.

'Reg wouldn't hurt me' she told him confidently.

'Can you risk that? He's due out in a few weeks if he plays his cards right'.

'It's not a risk at all' she said firmly. 'He's like a lamb really. Will you come round this evening? I've missed you'.

He looked into those lovely blue eyes and wondered what was going on in the brain wired to them. 'I'll try' he said and took her hands. 'Kay, love. You've been over the top of late. You must understand I'm a working man'.

'A working man who's shagging his wife! How do

you suppose I feel? What am I? Someone you can just pick up, fuck and throw away? I won't have it!' she threw back as she walked stiffly down the hallway.

Masters knew when it was time to leave. He left.

Back at the nick, decision made about her old man, he called Len Spence.

*

Sheila Walters had sensed for several days that he was suspicious. Probably not because of Charlie's break in, it was more………..yes, that was it, he had done some odd things. And just the evening he had pulled the bedclothes back and stared down at the bed. Sheila did the wise thing and stayed a little longer in the bathroom until she judged he was in bed. The brief kiss good night on the forehead that followed was so totally unlike him that she experienced foreboding.

Chapter nineteen

The Judge made it clear that the appeal by Gardner had been lodged on the basis of evidence not available to the trial Judge. 'The appellant, he intoned, sought to put before the court evidence that refuted the prosecution case in two particulars, each relating to the gun and the bullets' He stared at counsel.. 'Mr. McDonald. Are you ready to proceed?' he peered over his spectacles at the lawyer.

The oily man rose to his feet, shrugged his gown and fingered documents before him. 'M'Lord. The appellant Gardner alleges that the evidence given by the police at the trial in relation to the gun and bullets is false. I shall bring evidence to show that the gun, and therefore the bullets, were not, as claimed by the police, in the possession of the appellant at the times stated on oath by the police officers. I call Brian Fellows'.

The barrister studied Fellows being marched to the witness stand by a prison officer to whom he was handcuffed. After a bad tempered exchange between the prisoner and the court clerk, who did his best to explain he had to take the oath, he explained to the Judge that the witness was serving a term of imprisonment for armed robbery. Turning his grave features to Fellows he asked 'Mr. Fellows. Please, in your own words, tell the court what you know about the gun'.

The exhibit was held up by the court clerk for him to see.

'In my garage it was'.

'And when was that?' The barrister looked from Fellows to the judge, his expression constructed to convince him that gold-plated truth was imminent.

'When I got nicked'.

'And when was than?'

'Before he got nicked', he gestured at Gardner.

'Quite. And where did you get the gun from?'

'Can't say can I'. Fellows tugged back at the handcuffed warder, who had inadvertently jerked his arm.

McDonald reminded him he was giving evidence to establish the history of the gun. He tried again 'Have you been intimidated?'

Fellows' nerves had settled and his natural arrogance shaped his face into sneering contempt for the proceedings. 'No one intimidates me!' He jerked his handcuffed arm again and glared at the warder.

'Mr. Fellows. I must ask you to show respect for the court' the stern, icy-faced Judge felt obliged to warn.

McDonald tried again 'How long was the gun in your possession?'

Fellows shrugged. 'Dunno. Weeks I reckon. I've already said it was in my garage when I got nicked'.

'Did you at any time handle the gun?'

'Stuck it in a drawer didn't I'.

Thank you Mr. Fellows. Stay where you are'.

The case for the Crown was in the hands of a QC who belonged to the same London gentlemen's club as the Judge. The reader will understand that impropriety is not intended. Working class, shopkeepers and people engaged in professions know where they stand in the order of things. So is it with the judiciary . Lawyers have a class structure which would be the envy of those stalwart people. Oily McDonald was deemed lower class; the Crown QC and the Judge were, naturally, upper class. That's how things are and nothing, no matter who tinkers with the legal system, can change it. Its the way things are.

'Mr. Fortesque'

The QC rose, shrugged and smiled to the Judge who

smiled in return. Turning to Fellows he constructed a brief smile and asked 'Are you a friend of the appellant?'

'Who?'

'I do apologise'………He turned to face Gardner and point to him 'That man'.

'Know him'.

'How long have you known the appellant?'

'Couple of years'.

'Is that why you are here today –to help a friend?'

'Yeh. Why not. He's been fitted up'.

'Quite. The gun, Mr. Fellows. You answered counsel by saying 'stuck it in a drawer didn't I' You recall saying that?'

'Something like that'.

'No, precisely that. Were you wearing gloves at that time?'

'No…Yes.. I don't remember'

Mr. Fellows. Your fingerprints are not on the gun'.

'Must have worn gloves then, right!'.

'Why would you have done that?'

'Where's this going?'. Fellows stared at the QC, then at the judge.

Fortesque smiled disarmingly at Fellows and continued. 'Let me see if I am understanding you correctly. A person who you refuse to name gave you the gun. And the gun was in your garage at the time of your arrest; it did not bear your fingerprints; and not, as I understand the allegation of the appellant, in his possession at the time of his arrest as accepted at the trial'.

'Dead right. It's a fit up' Fellows shouted as he pointed at Masters. 'He's fitted up me mate!'.

'Stay there for a moment'. He turned to the Judge, bowed, and sat down.

'Mr. McDonald. Have you any further questions for

this man? Any more witnesses?

'No M'Lord'.

After a lunch recess the Judge didn't mince words. Dismissing Fellows evidence that the gun was in his garage when he was arrested he addressed the court. 'Nothing I have heard today undermines the credibility of the evidence given at trial by the police officers. The trial Judge was aware of this allegation; and the evidence given today by the new witness tends only to corroborate that allegation, it does not alter the facts accepted by the jury. This appeal is dismissed'.

Lakey was next up. Clad now in prison garb he looked decidedly one of them. The 'us' stared at the subdued man and waited for the proceedings to begin. It turned out to be a formality. Via his counsel he admitted to being a right shit so far as women were concerned, but a killer- definitely not.

Miller's evidence slaughtered him. No way would Miller admit planting the belt. If anything, he embellished his evidence by remarking on the texture of the underside of the belt which, he mysteriously explained, knowing it would be so, the scientific evidence might corroborate.

A woman from the science laboratory indeed partly corroborated his version: the rough texture of the underside of the belt could have caused the weals imprinted on the woman's neck; and the buckle pin the abrasion found.

The judge, viewing the appalling events from his lofty perspective, decided that the appellant had not established that detective sergeant Miller who, he added gravely, had an unblemished character, had planted the belt in the car. He dismissed the appeal.

*

Don Masters was tired. Bloody tired. He looked across at sergeant Miller and asked him if he felt the same.

'Right now, guv, I could do with a straight eight hours in bed'.

Masters checked his watch, surprised to see it was already ten o'clock. 'Dusty. Sometimes this job pisses me off. We've got that many jobs on the go I could go out and just get drunk. Fancy a pint?'.

'Great idea' said Miller when he hauled himself out of his chair. 'Let's go to that boozer round the corner. I fancy walking. Need a dose of fresh air'.'

An hour and two pints later Masters was more settled and brought up the subject of the belt. He looked keenly at Miller, who was downing the last of a pint. 'Smithery wanted you suspended back then. The DCS was with me and talked him out of it. Anything you want to tell me?'.

Miller put his glass down and shrugged. 'What's to tell, Don. He was an idiot to leave it in the car'.

Masters nodded apparent agreement but studied his friend's demeanour and wondered...........but no. It couldn't be. He changed the subject to the Bateman murder, and Williams in particular. 'All we've got on the bastards is dabs. They don't know we can't prove when they put them there, but a good brief will hammer us. If Doris goes bent we've got nothing on Jakeson that says he pulled the trigger. The bastard is laughing at us and likely to spill the beans on Lindley'.

'He's in Strangeways isn't he?'.

'Yes. Why d'you mention that?'.

'We've got someone in there. Remember the finger who's on remand for beating up a bouncer at the Golden Goose?'.

Masters looked at Miller while he digested the comment and thought back. 'You're thinking about Dougie Spencer?'.

Miller nodded. 'We did him a favour on that blagging six months back, guv. He owes us one'.

'You dealt with him. Will he play ball?'.

Miller smiled and nodded. ' If he wants out of his present GBH charge he'll do the business for us'.

'Which nick's dealing?'.

'West End Central'.

'Can you square it with them?'.

No trouble, guv'.

*

Kay's husband Reg, also in Strangeways, was in the toiler block when a blow to the back of his head sent him down with a wallop on to the tiled floor. Dazed and unable to move he was savagely beaten up, his two attackers taking it in turn to outdo each other. Days later, in the hospital wing, he was told he arms were knackered and his head had taken a hammering. The usual brain scan was awaited

*

Chapter twenty

It was just before midnight when George Stillwell, Tims late turn shift replacement, looked at the well dressed man, around thirty he judged, who had walked into the station and was staring at him. Leaning his arms on the counter he smiled. 'Yes, sir?', he asked.

Sheila's husband shifted his feet and looked away, undecided what to say. 'I think I should probably speak with a senior officer. It's a private matter'.

'Your name sir?'

'David Walters. You have a detective here, John Barton, he's an acquaintance'.

'Is that relevant sir?'

'Possibly. I don't know. May I see an inspector?'

'If you would give me a few details, sir?'

'I'd rather not'.

George studied the troubled man for some seconds before suggesting he went to the interview room he pointed out. With the man's back disappearing into that room the sergeant made the call that brought inspector French from his comfy office to stare quizzically at Walters, who stood up when he entered and then sat down again. Holding out a hand and introducing himself he asked 'You wanted to see me?'

David wasn't sure and said so 'I suppose I shouldn't be here really…..' he tailed off and studied his hands in his lap.

'Why do you say that? Is it a police matter you want to talk to me about?'

David nodded.

The inspector decided to sit down and be patient. 'Well, Mr Walters?'.

'It's about my wife you see………' again he left his meaning unfinished.

'Has she been attacked………or hurt in any way?'

'Oh no. She's fine. It's just that……..'

'Please Mr. Walters. If I am to be of assistance you really must tell me what's troubling you'.

Walters looked at the inspector and his anguish came out in a rush. 'My wife Sheila is having an affair with John Barton, a detective here'. With the accusation out in the open Walters stood up and faced the inspector who also stood. 'Do you think it's right?'. He saw that the officer was digesting the news and pushed on with what had been troubling him for some weeks. 'My house was broken into a few weeks ago. John, that's John Barton, one of your detectives, he arrested the man who did it and nothing, I mean, well, nothing has happened to the man and I am convinced it's because Sheila is having an affair with your detective'.

The inspector was puzzled at the connection.'Why do you connect the break in with an affair?'.

David hadn't fully developed his theory beyond the testosterone-driven certainty that if another man so much as smiled at his beloved something was afoot in the bedroom area. 'Well. I just do'. His previous certainly was fading fast within the claustrophobic, clinical, mind-clearing confines of the room.

'Shall I get Mr. Barton here? Would you prefer to talk it through with him?'

David felt a little foolish and smiled sheepishly. 'I'm, well, I'm sorry if I have behaved foolishly. This has been on my mind for that long. No need to trouble John. Thank you for seeing me'. He held out his hand and shook the inspector's. 'I'm sorry for bringing my worries here'.

*

'David. I've been so worried'.Sheila helped David out

of his top coat. 'You went out without a word. Where have you been? It's gone midnight'.

He looked at his beautiful wife and could have cried at his stupidity. He loved her so much and held her tightly to him. 'I've been a fool' he whispered to her. 'A bloody fool. Let's go to bed'.

*

Responding to the suggestion by Inspector French, Masters took John Barton's file on Charlie's break-in to the Walters' home with him and listened while the inspector recounted his conversation with the man.

'I know you have your way of doing things, Don. But what's the score with this one?' French leaned back to study the DI's bland expression while he was settling himself in a chair.

The DI patted the file 'Cleared at the top, Bill. The villain is one of John's snouts. The DCS saw fit to wave a wand over this one. The nicked cash was recovered and returned to his wife. I told Barton to have a word with the man. Let him know Hobbs was helping us with other matters. Apparently he didn't do that'. He grimaced. 'This is the result of not carrying out an instruction. I'll have a word with John. Is that all?'.

French stood up and shrugged. 'Unless your man is having an affair with his wife, then no'.

Masters got up as well. 'Who knows, Geoff. Did Walters suggest he was?'.

'Yes and no. I suggested he got together with Barton but he declined'.

'Leave it there shall I?', Masters queried when he was at the door.

'He's your man, Don. I don't think Walters is going to stir the pot'.

Masters raised a hand and smiled. 'Thanks Geoff. I'll have a chat with John'.

*

The following evening, for the second time in an hour, it was inspector French's turn to hear Kay's tantrum on the phone. 'He must be there! Put me through to him now!' she demanded, her voice shrill with demented frustration.

The inspector shook his head at the nastiness at the other end of the line. 'When he arrives here I'll let him know you've called. I can't do any more than that' he told her again.

Like the CID team he now knew all about Kay and her nasty ways. He'd had her pointed out in the High Street once and he well understood the DI getting mixed up with her.

*

Bill Gore sat passenger to Charlie in his Viva and watched the street lights go past and the sleet come down. He was by now convinced that Charlie was right. 'Get out there and nick it' he had been told only the other evening. 'Always been my solution to running out of bread'. They were on their way to burgle a drum that Masters had arranged for them. Charlie had cased the house with Masters and memorised the set up and his escape route.

'We walk from here'.

Bill clambered out and stood for a few seconds eyeing what he could see of the street. 'You're sure about this?'

'A doddle, Bill. The geezer's rolling in it. Let's get going'.

It was a detached house in a row of individually designed Edwardian houses with a fairly short front gardens. Charlie knew but Bill didn't that Don and Ted were hidden up behind bushes near the front of the house.

'Stay close, Bill. I'll jemmy a window'. Charlie pulled the tool out from his waistband and got to work.

Within minutes they were in and Charlie told Bill to scout around upstairs. 'Be careful with the torch, Bill. I'll see what's on offer down 'ere'.

Wised up by the DI, Charlie left it for several minutes before he stepped onto the mat over a pressure alarm just inside the front door. When the alarm rang out Charlie scarpered out the back and Bill, running downstairs with torchlight weaving all over the place, was collared by Ted as he shot out of the front door to hear, 'So who's been a naughty boy then' as the cuffs were snapped on.

In a state of speechless shock Gore stayed silent on the drive to the police station. "Charlie had been so sure................"., he told himself over and over,

Half an hour later when Don and Ted came with Bill Gore in tow the DI was told by sergeant Stillwell about Kay's latest calls. 'You've got to do something about that woman, Don. We can't have her constantly phoning and abusing officers in this station'.

Masters knew that the sergeant meant well. 'I'll have words, George', he said quietly. 'She's a bloody nightmare'.

'Sooner you than me, Don'.

Masters smiled faintly and nipped up to his office and phoned her.. Between earfuls he got her to agree he could pop in the next day.

*

Bill Gore was 55 but looked older. His wife Mavis was used to his funny ways –after 30 years of marriage you'd expect that. His criminal life started late: when he was 30 in fact. Caught leaving via a factory gate with two bottles of brandy he'd half inched from a carton on the loading dock he got away with 12 months probation. Between then and now he'd had a few set tos with the filth but had managed to avoid arrest. The reader must understand that life in the Met area for a villain wearing an L plate was easy or hard depending how he responded to questions. Bill was not what you might deem educated but, when dealing with the filth, he was an outstanding student. Now and then he came against a genuine copper. Respect him? Yes, of course, he would agree after a bit of an argument, but it gets you nowhere when all you want is to avoid going to prison. Bill learnt that if his crimes were to go unpunished at court he should listen to the advice of and invest in the CID. Anyway, enough of that. Bill has been caught bang to rights on a burglary and, the following morning, he was staring at the smiling face of Masters and wondering how he was going to get out of his present predicament.

'Had a breakfast?'

Gore nodded.

'Anything to say for yourself?' Masters opened with as he stared across the table in the interview room at Gore, trying hard to smile back.

'Nothing to say is there'.

'You're right there, Bill. Why that house?'

Had Charlie walked into the room then Bill would have flattened him but he was no grass 'Spur of the moment guv. Saw the house and just well, sort of thought why not'.

'The DI gingerly fingered his grazed face. 'The bloke who hit me, Bill. Youngish? Got a name for us?'

'Can't do, guv. You know how it is'.

The DI nodded. 'I respect that Bill. Your mate must be shitting himself'. He stood and paced the room for a few minutes, from time to time shooting looks at Gore, who kept his gaze on the detective. His mind apparently made up he sat down again and hunched towards Gore. 'This is how it'll go, Bill. I'm going to bang you up for a few more hours - give myself a chance to work out a way forward. Understand me Bill?'

Bill didn't but wisely nodded.

*

'Let's see'. The next morning Masters was scanning a report and looking at Gore from time to time. 'You started with Wrights Transport about three months ago?

Bill nodded 'Ad in the paper for a driver'.

'My enquiries say you've held an HGV licence for 15 years. Move about a lot Bill'?

'The missus. She gets fed up with long hours. Nights away, that sort of thing'.

'That's why you took the job at Wrights?'

Bill nodded

'Not quite right that Bill. Want to try again ?'………..'Bill…..Lost your tongue?'

'It was an advert, guv'. Gore was trying to get the hang of the way the chat was unwinding.

'I'm not doubting that but I'll give you a name and you give me a nod. Justin Swain?'

Unprepared to hear that name, Bill stared at Don and his face paled. He nodded.

'Talking the same language are we Bill?'

A dejected Bill nodded again.

'Known him long?'

'Couple of years'

'What's he got on you, Bill? He's out of your league'.

'Can I trust you guv?' Gore had leaned forward, looking for an out.

'Depends'.

Bill was staring hard at the detective for any indication he could do some sort of deal but saw nothing in Don's bland expression. He took the plunge, 'Last year, I dunno, about six, seven months ago, I nicked a loaded lorry out of Wrights yard. Swain put me up to it. He's got something going with Jimmy Holden. He got me the job –it was advertised but that's not how I got in. I know where you're coming from. Justin's shopped me, aint he, for the silver job'

Which, of course he hasn't thought a satisfied detective. 'Bill. I'll bang you up again for a while. I'll have another chat with my guvnor. What I want you to think about is clearing your slate. I want to be able to tell him you're cooperating. Make a statement that I can show him, that should do it'.

*

Sheila was tearful the following evening and try as John did she couldn't be consoled. He looked at the other diners –a couple at the next but one table were showing interest, the man was giving John the stare.

'Honey darling, please…………it'll be alright, I promise you'.

Sheila Walters' guilt was overflowing and John didn't understand. '.You don't understand' she told him tearfully. 'David…….he……..he's been so understanding. So loving' she added, which to John implied it was all over between them..

Like any man in his position he was in a fix. He loved

the woman and he had, until that evening, believed she loved only him. Throwing her old man in his face as she had just done seemed to be implying she loved him as well? As well! Never!.

'Do you still love David?' he asked, more to hear her say no but he couldn't have used that simple deduction at that moment. His testosterone told him her bloody husband had turned her against him. What an arsehole!

'John……..I'm so……..so mixed up. He's been so sweet lately. Like the man I married. John', she reached across the table and took his hand 'You do love me. Tell me you do?'. Her desire to be constantly loved had conflated their love, confusing her.

John wasn't into psychology but with Brenda as a reminder he sussed that Sheila was throwing a wobbly, dragging her bloody old man into the frame. His mates had told him that women were wired from birth to choose and stay with a man who sired her children. He looked at the love of his life and wondered what the flipping heck was going on. She didn't have any! So why mention him? Was it guilt?. 'I love you with all my heart, Honey', he offered in the silence between them.

'Oh, darling. And I love you so much too'.

*

Gillian Barton was content with her five year long marriage to John. His passion of the first couple of years had waned a little, but she knew in her heart that he loved her dearly. The unexpected presents of late were always a delight. Sometimes flowers; sometimes costume jewellery: he seemed to know when she was low and the little present always lifted her spirits. It wasn't their value: that he was thinking of her when he was buying them was the real present. 'My John', she told herself 'is all I ever wanted in the man who loves me. It's such a pity he has to work such long hours'.

*

Phil Jakeson's luck ran out the moment he went to the shower block. The knife jabbed into his chest caught him unawares and he stumbled forward, his face hitting the tiled wall as he slid to the wet floor. He stared up at the man looming over him recalling, as his image was fading, the threat of the day before.

His attacker dropped the knife and, stepping back to avoid the seeping blood, looked across at a heavy set man holding the door shut and nodded. ' Let's get out of here'.

*

'Is he dead?'. The warder who asked the question was edging gingerly away from the seeping blood.

The prison doctor shook his head. 'Missed the heart. Lucky bastard this one'.

*

Detective constable Edward Read and Lucy Whitelaw were deeply in love. Their initial sexual interlude had blossomed to the extent they needed to spend every possible moment together. Ted knew the knicker episode that brought them together was the crucible forging his love for her. The visions he had of her in those early days of their relationship were seared into his memory. So very beautiful, so vulnerable, and so willing to share her body with him; these had been enhanced by the bliss of simply being in her company.

Ted had never been a ladies man. Even with Brenda

he couldn't commit: which was why, he lately reasoned, she had shot off with another bloke. With his mates he'd many times enjoyed the pleasure of evenings with young women. But with Brenda gone it always ended there for him.

Ted was enjoying his work out at Gyms Place: John Barton had egged him to join many weeks before. The same two beautiful young women he had seen for many weeks were working out on weights again. One, a bit like Lucy he thought, was exercising, the other holding her shoulders and smiling constantly when her friend pushed up the weights, muscular boobs contracting and expanding with the effort of it all. Later, he noticed, she was steadied on the rowing machine. About 25, Ted reckoned. Nice looking, the pair of them. They always came in, hand in hand, exercised together and left together, hand in hand again. It was nice to see. Really nice women. Rubbing each other down with towels. Holding hands a lot. Nice.

*

Lucy at 28 was a radiant beauty. Her divorced husband was a brute, she told Ted, who had never loved her. Eighteen when she got married she was too young to understand the true love of a man. She couldn't clearly explain to herself let alone to Ted how she had drifted into a loveless marriage. Maybe it was because her mother had told her to leave home when she was fifteen. 'Oh yes', she assured Ted. 'Mum had always told me that when I left school I would have to leave home'. He was a gambler, she explained to Ted. He never had a regular job; and any money she earned he would take and gamble away. Five years the marriage lasted. 'Leaving him was an escape from a cruel , loveless world', she explained to our Ted, who's eyes had moistened at the tale.

*

Kay stood back from the open door and let Masters squeeze past and go into the living room. Not a word was spoken. Don by then knew he was looking at the other Kay who kicked police station doors and yelled abuse down the telephone.

Following him in she settled in an armchair, placed clasped hands in her lap and stared. The vibes coming from her were disturbing.. At that moment he was unaware of his own tense expression because he was trying to understand what had gone wrong. Still standing in front of her, staring down, he rationalised for the first time thoughts that entered and left his consciousness many times over the months were probably right: Kay was mentally unbalanced, schizophrenic even. And the Kay he was staring at was surely capable of anything.

'I won't stay' he said coldly. 'Ring me when you're in a better frame of mind'.

Equally coldly she said 'So that's it is it?'

'Kay. What's gone wrong? Jesus, you know I have a job to do. I can't be at your beck and call'.

'Then go'.

*

Makepeace and Masters were at Essex Headquarters in conference with their officers dealing with the stolen lorries discovered at the Galleywood run in. Masters reported that Gore, the driver of the 17 tonner had been charged with conspiracy to rob. 'Interestingly' he told the assembled officers 'Gore has thrown up his hands to nicking the lorry from Wrights Transport. You've identified its cab but its £50,000 load of cigarettes has disappeared. We haven't given up hope of rounding up the conspirators'.

'Have we got enough to charge Swain and Finch in relation to the theft of each vehicle and its load?' asked an Essex DI.

DCS Makepeace was shaking his head. 'No. As it stands at the moment DI Masters has uncorroborated evidence that both the 17 tonner and the artic stolen from Wrights Transport earlier last year involves the owner of the firm, James Holden and the prisoners Swain and Gore. We are waiting to hear from our legal department whether we have enough to pull Holden in on a warrant. What have you established regarding the two other vehicles?'

It transpired they had been hi-jacked in London. The loads were TV sets and yet again cigarettes. The Essex enquiries had identified the transport firms involved; and where the lorries had been loaded. The Met CID for each area was involved in the enquiry, Makepeace was told, and tabs kept on the drivers.

'Still driving for their firms?'

'No, sir. But we've got them housed'.

Makepeace was taking in faces of the assembled detectives 'If James Holden is the ring leader he's a clever bastard', he told them. 'But we'll get him'.

*

Chapter twenty one

With the Jaguar's windscreen shattered and a shoulder numbed from the impact of a bullet, The DI managed to steer the car to a standstill and sit in a state of shock. He reached across and pushed a hand under his jacket and drew it back to look at the bloodstained palm and fingers. His radio was on the passenger seat but he managed to reach across and send a message.

*

'How bad is it?' asked Makepeace, looking up at the doctor who had just left the operating room
'Flesh wound. The bullet missed vital organs. It's in a tray beside the bed'.
'May I go in?'
The doctor smiled reassuringly 'Why not. He's wide awake'.
Makepeace hauled his bulky frame out of the chair and popped his head around the door. The DI, propped up on pillows, smiled weakly at Makepeace and gestured to a chair beside his bed. 'Pissed off somebody' he quipped to the DCS with a faint smile
'Don. You piss off everybody!'
Masters looked quizzically at him and realised it was meant as a light-hearted comment.
'You're a lucky buggar. Any idea?' Makepeace glanced around at the other patients.
Masters mind was searching for the most likely villain. Top of the list had to be Gardner. Or possibly Kay? Her angry face swam into his mind.
Makepeace's eyes were back on the DI, who was shaking his head. ' Who're you thinking of?'
The DI smiled briefly 'Gardner comes top' he

replied.

*

Spence and the DI were in their arranged café when he confidently told the DI a Phil Downey from Hinkley pulled the trigger. 'The word is Mel Gardner arranged the shooting'.

'How d'you nail him down so quickly, Len?'.

'A mate in the same prison as Gardner slipped me the info'. Spence grinned at Masters' obvious surprise. 'Your lot aint the only firm hoovering up info, Don!'.

'What's his form?'. Masters looked keenly at Spence.

'I don't know too much about him. Did bird for GBH in the same prison as Gardner. Came out two months ago'.

'Sure it's him?'

'Positive'.

Masters stood and leaned across to shake Spence's hand. 'Well done, Len. Now the ball's in my court'.

*

Masters drew Downey's file from CRO and saw he was the usual blaggard with cons for violence. He was an ugly bastard, Masters thought, as he looked at his mug shots. His last arrest was seven years before for slicing off a bloke's ear in a pub brawl. Nice one. The Hinckley address was there and Masters reached for the phone and asked the station officer to get Hinckley police station on the line for him. The information he got was brief. Downey was dossing down in a probation hostel. His wife had divorced him while he was imprisoned and moved away. No family on the town.

'What d'you want us to do? The detective sergeant at the other end asked.

'How well do you get on with the manager of the hostel?'

'Alright. He's an ex copper. Retired several years ago'

'Be nice to know what gear Downey has. Mates. Car. That sort of thing. Can you manage that on the QT?'

'I'll see it gets done'.

With the assurance the enquiry was in good hands Masters dropped the hand set in its cradle and sat back. Kay's image was there immediately.

*

It was a month since Don got shot. Because he had been determined to get back to work Jean did the same. On Wednesdays she always finished work at 4pm. On that fateful Wednesday afternoon Jean was driving home from work, paying no attention to the blue Rover saloon that dropped in behind her as she left the firm's car park. Out of town she drove along the quiet B road and became aware that the car was close behind her. In the interior mirror she could see it was a woman driver who was steering her car as if to overtake and then dropping back. Jean did the sensible thing and pulled into a nearside overtaking bay, expecting the car to carry on. It didn't. Kay slotted in front of Jean's car and backed up, almost bumper to bumper.

Jean started to open the door but something in the determined stance of the blonde haired woman strutting towards her car stopped her. She looked up at Kay, who by then was standing immediately beside her door.

'What do you want?' Jean asked, alarmed by the aggression in the woman's stance and instinctively pressing down the door button when she believed the woman meant to hurt her.

Kay kept trying the door and was glaring at Jean. 'Open this door!' she shouted as she tugged futilely at the locked door.

'Who are you? What do you want?' Jean was petrified and scrambling to get the car into reverse while she flicked frightened stares at the manic woman.

'You bitch!' Jean heard Kay scream but, thankfully, by then she had the car in reverse and shot back into an overgrown hedge. In first gear now and engine racing she pulled out of the slot and aimed at Kay, who managed to dive out of the way.

Driving automatically, unaware of the last leg of her journey, Jean was relieved when she pulled into her driveway and scrambled out and ran indoors where she grasped her phone and got through to Don's police station.

*

The crew of a patrol car were making notes as Jean described the woman as best she could. 'It was all so quick. Once she was out of the car she was screaming at me. About 35 I'd guess. Blonde hair up at the back. Slim. She was wearing a black leather belted jacket and slacks, oh, and high boots'.

'Was she wearing gloves?'

'Yes. I'm sure of that'.

'You've done very well, Mrs. Masters'. The patrol officer's pen was poised over his notebook 'Did you get any details of her car?'.

'Blue, yes blue. I wouldn't know its' make. I'm sorry' she smiled ruefully 'I'm not very good with cars'.

The front door slammed shut at that moment and

Jean told them it would be Don. He came into the room quickly and took her hands and smiled an acknowledgement at the officers. 'You're alright, sweetheart?' He had been given a brief account of what had happened over his radio and knew straight away it had been Kay. He led her to the settee and sat beside her, taking in what she was telling him, more certain from the description she was giving it had been Kay 'Would you know her again, darling?'

Jean shuddered at the thought of seeing the woman again but nodded.

'We'll be off, sir'. The officer who spoke had nudged his partner.

Masters walked them to the door and thanked them. 'I'll write up the report when I get back', he told them. Back in the living room he could see that Jean still wasn't herself. 'I know, darling. I know'. He sat beside her again and took her hands in his 'You've had a nasty shock' he said and then cuddled her, nuzzling his head against her cheek. 'I'll get it sorted. Changing his tone and smiling he got up and said. I'll make us a cup of tea. Would you like that?'.

Jean smiled wanly and nodded and reached across her shoulder to the ache in her back. She stopped rubbing the spot and looked up at him 'It's started to hurt again. What should I do?'.

'We'll see your doctor. I'll ring the surgery now'.

The next afternoon Masters took time out to see Kay at her flat and didn't mince his words. 'What got into you, you bloody cow?', he demanded, starring down at her. She had let him in and walked stiffly ahead of him and had flounced into an armchair and was staring back at him, outraged at his angry tone.

'Who do you think you are? You come here and fuck me and think you can just walk away from me! We shall see!'

'Walk away?. Who's walked away? Just lately all you've done is behave nastily'. He kept his anger out of his voice but his icy tone was betraying his feelings.

'And why shouldn't I? You come here when it suits you. You go back to that slag and fuck her as well! Well, I'm not having it!'.

He stared at her now very familiar pose in her favourite armchair, her fisted-hands in her lap, and wondered how he ever got mixed up with her. 'What is it, Kay? Why are you behaving this way?', he asked, desperate to keep her calm.

'I want you here with me, not with that cow'.

'Is that what this is about?'

She sat tight lipped and looked away. 'Just go'.

An hour later Masters was reading a teleprinter message from Hinckley CID that briefly indicated Downey's movements for the day of the attack could not be verified; that he had a three year old Vauxhall; and the unofficial search of his possessions hadn't revealed anything to connect him with the attack on Masters. To all intents and purpose the Hinckley enquiry had hit the buffers.

It was a long shot but he gave the details of the Vauxhall car to the traffic branch asking that enquiries be made. It was a long shot but it might have been ticketed in London.

*

Gardner's confidence that Downey could take out the detective had turned to frustrated anger. Night after night he had lain on his bed and stared angrily at the ceiling. Days were meaningless and weeks passed "Not to be considered for parole for thirty year" the judge had said. Thirty years! He had to escape or go mad. He had to find a firm to get him out. His word was out on the wing that he was looking for a firm to do it and that word reached Alfie, the brother of Bert George who Gardner had shot in the Blind Beggar pub.

*

Alfie had form. He was a south London villain you steered clear of: a bit like his dead brother, "may God rest his soul" he always added to his missus whenever they discussed Bert's demise. His blagging firm was on the flying squad's radar, he was well aware of that but, whether by good fortune or the money he handed over periodically to a particular flying squad, Alfie's firm hadn't had a collar felt for two years. Right then they were in their favourite pub working on the details of their plan to spring Gardner. It was a simple plan that relied upon Gardner convincing the screws he was seriously ill.

*

Inside the ambulance taking him to hospital Gardner was stretched out on the bunk handcuffed to a prison warder, his convincing groans keeping the second member of the crew on his toes with the worry of it all. The driver saw the stationary ambulance up ahead and what looked like a first aid bloke waving his arms about. He stopped and wound down the window.

It happened so fast, the driver told the policeman much later at his hospital bedside. One minute there he was smiling at me and the next I had a gun in my face. 'Dragged out I was' he stated firmly. 'That bit I remember. Nothing else'.

The hovering doctor had advised the police officer to let his patient rest. 'He's had a nasty whack over his head with a blunt instrument'.

*

Gardner was on his feet the moment he heard the kerfuffle up front and whacked the warder with his free hand several times until, the rear door open, he saw his rescuers clambering in and swiftly handcuffing the first aid man to the warder.

'He's got the fucking key!' Mel shouted.

Freed, he had it away on his toes with the others to the ambulance up the road. Once on board he thumped his fist down on the bed and yelled 'frigging well done!'.

*

After they did the business, Alfie and his mates abandoned the ambulance up a lane off the main road and transferred to the waiting car and were gone. 'Sweet as a nut that' Alfie reckoned to his mates

*

There were four of them watching the doctor in the ambulance peering down at a very dead Gardner. The doctor turned his head to the waiting CID officers and shrugged. 'Two shots to the back of the head. Quite recent. Possibly within two hours. Body's still warm..........but then you already know that'. He clambered out and added 'The post mortem will reveal all'.

It did. Some of Mel's brains were missing of course having shot out and smeared against the wall of the ambulance. One of the bullets was still in the head but the brain was pulped. With the sawn off skull and scalp back in place, head shrouded and his chest roughly stitched up Gloria Gardner was offered the opportunity to identify and say her farewells to hubby.

Once outside the building she teamed up with the waiting Kathy Peel and, together now, they sloped off to a café up the road a bit for a council of war.

*

Author's note:

Digression is needed at this point in time. We have here the wives of two of London's villainous desperados. Loyalty is a given. Revenge natural. Over the course of their married lives they had rubbed shoulders, along with their men, with London's very successful scum which included bent CID officers; and had access to an information network that included police officers willing to earn a few bob now and then. Remember, we are talking real life here: these things do go on.

*

Kathy was naturally nervous for her Les. He didn't pull the trigger but he was on the jobs and that, she knew, now that Mel had been done, put him at the top of some bastard's hit list. 'D'you reckon it?' she posed rhetorically. Both women had fingered the Swain and George families during their chat and their belief had hardened.

'Who else?'

'We'll put a word out' Kathy said firmly. 'My Les aint going the way of your Mel'.

'Too right, Kath'.

*

The scientific examination of the stolen ambulance threw up nothing to help identify the killers. Fingerprints were dusted but it seemed to the SOCO officer that half of London's population had ridden in it. The vehicle had been stolen from outside a house in the back streets of Hammersmith a week before the snatch. A sharp pair of searching eyes found one of the bullets that did for Mel on the floor.

Door to door enquiries revealed a dark saloon, possibly a Ford Consul, might have been involved. A man with dark hair was seen to get out of that car and was peering into the cab of the ambulance as the witness walked past.

'How did they know the ambulance would be there that day?' posed one detective

'They followed it' suggested another.

'Duplicate key job' another offered.

*

Chapter twenty two

What to do about Kay was uppermost in Masters mind. It was Saturday and a week since the frozen meeting; and several times he had wanted to go round and have it out with her once and for all and make a clean break. Sitting back in his office chair he was taking stock of his predicament. Her reaction, he knew, if he made a clean break was unpredictable. So far he had been lucky. She hadn't contacted him at home but he realised that situation could change overnight if she wanted to go down that road.

God knows what Jean will do or say if she does, he reminded himself. That was his biggest fear but, so far, he hadn't been able to muster the courage to confess to her. He shook his head in despair at the thought of hurting Jean but.....he stood up. It had to be done and the sooner the better.

'All quiet?' he asked Tims when he got downstairs

'Until the pubs turn out, guv'.

'I'm off home. Bell me only if it's urgent'..

*

In a state of shock Jean sat unmoving in the armchair and gazed up at the man she loved, who was telling her, and now looking anywhere but at her, that he had been seeing another woman for the past six months! He was still talking to her but she was no longer able to concentrate but a word registered.............. unpredictable.............? The doctor had told her only that morning that she was to attend hospital to have a biopsy. "We need to know, Mrs. Masters" he had said "what kind of tumour you have".

'Unpredictable?' she repeated as she looked up at

her husband. 'What do you mean?'

'Jean , sweetheart. I don't know which way she'll go. I've told her it's all over but.........'. He sat down beside his wife and took one of her hands. 'I truly believe she's gone round the bend. She's capable of anything'.

'Do you love her?'. She withdrew her hand as she spoke.

He knew what the gesture meant but had to get it said. 'I thought I did, darling, but I was kidding myself. I know it hurts to hear this but it was just sex'.

'How did you meet her?'. She was dabbing at tears and staring at the wall.

He told her her husband was in prison and invented a lie that threats had been made against her. 'That's what got me round there in the first place'.

'Was she the woman who....who I thought, was going to hurt me?'.

'Possibly'.

'And you haven't said a word!'. Shocked, she stared unbelievingly at her husband, her confusion and growing anger evident.

'I'm so sorry, darling. Really I am. But it's over. I'll ring her now'. He reached for her hands but she drew them away and broke down in a flood of tears.

*

Kay put down the receiver and, in a state of shock at hearing him say it, sat perfectly still, her thoughts ranging from hate to murder. "Dumped by the bastard!", her tormented mind was telling her, his words ringing in her ears until she couldn't think straight. It was his wife, she knew for sure once her brain clicked into overdrive. The cow has turned him against me! A very, very angry Kay climbed out of the chair resolved to do something about it.

*

Ted was deliriously happy. His love for Lucy, his beautiful wonderful Lucy, had taken over his life. Sitting across from her in the restaurant, looking so beautiful in her new dress, he was staring and not eating; content to be there with her, to experience for the first time in his life that wondrous feeling of overpowering love for a woman.

'You're not eating, sweetheart' Lucy observed, her knife and fork poised over her plate.

'Oh. Sorry'. He started to move the food about again with his fork.

'Is something the matter?'

He wanted to ask but the thought of rejection stopped him. He looked at her again and once again lost courage and forked his food.

'There is something isn't there?', worried Lucy asked encouragingly.

He took the plunge and stared across at her worried expression. 'Lucy darling.........'.he began and then abruptly lost courage at the enormity of what he wanted to say to her.

'What is it, darling?', she asked gently as she reached to hold his hand.

'Sweetheart............will you marry me?' he blurted.

'Oh, Ted!'. She got up and came round to him 'Ask me again!'.

'Will you marry me?' he asked hoarsely as he looked up into her lovely, smiling face.

She leant over and kissed him 'My darling. I've been longing to hear just those words'. She smiled over his head at a couple sitting at the table nearest to their own. They raised their glasses and smiled back.

*

David Walters had grudgingly accepted John Barton's tale that Charlie was helping the police with their enquiries into other matters. Playing squash with him pushed his fear to the back of his mind but, nevertheless, his determination to beat John was stronger now than before his suspicions were aroused.

John, on the other hand, before he started his affair with David's wife, had managed to hold his own, even though he acknowledged David was a better player. Gradually over the recent weeks his natural desire to compete faded and David won easily. And on this occasion it was happening again and David was all smiles at a vanquished detective constable.

Sheila had changed. John was sure she still loved him but he felt........sensed, was a better understanding he decided, that she had become introspective, speaking of her husband more often. Even when they were making love her mind wandered because, on one occasion she had called him David, immediately clinging tightly to him and apologising again and again. John understood because he knew she loved only him. She was bound to make that mistake. She had asked on several occasions recently whether he wanted to live with her, so he knew she loved him more than she loved her husband...................

*

Kathy was on a visit to hubby Leslie in Wandsworth prison, hunching over the table to have their chat. Les was wearing that coloured thing again 'They've marked me a high risk, love' he told her. 'Who the frigging hell am I going to hurt in here?' Other inmates and their visitors were at other table and two screws were over by a wall with eyes everywhere.

'Are you alright, Les?' Really – are you?'

Never a one to moan about life when he was with Kathy he shrugged but it was obvious he had lost a lot of weight.

'Terrible about Mel, love. What's being done about it in here?' Kathy was looking anxiously at her husband.

'What can they do?' His dejection was more obvious now.

'Well, love. One day he's in Pentonville alive an' the next he's out there dead! Have the screws talked to you about it?'

He shook his head. 'Why should they?'.

'Because, love, you went down for the same jobs. Come on, love. Think of yourself! Put the word about. Someone must know somefink'.

Les had shut off. All he had done since hearing about Mel's murder was think about himself. Everywhere he looked screws and lags seemed to be staring at him. He'd even got to the point where he was worried to have a shit.

'Les?', she asked him softly, naturally concerned for her old man who was obviously under the weather.

'Sorry Kath love. I'm doing my nut in here. Fifteen more frigging years of this an' I'll go round the bend'.

Kathy wanted to pat his hand but the screw was ever watchful. 'Me an' Gloria will fink of somefink'.

'I know, love. I know. But what can I do stuck in here?'. He glanced at the warder and then back at his wife. 'Look, love. We've got cash stashed away. Put the word out that I want to do a runner from this place. Do that for me?'.

With the warder moving closer and others getting up she stood and held his hand. 'You know I will'.

*

When word had got back to him a certain flying squad was looking to have a chat with him, Alfie George wasn't surprised he'd been given a tug by the sweeney. Straight off he sussed they were on a fishing expedition. Shoving a fag packet at him, smiling, dropping names for blags, hinting at back handers if he was a good boy; he rode out the few minutes in the back of the squad car until the door was pushed open. and he was told to piss off. Alfie had been pulled before by the same squad, so he knew when to keep it shut and ears open. Even so his firm had been ultra cautious and the squad, obviously to Alfie, had been on a fishing expedition.

His firm had been very cautious on the run up to Gardner's demise: the stolen car used to nick the ambulance had been run into a scrap dealer's yard and a handful of notes ensured it was crushed that same day; and because possession of a gun in south London was an essential bit of kit, and being blissfully unaware that vengeful Gloria and Kathy were on the prowl, he had foolishly stashed it in his attic, ready for the next emergency.

*

Author's note:

A bright pair of sparks are Gloria and Kathy. Men will never understand how women do it but information gathering is their speciality. To you and me, women gossip and make snide remarks about other women. Well no, actually, its never that simple. Women like Gloria and Kathy are naturally cunning. It's the way they go about getting at the details: it's genetic, has to be. Anyway, stay with me on this one because our two heroines hit the bulls-eye within days of setting out on their quest. Alfie George was in the frame and a nebulous plan had been hatching in their devious minds. Rest assured, I mean they're women for God's sake, the final plan is to do for Alfie in ways most horrific.

*

Gloria's aunt Daisy living at North Pickenham, a few miles away from Swaffham in Norfolk. She had often gone on about the smell coming from the factory up the road from her.

'God awful, it is', she told Gloria on the rare occasion of a visit. ' Somefink ought to be done about the place or we'll have to get away from here'.

On a second visit, not too long back, Gloria got a whiff herself. Auntie told her what went on there. 'It's no secret' she explained ' Dead animals and their bits and pieces are bloody well cooked in that place'.

Gloria, with Alfie's demise in mind, drove to the factory and stood in the open gated entrance and witnessed a scene which, to her, was one of horror unfolding in front of her eyes. A large mechanical loader was pushing animal carcases and slithering intestines against a steel wall before scooping up a load of the stuff, and depositing it into a hopper, which seemed to be part of a much larger machine. An overalled man, Barry Sheenan he later told her was his monicker, who had just jumped down from the loader, spotted her and wandered over and gestured behind her 'Move over, love' he advised as he pointed 'Lorry coming in here'.

She got out of the way and watched as the lorry manoeuvred in the yard before tipping a load of slimy animal body parts onto the concreted ground. When the lorry had gone she watched the loader again push the stuff against the wall and repeat the lifting operation, lifting and depositing, over and over again until the yard was clear. 'My Gawd' she whispered to herself.

With his job finished the worker clambered from the loader and wandered back and lit a cigarette. Standing close to Gloria he smiled. 'Bit curious, love?'.

'Not really. The smell got me here. Where's all that stuff coming from?', she asked.

'Slaughterhouse. We get all sorts here. Vets dispose of their dead dogs and cats as well. They all get cooked'.

'Cooked! Oh my God!'. Gloria stared at the huge machinery and then at Sheenan.

The man pointed to the machine she had been looking at. 'The stuff I load into that hopper gets minced up and fed into the oven at the end there', he was pointing to one end. He grinned and pointed at steam. 'That's what you're smelling. Nice, eh!'.

'Why is it cooked?'.

'Greaves and tallow, love. A money maker for the boss'. Sheenan thought is was funny and smiled at her discomfiture.

Gloria then shook her head in disgust at the scene and gestured to the open gates. 'I suppose they're locked at night?'

The man laughed. 'No need to shut the gates, love. Would you come poking about in here at night!'.

*

Masters had worries. The letter that morning had been addressed to him and the content typical Kay. In the form of an invoice it was a bill for services rendered. Kay had included a photo of herself in knickers and bra, holding up an unwrapped somewhat soggy condom. He had shown them to Jean.

'She's a tart' she responded angrily. 'How did you ever get involved'?

'This won't end here' he told her worriedly. His thoughts were ranging ahead: seeing letters, visits, and threats and.... 'I've got to put a stop to all of this right now' he said decisively but with no clear vision of how.

'Can't the police……., well, your superiors, deal with this?'

Don was shaking his head. 'It's a personal matter, sweetheart. My problem to deal with. I've got to nip to the station for a few hours paperwork. Don't concern yourself with her. You going to be alright?'

Jean nodded and watched him go, her mind a kaleidoscope of images she couldn't bring to focus, especially the nightmarish one of cancer.

*

Alfie, a cold blooded killer now, was a likeable, gregarious, bloke who was well liked down the pub. He splashed his money about. Good villains do that: prestige; it mattered. That evening, with his wife and mates, he was enjoying a few pints and getting slowly pissed. Betty, his beloved wife, had let herself go a bit and was holding forth about the perils of dieting. Alfie, urged on by mates, tried his hand at the dartboard and couldn't find a double. Six darts he had on the double, he was that far ahead, he still lost and smilingly bought a beer for the winner.

Gloria and Kathy were in the same bar tucked into a corner and enjoying the moment because if their plan went off, it was going to unfold in front of them.

'That smiling bastard over there hasn't a clue' said Gloria to Kathy as she raised her glass and looked across the saloon at Alfie and his missus. 'Here's to revenge'. They chinked glasses.

Kathy was concerned at Gloria's confidence. 'Are you sure we can pull it off?'.

'Don't go sour on me, Kath. It's a cert. Watch what happens'.

A wee digression here: you and I know a little about Gloria and Kathy. We know they have a plan of sorts to deal with Alfie. Remember, they are East London villains' wives. They are a breed apart who expect an enjoyable life to bear fruit out of the misfortunes of others. Compassion is for family and close friends. Alfie, as Gloria kept on at Kathy, is not going to be shown compassion because he did for my old man.

But back to unfolding events...............

'Phone for you Alfie' the barman called across to Alfie's table.

Gloria put down her glass and nudged Kathy and whispered 'See if he goes for it'.

Alfie held up his glass at the barman in acknowledgement, took a swig and sauntered to the bar. Taking the phone he asked: 'Yeh. Who wants?' He listened for a while and handed the receiver to the barman and tottering back to his wife's table.

'Who was that, love?' she asked with her glass at her mouth ready for a swig and a fag, ash still clinging for dear life, in the other hand.

Gloria nudged her friend.............

'Sweeney'. Alfie was still on his feet when he explained that to her. Seeing the alarm on her face he calmed her 'No worries me love. A few quid's probably wanted. I'll nip out and square it'. He finished his pint and smacked his lips and headed for the door.

'Be careful love. Don't trust the filth' Bet called to his disappearing back.

'Alfie alright, Bet?' asked a woman friend absently

as she critically eyed her wrinkle-concealed made up face in her hand mirror.

'Yeh', Betty answered absently as she picked up her glass and blew a stream of smoke while dotting her fag. 'Bit of business.................the usual. Those bent bastards never know when to knock it off do they?'.

'True, love. So true' responded an inebriated friend who was nudging her old man for a refill.

Betty watched her old man disappear from the pub and, unknowingly, as events were to establish, out of her life.

Gloria and Kathy, knowing the end game, finished their drinks and left to do the business.

*

The car appeared okay. The back door being shoved open for him was typical squad. Alfie slid onto the back seat and was immediately chloroformed and the car was away. He didn't know he had been out for some time but when he was able to focus, Gloria's hazy face swam into focus.

'Hello Alfie' she addressed him, determined to keep to the formalities the occasion warranted. He was about to be snuffed for God's sake!

Alfie tried to move before realising he was tied to a chair. Staring at Gloria he shouted 'Who the frigging hell are you?'.

She stared down at him and told him, coldly 'Your nightmare, Alfie'.

'Don't muck about. Untie me', he shouted as he struggled with the ropes.

'What d'you reckon, Kath. Right bossy bastard aint he!'.

Alfie looked from Gloria to Kathy, who was speaking while he was staring. 'True Gloria, true'.

Alfie seized on the name 'Know you don't I ?'

Gloria stared at Alfie, her cold expression and her follow up words enough, if he could have truly concentrated, to inform him his life had reached it's use by date, telling him: 'You frigging bastard, you killed my Mel'. He saw her turn away from him and cross to the door and open it, beckoning Joe Keel and Ron Jackson into the room..'Untie him and hold him' she told them quietly. She watched Alfie struggle but it was useless in the grip of the two strong men. 'Get the bastard on his knees facing me' she told them, her steady gaze on the terrified, helpless man.

They forced Alfie down and he looked fearfully up at Gloria., who had produced a gun and was looking at it. Turning her attention to Alfie she said, 'Two in the back of the head for my Mel wasn't it Alfie. Remember that?'

Alfie bottled it, sudden knowing who she was and what was definitely on the cards.

'Have a shit as well, Alfie' Gloria said coldly when she saw the pool of water forming between his legs.

Shaking with fear he farted and watched her wiggle the automatic as she stepped close to him. He tried to loosen the men's grip but gave up as he stared up at her pitiless expression, experiencing the certainty of imminent death.

'One or two Alfie. What do you think?' she taunted him, her rhetorical question heightening his fear because she had stopped in front of him, the gun steady and pointing at his head.

Ashen faced and definitely unable to speak, he stared at Keel, then Jackson, then Kathy Peel and, when the gun was close to his head, at Gloria, who inched the gun forward until it was against his forehead., the coldness of the metal the last sensation he was to experience before she pulled the trigger.

The impact forced Alfie out of the grip of the men to spread-eagle him on the floor.

'Get him in the bag ' Kathy said quietly as she stared down at Alfie. 'He got what he deserved'.

Alfie's lifeless body was rolled into the open body bag and zipped into place.

'Get him in the car' Gloria urged the two men.

The ungainly burden was taken outside and, with the help of Derek who had stayed in the driving seat until he saw them struggling with a lifeless Alfie, was squashed into the boot of the waiting car.

*

The trip took two hours to reach the factory and the entrance gates, as Gloria had told them, were wide open. Derek Stockhart parked up and left the rest to Ron and Joe. Knowing from Gloria what they were getting into they had come prepared. They donned boiler suits, rubber boots and gloves before dragging Alfie out and lugging him across the moon and sodium lit yard to the heap of slimy intestines. Derek was unzipping Alfie when Barrie Sheenan approached them and watched open mouthed at the goings on.

'What the hell are you doing?' he demanded incredulously as Alfie rolled onto the concrete.

They straightened and expressionlessly stared at him.

He stared back and then stepped close to look at Alfie's obviously dead body. 'What happened to him?'.

Jackson took his arm and led him to one side. 'Look mate', he said in a persuasive, threatening tone. 'He's a mate what got done in a pub fight. We don't want the old bill sniffing around so...', he stared hard at the worker, 'there's a ton in it for you if you stick him in that machine'.

Sheenan couldn't believe what he was hearing. Staring at Alfie while Jackson was talking he broke out in a cold sweat, aware his hands were shaking. The men, who had rolled up the bag, were by then giving him a hard, uncompromising stare. Having no choice but to do as he had been asked he walked over to the loader and started it up. Backing up and aiming the shovel at Alfie, he edged him forward, almost burying him in the slime of an untidy heap of body parts, until his blade touched the steel wall and he tilted the shovel and raised it, dumping Alfie, by then part of a mixture of animal guts and carcases, in the mincing auger that was to propel Alfie's bits and pieces to the oven.

Backing up and jumping down, he looked at the men who were smiling at him.

'Ta, mate'. Jackson said as he handed over the hundred pounds. 'Not a word about this. Right?'.

*

Chapter twenty three

The Essex detective chief superintendent and DCS Makepeace agreed to Masters request to bring Keith Mooney in for questioning. As it stood they only had his cheque for £2500 paid into Justin Swain's account, but Mooney didn't know that and, with him under arrest, his house and office were searched.

Caged in a cell and denied access to a solicitor he paced his cell and waited for someone to question him, about what he had no idea. In the meanwhile, the search completed, Masters decided the time was right for a chat. Mooney was escorted up from his cell.

'Detective inspector Masters'. Smiling, he reached across the desk and shook Mooney's hand.

Mooney automatically gripped it before his nervousness reshaped his face. 'Why am I here?', he demanded.

'You're here, Keith, because you are involved in placing nicked gear'.

When Mooney started an obvious protest Masters fluttered a hand to him. 'No need to deny, Keith. In fact I don't intend to put any questions to you about your part in the thefts. There's something bigger at stake. Justin', he broke off and added as a prompt 'You know him —you're part of his hi-jacking team. You know we've arrested him and Bert Finch —red handed actually'.

'What's that got to do with me'?

'I'll leave that for now. Read the papers lately – Bloke called Gardner shot'?

'Seen that. I don't get involved in violence so why talk to me about it'? Mooney looked around the sparsely furnished room, nodding at Miller who was, as usual, by the door. Turning his attention to Masters he asked 'Why mention Gardner? Look -what's this all about?'.

The DI hunched forward and studied Mooney's composed features for some seconds before saying, his tone convincingly grave 'You're in the frame, Keith. Justin's put a contract out on you'. He sat back and watched the reaction. Mooney's eyes widened, he paled, and started to get up. Miller, who had moved behind him, pushed him down.

'You're safe here, Keith. I've had you brought in to protect you'.

'This is a load of bollocks! I don't know the bloke. What's his name again –Justin?'.

Masters nodded and took a photo copy of a cheque from the file in front of him. He pushed it front of Mooney and watched his reaction. 'Still don't know him, Keith'?

Mooney studied the copy for a while before sitting back and staring at the unsmiling detective.

'Justin had Gardner shot'. The DI lied easily and leaned across his desk to point at Mooney 'He believed he was the grass who set him up. Now the word is it was you'.

'Where's all this coming from?'. Mooney angled on his chair and looked from one detective to the other before glaring at Masters. 'Load of bollocks this isn't it? Why are you giving me all this crap?'.

'Bollocks for you maybe, Keith, but the word from the prison grapevine is you're in the frame for grassing Justin'. Watching the man the DI saw the beginnings of doubt and said nothing more to him but suggested to Miller it was time for coffee.

'Fancy a cup, Keith'?

Masters' sympathetic attitude was working wonders in Mooney's mixed thoughts. He gave an involuntary nod which the DI hoped meant he had broken the man's train of thought. He kept up his pressure 'This is a new situation for us, Keith'. He smiled. 'Nicking villains is our game –not baby sitting!'

The DI's confident manner had caught Mooney off guard. He was well aware of the Galleywood run in but it hadn't been mentioned. The cheque to Justin Swain made it obvious the police had made the connection. He leaned forward slightly and quickly studied the photo copy and sat back. In 1970 he'd managed to avoid being charged, but this was 1974..................

The coffee arrived and Masters pushed a cup towards Mooney. 'D'you smoke' On a nod he pushed his packet across the desk and stood his lighter beside it. Watching the man light up and blow smoke to the ceiling the officers waited for the man to question them. The waiting game stretched into a few minutes before he did.

He gestured at the photo copy 'Alright, that's mine. What's your point'?

Masters took his time answering. He lit a cigarette and lobbed his packet to Miller, who lit up as well. Then he turned his attention to the troubled man 'The cheque is why Justin has fingered you. He knows we've got it. Work it out for yourself'. The lie was a gamble but, if the detectives were right in their assumption, they had another member of the hi-jacking conspiracy sitting in front of them.

After a few sips and still holding the mug Mooney said 'I've had no dealings with Gardner. Until the bit about him being shot I'd never heard of him'.

'Not the point, Keith'. The DI was now well into it. 'Gardner knew about Justin's scams. Think of yourself. Look', the DI gestured for Miller to draw up a chair at the desk 'Make a clean breast of it now. My guvnor doesn't piss about. If I can show him you're cooperating he'll work out a way to protect you'.

Masters saw that Mooney was going for the lie.

'If I make a statement I want your word you can protect me'?

'Goes without saying Keith'.

*

Charlie was at it again and had roped Janet in. Right then she was sitting in the driving seat of his clapped out Viva waiting for her hero to return from his latest tickle. Back he came and away they went.

'What did you get?' she asked

'About a ton', he told her as he pulled crumpled notes from a pocket and tossed them into her lap.

Janet eased the car into the main road traffic and glanced at him. 'What shall we do now?' she asked as she moved to overtake a cyclist.

'Let's nip down the Hare and Hound. I could murder a lager'.

The pub was its usual full self. Some of their friends were already there, the men on lager and the girls sipping vodka and lime and deep in conversation with each other and enveloped in cigarette smoke because the whisper fan wasn't working.

'Charlie mate. What's yours?' asked one of the youths who had just got to the bar. Charlie told him.. 'Make that another lager' the barman was told.

'See who's in the next bar?' ginger Bert asked, angling his head over the bar at the adjoining room.

Charlie peered past the barman and spotted Ted Read and John Barton with Lucy and Sheila near the bar.

'Nice birds' Charlie reckoned. 'Tasty'. He added, and found himself eye-to-eye with Barton.

*

Anything new?' the DI queried of tired Tims when he walked into the police station.

'Two in the cells for GBH –came in this afternoon. Punch up in the middle of town, apparently. Oh, yes. A woman had just phoned in a burglary at her house. Pimlico Road. Nice houses out that way Don. She's already had a chat with next door. An oldish Viva was parked up just past the neighbour's place. Female in the driving seat. No description. Might mean nothing. Shall I pass it upstairs?'

Masters nodded his head knowing Charlie had been at it again. 'Do that' he said 'I'll get one of my lads to look into it'.

*

Masters stood in the cell and stared down at Charlie. 'What is it with you?, he demanded. ' Now you've involved Janet'

Charlie Hobbs was slumped forward on the bed but raised his head to look up at Masters.

'Well?'

'Why are you having a go at me Don', he protested.

'You were seen Charlie. With Janet, for Christ's sake. We've got a bloody witness who clocked your car. And two of my men saw you in the Hare and Hound. Hand over the cash'.

'I 'aven't got any bleeding cash, Don'.

'That might be good enough for the duty sergeant. Now, don't piss me about Charlie. Hand it over'.

'What about Janet? She going to be alright?'

'The cash, Charlie'

The youth took off the usual sock, pulled some bank notes out and slung them on the bunk.

The DI counted them. '£45 missing Charlie'

'Well, I spent it didn't I. How do I stand on this

Don'?, he pleaded.

'Can't help you with this one. Charlie. I warned you to behave and you know my rules. The only help I can give you is when you get to court. . With decent antecedents I can help a bit' He sat and stared at a chastened Charlie. 'Why, Charlie. For God's sake why? You're on probation. They'll throw the breach at you as well'.

Charlie already knew it and was thinking about Janet. 'She'll be alone in that flat, Don. I don't like that'.

Masters refrained from saying the obvious, but patted Charlie's shoulder.

'I know, lad. I know'.

*

After the remand hearing the next morning the DI let Janet into the cell to say her goodbyes. When he saw her standing wet eyed in the interview room later he tried to console her. 'I'll do my best for him, Janet' he said quietly as he squeezed her shoulders. 'Keep in touch with me. If there's anything I can do I will'.

She searched his face for hope for her Charlie and saw a genuine concern, and believed him.

*

The plaster casts were off and Reg Bruce was feeling much better but still angry at Kay having it off with a copper. Lesson learned he kept shtum but his desire to sort out her and Masters had gone deep, festering over the passing months. It was his parole hearing that day. The doctors at the hospital and the visiting psychiatrist's report were going to help at the hearing, a screw had told him. Anyway, that's what other lags reckoned as well. Standing there that afternoon he watched the three of them, one a woman with glasses on, peering at papers in front of her, from time to time glancing across at him and muttering to the others.

'You are much better now?' one of the men asked.

He nodded.

'Hmm'.

Reg reckoned the woman, who had specs perched on the tip of her nose, was a right frigid cow. She looked across at him and tapped the paper in front of her. 'You did not have a trade. Why is that?'

Reg shrugged and suppressed a smile. Being a robber wasn't likely to impress. 'Bad start in life, I suppose'.

'Were we to recommend you for parole, what work would you do?'

'Hard to answer that one. Building sites –that sort of thing. Bound to get a job with all the houses going up I've read about'.

'Hmm'. She looked to the others, who shook their heads. 'Thank you. You may go'.

At a gesture from the warder who had brought him he turned and left.

'How'd it go?' he asked him.

'Didn't ask you much. Alright I reckon'.

*

Makepeace, on top of the world, was in conference with his Essex counterpart. The enquiries had brought in enough evidence to bring in James Holden for questioning and that task had been delegated to Masters and Miller. The small net they had begun with had expanded and three other Met police stations were in the net dealing with six other stolen lorries. Five men had been remanded in custody for their part in the thefts; and eight for their involvement in receiving. Deals had been done putting Justin Swain in the frame for receiving other lorries and their loads. That part of the enquiry was under wraps until the two officers decided on an appropriate time to re-interview the man.

*

James Holden did not have a criminal record. He was 45 and a going-to-fat six footer married to Doreen, ten years his junior, with two sons aged 10 and 12. A one-time lorry driver quick to see an opportunity he borrowed enough dosh some years back to buy a lorry and go it alone. Years in the haulage game opened doors to earners because he could be trusted. Carting parts of stolen loads from here to there set him up with enough cash to buy outright the land where he set up Wrights Transport at Enfield, an off-the-shelf company that had ceased trading; and invest in four more lorries.

Trusting nobody, he and his wife took care of the book keeping. Not the tidiest, and certainly not the most efficient of clerks, their filing system lacked the expertise of an uprightly honest company. This was to be his downfall. The thorough search by fraud squad officers uncovered a blatantly corrupt company. The books showed it hauled goods for others firms very few of which actually existed.

The evidence coming in from the larger field enquiries revealed the loads from several lorry hi-jackings had been funnelled through his company. Tying in that evidence with documents found at his home brought Justin Swain further into the picture. Some of Holden's own lorries were evidenced as having delivered goods to the run in. Phone tap information had led to some of the other arrested men and the various stolen lorries. Masters knew well enough the phone tap information could not be used at court. Now, looking across his desk at Holden, with the confidence of the documentary evidence to hand, he leaned across and offered a hand to the man. 'Might as well get off on a friendly, basis, James. DI Masters'.

Holden shook the offered hand and waited. He had been in custody for two of a seven day remand to cells. He could see that Masters had a thickish wad of paperwork before him which he was flicking through. Miller arrived at that moment with the coffees, which were handed around.

'Let's get started. Is it James or Jimmy?', Masters queried

'Jimmy'll do'.

The DI nodded. 'This lot has done for you, Jimmy. There's enough evidence here to tie you in with several nicked lorry loads, receiving, etc,etc'. He pushed the file to one side and stared at Holden, knowing that he needed a statement from him to validate the phone tap evidence against many other villains.' From here on in, Jimmy, it's up to you. You needn't say anything about this lot –it speaks for itself'. He nudged the file. 'You're at that time in your life when you need to work on your priorities' He carried on looking thoughtfully at the other man who was clearly thinking something over. 'Want my advice?'

'Which is?'

'Make very clear your part in all of this. Others have done so –that's why you're sitting there and I'm sitting here. I've been years at this game, Jimmy. Make a statement and tell all, as they say'.

'What have you got there?' Holden asked, his voice betraying nervousness at the way the interview was going.

'Every deal you were involved in; every pound you earned out of them; all their names: you've been very thorough, Jimmy, but I'm afraid too thorough. Do you want a solicitor here?'

'Not much point. Can we leave this for a while? I'd like to talk it over with the missus. You're not going for her as well are you?'

'Down to you, Jimmy. Dusty and me -we try to keep women out of the loop if we can'.

*

Chapter twenty four

David Walters job in a travel agency in the High Street gave him time to mull over his worry for his beloved Sheila. She had become tearful. The slightest thing was setting her off. Only that morning she had burned the toast and was reduced to a flood of tears. It was just one of many such minor events that had that effect upon her. And she had become very attentive. For ever ironing and cleaning the house and fussing over his appearance before she would let him leave the house: it appeared to David that Sheila needed to fill every second of every day with activity. They hadn't made love for weeks. He wasn't upset about it: their long cuddles of an evening had become a ritual he enjoyed because she was so obviously happy to be in his embrace: and that's what he wanted for her; happiness and contentment. In bed it was the same. She would slide into his embrace and lay her head on his chest and, from time to time, stroke his face. Sometimes she cried. They didn't talk much either. None of this was the Sheila he had married but he couldn't bring himself to say so to her.

*

Sheila was unaware that the two men who loved her were concerned for her state of mind. A submerged guilt had entangled her awareness of their love for her and her love for them: the conflated whole was an entity making it virtually impossible for her to assuage the unconscious guilt which, from time to time, entered her consciousness and reduced her to the tears that David was seeing. Keeping busy was the palliative helping her through her days. Giving up John or leaving David to be with John were not conscious resolutions. She truly loved two men who, she believed beyond any doubt, truly loved her and, as she waved to David from the doorstep, her guilt and her helplessness trickled and she turned and shut the door and let sadness flow.

*

Detective constable John Barton's love for Sheila, his Honey, had crossed the divide from rational thought to fantasy. He loved his wife dearly as much as he loved Sheila. He had reached that stage in the affair when he was consciously aware of confusing, intermingling, emotions: he could not acknowledge guilt; he was, in fact, he told himself firmly as he sought to get a grip on his reality, not guilty of anything. But discarding Sheila from his life was a non-starter. He recalled the stories of some of his friends who had had relationships. Mistakes they had called them because, they alleged, at the end of the day, it was the women who had led them on but not, John readily admitted to himself, in his case. John had tried to put himself in his wife's position listening to his confession. What would he do in her place? Stay or go? Would she kick him out?

*

Gillian was unhappy. Having no evidence of John's affair she intuitively knew that his love was on the wane. Even those little surprise gifts were no longer given. She needed to be loved as all women do. She had a right to expect the man she married to continue a loving relationship because her love for her man was unconditional. She hadn't rationalised that line of thought because for a woman it is a given. These various emotional thoughts flashed through her tormented mind because she was dragged down by the leaden weight of uncertainty; a punishment she did not deserve and should not be suffering. Talking it over with John was not an option because................at this moment in her rationalisation her confused mind became concerned because she worried it would bring into the open what she feared; and dealing with another woman in John's life would be too painful to bear.

*

Jean Masters has resolved her dilemma. Don had been a constant, caring husband for the ten years of their marriage and their love life had been a shared devotion. The other woman in his life -she couldn't bring herself to give her a name – she was sure had been a passing fling. Jean was not a fool. She was aware that men strayed. Until the bombshell it had always been other wives' men. It had been difficult for her to come to terms with but she had. Forgiveness was never mentioned because it was an empty word that could never heal emotional harm or erase the affair from Don's thoughts, or her mind. If those thoughts were in his mind she would live with that possibility; but her constant concern was the specialist's diagnosis her lung cancer was malignant; and her fear of the effect it would have on Don when she told him. She went to the bedroom and opened her drawer and looked at the differing coloured pills and cried.

*

Don Masters knew only too well the hurt he had caused. He also knew he was a randy arsehole who had enjoyed sex with Kay. It was over, yes, but she was still out there, still Kay with that lovely body and her love for sex with him. But he had since done what all men caught with their trousers down have done, he became moral. To assuage his guilt he naturally blamed Kay. If she hadn't been so demanding for sex he would never have strayed. It helped that she had become nasty and dangerous because it made it so much easier to move on and to put to oneside his lust for her body and their thrusting sex................................

*

Don had got her background from Charlie in bits and pieces over time and knew that Janet, this beautiful young woman, had been brought up on a council estate. Her dad had buggered off early in her life; Iris, her mum, had slaved away to scrape the necessary pennies together to keep them going.

A product of comprehensive schooling which others knew, but she did not, that if you came through the imposed Labour Party system you were likely to be blighted for life. Her proud mum naturally wanted the best for Janet, an aspiration she knew was not an easy option because it couldn't be achieved in her circumstances on that council estate. Janet didn't know it but she had inherited her mum's intelligence; yet she left home to breathe. Charlie explained she felt suffocated living with mum; neither knew that leaving would twist a knife in her mum's heart every day she wasn't there. And then she met and fell in love with Charlie, an unfortunate choice in partners, whose villainous way of life was to drag her into petty crime. With Charlie locked up, the DI knew Janet needed the stability he had given her. She was, in fact, a lost soul who was in a café holding a cooling cup of milky coffee pouring out her worries to Masters, who was holding her hands and wondering if she was going to be a thorn in his side. She clearly had no idea of Charlie's criminal involvement with him.

'Will you go back to your mother?', he asked sympathetically.

She shook her head and pulled free from his hands to pick up a photo of Charlie that was on the table between them.

'Can you afford to keep the flat going without him?' Masters asked when she put Charlie's photo down.

'Just about. I work in a hairdressers' shop. Full time it'll have to be now that Charlie's gone', she said through a burst of tears.

'Look'. He studied her weepy face 'If you get stuck for money give me a ring. I like Charlie. He would want to know you're all right. Will you do that?'

Janet perked up at the mention of money and nodded, surprised at the offer.

The DI stood up and gently ruffled her hair. 'Charlie left my number with you?'

Janet search her handbag. Pulling out a scrap of paper she read out a number. 'That it?' she asked

'That's the one. Now Janet..........' he looked kindly at her 'Don't get yourself into a muddle. Ring me if there's anything Charlie or you want. Will you be okay?'.

'Fanks, Don. Charlie'll appreciate that. So do I'. She stood and moved close to the detective, taking his hand and gazing into his face. 'Charlie reckons you, Don. And so do I'.

*

The Prison Authority, being able to move prisoners around the system, brought under the same roof Leslie Peel, Ronnie Silver, Jimmie Pollard, Reg Cook and Brian Fellows. The screws agreed with each other when they were sinking a few pints at the prison bar: a more charming bunch of recidivist blaggards you couldn't find under a rotting fungus. Unbeknown to these men they were soon to be joined by Jimmie Holden and Bill Gore whose trials were over and sentence awaited. Those two reprobates had fingered and been fingered by other low life, who themselves were awaiting the judge's pleasure. All in all, Masters and the many other detectives crawling around the slime of thieves and robbers, had had a very good haul. In the course of the many tortuous journeys various officers had done the right thing and took bungs; Masters and Miller included, because many of the villains questioned insisted on rewarding the detectives for bending, sometimes the laws of evidence, sometimes the evidence itself, in their favour.

This is as it should be because those officers sought and duly caused the punishment of deserving villains. Lighter sentences were sometimes dished out at court to those who chose the Masters' pathway to justice.

*

Author's note:

Were the readers of this chronicle to recap it in its entirety he/she would realise that, with perhaps a few exceptions, only those deserving of arrest and subsequent punishment were in fact so dealt with. We are back at the core of an important thesis underlining the work of detectives: do the ends justify the means?. Consider Alfie George. He murdered Melvyn Gardner who the state allowed to live even though he had been found guilty of two murders. Mel was due to stay in prison for thirty years. The cost of keeping him alive would have risen exponentially over that long period. Up pops Alfie to carry out a deed that, some would argue, a majority of the population would agree with; and one that should have been carried out by the state authority. The state benefitted. The Chancellor of the Exchequer was able to reduce the funding for prisons. A vacancy occurred in a prison for a more deserving inmate. Then consider Gloria Gardner and Kathy Peel. Murderesses yes but Alfie got his comeuppance. Justice was done yet again; Exchequer money saved; and space yet again made available in a prison. You could properly point out that they were not arrested for the crime. Let me explain. Detectives dislike nicking women for any crime. If another way can be found to solve their crimes it will be sought out. It may turn out that Masters & Co will solve the murder of Alfie. We must wait and see. Most of the reprobates dealt with by the police and the courts only came to notice due to Masters' rule bending. Back handers resulted in villain shopping villain. Crime after crime was solved using this tried and tested method of detective work. To continue...................

*

Physically recovered and out on parole, Reg Bruce arrived in a taxi and for a few moments stared up at her first floor curtained windows, unsure if she was looking down at him. He'd belled her from the railway station and was surprised at the mellow tone inviting him home. In he went and up he went and rang the bell and there she was, in the open doorway, smiling the lovely smile he remembered.

Warily, he stood still when he opened up with a nervous 'Hello, Kay'. Unaware of the type of welcome he was going to get he spoke quietly. But unknown to him her mood had switched from the psycho who now hated Masters, to welcoming. She reached for his hand

and led him inside her den.

*

Chapter twenty six

Charlie Hobbs had been weighted off and was serving a three year stretch. Three weeks into his sentence he got to know Leslie Peel and was intrigued at the yarn he spun about his missus and a bird called Gloria doing for a bloke called Alfie. Charlie being Charlie soon found out why Alfie had been done in. He told Janet on her next visit about the murders. 'Get a message to Masters. Tell him to arrange a visit here', he told her. 'It might do me a bit of good and get me out of here'.

It was thrilling stuff for Janet. On her way home she fantasised about Charlie being home. She could hardly wait to tell the detective what Charlie had said.

The DI met Janet in the same café and put his arm around her shoulders, giving her a friendly hug on their way to a table.. 'Been okay , Janet?'. He gazed admiringly at her slim beauty in the short skirt and tight top as she smoothed the skirt when she sat. 'You really are beautiful, Janet. Charlie's a very lucky man'.

Thrilled at his admiration she lowered her eyes and thanked him. 'But I miss Charlie so much' she said, looking across at him 'and I worry about Charlie all the time. I don't like it wiv him in that place'.

Masters reached across the table and squeezed her hand. 'Tell me about Gloria and Kathy'.

Janet picked up her mug and sipped the coffee and put it down and then looked directly at Masters.

Instead of answering his question she said 'Can you 'elp Charlie?'

Masters had no positive answer for her so avoided her searching gaze while he sipped his coffee.

'Depends on how things turn out, Janet' he said, after a short while. 'What is it Charlie wanted me to know about the two woman'?

'Well, there's Kathy first. And Gloria. Kathy's married to Leslie Peel she is. Charlie's been listening to 'im going on about his missus doing for Alfie. Does that mean anything to you?'

It certainly did. Alfie George had gone missing according to his wife, Betty. The local police station had picked it up from chit chat in a pub. The word coming back was that the flying squad had belled him in the boozer for a meet outside. He went out and never came back.

'Yes, Janet, it does. And this other women -Gloria?'

Janet came over all conspiratorial and leaned towards Don. 'This bloke Les told Charlie her and his missus took this Alfie for a ride and blew his brains out'. She grinned. 'Like the cinema aint it'.

Masters patted her hand. 'It is, Janet. Indeed it is'. He looked into her empty cup. 'Another coffee?'

'No fanks, Don'. She looked embarrassed for a moment 'Charlie always calls you Don. Do you mind?'.

'Don's fine, Janet. So this Gloria. Did Charlie have a last name for her?'

'Yeh. I've got to 'fink........Garding?. No.... Gardner it was. Charlie reckons this bloke Peel said it was his dead mate's wife. But wot about my Charlie? Can you 'elp him?'

'It's a possibility, Janet. I'll fix a meet with him soon'.

*

Charlie was brought to the room the governor of the prison had laid on away from the cell block for his meet with Masters. His 'hello, Don' came out with a relieved rush the moment he saw the detective.

'I'll be outside the door' the warder told Masters. 'Tap on the door when you're done'. The moment the door closed Charlie asked Masters for a cigarette. 'Gold in here they is'.

The detective handed over his packet and an unopened one and gestured to the table and chairs. 'Take the weight off Charlie. How have you been?' He sat down opposite the young man and offered his lighter.

Charlie grimaced. 'I'm not, Don. It's doing me 'ed in'. He sat and took a deep drag on the fag and looked across at the detective.

Masters could see Charlie was depressed and his engaging cockiness was gone. 'So tell me -what's Les Peel been telling you?'

Charlie became animated and sat forward. ' I tell you, Don, it's right gruesome. Mel's missus and Kath', he paused 'That's Les's wife. 'They had a bloke called Alfie away from the Greyhound pub and done for 'im. Shot 'im'.

The information added a dimension to what Masters had gleaned from the police grapevine about the abduction. 'What did they do with the body?'

Charlie chuckled. 'Minced the poor sod!'

'My God! How'd they manage that?'

'Some factory Les reckoned. Animal place, somefink like that'.

Masters was shaking his head 'Something wrong here, Charlie. Two women can't abduct a bloke from a pub and mince him!! Who else was involved. Did Les say anything more?'

'No, but I can find out if you like'.

'Be careful, Charlie. Don't show out. I shouldn't for your sake keep meeting you in here. If you can get any more slip the info to Janet. Do that?'.

Charlie nodded. 'Got any more fags I can 'ave Don?'.

Masters fished out the last packet he'd kept back 'Slip them out of sight of the screw who brought you'.

Masters got to his feet and shook Charlie's hand. 'Just be careful' he warned as he crossed to the door and rapped.

*

Detective sergeant Brian Fountain had heard a lot about Masters and his ways and worried that one day he himself would fall into a net set to catch the man. Because Masters was more outspoken of late, especially in the canteen when he was chatting to Miller, he considered it highly likely the rubber heels were bound to be sniffing around, bearing in mind what happened to Sneed at Leytonstone.

Determined to keep his nose clean he'd requested and been granted a meeting with Makepeace. Sitting opposite him in his spacious office was a nerve racking moment because he hadn't thought through consequences. "Don's bent" was a non starter. He hadn't a clue where the DCS stood on corruption.

'So, sergeant. What is it you want to discuss with me?'

Fountain, now lost for words that would resolve his dilemma, looked at the questioning face and regretted asking for the interview.

'Something's troubling you, sergeant. Out with it man'.

It was sink or swim time and Fountain took the plunge in the deep end. 'Don tells us he gets good information, sir. On the blagging recently two had it away; and the man who brought the other car has never been identified'. He held Makepeace's steady gaze with his own but couldn't read it; and the DCS wasn't saying anything. 'The man who placed the first get away car was nicked only because the prat had left a union card in the car'. The sergeant suspected he wasn't getting anywhere and stopped talking.

For several moments the men stared at each other until the DCS asked 'Is this a matter you want pushed upstairs, sergeant?'

'No sir'. Fountain was unexpectedly relieved. 'It's off my chest; I wanted you know my view about the way things are being done at this station'.

Makepeace inclined his head. 'Am I to leave it there?'.

Fountain thought he got the end game of the interview and stood. 'Thank you for listening to me, sir. Maybe I'm getting the wrong slant on the picture'.

'Maybe so, sergeant. But thank you for sharing your view with me'.

*

With the sergeant gone Makepeace eased back in his comfortable chair and did a mental comparison of Masters' methods and his own in his younger years. He smiled at one point, recalling the many occasions he had taken the advice of his senior CID officers and crossed the divide. The then and the now were moral frontiers he had adapted to easily. But the now was his to control and, being a detective chief superintendent, he accepted his responsibility to keep a steady ship. Masters and Miller had the propensity to sink the bloody thing. Miller especially, he reminded himself, the belt issue floating into his mind.

*

Janet was very excited. She was on a visit and Charlie slipped her three names to give to Don.

'They're the team that kidnapped Alfie George!' he told her, all excited, she could see. He wanted to reach out and tough her hand but saw the screw hovering. Whispering now he said 'Have a meet with Don. Tell 'im'.

She promised she would but of more importance was her Charlie. 'Be careful darling' she whispered. 'These men you're in wiv. They could 'urt you if they found out, like'.

'Nah. I'll be okay. Careful I am. Stop worrying'.

Their time together had already slipped away and Charlie had filed out with all the other inmates and Janet, worried for him all the way back to the railway station, made up her mind to ask Masters to get Charlie out.

*

Holding her cup of milky coffee she spotted Masters through the café window and waved. Smiling, he waved as he entered and crossed to the counter to buy his mug of coffee before wandering over to sit opposite her. He gave her a friendly smile and liked what he saw. 'Like the outfit, Janet. Very sexy'.

She lowered her head but was pleased he had noticed. She had spent more time than usual that morning doing her face and hair and choosing the short straight black skirt and matching top he had admired the last time. The silk stockings, held up by garters and a suspender Charlie reckoned were sexy, set off the whole ensemble and she knew, after a few twirls in front of her mirror, that she looked stunning. She knew Charlie's preference was rolling them down her legs as the beginning of his foreplay, which ended with him licking her legs all the way to the top. She shivered at the revived memory She hadn't thought deeply about her feelings for the detective inspector but her feminine yearnings were awakened when she looked across at his handsome, lean features, her imagination doing the rest.

'So, Janet. What has Charlie got for me?' Masters asked, completely unaware she was aroused.

She reached across the table and took his hand, placing a piece of paper in it, yearning for him to say something, to squeeze her hand, anything............

Masters again failed to recognise her arousal and took her hand, feeling her warmth, but his imagination was captivated by the previous sight of her stockinged, slim thighs.

'Those blokes are the ones wot done for Alfie' she told him when he was reading the note. 'And Charlie says to tell you there's no doubt'. She held onto his hand 'You're listening aren't you Don?'

He was, but her beauty and his growing lust was making it difficult to take in what she was saying. Dragging his thoughts from the carnal images he had conjured up he leaned forward, making a point of truly listening. 'Carry on, Janet. Of course I am'.

'I get me names mixed up but I fink this's right: Gloria shot Alfie and those blokes took him to a factory in North Pickington...or was it Pickenham? Anyway, Don, that's in Norfolk Charlie reckons. there's a bloody great mincer thing there that chopped Alfie into tiny bits'. Well into the delight at relating the gory tale she added: 'an' 'e was cooked!'.

Masters looked at her smiling, lovely face and wondered what she must have experienced for such an horrific tale to have no apparent effect upon her. He already knew most of the tale from Charlie himself, but the three men were knew to him. 'I'd better be getting back, Janet'. Standing, he looked down at her. On impulse he told her 'You're truly stunning, Janet. You should be proud of yourself. Charlie's a very lucky man to have you in his life'.

Getting up she smiled, pleased that he had noticed her in that way. 'Ta, Don' she said coyly. On an impulse she asked him to drive her to her flat.

'Love to, Janet'.

*

It took a couple of days before CRO sent the files of the three men to Masters. He and Dusty were reading through them. Joseph Keel aged 30, Ronald Jackson aged 41 and Derek Stockhart aged 44 had conviction going back to their youth. Jackson and Stockhart were cross referenced for a blagging job they'd been pulled for two years back. A £20,000 wages snatch on the outskirts of Croydon. "A three man job -driver and two with shotguns -no shots fired. Driver and guard beaten. No charges brought". The entry was clinical in it's brevity but to Masters and Miller very informative indeed and they fitted the bill for Alfie's demise. All three men were London villains who were, if Charlie had got his info right, for hire to the right person and firmed up with a flying squad team.

'Shall I bell Plumstead nick, Don? Check if they're still at these addresses?'

Masters had been mulling over just that point. He shook his head. 'Our job, I think Dusty. There's sod all on their files that says they're still active. I don't believe it. These blaggards are always at it. Why nothing for two years on their files? No' He studied Miller's reaction 'Dodgy that. What d'you think?'

Miller got the drift. 'Possibility guv I agree. We do it then?'

Masters grinned, pleased that another enquiry had opened up. 'I think you and I can handle it'.

*

With their enquiries showing that Jackson and Stockhart ran transit vans the detectives' interest was in a Rover car owned by Joe Keel garaged at the back of No.38 Westgate Street, close to the Blackwall tunnel. Dave Watson, a 25 year old villain on Masters' payroll, carrying a small holdall, was dropped off soon after midnight by the DI close to the street and walked the rest of the way to the garage. Several curtained windows were lit up but he wasn't troubled. Number 38 was in darkness. He walked around the back of the terraced houses to the garage block, his target one of a block of six. With nobody about at 1am that morning, armed with a pair of bolt croppers he snipped off the lock at the bottom of the door and pulled the up and over door open. He opened the driver's door and, squeezing between it and the wall, he slid into the driving seat and placed his powerful torch on the passenger seat, angling the beam at the dash board. Working quickly he deftly cross wired the ignition and the engine sprang into life. Having backed the car out he drove towards the Blackwall tunnel and, once east side, headed for Canning Town and the target car park which he knew was beside a cinema. He drove at a steady 30 miles per hour, which the detective had stipulated, located the car park, and drove to the far corner, where he removed his wiring, stopping the engine. As per his instructions he walked away and caught a taxi.

The DI and Miller, watching the car's arrival, climbed out of the Jaguar and walked across the almost empty car park and gave the Rover the once over. 'Let's get started', Masters said quietly, as he reached for his radio.

It had been a long night for the detectives. By now it was 4am and they stood in the large garage at divisional headquarters watching the fingerprint and scenes of crime officers at work on the Rover. The detectives left them to it and drifted to the canteen for a cuppa and a cigarette. By 7am the job was completed and the expectant detectives left to begin the waiting game for corroborating evidence of Alfie's route to his minced fragmentation.

*

'Some bastard's had my frigging car away!'. Joe Keel was not a happy bunnie as he stood with his missus staring at the empty hole. 'If I lay me hands on the bastard I'll scrag 'im'.

'Wot d'you reckon, love?'. Doris wasn't into cars but she was shrewdly working on the idea that Joe had pissed somebody off. 'You must 'ave some idea?'.

'Wot d'you mean wot do I reckon?. I haven't a bleeding clue why some toe rag 'alf inched it'.

'Call the old bill, love' she urged. 'Fink of the bleeding insurance'.

Keel nodded at that but his anger had stopped his brain from working rationally. On the walk back to the house his brain engaged. 'You know wot I fink? I reckon a firm is setting up a blag and my car figures in it!'

Doris saw the danger to her man and tugged at his arm 'Let's get home and give the old bill a bell, love. I aint having you mixed up in some uvver firm's blagging. Not right that aint'.

DCS Makepeace was casting his suspicious eyes at the two detectives, resenting their bloody nerve for dragging him into yet another of their scams. He had heard it all before. This one was a variation on a Masters theme of catch 'em and do it to 'em before they do it to someone else. He held his tongue until the end of the tale and then looked from Miller to Masters and back again.

'This is unbelievable!. You expect me to swallow your story that a nameless chappie bells you and bingo, we have the car and the men who carried Alfie away! For Christ's sake, Don. Enough is enough!'.

Masters years of experience was controlling his expression as he gazed serenely back at Makepeace before turning to Miller and smiling 'Fag, Dusty?'. He held out his packet.

'Ta'. Equally nonchalant, Miller took one and lit up.

'Look at the pair of you!' Makepeace was doing his best to keep his disbelief under control. 'Alright. I've listened. Now then: how strong is the evidence Alfie was in that car?'

'One hundred per cent, sir'.

'So what does that prove? He could have been in the bloody thing at any time'.

"Fraid not, sir. We've checked with Betty, that's his wife. Alfie's firm would rather push Keel under a bus than help him. We're on firm ground there'.

Makepeace nudged a report on his desk 'He reported it stolen it says. Nicked out of a locked garage it says'. His stare was fixed on Masters 'You know what I'm thinking don't you'.

'Sir?'

Makepeace was leaning forward, thrusting his angry face at the DI. 'If I ever find out you did this

I'll, I'll'............. words failed him. 'Just get on with it. But do it right for God's sake!'.

*

Briefed by Janet, Charlie got on board with Les Peel as often as possible. Slagging off the old bill was always good for an introduction and it worked for Charlie, helping him join Les's small group of landing associates. Probably because he was that much younger they took to him. Most people did. Charlie had that way about him: always ready with a quip and a cheeky grin; if you were down he'd lift you. A gift in a way; and Charlie listened avidly when Peel often relived the tale of the two murders and his anger against Alfie, the brother of Bert George he wanted his listeners to know. His temper was kept on the boil by Charlie's eager questioning. 'Friggingwell deserved to be topped' Charlie opined many times as the story got retold. Les was grateful to Charlie for that understanding opinion. Seemingly casually our Charlie plugged away at Les, at one time suggesting the blood and brains must have taken a hell of a lot of scrubbing to get rid of? Still there, Les reckoned. Gloria and Kathy done the job in the basement of an unoccupied house in East Ham. Bit risky that, Charlie reckoned, because you never know who would move in do you? True, a relaxed Les agreed.

"Friend's house?" Charlie supposed and got a nod and Vincent Paul's name.

*

Vincent Paul, Masters had been pleased to find out, was doing a two year stretch for receiving and his address at the time of his incarceration was 108, Firth Street, East Ham. With scenes of crime investigators brought along to help, Masters ensured a thorough search for evidence that Alfie and the abductors had been there.

Somebody or something had lost a lot of blood and bits of bone in the basement; a tipped over chair, lengths of adhesive tape and a roll of that tape were on the floor. Charlie's information had been spot on.

Masters came away satisfied the search was going to establish Alfie's route from the pub to the rendering plant in Norfolk.

*

Joe Keel's Rover had turned up the fingerprints of Alfie and the other two. The basement of the East Ham house had turned up the dabs of Alfie, Keel and Jackson; the jemmied rear door Stockhart's prints. Among the many unidentified prints Masters was hoping they had the prints of Kathy Peel and Gloria Gardner.

All this information and speculation was on the table when Masters was sitting across from Makepeace running through the options open to the investigation. He favoured a prison visit to question Paul. 'We must be sure that none of the fingers had lawful access to the East Ham house. With the right approach I feel certain we'll get the truth out of Paul, sir'.

'Right approach, inspector?'

For God's sake man, the DI thought angrily but said instead. 'Straightforward questions to get straightforward answers, sir'.

Irritated but mollified the DCS agreed. 'You have my authority to set up a prison meet with Paul' he confirmed.'What are your intentions about these alleged abductors?'

'I have to wait. Until Paul's been seen we can't bring them in. On it's own the car evidence may not be enough. With the right barrister the car evidence can be rubbished on various grounds, you know: "who keeps a record of who gets into a car" sort of defence. But tied to the house evidence I've got the bastards. As I said, sir, presuming Paul hasn't been got at I feel sure I can get them on a murder charge'.

Chapter twenty six

'Put up Jakeson'.

'Up we go son' said the elderly warder, nudging Jakeson up the steps towards the dock of court four at the Old Bailey.

Still handcuffed to the warder lagging behind he shuffled into position and stared around the court for familiar faces, clocking Lindley's. Then he looked at the impassive face of the judge and waited. It didn't take long.

'Jakeson. The jury unanimously found you guilty of the premeditated murder of Mark Bateman. You will go to prison for life. My recommendation is that you serve a minimum of 25 years. Take him down'.

His co-murderer, Bill Williams, listened to the the judge who was saying: '....... I have taken into account the jury found no evidence that you assisted in the murder of Mark Bateman. They quite properly found you guilty of being an accessory to that murder. For that crime you will go to prison for life with my recommendation that you serve a minimum of fifteen years. Take him down'.

*

Vincent Paul, a well built product of the local weight lifting club, has scraped a living odd-jobbing on building sites and packing boxes in factories. He was forty when he went down six months previously on a two year stretch for receiving copper piping stolen from his last building site job. He had nicked the stuff himself and stashed it, lorry and all, in a mate's yard he'd rented, but resisted the old bill's attempt to knock a confession out of him but, lacking the readies to buy his way out, he had to settle for a spell inside. Prior to the copper pipe job Vincent had followed a path villainous youngsters of his generation had chosen and spent time in remand homes, remand centres and prison. The two year sentence was water off a duck's back.

The detectives sat opposite him in a small room on a pre-arranged visit at Pentonville and Paul, dumped in the room by a surly warder, stared at Masters and Miller. He gestured to the cigarette packet Miller was twiddling with. Wearing a broad smile he quipped: 'do with one of them I could'.

His grin was infectious and in spite of himself Miller grinned and slid the packet across the table. 'Keep it'. he said, and waited patiently when one was shaken out and lit from Miller's offered lighter.

The detectives lit up themselves and blew smoke and watched Paul who was by then relaxed and glancing around the sparsely furnished windowless room.

'Had your house long, Vincent?' the DI asked.

'Nah. Couple of years. Got it cheap. Why you asking?'.

'I'll get to that. How come it was cheap?'

'Derelict wasn't it. Me and me mates sorted it'.

Masters nodded. 'Did a good job'.

'Been there 'ave you?' Paul's surprise was obvious 'Why d'you go there?'

Masters hunched forward and bridged his hands. 'Routine stuff. A neighbour reported a break in. No sign of damage -not tipped up; a tidy job. Considerate that! You know how toe rags are. Any ideas?'

'That why you're here is it?'

Masters nodded and took time stubbing out his dog end. 'Yes. Have you arranged for someone to look after the place while you're in here?'

Paul shook his head 'Can't trust no one these days

can you!'. He was grinning again.

'True. Very true. So nobody has your permission to go in, or rent the place?'

'Course not'. His brain had obviously worked on the line of chat and suspicion clouded his face. 'There's something you're not telling me aint there?' The detectives' changed expressions was confirming his doubts. 'What's the score?'

'The body in the basement, Vincent'.

A shocked Paul was instantly half way out of his chair. 'I'm being fitted up aint I! What frigging body?'.

Miller, sensing likely trouble, had moved quickly around the table and, his hands firmly on Price's shoulders, pushed him back down again.

'No fit up, Vincent. Just listen'. the DI tapped the packet on the table. 'Have another one. Help yourself'.

With Miller still behind him Paul did and lit up with a shaky hand.

'Okay?'

Masters got a nod.

'Your basement was used to execute a bloke, which puts you right in the frame...............'

Paul broke into Masters explanation 'Execute! Hang on a minute! I'm stuck in here and you're going on about a body in the frigging basement. Do me a favour!.

'It's a fact, me old mate. Shot through the head. Brains everywhere'.

Paul, about to get out of his chair but restrained by Miller, said angrily 'When was all this? I've been in here six months'.

Masters told him. 'Which makes you a very lucky man. However' he stared into the eyes of the other man 'Accessory to murder is on the cards'. Paul started to speak but the detective held up hand 'Answers to a few questions can sort that'. He read out the names of the suspected abductors. 'And the shot man was Alfie George. Know any of them?'

'No'.

'Gloria Gardner -know her?'

'Yeh. Met 'er and 'er old man a few times'.

'Been to your drum?'

'Nah'.

'A statement'll sort out your problems, Vincent. My boss reckons that. Do that shall we?'

*

Joe Keel's suspicion his car was stashed away for an upcoming blag lurked in his troubled thoughts. The local CID and the flying squad team he was on board with hadn't helped, which pissed him off, considering the dosh that had changed hands over the past couple of years. Doris was more concerned about the insurance claim.

'The bloke they sent down to deal with the theft was bloody rude', she told Joe. 'Got the idea, I did, that he fought we was up to somefink'.

A couple of evenings after the car got nicked Joe was down the local with his murderous mates Ron and Derek sinking a few pints. Ron mentioned the car and suggested how it was queer it got 'alf inched out of a locked garage. 'What tea leaf after a car'd do it that way, Joe?'. A couple of pints later the car was still the main topic.

'You don't think the old bill are up to tricks do ya Joe?' suggested Derek.

Joe had an alarming thought when that was said. 'You mean..........doing for Alfie?'. Until Derek mentioned the old bill the thought hadn't entered his head.

'It's on the cards, Joe. Those bastards never give up

do they'.

*

Kathy, Gloria and Doris were having a girls' night out down at their favourite watering-hole sipping vodka and lime and mulling over Joe's concern the police were sniffing into Alfie's disappearance. Gloria suggested they pop over to East Ham and have a word or two with neighbours of Paul. If the theft of the car was in some way connected with Alfie and the old bill had been to the house, it would point to the old bill making the connection, Gloria reckoned.

'But why? What's gone wrong? Why would the old bill be sniffing about?' Doris was looking from one to the other for the answer, worried that Joe was in the frame for something.

Gloria shared a quick look with Kathy before asking Doris, 'Joe not told you?'

'Told me what?'

Gloria reached for Doris's hand 'Him, Ron and Derek kidnapped Alfie George from a pub'.

'Oh my God!. Doris's blood ran cold as she stared at two very calm women 'And...and...was he in on the killing?'

'Keep your voice down, Doris' Kathy warned . 'Me, Gloria, your old man, Ron and Derek, we all did it'.

Doris looked ready to faint. After a while and some swigs of her vodka and a top up and a fag she'd recovered sufficiently to ask 'The car........it was Joe's car wasn't it?'

Both women nodded.

Doris downed her drink in one go, shuddering as she put the glass down and, forgetting the one in the ash tray, reached for her fag packet again.

'you've got one on the go, Doris', Gloria reminded

her.

'I can't think straight' Doris said after she'd lit up from the old and filled the air with smoke..

Kathy took command 'East Ham is it?'

The following afternoon with Gloria driving Mel's Ford Zephyr, the three women drove to East Ham and parked down from 108.

'Now what?' Doris asked while the other two sat silent staring down the long road, wondering........

*

Door to door police enquiries in Firth Street, East Ham, had turned up a sighting of a Rover car, dark colour, "but it may have been a trick of the street light" stopping outside 108 on the evening of Alfie's abduction. The witness, a Mrs. Joan Rivers who lived at No.105 nearly opposite was sure of the make of the car because it was the same as her husband's previous one. She remembered the time because her daughter came home at the same time and got into an argument with her on the doorstep just as the car arrived. One man got out and disappeared round the side of the house. When he came back two others got out and carried what looked like a rolled carpet and went round the side of the house as well. She remembered the time because the ten o'clock evening news was on. Her daughter, not into TV news, agreed because of their row it had been somewhere around ten.

The woman who lived next door at 110 Firth Street, Mrs. Mavis Smith, remembered a car being there when she came home from bingo around 10pm that same evening. She couldn't say what its make was because another car, she believed it was a Ford Consul or Zephyr was parked behind it. She remembered the cars being there because nobody lived in the house.

*

Detective constable Ted Read took the call from Mrs Smith. From her tone he got the impression she was excited but she wasn't making sense.

'Next door, you must know!' she said impatiently.

'Where do you live?'

'110 Firth Street, East Ham'.

The penny dropped. 'Oh. Sorry about that. What about next door. Woman you said?'

Mavis Smith described Gloria to a T and told him she'd been there just that morning. 'Asking about 108 she was. I asked her if she was another detective and she said no like. She wanted to know where Vincent was'.

'Did she say that "Vincent"'.

'Dead right she did'.

'Make a note of the woman, Mrs. Smith. Write down all you can remember about her and what was said.. Did she have a car?

'Can't say to that'.

Thank you for the call', Ted told her, ' someone will call and see you'.

*

Masters and Ted Read kept an appointment at the offices of the Watton abattoir with the youthful company secretary, who confirmed the company owned a rendering factory at North Pickenham, operated by six men on two, three-man, twelve hour shifts. Questioned about the loader Janet had told Masters about, he confirmed one was necessary to load an auger. 'Can you tell me what your enquiry is about?'.

Masters kept it brief but even so the information shocked the secretary. 'We need to see for ourselves.

Can a visit be arranged today?'.

'Of course'. He broke off to smile at the young woman hovering in the open doorway and glanced to the detectives 'Coffee?'. Getting their nods he smiled and nodded to her.

'Thank you. Can you arrange a cover story: we don't want our enquiry bandied about'.

The secretary nodded. 'They're used to the Ministry calling at all hours. I'll fix you up with protective clothing -you'll need it I assure you'. He reached for the phone and spoke for a few moments. Putting the receiver down he told them he would get someone to take them across to the store.

'One more thing' Masters asked 'Can you find out who was the loader on this particular night shift, and confirm if he is presently in employment at the factory?'. He pushed a note across the desk.

'No trouble at all. When you're finished at the factory give me a ring. I should have that information by then' He shook the hands of the detectives and smiled 'What should I say...........good luck I suppose?'.

*

The two officers spent a grisly hour being shown the workings of the factory and were able to visualise Alfie's passage through the massive wormed augered mincing machine that would have fed his remains to the cooker. In the yard they witnessed at first hand the loading shovel at work; and an overalled man shoving drainage rods down a drain. The smell of the wispy steam from the chimney was indescribable. When he was satisfied they'd seen enough they handed over their protective clothing and Masters rang through to the company secretary and got the information he needed. By late afternoon the same day, having shown their warrant cards, Don and Ted took the bull by the horns and were sitting across from Barry Sheenan, the machine operator on the night in question, in his cottage a few miles from the factory. From his body language it was obvious he was clearly worried.

Masters didn't waste time on preliminaries. 'I'll get straight to why we're here, Mr. Sheenan. We know that you helped men from London dispose of a man's body at the North Pickenham factory. We could arrest you right now but we're prepared to hear your explanation. Have you anything you want to tell us?'

Sheenan clasped his hands, licked his lips, and looked from one officer to the other. He was completely out of his depth having never been spoken to by a police officer before.

Masters wasn't going to give him an opportunity to think his way out. Standing now he demanded 'Well?'

With his mouth dry and tears welling in his eyes Sheenan was overwhelmed by guilt and wishing his wife was there. 'He.......the man said.......he said, the man died in a fight'. He stared at the detectives for understanding. 'The man was dead. He was! His head.........it.........it was, it wasn't all there'.

'What were you asked to do?'

'Get rid of the body'.

'Did you?'

'Yes. I shovelled him into the auger. I'm in trouble aren't I?', he added, his naivety painful to see.

'Did money change hands?'

Sheenan nodded. 'A hundred pounds. What happens now?' he asked in desperation, inwardly praying his wife wouldn't be long.

'Put the kettle on. We could do with a cup of tea'. Masters suggested. 'We'll wait for your wife. Picking up the kids from school is she?'

Sheenan nodded and got up to go to the kitchen just

as his wife came in with their two little daughters. Seeing the officers she stopped and stared 'Who are you?'. Without waiting for an answer she stared at her shaken husband who had stopped when he heard her at the door.

'They're police officers, Audrey, love', he told her. 'Come and sit down'.

The detectives waited until Sheenan led his wife to the settee and sat beside her and stared up at them before skirting around the real reason for their presence. Looking kindly at the man's worried wife, Masters told her Barry had to go with them to Dereham police station 'to clear matters up', the DI added as he reached and patted her arm 'You're not to worry. When we've finished we'll pop him back here'. Masters angled his head at Sheenan and stepped to the door behind the man, with Ted following up.

In the police station Sheenan was glad that Ted was writing it down. Every since he'd pocketed the hundred pounds he had worried about what he had done. Keel and Jackson's faces were burned into his memory. Several nights since that evening he had woken in a cold sweat, his nightmare of Alfie sliding from his loader bucket into the hopper running on a continuing loop. 'Yes', he told Masters and Ted Read, 'he would certainly know the two men again'.

Twenty-seven

DCS. Makepeace was a contented man. Commander Stewart had praised him, impressed he had said by his ability to keep his team of detectives on their toes and get crimes solved. 'He actually said that', he told his wife. 'When he congratulated me he patted me on my back.'

Naturally, they knew the praise was merited; and his wife, dear Martha as he would refer to her when with his fellow senior officers, was overjoyed he was being recognised. She had always told him when he got a bit low that the promotion he yearned for would definitely come.

'He only told me I had done well, Martha'. He replied modestly.

'But from a commander, darling. I mean..........!'.

With the glow of recognition lifting his mood he was chairing a meeting with his CID officers, listening to Masters recap on the hunt for Alfie's killers, but from time to time slipping into reverie that had him at the Yard......... as a commander.................'So all in all' Masters was concluding, it's been a very successful enquiry. We've got enough to lift a few fingers and get the file together'.

*

Janet phoned Masters, an edge of worry in her voice. 'Charlie's in trouble, Don. He finks they're onto 'im. What can you do?'

'What has he told you?'

'It's Peel, Don. Charlie finks from the way he's going on he suspects him of grassing up the three blokes. Somefink to do wiv a car being nicked from a garage'.

Any names mentioned?'

The question didn't register in her troubled thoughts. 'You've got to do somefink for 'im, Don. You 'ave'.

'I will Janet, I promise you that'.

'Wot are you going to do?'

Masters recognised her fear and made a swift decision. 'Get him moved to another prison, if possible'

'Can you do that?

'I'll pull out the stops, Janet. You can let Charlie know that'.

*

With the murder enquiry underway and the urgency of getting Charlie moved to another prison uppermost in his mind, Masters was discussing the possibility of the move with Makepeace, who needed an assurance that Charlie was in danger where he was.

'He was the key to solving Alfie's murder, sir. And he's on the same landing as the husband of one of the killers. He's a good lad and he wants to help us. Without his help we wouldn't have known about the finger's he put up for the job, or the disposal of Alfie's body. I want to look after him, sir'.

Makepeace was impressed. He was seeing another side to Masters character; kindness not being a trait he had ever detected in the man.

'Very well. I'll get onto to it straight away'.

*

Janet was on a visit to Charlie and told him Masters was going to help get him moved to another prison. 'He's being real nice, Charlie. He finks a lot of you'.

'Where do you meet?'

'In that caff we go to. I give him a ring like you tell

me to and he comes over'.

'Good bloke that Don' Charlie reckoned . 'It's not his fault I'm in here. He warned me but I didn't listen did I'.

'You never told me how you met did you?' Curious, she stared at her lover.

'Met him from time to time like, but it started in a cell.....at the nick', he explained. Charlie chuckled. 'An eye opener that was'.

'How d'you mean?'

'Did a deal didn't I. He helped me at court -got me probation'.

'Wot sort of deal, Charlie?'

Charlie could see that Janet was dead curious so told her the truth. 'Did a housebreaking job for him'.

Her shocked expression made Charlie explain a bit more 'He knew some blokes were at it, you know, burglary. I got in wiv them and got them nicked'.

'Oh Charlie! How could you! Did you know them?'

'Yeh.............well, not at first'.

Dead curious now, she had to know the rest. 'What happened to them?'

'A couple of 'em got a few years. One got probation I fink'.

'Charlie. I'm more worried now'. She looked at the warder over by the door ' 'e can't hear can 'e?'

Charlie shook his head and squeezed her hand 'They don't know I set them up, sweetheart. You're the only one who knows, apart from Don that is. You mustn't worry'.

Janet's concern for Charlie was increasing when the explanation sank in. Her face now registering her fear for him she had to know more. 'What about these other blokes you've told Don about? Charlie, I'm scared for you. Last time I was 'ere you said you reckoned Peel, that's his name isn't it?'

Charlie nodded.

'You said you fought 'e was onto you'.

Charlie saw that the warder was heading their way and stood up. "Stop worrying .I'll write when I know my new prison, sweetheart', he whispered. ' Keep in tough wiv Don. Be friendly wiv 'im -we might need his 'elp one day'.

' 'ow d'you mean friendly, Charlie?'

' 'ave a meet now and again. I don't want 'im to forget about me stuck in here'.

*

From the tone of her voice Masters believed Charlie was still in trouble and drove quickly to the café and parked up nearby. Seeing him approach she waved through the window. Once inside he went straight to her table and sat opposite. 'What's wrong, Janet?', he scanned her troubled expression for an answer.

She reached across and took his hand and unburdened her fear for Charlie. 'Will it take long, Don, to get him moved?'

'Has something happened?'

She shook her head and told him everything Charlie had explained to her. 'Charlie wants me to keep in touch wiv you, Don. He's scared you'll forget 'im in that place'.

Masters smiled and reassured her Charlie would be looked after. 'Try not to worry. It won't be three years: he'll be out long before that'.

'Come back to my place, Don. It don't feel right wivout Charlie being there'.

The DI decided to leave his car where it was because it was only a ten minute walk. Janet held Don's hand tightly all the way until she opened the front door beside the chip shop.

'I don't like being on my own Don', she explained

when they were in her flat. ' Wivout Charlie it's not right. Stay a while, please. I'll put the kettle on. You'll stay for a cup of tea won't you?'. Without waiting for an answer she disappeared into the small kitchen. The DI looked around the sparsely furnished room and dropped into the settee as Janet came back with two cups and a sugar bowl on a tray and put in down on the small coffee table in front of the settee.

'Fanks for coming, Don.' She smiled at him. 'D'you mind if I sit beside you?'.

He shook his head and watched her arrange her smooth tight skirt. . It was short and had ridden up when she sat and Masters, in spite of himself, felt himself hardening at the sight of stockinged thighs and a button of her suspenders pressing against the material.

'Sugar, Don?'

He shook his head and accepted the cup she held out to him. She sipped from her cup and studied his face for what seemed to Don a long time. He took a few more sips and studied her's in return. 'I'd better go' he said suddenly as he put the cup down.

She put her cup down and reached for his hand. 'Please don't go, Don. Can't we be friends like Charlie wants. I'm so lonely here' she whispered, her confused mind conflating Charlie and Masters in her desire to be comforted.

'Janet. You don't understand what's happening here do you. I really ought to go, right now'. He released her hand and stood but she got up and pressed close to him and placed her head on his chest and her arms around his waist, her mind a confusion of images and desires.

Don hugged her and tried to ease away but she clung to him and raised her face and kissed him. Masters responded and their kiss became passionate until Janet broke away and led him to the bedroom. Aroused, she stepped out of her skirt, pulled off the tight top and laid back on the bed with her arms outstretched to him.

The DI stared down at the invitation that was sending an urgent message to his groin. The temptation was irresistible. He moved to the side of the bed and leaned down to kiss her tenderly.

'Come to bed' she whispered, knowing it was Don but wanting it to be Charlie seeing her wriggle on the bed as she removed her bra, suspenders, stockings and knickers and offer her welcome with outstretched arms.

Masters stripped off and at first laid beside her, her arms sliding around him, pulling him close.

'I need you Don' she whispered. 'I need you so much'. Her desire for Charlie's love was transferred to Don in the ecstasy of the moment and she yearned to be caressed and held in a loving embrace again. She closed her eyes and experienced his warmth and shivered when his hands caressed her body. 'Make love to me', she whispered.

Don eased himself on top and immediately experienced the exquisite feeling of her supple slenderness while he guided his penis inside and eased his hands under her body, pulling her tightly to him and thrust, slowly at first but more quickly when his movements brought a thrusting response against his body.

A fulfilling desire enveloped her body and she clung to him, murmuring her pleasure, whispering Charlie's name. He slowed, enthralled at her passion and not wanting to go until she was ready for him. She too moved more slowly now and Don, holding tightly to her and sensing it was time, let himself go, his and her climax coinciding and he continued to thrust, not wanting the moment to end until, still inside her and still on top, he kissed her and propped himself up to gaze at her rapt expression, her eyes still closed and her hands caressing his body.

'Oh, Charlie. That was so wonderful' she breathed into his ear when they were side by side, his hands caressing her slender body until he reached and held her face and kissed her tenderly. 'You're a truly lovely young woman, Janet' he said. He understood her desire for it to have been Charlie and smiled, letting go to tickle her nose. 'Now, I really must go'.

'Do it again Don, please.....'

He turned onto his back and Janet eagerly slid on top and held his hardening penis and put it in, moving forward and down as she did so 'Don. Oh Don! That's.......**so**.........**beautiful!**' she gasped as she fulfilled herself again and continued to move slowly against him until she felt his erection slackening. Easing herself away she moved to lay beside him, reliving the ecstasy of fulfilment.

Masters cupped her head and kissed her tenderly and smiled. 'I really must go, Janet. I really must'. He slid from the bed and slowly dressed, looking down at her beautiful body, her half-closed eyes, and the smile that said it all. She opened her eyes and watched him finish dressing and stayed motionless in her nakedness. 'Can we do that again soon, Don?', she whispered, her longing for Charlie slipping from her consciousness..

Dressed now he sat on the edge of the bed and took one of her hands 'You are taking precautions aren't you, Janet'

'Course. Charlie wanted me to'.

Shouldn't we be thinking about Charlie now?' He was smiling but the thought was there, and the complications it might bring.

'I fink about him all the time but he's going to be gone a long time, Don. We will do it again, won't we?'.

He squeezed her hand 'I understand, Janet, I really do. Maybe we can'.

'I'd like that. It won't be too long will it?' She was squeezing his hands between hers now and looking longingly at him.

'We'll see'.

*

The investigation into Alfie's abduction and murder had resulted in Masters' comprehensive file of evidence being submitted to the Director of Public Prosecutions. The covering report included his opinion, backed by that of Makepeace, that each suspect should be arrested forthwith on a holding charge of abduction until a decision by the DPS relative to a murder charge was taken.

Two weeks later, acting on that decision, the operation to coordinate the arrest of the two women and the three men for Alfie's abduction and murder was under way. It was arranged that simultaneous raids at their homes at 6am that day would take place to arrest them. Masters wanted each suspect to be detained at a police station close to the arrested person's home to ensure they were denied the opportunity to get stories straight. Apart from the formal arrest procedure the suspects were not to be questioned; nor allowed a solicitor unless sanctioned by Masters. Procedures for arraignment before a court for remand procedures would be undertaken by a CPS barrister.

*

Slim 45 year old Gloria Gardner was naked in bed when she heard the front door being battered in and was trying to cover her modesty when a burly detective entered the bedroom, yanked the sheet away, told her she was nicked, and dragged her to her feet. The police woman who had followed him in picked up knickers and a bra from the floor and threw them at her, and watched her put them on. Too stunned to speak Gloria had pointed to clothes on a chair near the bed and watched the police woman pick them up and throw them at her as well. The detective waited until she had donned them before cuffing and hauling her unceremoniously down the stairs and out the door, pushing her into the back of the police car. The waiting SOCO team traipsed into the house and started their scientific examination.

*

Kathy Peel was similarly taken by surprise. More modest than Gloria the 46 year old was clad in a nightdress when she was hauled out of her bed. The bellowed 'you're nicked' was followed swiftly by an order to get dressed, which meant her modesty was compromised by the ogling man watching her shed the nightdress to stand naked while the accompanying police woman searched around for clothing. Dressed, cuffed and hauled down the stairs just like Gloria, she was shoved onto the back seat of the police car and driven off, leaving another SOCO team to do its work.

*

Joe Keel, Ron Jackson and Derek Stockhart got the well rehearsed treatment dished out by the Sweeney. Just as the women were taken by surprise so were they. The squads didn't muck around with villains. Front doors were hammered in and guns were in hands when they raced up stairs and bedroom doors were kicked open. The men's surprise at the suddenness of it all was swiftly followed by the pain of arm wrenching and body thumping before handcuffs were in place and they were dragged down the stairs and whisked away, leaving a stunned Doris and the other two wives frightened for their man's safety.

*

Shortly after 7.30am Masters was informed by each team of detectives the suspects had been detained, charged with abduction, and the addresses were being searched.

Masters had Gloria brought to Walthamstead police station for her grilling. He and a female detective sat side by side at the desk and Miller by a wall. Gloria's chair was opposite to the detectives' beside a chair for her solicitor.

The long night in the cell and the absence of Kathy Peel had undermined her resolve to face out the interrogation she knew was to come. Staring into the hard unsmiling face of Masters, and the coldness of the female officer, a bit more of the resolve drained away. She watched the detective turning pages, occasionally, as the seconds ticked away, catching his eyes when he looked towards her. Miller crossing his legs caught her attention and she stared into his granite-like, sneering face. Her gaze now back on the DI she saw he had stopped turning pages and had bridged his hands under his chin and was studying her.

He was finding it difficult to imagine her as the cold blooded killer of Alfie. With the totality of the evidence against her, answers weren't necessary but a confession helped.

'Mrs. Gardner.' he began with. ' Shall we dispense with the surname?'

'Suit yourself'.

'Gloria then. I want to make it crystal clear why you

have been arrested. We know that you and others kidnapped and murdered Alfie George. We also know what you did with his body. The arresting officer would have cautioned you and explained to you that you did not have to say anything to him. Is that so?'

She shrugged an acknowledgement.

Masters glanced towards her solicitor, who inclined his head.

'Gloria. Will I be wasting my time talking to you?'

'Depends'.

'Would you like a tea or coffee?'

Surprised, she nodded. 'Coffee. Black, no sugar'.

Masters glanced to her solicitor 'What would you like?'

He smiled back and said a black coffee would do fine.

The detective waited for the cups to arrive and each had taken a sip or two before going ahead with the interview. 'Gloria', he began 'We can end this here and now if you wish. Take advice.......' he gestured to the solicitor 'before answering any questions'.

She looked at her solicitor.

'Listen to what he has to say Mrs. Gardner' he advised.

Masters outlined the case against her and her accomplices starting with Alfie being lured from the pub and taken to 108 First Street, East Ham, where he was shot and his body taken in a body bag to the rendering factory at North Pickenham. 'We have evidence that you were in the basement of 108, Firth Street at the time of the murder; and that you went back there after the murder making enquiries'. He paused to look at her reaction before adding 'Gloria, we have the gun you used to shoot Alfie and hid in your attic. Do you want to say anything to me? You don't have to say anything at all'.

Gloria turned to the lawyer 'What should I do?'

The solicitor looked at Masters for a few seconds before answering Gloria, but directed his comments at the officers. 'I am advising my client to say nothing at this stage. This is a very serious charge and one which, I believe, invokes the need for considered thought'.

Gloria was nodding and said when he had finished 'No comment then'.

Despite the apparent weight of evidence against her Kathy Peel too took the same line and Masters, she told him, could stuff himself. 'I'll take my bleeding chance in front of a jury, thank you very much'.

It was much the same with Joe Keel: he was heavily into swearing and his hatred for the filth shone through his every utterance. Ron Jackson and Derek Stockhart listened and 'no commented' everything Masters put to them.

With them banged up Masters was later able to enjoy a pint with Miller and toast their success and think about Janet and their lovemaking; and Charlie; who would soon be tucked up in his new prison.

*

It was two months since his parole and Reg Bruce was working part time as barman in a local pub frequented from time to time by members of the CID. Kay, on this particular evening, was perched on a stool at the bar when she spotted Don Masters in the adjoining bar with detective sergeant Miller. Gesturing to her husband she pointed Masters out. 'Just so you know' she said icily, not really knowing why she did that but possibly because she was four months pregnant and angry, very angry, with Masters for putting her in the club. Her periods had initially been irregular but then stopped altogether. She had presumed she was experiencing the change of life but, even so, she blamed herself for leaving it late to confirm the pregnancy. It was too late for an abortion but a baby was not an option and the detective she was staring at with hate in her heart was going to suffer for her condition

*

Jean Masters was confident of her relationship with Don. Since his confession he had been loving and attentive and the Don she had married. He had mentioned she was losing weight, but she brusquely brushed that away for fear he would ask the questions she didn't want to hear, which would open her mind to the reality she was suppressing. Her doctor had only that day confidently said that the chemo was working. Her breathlessness, he told her, was most likely the asthma he had mentioned weeks before. Jean understood what a drain Don's job was. Many a time she marvelled that he was able to make love at all what with all that the job threw at him. Her Don was perfect in every way. She had pushed thoughts of Kay into the dark recesses and knew he would never let her down again. But her pain and her breathlessness was worrying.

*

'Oh Don!'. Janet was experiencing moments of pure ecstasy as he pushed inside her again and again.
   'Oh Don', she whispered. 'That was so...........**beautiful**!'. Fulfilled and loving every second she clung to him, not wanting him to stop. With nature setting the pace and slackening his erection she giggled and kissed him and eased herself from him and snuggled beside him, nestling her head on his chest.

'Fanks Don for coming over. I Don't know wot I'd do if you didn't.' She peered up into his face and asked about Charlie 'When will 'e move, Don?' she pleaded.

Masters eased away from her to think. 'Any time now, Janet, I promise you'. Knowing that Charlie's relocation was taking place that week to Pentonville Prison he added reassuringly 'You'll be able to visit him more easily'.

She leaned over him and took his cigarette packet and shook one out for herself and one for him. Don lit his and she lit hers from his glowing end. 'I'm so happy now Don'. She leaned across again and kissed him tenderly, her expression a reflection of her contentment at their togetherness.

He contemplated the spidery-meandering- cracked ceiling which, he thought, when he slid to the edge of the bed, tended to mirror the way his life was heading.. 'I'm pleased for you Janet' he said absently, but his mind was trying to unravel its tortuous path and to imagine its ending. Shaking his head at the worrying train of thought he smiled and said 'Promise me you won't start using perfume when we're together, Janet'.

'I promise, Don'.

*

Twenty eight

Reg rolled off Kay and patted her stomach. 'Putting on a bit weight, Kay', he said bravely but nastily, remembering how slim she had been when he got nicked. He reached for his fags and offered her one and got no reaction. Lighting up he worked himself into a sitting position and looked across at her. 'So tell me', he said even more bravely now 'How come you let that copper put you in the club'?

The question hit home and Kay turned her unblinking gaze on him, watching him smirk and drag on his fag. Without a word she got up from the bed and again stared at him while she donned her usual dressing gown, keeping her cold gaze on him until suddenly turning and stalking from the room.

Reg watched her leave and smirked again. Dotting his fag end, he eased himself down under the covers, pleased with himself for getting a reaction from her, but oblivious to the likely consequences of his rash words.

She guessed what he would do and left him alone for a while. Standing now in the kitchen she stared at the saucepans, each on a hook suspended from a pine support beneath the ceiling. The bastard, she recollected, had bought them years before because he said her cooking was "fucking rubbish". She snatched one off it's hook and hefted it, raising and lowering it, testing her grip, remembering those earlier words which, now that they were sitting there in her consciousness, had to be assuaged. Not a one to leave matters unresolved she strode back into the bedroom and stared down at the slumbering body of a man she hated.. Balancing herself, she practised two swings at his head before, raising the saucepan above her head and, with all the force she could muster, brought it down on his head and felt a satisfying judder up her arm when metal hit bone.

The shock of the blow brought him out of his slumber just in time to parry the descending saucepan a second time and try to fight her off. He got a grip on the hand holding the saucepan and with his other hand punched her in the face, swearing at her as he battered away. Kay wrestled free of his weakening grip and managed to land two more blows on his head until, satisfied, and dropping the saucepan, she stared down at her battered, groaning husband. Flooded with joy of a job well done she turned away from the bed, unaware that Reg was hauling himself up until she felt the tight grip of his fingers on her shoulders. She tried to break free but he managed to spin her around and rain punches on her stomach, each punch weaker than the last as the adrenalin pumping through him was diminishing but, still having some left, he managed to drag her to the bed and inch her onto it. He punched her pregnant stomach several more times before, weak from the blows to his head, he flopped on the bed beside her and looked at the result of his temper unaware, as he began to slip into unconsciousness, that the saucepan had fractured his skull.

*

The ambulance chappies, alerted by the worried neighbour in the flat below, and allowed in by Kay, were staring down at Reg, who was clearly unconscious. 'What happened here?' one of them asked Kay, whose face was hidden behind the hand towel she was using to stem the blood dripping from her battered nose.

She gestured to the saucepan on the floor 'I hit him with that'. Looking decidedly fragile she turned away and tottered to the bathroom to clean up.

The men looked at each other in disbelief. 'What d'you reckon. Police'? One queried

'Definitely' his mate reckoned.

Turning their attention to the slumbering man they worked him into a neck support and onto a stretcher. When they were on the landing they saw through the open bathroom door that Kay was vomiting into the loo. 'Let's get him in the ambulance. I'll sort him out while you nip back for her. I reckon she needs the once over',

*

Charlie once again made new friends quickly. In Pentonville he had regained his composure and confidence and put himself about and became an eager recipient of the prison grapevine that reckoned a new inmate, Jakeson, had a score to settle with the flying squad; and another bloke on his landing was running on about a copper called Masters. Charlie did the usual and got the bloke's monicker and realised at meal times he was sitting close to one of the three blokes who'd done for Alfie. Biding his time it took several days before Charlie was sitting beside Ron Jackson and hearing from him what a prat Masters was. A patient Charlie heard that this frigging dick of a detective inspector reckoned on having Ron bang to rights on fingerprint evidence.

*

When Kay woke up she was in a recovery room with the fuzzy face of a nurse becoming clearer. 'What's happened to me' she croaked.

'You've had an operation, Mrs. Bruce. You're fine.

You've nothing to worry about'. The nurse fussed with the sheet and plumped the pillow. 'There. How does that feel?'.

'Operation? What for?'

'I'll get the doctor. It's best he explains the procedure'.

Kay became aware that her stomach was hurting and gently ran a hand over it and let it lie there. Her bump had gone!

*

Reg was in a bad way. The blows from the saucepan, taken one at a time wouldn't have done much damage but Kay had expertly, or most likely by chance because it was a first time for her, managed to hit the same spot each time. They had caved in his skull and the fractured bone was bearing on the brain of the poor sod, as Masters said to Miller when he was reflecting on the diagnosis. The surgeon carrying out the emergency operation had told him he was wasting his time. "Come back in a week's time. He might have recovered sufficiently to talk to you by then. It's possible he won't have a memory of the incident".

Masters later got the down on Kay's miscarriage and went home in a cheerful mood. It was still only 7pm so he suggested to Jean they drive out to a country pub for a meal. She was thankful he was more relaxed than he had been of late; and appreciated the little token moments of loving consideration when he pulled back her chair and took her coat to the cloak room. My Don, she told herself, was his old self and I love him so much.

*

A couple of days after Vincent Paul put in a request to see him it was granted and he was ushered into the governor's spacious office. Taking the advice of the warder he stood to attention in front of the grey haired slim man sitting behind his large desk. Looking up from his record in front of him he offered a fleeting smile before asking what Paul wanted to see him for.

'I want to see a police officer, sir'.

'Why?'

'It's difficult, sir'.

The governor was experienced dealing with strange requests and had a shrewd idea the man was being threatened. 'Can you be precise, Paul. Is it a particular officer you want to see?'

'Yes sir. Detective inspector Masters............he's the one dealing with a murder that happened in my house'.

The governor turned his attention to Paul's file which made no mention of a murder and looked intently at Paul. 'Are you involved in a murder?'

'No sir. I can't name names but its about the murder. And its important' he added hurriedly.

'Hmm. I see, right. I'll see what can be done'. He gestured to the warder beside the man 'Take him back'.

*

Miller offered a cigarette to Paul and offered the packet to Masters who shook his head and waited for Paul to light up and look his way before speaking. 'So, what's the problem, Vincent?'.

Paul was staring at the DI but his thoughts were about the threat from Jackson. He took a deep drag on his fag and blew out and shook his head with the worry of it all. 'It's me house, guv. I wish I'd never bought the bleeding place'.

The detectives exchanged a puzzled stare and

Masters looked back at Paul. 'Can you be a bit more specific Vincent. Have you been threatened?'

'You could say that. A bloke you've put in here knows I've made a statement about the body in the basement and, well, the word is out that he's right pissed off with me'. He stopped and stared at Masters and then at Miller but he wasn't getting the vibes he wanted. 'This is bleeding serious, guv! Know what I mean?'

'What is it you want from us?'

'I don't know what I want, guv, and that's the bleeding truth. I'm in the shit, deep shit, and you've got the bleeding statement. Where do we go from here?'

'We go to court, Vincent'.

'No we bleedingwell don't! No way, guv!'.

Because the man was an important witness in the case Masters reassured him as best he could. 'Every evidential document has to be copied to the defence, Vincent, The lawyer would have passed on the detail of you statement. But until you actually appear in court he won't know for sure you'll be giving evidence. Anyway, you'll most likely be out of prison before the court date is fixed'.

'Parole you mean?'

'Why not? It's possible and', he leaned forward to emphasise the next point. 'With a nudge from us it might be probable'.

'Can that be done?'

'If necessary, in the interests of justice, yes'

'So what are we saying here, guv?'

'Keep your head down and say nothing. If you're got at put the word out you've backed out from giving evidence. Just go along with what he wants to hear'.

Paul got to his feet, dotted his fag, and smiled for the first time 'That's a bleeding relief, guv' he said as he stuck out his hand. 'Ta', he added when it was shaken.

*

Reg Bruce's injury was serious. The blows that had fractured his skull had caused a coup lesion at the site of the blows; this had caused epidural hematoma. The blood clot had formed underneath the skull on top of the dura resulting from a tear in the middle meningeal artery. The surgeon reduced Reg's intercranial pressure by inserting a catheter into the fluid filled ventricle between the brain and the skull and placed him on a monitor. With the swelling reduced he was wheeled into a ward with other blokes in beds opposite and to both sides. When he eventually surfaced he stared out from under bandages at his immediate surroundings, his foggy brain doing its best to help him understand what he was doing in bed with all these other blokes in their beds. giving him the eyeball treatment.

*

Kay had got off better than her old man. The reflection of a swollen face and black-turning-green puffed eyes in the mirror above the dresser in her bedroom determined her, there and then, in an unstructured haze of fury, to get the bastard.

'And that bastard copper!' she said aloud when the thought of him with his wife swam across her mind's eye.

*

Chapter twenty nine

Lucy was ecstatic. They were in their favourite pub and Ted had shown her the ring and transformed their betrothal into the blissful reality she had yearned for, opening the door to the life of love she had craved since................ her mind raced back in time to her dolls and the dresses she had motheringly clothed them in until her mother's stern face was imaged and she remembered her subsequent childhood sadness.................

'What is it, darling, Ted asked when he saw her sudden sad expression.

'Just sad memories, sweetheart', she told him as she held tightly to his hands. 'Before your time. Let's toast the future, darling. "to us and our wonderful life ahead". She raised her glass and chinked his ' I love you sweetheart'.

He reached and held her hands and his love for his darling Lucy misted his eyes.

*

Because Sheila wasn't into football, David Walters had gone to a friend's home to watch a televised match. The opportunity was too much to ignore and her thoughts were instantly of her beloved John. She telephoned his station and luckily for once was put through to him. ' David is out for the evening', she told him, her desire for him obvious in her husky voice. 'Can you come round? We can go out somewhere if you like. Can you get away?'.

Half an hour. I'll be there'.

"Please don't be late. I miss you so much'.

John shoved his current case files away and,

knowing what was waiting for him, had cut thirty minutes to twenty-two and now, with Sheila in the driving seat, he sat beside her and was content to gaze lovingly at her while she drove to their favourite place, parked, transferred to the back seat for the cuddle they were both longing for, and enjoyed the contentment of their loving relationship.

Sheila, with her John snuggled close, laid her head on his chest and welcomed his arms closing around her. The bliss of the moments was heaven for her because John was so undemanding and so loving and so understanding that, just being with him, banished the guilt that ate into her mind when they were apart.

John, cuddling her and aware that he would never be able to find the words to explain to himself why he loved her so much, was content to feel her responsive body under the silky dress and bury his head in her hair and be captivated with her scent. He was, he knew, as all men know when their testosterone is up and running, at the pinnacle of love for a woman.

*

Gillian Barton was hoovering and unhappy because John was working such long hours and had changed. She was beginning to hate his job. John would never say so, she knew that, because he loved CID work. She sometimes tried to imagine what it must be like to be dealing with all those nasty people he got involved with. Some were women, he never said so but she read the papers and knew he had dealt with so many.

On one occasion, she recalled, he had mentioned a burglary at a David Walters home. Sheila was his wife, she recalled him saying. She had sent the Christmas card: that's right, John had described her once. Why was that? She stopped hoovering while she recollected.

Oh yes, that was it, she recalled and started hoovering again, he had answered her question about the burglary and went on to say how pretty she was. She stopped the machine and sat down in an armchair to think while she was trying to push hazy images of the woman from her mind. Why am I concerned? Why? It was there but just out of reach..............it was something John had said................suddenly she knew:: they was making love and he had kissed her tummy, jokingly mentioning her mole had disappeared!

*

John was dropped off near Sheila's home and reluctantly clambered in to his own car and drove home. Gillian took his top coat and had a good sniff at Sheila's whiff before she hung it up. He didn't know it but her nostrils were on full alert and her smile hid the danger he was in. He'd been to the fridge and collared a can of beer and was lounging in an armchair when she came back and leaned over him and had another sniff at the whiff and moved to face him 'Did you fuck her?' she asked as her eyes bored into his head.

'No'. The word was out before he realised the enormity of his words. With her eyes wide and staring and her expression changing from challenge to hate he dropped his head and his brain froze over.

'Sheila was it?'

The can of beer was a frozen nothingness in one hand. John did his best to come to terms with the sheer bloody stupidity of his answer and found just enough energy to nod.

'Why?'. Gillian's tone was icy.

John stared back but his mind had blanked. Seconds passed before his brain got back into gear but its slipping clutch couldn't help him out of his pitiful state.

Gillian broke the silence 'How long?' she asked, suspecting the bastard had been screwing Sheila for some time. Getting no answer she pushed on 'Months?'

An abject John nodded.

'You utter bastard' Gillian said coldly.

*

'Why are you crying, sweetheart?'

Janet dabbed a tissue against her eyes and looked across the table at Charlie's concerned face and felt so very guilty. She couldn't tell him she was making love with him regularly because that was her truth, her reality; that Don was Charlie fulfilling her desire; that when they made love she assuaged her guilt by closing her eyes and seeing Charlie bringing her to fulfilment. 'I want you home, Charlie' she whispered. 'When are you coming home?'

'Keep your pecker up, sweetheart' he told her kindly, worried by her tears. He looked across to the warder who was looking elsewhere and briefly touched her hand. 'Don'll get it sorted. A bloke the other day compromised parole because he was getting threatened in 'ere. Don knows the score. Trust 'im'.

'I do, Charlie, really I do. I see him a lot. You know that. You told me to be friends with him'.

'You're a good girl, sweetheart. Don't know wot I'd do if I lost you. Sweetheart' he added softly, worried because she had started crying again. 'Wot is it?'

'I miss you, Charlie, that's all. I really do', she whispered, her guilt adding an edge to her words.

*

Prison grapevine being what it is Gloria was a star attracting vicarious emotions among her fellow inmates. The thrilling bit of her attraction was mincing Alfie. Egged on, she recounted the tale many times but stopped going on about him when McDonald told her on a visit to keep shtum because he was working on a defence to the murder charge.

Kathy Peel was relieved at that because Gloria's constant bragging was getting her down. The remand was more like a sentence because it was weeks since being banged up and the chance of a not guilty result had faded as the weeks passed by. The two discussed their chances at meals and exercise and realised it came down Firth Street and fingerprint evidence. When Jackson got words to them that Vincent Paul was wavering and could be bought off they cheered up.

'What if he won't?' Kathy asked Gloria when they were in the exercise yard.

'Won't what?'

'Take a bung'.

Gloria stopped walking and pulled Kathy closer 'He'd better if he knows what's good for him'.

'Meaning?' She stared at her friend until the penny dropped. 'For Gawd's sake, Gloria, not again!'.

'Come on Kathy. Get real. With Paul out of the way we'll stand a good chance of walking out of it. Look', she added, earnestly now, 'the whole bloody case against us starts in Paul's basement. They've got our dabs, right?

Kathy nodded

'With Paul out of it our dabs could have got there some other time, right?'

'Oh..........yea, I get it. What about your gun?'.

'Some other geezer left it in my house. Why not', she added when hre friend shook her head. 'Let the filth prove otherwise, Kath'.

Kathy remembered the factory and shot another worried glance at Gloria. 'Didn't you talk to a bloke at that factory?'.

'So?'

'So, what if the filth dig up that meet? And your aunt -she lives in the village don't she?'

"Oh my bloody Gawd", Gloria thought, "she's right". Until then it hadn't occurred to her that the filth would dig that far back She tried to recall the bloke's face and age and failed and her worry grew. That something had to be done was bloody obvious. 'I'll get the word out Kathy. Thank gawd you mentioned it'.

*

His plea for solitary confinement was granted and he took his meals in his cell during his last two weeks in Pentonville. Before that it was a frightening experience so sure was he that Jackson was going to have him done. With his parole agreed at the highest level and kept secret until he was let out, Vincent Paul was able to relax for the first time and allow himself to be led to an unmarked police car and be driven away, with Masters' assurance it was to a safe house out of the East Ham area of London.

*

Audrey Sheenan had been on tenter hooks since Barry had let her read Masters brief letter advising him of the start date for the trial. He was on the day shift at the time and her concern for him deepened as the weekend and a week of night shifts drew nearer.

'You will be careful, Barry', she told him.'I worry for you being at that place knowing what they got you to do'.

He laughed it off. 'You've no need to worry, darling. They're tucked up in prison'.

Audrey's mum Beryl knew her better than Barry did. "A worrier. Always was and always will be" she would tell Audrey's dad Fred whenever he talked about their daughter's constantly sad expression. On this occasion, though, she knew her daughter had cause to worry and she reminded her husband of that. 'They shot a man and Barry................'

Hubby broke in there, saying: 'Don't I know! He shouldn't have done that, Beryl'.

'Oh. And what would you have done then?'

Fred mulled it over while Beryl nipped off to the kitchen saying she was going to make them a cup of tea. In his heart he knew he'd have done the same and told his wife that when the cups were on

the side tables. 'Worrying won't help Audrey, love' he added. 'They'll be alright'.

*

The following Saturday evening, when he was on his way to the factory to start a week of night shifts, Barry saw the flashing blue light from a distance. As he approached the factory gates he saw the police car in the yard and a uniformed officer bending over someone on the ground and one of his shift workers standing nearby smoking.

He parked his car and went over. 'What's happened?' he asked

His co-worker pointed to the man on the ground. 'Don't know. I heard shouting and a bang and came out and found Brian lying there'. Seeing Barry's concern he told him he'd called for an ambulance and the police. ' He turned up first' he pointed to the policeman, who was making Brian comfortable.

Barry stepped closer and peered down at Brian, who appeared to be unconscious, and saw a blood stain spreading across his chest.

'What d'you think? Stabbed?' he asked the police officer bending over him.

'Shot I'd say' the policeman reckoned. 'I'll get CID here'. He radioed the request and looked from one to the other ' fell out with his missus?' he asked smilingly and turned his attention to Barry's workmate. 'See anyone about?'

'Not a soul. Heard a car though'.

Barry was still staring down at Brian and chillingly thinking it had been intended for him. His wife's worry swept over him. He looked at his shaking hands and started walking to the factory. 'I've got to make a call' he said.

*

Makepeace listened and his concern increased. 'Where is all this going, inspector? First I go upstairs to get Paul paroled and into a safe house, and now you're telling me you want -what's his name.......?'

"Barry Sheenan, sir'.

'This chappie Sheenan moved as well! Convince me. Try!'

'Well sir, as I've told you, the wrong man got shot..............'.

'There you go again! What do you know about this, this, Brian what's-his-name? Couldn't he have enemies for God's sake?'

'True sir, he could. Do you really believe that though? We're dealing with a bunch of murderers who'll stop at nothing. What about the sighting of a stolen car turned up by Dereham CID that was seen in the area fifteen minutes before the shooting? Nicked from Whitechapel a week ago. How does that square with the shot man having local enemies?'

The cost-conscious DCS saw which way Masters' wind was blowing, and recognised immediately the downside implication if he denied the DI's request. 'It's you and me to the Yard, inspector', he said abruptly as he stood. ' I'll arrange a meeting with the commander. It'll be his decision'.

*

John Barton and Don Masters had chosen a corner table in a favoured pub for John to unload his worry onto the detective inspector. As Barton's tale unfolded Masters knew only to well what he was hearing could just as easily be his tale of woe any time soon. Jean thankfully hadn't cottoned on to Janet. But it could happen. Women had an instinct, he knew that only too well, for sussing out what blokes got up to. 'How did it come on top, John?' he queried when Barton stopped talking to cuddle his pint. It was important he knew how he had slipped up.

'Perfume, guv'.

Masters nodded. Kay had tried to nail him that way.

'On my clothes. What am I going to do, guv? I love Gillian'.

'And Sheila. Do you love her as well?'

John nodded. His eyes had filled up and the DI cast a wary eye around at the nearby diners.

' Does Sheila know it's come on top?'

Barton downed his drink and shook his head. Looking hopefully at Masters he asked, his confidence shattered, 'What should I do?'

'John', the DI gathered their glasses as he was speaking. 'You've got to talk it over with Sheila. Rest assured Gillian will get round to it. And what about her husband? Where's the fall out from this going to land? Think about that while I get the drinks in'.

John nodded miserably and watched the DI go to the bar, and come back minutes later with their drinks.

'Thanks, guv'.

The two men sipped for a while, each buried in his own concern. Masters knew only too well his dalliances with Janet were likely to come on top - and with Jean worried about her lump.....................he shook the worry away, took another sip, and studied the younger man, who who also deep in troubled thought. 'Tell me, John. When you, Ted and Dusty opened Lakey's garage- who had the key?'.

'Sergeant Miller, guv. Apparently he got it from the leasing agent'.

'Was the car locked?'.

'No, guv. Sergeant Miller told Ted to search the garage. He told me to search the boot. Something wrong, guv?'.

Masters shook his head and patted Barton's hand. 'Filling in holes, John'.

*

Brian Snow, shot by mistake at the North Pickenham factory, had recovered well from his wound and made a statement to a detective from Dereham. Forwarded to Masters he read that Snow was the yard machine operator of the day shift that day. "He was approached by a man wearing an anorak inside the gated entrance to the factory who asked if he operated the front loader. When he said he did the man pulled out a handgun and shot him. The last memory he could recall was of the man walking away to a car. He described the gunman as white, medium height and around 40 years of age. He would not be able to identify the man again; not could he describe the make of the dark-coloured car.

The communication included a statement from a

SOCO officer who had found and photographed in situ an ejected cartridge case; the ejected cartridge in it's bag; and the bullet taken from the shot man's chest at the hospital. A statement taken from the surgeon who removed the bullet from the man's chest was attached to the report, completing the evidential chain in respect of the bullet.

Masters drove over to divisional headquarters and showed Makepeace Snow's statement. Once it had been perused the DI made a firm point that Barry Sheenan and his family should be protected. 'It'll get back to the villains the wrong man got shot. As I see it we shouldn't allow Sheenan and his family to sit it out in the countryside waiting for a bullet'. While the DCS was mulling it over Masters made his serious point. 'Their protection is more important than the trial. He's a vital witness, yes, that's a fact, but his life is in our hands. I believe we should move the family out of the village until the trial's over'.

Makepeace knew the detective inspector was correct in his risk assessment, but foresaw likely difficulties ahead. 'And if Sheenan won't be moved out?

'We can't make him, obviously. I believe I have a duty to spell out to him our fears for his and his family's safety. We've got five lined up to stand trial for murder, sir. Any one of them could have arranged for the hit'.

'I understand, inspector, and I accept it was meant for Sheenan. Very well. Arrange a meeting with the Dereham CID and get up there and come up with a solution to this'.

'Right, sir. One other thing. Would you get Norfolk police to give a press release about the shot man. In his interests it could say he is making a good recovery but it should make it absolutely clear that he could not identify the gunman'.

'Fair point, inspector. I'll get onto it'.

*

By appointment Masters again met with the company secretary of the abattoir. The official listened carefully to what Masters was saying and indicated he was prepared to assist in any way.

'Can you find a replacement for Sheenan?', Masters wanted to to know.

The company secretary was smiling at the request but nodded. 'It can be done but' he touched his nose and smiled again 'I won't get a volunteer!'.

'If money comes into it, as it probably will, the Metropolitan Police Authority will cover the upshot of ensuring the family's safety. Will the company keep Sheenan on the payroll until the trial is over?'

The other man spread his hands. 'This is a cut throat business, inspector, and the truth is I don't know. I'll have to discuss the matter with the directors. What he did was a criminal act'. He smiled at Masters. 'There I go telling you your business!'.

'Can the company keep his job open until the trial's over? If he loses his job what could he do for work in that area? We have to ask ourselves what would we have done. In the dead of night men turn up with the body of a man obviously shot dead. He must have been scared to death'.

'Fair point, inspector. Barry is a good employee and the company would not want to lose him, in the normal course of events. As I've said: its a matter for the directors'.

*

Audrey and Barry Sheenan were perched on the edge of

their settee holding hands as if their lives depended upon it. They listened intently and understood that Masters was right, and his suggestion that the parents would have them stay for a couple of weeks was also right.

'Shall I phone them now?' Audrey asked, desperately in need of someone to take responsibility, to tell her what to do.

Masters reached across from his chair and patted her arm 'If you're sure going there will not be a problem. You mustn't alarm them but I want you gone in the morning. The school: would you like me to let the headmaster know the children will be away for a couple of weeks?'

Barry and Audrey looked at each other and then back to Masters 'Would it be best if you did that?'

He assured them it would be. 'An officer is on standby to stay here tonight. I'll arrange that now', He used his radio and confirmed it. ' Try not to worry. Everything'll be alright'.

*

The hitman was Gloria's older brother Adrian Fletcher who had never done time. He was a very dangerous individual. This remarkable achievement was down to a sharp, cunning mind that kept him a step in front of the filth. Adrian was known to a couple of the sweeney squads, in particular DI Lindley's. His contractual arrangement with them gave him a free run in London but on this occasion he'd overstepped the mark. Masters' Yard connections opened the door to Adrian and the distinct possibility that his sibling relationship with Gloria stuck him up as suspect No.1 for the Norfolk contract.

Masters, Miller and Don's mate Derek Lynham,

another flying squad detective inspector, were sitting in the Yard canteen running through options open to them but knew that steaming in was probably not the best course of action.

'How d'you want to play this one?'

Masters drummed fingers on the table and stared at his bacon sandwich while he thought. 'He at this address?' he asked when he jabbed the sandwich at the paper the squad DI had handed to him.

'Definitely. We housed him yesterday. One of my team followed him there. It's a ground floor flat close to Hammersmith Broadway'.

Masters nodded and munched. 'I'll work something out and get back to you'. He glanced at Miller before turning back to the squad DI and then to his sandwich, a soggy remnant of its earlier life. 'I reckon we can come up with a plan of action', he said. 'And thanks for what you've done'.

Miller waited for Masters to finish the sandwich before downing his coffee. 'That it, guv?'.

*

Chapter thirty

Mr. Cecil Fortnam, QC, rose theatrically to his feet, shrugged his gown, smiled at the Judge and turned to face the jury, adopting the serious persona he reserved for occasions such as this. 'Members of the jury', he began. 'The accused persons in the dock are charged before this court with murder. You are going to hear details which may shock you. You must steel yourselves and be objective at all times. You may already have read in newspapers or seen on television details of the murder of Alfred George. You must put these details out of your mind and try the case on the evidence put before you'.

Cecil told them that the train of evidence began in a public house on the night of the dead man's kidnap. 'I shall call witnesses to establish George was present in that public house on that evening; that a telephone call caused him to leave the public house and not return; and that he was taken by automobile to an address in London and shot dead. The evidence you shall hear will prove beyond doubt that the accused people were complicit in that kidnap and murder. Furthermore you shall hear evidence of the most horrific nature. The three male accused conveyed the body of George to a factory in Norfolk and caused it to be minced and cooked'. Pausing to consider their reactions to this latest twist in the tale he went on to tell them that he would produce evidence to prove that Gloria Gardner had arranged for the kidnap and murder and the subsequent disposal of the body at that factory.

'I call my first witness, Mrs Betty George'.

Alfie's wife had done herself proud. New hair do, new two piece, make up filling in facial cracks, all in all, very presentable. Alfie would have been proud of his missus. She didn't need reminding by Cecil of the events of that evening. "aving a quiet drink we was. The barman told Alfie he was wanted on the phone, like'.

'Did he say who wanted him?'

' No'.

Cecil turned to the judge 'M'lord. In the normal course of events the answer to my next question would be hearsay. Your direction is necessary because the answer establishes why her husband believed it safe to do as the caller wanted'.

The judge, in possession of all the papers, nodded 'Put your question to the witness'.

'What did your husband say?'

' 'e said the sweeney wanted to 'ave a chat wiv 'im outside'.

'The sweeney Mrs. George? Can you enlighten the jury on that word?'

'Yeh. The flying squad'.

'And did he leave the public house?'

' 'e did'..

'Did he return?'

'No 'e didn't'

'Stay there, please'.

Mr. McDonald, QC, for the defence popped up and said he had no questions for the witness.

'I call Stuart Biggs' said Mr. Fortnam

Biggs confirmed he was the barman who took the call and handed the receiver to Alfie and, no, the caller hadn't identified himself.

No questions, was McDonald's response to the Judge's question. He listened when a fingerprint officer from New Scotland Yard confirmed the fingerprints of Alfie and each accused had been found at 108 Firth Street, East Ham; and that Alfie's prints and the three accused men's prints had been found in the car belonging to Keel.

Vincent Paul, shooting a fearful glances at the men in the dock, confirmed he was the owner of 108 and withstood pressure from McDonald, refuting his allegation that his clients' had accessed the property prior to the night of the killing.

Barry Sheenan was a good witness, identifying Gloria as the woman who had spoken to him several evenings before the incident with the body bag; and pointed out Keel and Jackson as the men who had unzipped naked Alfie and had paid him £100 to tip his body into the mincer.

The firearms expert confirmed that the bullet found on the floor of 108's basement was fired from the gun recovered from Gloria's home. Medical evidence was given that samples of blood taken from 108's basement were of a type similar to Alfie's.

When it was Masters turn to be cross examined McDonald stared hard at him knowing him to be a crafty sod. If he was going to tip him up it was going to be regarding Joe Keel's car.

'Inspector. You have stated a car owned by Mr. Keel was found abandoned in a car park in Canning Town. Is that so?'

'That is so'.

'How did you know that?'

'Sir?'

'How did you know the car was in that car park?'

'Phone call, sir'.

'Oh. Did you have reason to believe the car had been stolen?'

'No, sir'.

'And did you log that telephone message?'.

'I did'.

'Tell the court the name of the caller'.

'Jesus Wept'.

'Pardon?'.

'It's the code word of that informant, sir'.

'No, inspector. His actual name, please'. He turned to smile confidently at the jury before staring at what he presumed was a cornered detective.

'The informant's name is unknown'.

McDonald studied impassive Masters and turned his attention to the jury when he next spoke ' Let me get this clear, inspector. An unknown person telephones you and a car you do not know to be stolen is reported to you as being in a Canning Town car park'. He turned to face Masters 'That is what you want the jury to believe, is it?'.

'That is so, sir'.

'Have I missed something, inspector? Why would someone want you to know that?'.

Masters looked at the Judge and asked 'Should I answer that M'Lord?'.

The judge gestured to McDonald to approach him and they spoke in whispers before the Judge directed Masters to answer the question.

His face composed and unsmiling Masters kept his unblinking gaze on McDonald while he answered. 'The word was out among my informers that Joseph Keel was a murderer. A snout belled me about the whereabouts of his car, sir. Naturally, I logged that call'.

Keel was on his feet yelling abuse at the detective; and McDonald had slumped in his seat and glared at the detective. The Judge, in a quandary, told the jury to disregard Masters reply but the damage was done. 'Inspector. He said sternly, ' You must place that log in evidence before the court'. Turning to the lawyers and then the jury, he said, looking at the wall clock, 'This court will adjourn until 2pm. Take the prisoners down'.

Later, the following afternoon the Judge summed up. 'You have heard the testimony of the police officers;

and the scientific evidence confirming the presence of the murdered man and each of the accused in the basement and on an external door of 108 First Street, East Ham; and of the deceased man and the three accused men being in the car belonging to the accused Keel. It is for you to decide who has told you the truth in regards to the presence of the fingerprints. The witness Paul stated that none of the accused had previous access to the house or the basement of 108 Firth Street. The accused have stated the opposite. I draw your attention to the fingerprints of the dead man in the basement and the car. Did they get there on a different occasion to those of the accused? You should consider the gun proven to be the killing weapon that was produced in evidence. It was recovered from the home of the accused Gloria Gardner and bore her fingerprints. Did you accept her testimony that she had loaned it to a friend who, you will recall, she declined to name. You may feel that the identification testimony of Sheenan convincing enough corroboration of the prosecution case regarding those fingerprints, some of which, you were told by the scientific officer, were blood stained of a type similar to that of the dead man. Sheenan admitted to this court his involvement in concealing the death of George and the possibility of involvement as an accessory to George's murder. That admission and that possible involvement are part of a separate investigation. It is for you to decide which of these witnesses has told you the truth. Ask yourselves who, if anybody, stood to gain by telling lies? Detective inspector Masters produced written corroboration of the call that led officers to Keele's car in that Canning Town car park. Finally I must tell you that if you decide upon a guilty verdict it must be unanimous and it must be beyond reasonable doubt. If doubt exists you must find for the accused. Retire now and consider your verdicts'.

It took four hours of deliberation to reach their verdicts. The jury was unanimous. All except Derek Stockhart was found guilty of Alfie's murder. His luck was that his fingerprints, although found in Keel's car, were only on the frame of the rear door of 108 Firth Street; and Sheenan had not seen him at the factory. Nevertheless, with each of the others, he was found guilty of a second count of conspiracy to kill Alfie. The Judge sentenced each to life imprisonment, with a recommendation that the killers serve a minimum of 25 years and Stockhart 15 years.

*

Chapter thirty one

Two weeks after telling John what a bastard he was Gillian was at work and desperately unhappy. Their separate lives, in the same house, were taking their toll; and she could see that John was suffering. The two weeks had given her time to think about her future. She had sometimes lain awake during those difficult, emotionally lonely nights, and sat through her working days, trying to visualise life without him. Her deep love for him always got in the way of a clear decision because, in those deeply anchored thoughts, he was ever present and part of her. Their marriage had brought about a bond that disarmed the weapon of instant hatred she had used to castigate him. Unconsciously it was that bond which was helping her to come to terms with what he had done and look for a reason for his behaviour with another woman, because he had always been so loving and caring. Why had he gone to Sheila? Why? Did he love her? Was it just sex? These entangled thoughts were painful to bear because she had always accepted his love was only for her; and their sexual relationship the expression of their bonded love for each other. She glanced out of the window at the spring plants and the resurgent grass and knew, if their marriage was to last, she had to forgive and try to forget and do her utmost to ensure that their bond was everlasting.

*

Because his shocked libido had shut down his sexual drive when he had been confronted, John Barton found it easier to come to terms with the hurt he had caused Gillian. Being a mere man he didn't experience the soul-searching a woman found necessary to cope with emotional hurt because, his reality told him, his love for two women, quite natural of course, he knew that, absolved him from blame. Gillian was his soul mate. Their years together had bonded them, not as Gillian understood, but as partners in the pathway of settled, mutual love that he found acceptable, enabling him to enjoy his dalliances with Sheila from time to time. It was natural that when he was grumpy Gillian should understand: hadn't his mother always understood and forgiven him? His dalliances with Sheila................oh, what dalliances, he recalled, when he imaged her urging him on, and on...........that was special because he had never as a teenager met a Sheila........... He shook the thought away and looked at an unsolved case file and sighed. 'If only women understood men' he thought.

*

Janet was in heaven again and it was thanks to an untiring Don whose love-making was way above Charlie's and he, she had previously known, was a sex god. She stroked Don's face and actually saw him instead of Charlie.. She let him know that 'You're not Charlie now' she whispered. 'I love you Don'.

In the normal course of events that would have confirmed a notch on Don's belt but, with Charlie due out in a matter of weeks, it slackened his old man and he slid off her beautiful, glistening body and his mind went into reverie. His fanciful mind-state had Charlie wielding a hammer on his head while Janet tried to grasp the hammer demanding that Charlie leave her lover alone.

*

Reg Bruce had no memory of the whacking. Since the operation he had experienced a severe headache and repeated bouts of nausea and vomiting and, to cap it all, his speech was slurred . Nipping to the loo was not for him. He'd tried it once and nearly fell over because his legs didn't coordinate when he attempted the short walk with the bottle-laden trolley.

The policeman detailed to get a statement from him was patient but had to give it best and returned to the police station.

*

Kay's broken nose had been set and the swelling had gone down but the damage was lasting. Glaring into the mirror at her disfigured nose, as she did many times, she vowed vengeance on Reg and determined to see it through. Just what hadn't crystallised but it would come with time and, if there was one trait she possessed above all others, it was patience borne out of a vicious urge for vengeance. She smiled her thin smile at the mirror and told her nose. 'Just you wait' as she imaged Reg over her reflection, his hovering, gloating smile ever present in her determined consciousness.

The opportunity came sooner than she had expected. On a visit to the hospital she was given the news that Reg would be better at home: apparently he had improved, she was told, and could totter, with a zimmer frame but a wheel chair would do better, but his memory was impaired. 'The incident' she was told tactfully, 'may have been erased from his mind. I doubt he will ever recover it', the psychiatrist added gravely.

*

She didn't rush into it. Observation and patience, and

two weeks helping him totter about and pushing him around worked wonders. He got to like their morning and evening ambles that took them beside the deep lake where they fed the many Mallards that dipped and swam and came ashore for their top up of bread. As before, her plan from weeks of scheming and resolution, emboldened by hate for the bastard, saw her pushing him to the spot where the bank fell away sharply. As on those many previous occasions she gave him the bread to throw to the ducks that hungrily had swum along and frolicked in front of them.

He was smiling up at her when she gave the wheelchair the nudge and Reg had the merest of time to look fearfully at the darkness of the rapidly approaching water and back at Kay. In those seconds Mallards swum quickly to avoid the crushing weight of Reg and chair hitting the water and sinking.

Kay stared at the bubbles and the shrinking eddies and the surprised ducks until the bubbles ceased and the surface was smooth. Wiping an involuntary smile when she saw the man with his dog, she screamed and pointed to the water..................

Convinced by her assumed hysteria and pointing hand and tears he did his best to calm her. 'Right here?' he asked as he stared into the water. 'When?'.

Hand still shaking she continued to point, with tears streaming, she said ' Just minutes ago. I let go for a second and it went...........down there..............I can't believe it happened so quick. So quick'.

'I can't leave you here' he told her kindly. There's a phone box near the entrance to the park. I'll let the police know. Come with me', he said, offering a hand.

'You're so kind................thank you'.

*

Mention of Kay Bruce's name at the nick alerted Masters and he and Miller left to join the other officers already at the scene. They watched a diver ease himself into the water and disappear. Within minutes he popped up and pointed beneath him. By that time a fire tender was at the scene and its crew had slung a rope to the diver, who submerged and secured the chair and Reg to it. With their end secured to a winch, and on a thumbs up from the diver, Reg, his legs now tangled in it and the chair, were hauled ashore.

Pasapula, on call as usual, waited until Reg had been disentangled and spread eagled on the ground to perform a perfunctory examination and smile across at Masters. 'Drowned certainly. You can see evident signs of cyanosis, skin blueish. Time of death recent', he gestured at the water 'Pretty cold in there I'll bet, but from what I've picked up from one of your officers, he went for his dip less than two hours ago'.

'His wife has been taken home, guv', Masters was told by a uniformed constable.

The DI played it safe and took Miller with him to Kay's first floor flat. When she opened the door to them she was, surprisingly he saw, fully clothed. Without a word, she stepped back and let them pass before closing the door. Pushing past, she led the way to the living room. Ignoring them, she sat on the settee and clasped hands in her lap, and stared.............

Knowing full well how her volcano could blow unexpectedly the DI started tentatively. 'Mrs. Bruce I need to..............'

'Kay not good enough for you anymore?' she retorted tartly

Masters dropped into an armchair opposite the settee and gestured for Miller to sit down. 'Kay. I know what happened must have been a shock for you but, can you tell Dusty and me precisely what happened at the lake?'

'I've already told one of the constables what happened', she said icily.

Masters recognised she was into one and nodded, hoping to avoid a row. 'Yes. He told me what you said. But I need to get it written down. May I do that now?'

'What's he doing here?' She shifted her gaze to Miller.

Masters saw that Dusty was about to get out of his chair and raised a warning hand. 'It's what we do when we interview a woman witness. Now, Kay, may I take that statement?'

'No you may not! Who do you think you are?'. She turned to face Miller and, deliberately ignoring Masters presence, said icily 'You know he's been fucking me?'

Miller grinned into her hate-shaped face and let his true feelings for women show. 'Sooner him than me, you frigging slag!'

Before he had a chance to defend himself Kay had launched herself at him, her arms flailing as she attempted to scratch at his eyes. He grabbed her hair with one hand and held her at arms length, grinning into her widened blue eyes, shaking her like a rag doll. 'You bitch!', he shouted, as he landed a punch on her jaw with his other hand. Still holding her he threw her back onto the settee.

Masters got to his feet and bent over her clearly unconscious body before he looked across at Miller, who was obviously on a high, thumping a fist into the palm of his other hand. He stared back at Kay, his rapid thoughts ranging over their times together. Sprawled with her skirt riding high her sexual appeal was for once at zero.

Miller looked at Masters. 'We've got to do something', he said meaningfully, holding Masters' gaze.

It was so obvious that Masters waved away Miller's remark and stared down at Kay's body. He knew there was no choice; she could wake up and bring their careers to and end with one phone call. 'Its got to look right'. Masters said, his thoughts way ahead. 'What would she do before going out?'. He looked around the tidy lounge. 'Check out the kitchen. She would never go out leaving dirty crockery'.

Miller went through to the kitchen again and scanned it: no unwashed crockery; all pots and pans in place. 'Tidy in here, Don', he called and went back to the living room, in time to see Masters at the front door.

'Check the bedroom' the DI told him. 'And have another look around. Make sure things are as they should be'. He opened the front door slightly and peered onto the landing, cocking an ear before stepping out and going down the concrete stairway. He peered through a side window of the lobby : nobody was about. Luck was on their side. He ran up and went back inside the flat and stared at the woman who had become his nightmare. His mind made up he told his friend. 'She's got to go, Dusty'.

Miller nodded. Sure?'.

Masters shrugged away his lingering doubts and nodded. 'She'll bell the nick as soon as she comes round and that'll be you and me suspended. That's not going to happen. Is everywhere spick and span?'.

'Yep'.

'We've got to get her into that coat'. Masters gestured to one on a chair. He looked around. 'Shoes.....where are her shoes?'

Miller had opened a cupboard and was holding a pair of high-heeled shoes. 'What d'you reckon? Masters, caught up in the desperation of the moment, nodded his agreement. 'They'll do. Handbag. We need a bag...........and her keys'. Masters scanned the room and saw a handbag on a side table. 'That'll do' he told Miller, pointing.

'The sergeant picked it up and unclasped it. 'The keys are in it. Now what?'.

Masters was heaving Kay up. 'There's nothing for it, Dusty. It's got to be done. Give me a hand to get the coat and shoes on her'.

On the landing it was easier than Masters had thought. Holding her at arms length he locked the door and dropped the keys into the bag Miller had hooked over an arm. . 'We do it', he said quietly as he edged her forward and stared down the stairway.

Geoffrey Burke, who lived in the ground floor flat, found Kay's crumpled body when he came home that evening and made an emergency call. Fifteen minutes later one ambulance man looked across at another and pronounced 'She's dead', and looked up at hovering Burke. 'Broken neck at a guess', he opined. 'I think we should leave her where she is for the police to work on this one'. He tugged at his colleagues arm ' Recognise her, Fred? She's the bird from upstairs who beat up her old man recently'.

*

Sergeant Tims, like many officers in the police station, knew a fair bit about Kay Bruce and her swinging moods. Being dead was a new one worthy of being spread about. the police station. While he was bringing the occurrence book up to date with the ambulance control bombshell, Masters walked into the front office. 'You'll never guess, Don'. He broke off to point to the book. 'Mrs Bruce has taken a tumble down her stairs and snuffed it. Want to have a look? - they've left her as they found her'.

'I'll send John Barton', he replied, glancing over the sergeant's shoulder at his entry. 'He's got nothing on at the moment'.

Barton swung the lobby door inwards and saw Kay lying in a crumpled heap with her head at a funny angle and her dress riding high and knickers on show.. Radioing back on what he had found, Masters instructed him to stay until the police surgeon arrived. While he waited he looked up the stairway and could see how Kay might have taken her tumble. He ventured up and spotted blood on several treads half way up and realised, for sure he thought, what had happened: she'd tripped over high heels and wallop, down she went, leaving one shoe several steps up the stairway. Going down he opened her handbag he found the two keys on a ring that Masters had popped in. He went up and tried the keys; one opened the front door. He ventured in and imagined Masters in there. Her scent hung in the air of the bedroom and he stared at the quilted double bed, imagining his guvnor in it having it off with Kay.

*

'So what have we got?'. Kay had already been opened up and her scalp pulled down over her face. The mortician was cutting off the crown of her head with a small powered circular saw while Pasapula waited, puffing on his pipe.

'Right' he said to the officers 'Let's get started'.

Masters glanced at John, who was looking decidedly sickly.

'You've got to do this, John. Evidential train'.

The pathologist extracted Kay's brain and was slicing it, explaining as he did so: 'Routine stuff, Don. At first sight, no problem here. The lab will tell me more'..

He put down the rest of the brain and moved Kay's head from side to side. 'Neck broken. I doubt she felt anything'.

Masters didn't respond but shot a glance at Barton, who appeared queezy as he watched Pasapula, who had already chopped through and removed her sternum and removed and opened her stomach. While he was unpicking her intestines into a long, almost flat tube, he referred to the chewed contents of her stomach. 'Small eater I'd say, probably her last meal was steak and chips. Still in there. See..........'

'Cause of death?' Masters needed a decision.

'Pretty obvious. Her neck was broken, snapping the spinal chord'.

'A fall?'

'Not for me to say. From what detective constable Barton has said that conclusion is pretty obvious'.

'Not drunk. No drugs?'

'At this moment, no, but toxicology tests will reveal all'.

'Accidental death most likely then?', Masters offered

'Seems that way, Don. Let's get all this stuff shoved back and close her up. It's been a long day and I fancy a juicy steak with chips myself'.

That said he knocked his pipe dottle into Kay's cavity and waited while the mortician stuffed his wiping cloths into the brainless skull.

'Put the skull back, shall I sir?', queried the tired-looking mortician.

'Do that. And sort out her scalp'. Pasapula grinned across to the detectives 'Make her look presentable, eh! I'll stitch her up and call it a day'.

*

It took a week for the toxicology tests to confirm the absence of alcohol and drugs from her body.

Masters and Miller, in the canteen with Barton, egged him to speculate on Kay's demise.

'One of her high heeled shoes was halfway up the stairs. I reckon it's pretty clear she tripped'.

'Seems likely, John'. agreed Masters. 'The neighbour chappie on the ground floor. Did he have anything to say?'

'Bit shocked, guv, I'd say. He called for the ambulance. Saw nothing'.

'Did she have a visitor?'

'I checked next door. Some old biddy lives there. Saw nothing all evening, except you and the sarge, guv'.

Masters blood ran cold. 'Me, John?'.

'Seen you many times, guv. The red Jag. Can't miss it'.

'There you go', the DI responded,. shooting a quick glance at Miller. 'Always someone out there bogging at us. We popped round for a statement about her old man'.

Barton was thinking about Sheila and the chances he took and missed to significance of Masters' answer.

'Make your book up for the coroner, John. Keep it brief. The pathologist will cover the cause of death'.

'Right, guv'.

'How are things between you and Gillian?'.

'They're not, guv. Gillian's put me in the dog house: we live apart. I rarely get a chance to talk to her.. I'm gutted the way things have turned out'.

'Down the road?'

'Who knows. I don't want us to split up. I love her, guv'.

'And Sheila?

'Problem there. I haven't told her Gillian knows -

although she's probably worked it out by now. I haven't seen her for a couple of weeks'.

'Keep me posted, John', Masters told him.

*

Jean Masters put down the local paper and looked across at her husband, who was buttering toast. 'You never mentioned her death, Don', she said, remembering. She picked the paper up again and read aloud "Mrs. Kay Bruce, aged 39 years, was found to have fallen to her death at her home. Readers may recall, her wheelchair bound husband drowned in a local lake the previous day". She looked quizzically at Don 'Was it suicide or was it a fall?'.

'Can't really say, sweetheart. One of my detectives popped round there when we got the info. Broken neck, apparently. Is that the coroner's verdict you're reading?' He munched his toast and looked at her questioningly.

'Yes, darling.

'What does it say?'.

'What?.......oh, accidental death due to a fall'.

Don nodded. 'We all have to go at some point. I can't say I'll shed tears at the way she went'. He picked up his mug and took some sips of the coffee, looking at his wife expectantly. When she didn't respond he asked 'You're not working today are you?'. He got up and went round and kissed her forehead. 'Have a nice relaxing day, sweetheart'. He walked to the hall and donned his coat and turned to look closely at her 'You're very pale, sweetheart. Are you feeling alright?'

'I'm fine, darling. You mustn't worry'.

'And you're thinner. You're not dieting are you?'.

She gave him a smile. 'Stop worrying about me, darling. Get yourself off to work'.

When he had gone she stayed at the table. Holding

her mug she let her thoughts run back over Don's affair with Kay and immediately imaged her at her car. She involuntarily shuddered at the memory of her contorted face while tugging at the door.

"I'm glad she's dead" she told herself sternly but was immediately flooded with guilt. She crossed to the hall full length mirror and saw that Don was right. She was losing weight and the pain was getting worse.

*

Gillian had come to realise that if their marriage was to work they needed to discuss why it was that he had behaved so badly. From John's perspective, now that his relationship with Sheila was over he'd stopped mooning about her; and Gillian's intuition told her the first move would have to be from her.

She broke the ice on an evening John had come home dripping wet from a heavy shower and she had been there in the hall to help him out of his coat. That simple gesture opened John's bottled emotions and he pulled her close and sobbed and nestled his head against her neck and whispered his love for her and begged for forgiveness. Gillian put her arms around him and she too cried, but for her it was tears of relief that her nightmare had ended because the man she knew and loved was himself again.

*

For David Walters those same passing weeks had been traumatic because Sheila would burst into tears at the slightest incident. Of an evening they sat side by side on the settee and he cuddled her, wanting her to say what it was that was hurting her so very much. In bed it was the same: she would wordlessly cling to him while he stroked her hair and whisper his love for her, trying his best to soothe away her troubles, all the time wondering if she had been seeing John Barton.

For her those weeks had been torture. John had stopped phoning; and was not returning her calls to the police station. Being cut adrift from the man she loved had reduced her life to a listless marathon in which the unconscious normality of daily life became a conscious burden she couldn't shrug away. And she had nobody to turn to, least of all David, she had told herself many times when she had wanted to tell him about John. But that need kept returning more frequently because John had slipped out of her life. David's love for her was burrowing into her guilt and forcing her to face the wrong she had done to him. She resolved to confess and did so that night when they were cuddled up in bed.

'I'm so sorry, darling' She whispered afterwards, as she raised her head to look into his eyes.

David hugged her tightly and kissed her. 'It's alright, sweetheart. I knew really. At least I thought I did but didn't want to believe it'.

'Can you forgive me?'

'What is there to forgive?' He eased away to turn towards her. 'Sweetheart, loving you as I do I know what you did had to be for love. Do you still love him?'

'I don't think so, darling. I'm so mixed up. I want to put it behind me. Do you still want me?'

'Want you! I couldn't live without you!'.

*

Chapter thirty two

Anne had done a runner from the care home yet again and was with Janet in their usual café in Romford. Without make-up and staring around defiantly she looked out of place with Janet.

'I aint going back you know' she told Janet as she jiggled her cup in its saucer. 'I 'ate the place. The uvver girls are shits and the staff're bastards'.

'You can't keep running awf, Anne. I told you when I visited you that me and Charlie will do our bit but I aint no mum'.

'Wot can 'e do stuck in prison? Anyway, wiv 'is record I aint got no chance of being wiv you'.

'Is that wot you really want?'

'I want to be mates wiv you and Charlie. I liked 'im that time'.

Janet sipped her milky coffee and thought over what Anne was saying.

'You aint saying nuffink are you like' . Anne was staring at Janet, hoping she understood.

'Finking, Anne'. After a while she said 'I've 'ad an idea. Look, why don't you make it up wiv your mum. If you was at home we could meet when we liked, couldn't we'.

'Suppose'.

'I mean it, Anne. 'ow else you gonna get out of that place?'

'Wot do I do then, like?'

Janet took one of Anne's hands tightly. 'Let's get a bus to your place and 'ave a word wiv her. She's alright aint she?'

'Suppose. Yea. Alright'.

*

With his love life sorted John Barton had another worry. Ever since perjuring himself regarding the identification parade he had been troubled by what he had done. On a couple of occasions he thought about discussing his concern with Masters before thinking better of it. He couldn't see the DI being the type who would understand his concern. In any case, he realised, Masters would want a lid kept on the episode. Sergeant Fountain was a better bet, he thought. Brian had never got involved in any of the DI's cases. He took another bite from his bacon roll and wondered if he should go across to the sergeant's table and talk it over with him. On impulse he decided to do that and took his tray over.

'Mind it I have a word, sarg?'.

Fountain looked up and gestured to the opposite chair. 'Course not John. What's the problem?'

The detective constable sat down and leaned forward and spoke quietly ' It's about an ID parade, sarg. Remember the bloke and the union card? You know?', he added when Fountain appeared puzzled ' the bloke who ran a car down for the robbers?'

'Oh. Yes. The one that got away at court as I remember'.

'That's the one. The point is, sarg, I picked him out on the parade'.

' What's wrong about that?'

'I lied, sarg'.

Fountain stopped drinking his coffee and sat back in his chair and studied Barton while he thought over what he had just been told. 'Why are you telling me this?'. He could see that Barton clearly wanted to unload his worry onto him. 'Is there more to this?'

'There is, sarg'. John hesitated and his worries multiplied because there was no going back.

'Are you going to tell me, John?'

Barton took the plunge and revealed how Masters

had arranged for him to lie in his statement and at court. 'I don't know where this is going, sarg, but I had to tell someone'.

The sergeant's concern regarding involvement in any of the DI's scams came on top. He looked across at the troubled detective and wondered....................'Why me, John?'

'I don't know who else to trust, sarg. What should I do now?'

What should I do! He'd just been lumbered with Barton's criminal behaviour and was pondering what he himself should do with the information. He had to make a decision.

'John, who else knows about this?'

Barton was shaking his head 'Nobody else'.

Fountain made up his mind quickly and waggled finger at the troubled detective. 'If this is true you're in the shit. I'll tell you now that no way will the DI admit anything'. He drummed his fingers on the table for some seconds before adding 'Tell no-one else. Frankly I don't know what to do. Leave it for a while. I need to think this through because quite frankly, John, the only person with shit on his face if this gets out, is you'. He watched Barton walking away and recalled the frosty interview with the DCS. "And now this" he told himself.

*

Martha Makepeace was very concerned at the news her George had just given her. She saw how concerned he was and told him so 'You're concerned aren't you George?' she said as she held one of his hands and looked sympathetically at him.

George nodded his agreement and continued to worry. 'The very last thing I wanted to happen, Martha dear', he said while his mind was working on the likely fall out.

'What will you do, darling?'

George was grateful for her concern and reached to place his other hand over her's to squeeze it. 'Got to keep the ship steady, that's important'.

'Yes, darling. But how can you do that?'

'Sergeant Fountain is a good man, Martha. The ship needs him'.

Martha was initially puzzled at the change of direction but, knowing her man would know what to do, she smiled and squeezed his hand. 'Let's have some breakfast' she said as she got to her feet..

*

John had just unloaded his concern onto Gillian at the breakfast table and was staring, needing her assurance. 'What do you think will happen?' he asked, his face etched with worry.

'Oh, John'. She reached across and grasped his hand, instantly concerned. 'How could you? That poor man. Whatever made you do such a thing?'

'He was guilty, darling. The detective inspector told me he was. He found the man's union card in the car'.

'A likely story John. And you believed it?'

'Well, yes. I saw the card'.

Gillian withdrew her hand from his and her surprise at his naivety was obvious to him. 'What is likely to happen to you?' She looked intently at his worried face and knew from the way he was slumped in his chair that he was thinking the worst. 'You believe you're going to be charged with lying, don't you, darling?'

He nodded. 'Perverting the course of justice, sweetheart. That's what it was'

'What about the man. What happened to him at

court? Did he go to prison?'

John shook his head. 'Found not guilty'.

Gillian took his hand again. 'Listen to me, darling' she said firmly. 'What good will it do to admit to it now?'

'But I have. I told sergeant Fountain'.

'And what did he say he was going to do?'

'Well..............as I recall........... he told me to say nothing to anybody while he sorted what to do'.

'There you are then. Stop worrying. Why would he say anything to anyone and get you into trouble. I thought policemen stood by each other'.

The troublesome weight lifted. She was right. There was no need to worry. For the first time he felt able to rationalise his predicament: the other detectives were behaving the same as usual which, hopefully he told himself, meant Fountain hadn't mentioned anything and, so far as he could tell, the DI was being pleasant. But the worry that DCS Makepeace had sent an instruction for him to be interviewed at divisional headquarters that afternoon clouded his uncertainty. 'You're right, sweetheart', he said, mustering a cheerful tone.

'I know I'm right'. She patted his hand and stood up and gathered their plates.

*

Sitting in the anti-room, staring at the pictures on the walls and at the secretary sitting primly behind her desk, fingers of fear tiptoed down his back. 'Excuse me?', he said to the young woman who had said something to him.

'The detective chief superintendent will see you now'. she told him again.

Steadying his nerves, and licking dry lips, he opened

the door and nervously crossed to the desk and stood at attention.'Dc. Barton, sir', he said hoarsely.

Makepeace looked up from a document he had been reading and gestured to the seat opposite him.'Wondering why I've asked for you to come here today?'. The DCS smiled through the question.

John's fear had dried his throat but he managed a croaking 'Yes, sir'.

'Well, Barton, it's about your annual report. I have detective inspector Masters' and detective sergeant Fountain's reports here and I'm impressed. Speak highly of your initiative and work ethic'. The DCS turned over a page 'I see you passed your sergeant's exam last year. Well done. Very well done. I am going to recommend your promotion to detective sergeant'. He recognised the constable's astonishment and added 'Well done young man. Keep up the good work'.

*

'Come in', Masters called. He watched Barton enter and stop in front of his desk 'What is it John?'.

Barton was beaming. 'I want to thank you, guv'.

'Thank me for what, John?'

'My annual report. I've been told by the DCS I'm up for promotion to detective sergeant'.

'You deserve it. John. I'm pleased for you. Did he say when it would be confirmed?'

'No, guv. How do these things work?'.

'Weeks at the most. It'll be approved at the top - with the DCS's recommendation it's a cert to go through'.

He stood and reached across the desk and shook the constable's hand. 'Take the wife out and celebrate'.

Barton could barely contain his excitement for the rest of the afternoon and floated around on a cloud. He put his concern about Davenport from his mind and enjoyed the imminent prospect of becoming a detective sergeant. *Detective sergeant!* He reflected on what Gillian had said and she was right. He kept the news from her until they were in their favourite restaurant that evening.

'Oh, darling. What absolutely wonderful news!' she said, beaming her delight. 'Didn't I say it would work out!'.

*

Chapter thirty three

Detective Sergeant Brian Fountain was non-plussed. Applying to fill the vacancy at the Yard for a fraud squad detective inspector position would never have occurred to him but Makepeace was insistent. 'You're the right man for that job, sergeant', he was saying, 'put in your application and I shall support you'.

'But fraud, sir.....................'

Makepeace wasn't having any of it. 'Fraud, sergeant. With your approach to the job, well, it's right up your street'

'Will I stand a chance, sir?'

'Of course. It's yours for the taking. Promotion works this way. Onwards and upwards as my Martha would say!'.

*

Miller sank his pint and absorbed what he had just been told about Barton's underhand move. 'Why did he do that? Another one?'.

Masters downed his beer and handed his glass to Miller. 'Conscience Dusty. Thankfully the guvnor got it sorted PDQ. Brian's on the move, apparently; and John's up for promotion. Most likely he'll get Brian's job'.

With refilled glasses in front of them, Miller brought up Kay's imminent coroner's inquest. 'Has Makepeace said anything to you?'.

'He knows about the affair - who didn't the way she carried on. Our statements will be part of the enquiry. No choice there. The old biddy clocking us would have drawn us in - we had to admit we were there that evening'.

'We didn't get her statement did we. Did the DCS raise that with you?'.

'That was the easy bit. He understood our problem there - I reckon he'd been at it himself when he was younger'.

'So now it's down to the coroner. What d'you reckon?'.

'He's had the file for a couple of weeks. If he wanted further enquiries we'd have heard by now. No. I firmly believe we're in the clear'.

*

An hour apart, with Reg going through the curtain first, his and Kay's cremations were sombre occasions attended by two members of the local press Masters knew, and a man in his fifties who was, he was told by one of them, Leonard Passfield, Kay's older brother. The DI sat at the back and watched her coffin take his guilt through the curtains. The final notes of the accompanying music were still in the air when the DI walked out of the building and took in a welcome breath of fresh air, relieved that he and Miller had got away with her murder.

Standing by his car, he looked back to the crematorium and reflected on their risky decision to rely on the tumble to kill her. Her last moments were ever present in his memory: the push that had sent her head first onto the concrete treads; her body twisting to the side and then, slowly it seemed but was in fact very quickly over, somersaulting untidily to the bottom.

The risk had paid off but, as he climbed into the Jaguar, he resolved never to carry out unplanned solutions again.

*

Janet sat beside Masters in his Jaguar and stared expectantly at the huge prison gates. He had given her the wonderful news only that morning that Charlie, after eighteen months away from her, was coming out that day on parole. She had gratefully accepted his offer to run her to the prison and pick up Charlie.

'It's the least I can do' he told her.

On the trip to the prison Masters had explained to her that Charlie mustn't be hurt. 'So there's no need for him to know we've had sex, is there?'. Janet was relieved he said that because deep down she worried Don might tell Charlie about their friendship.

'There he is!' she said excitedly and clambered out of the car and ran to her Charlie, her sex God, who had just then come out through a small door in a big one.

The DI watched them hug and kiss each other and saw Janet point to the car. He got out and walked towards them and ruffled Charlie's hair. 'Good to see you again, lad', he told him and gestured to the car. 'Straight home or what?' he asked when they'd settled on the back seats.

'Back to the flat, Don. Fanks for bringing Janet'. Once Masters had the car under way he stared out at the passing scene. 'It's bloody great to be out!', he said, his face beaming with excitement.

Masters drove steadily through the late afternoon traffic and stopped short of their flat. He turned to look at Charlie, who had an arm around Janet. 'Get settled in, Charlie. Give me a bell in a week's time. By then I'll have sorted a job for you'. He pulled out his wallet and pulled out some notes. 'Here's a ton to tide you over'.

'Fanks, Don', Charlie said as he pocketed the money.

'That's really nice of you, Don', Janet said but, looking into his eyes she mouthed 'I love you'.

*

Alfie's killers had been inside a year when Adrian Fletcher, on a visit, told his sister she had lost weight. 'Fuck me, sis. You're skin and bones', he told her in his concerned sibling way.

'Adie' she said, she always called him that. 'If you'd done the job right I wouldn't be in here'. However, the passing months had mellowed her mind set and she patted his hand. ' Never mind. 'ow're things with you in that big wide world?'

He grinned. Always a good sign to Gloria when he grinned. 'Can't complain, sis' he told her as he recalled what happened when the squad had paid him a visit after the shooting cock up.

'What's funny?'.

'Nothin', sis. Well -not really nothin'. The sweeney gave me an out on that job'.

'How d'you mean?'.

'They found the shooter when they turned my drum over. A grand took care of it'. He could see that she had something else on her mind so asked 'What is it, sis?'

'Mel had a bloke paid to do for that bleeding detective inspector wot framed him and he cocked it up -bit like you, only he got the right bloke but did a bad bleeding job'.

'Why're you telling me this?'

'It's unfinished business, Adie'.

Adrian looked hard at his sister 'You want me to finish it?'

Gloria nodded and briefly touched his hand, 'Go and have a word with Doris Keel, you know, Joe's missus. I know she was keeping a scrap book about the trial. Bound to be a photo of that detective.

*

Masters had got Charlie a job in a cash and carry

warehouse he'd had his eyes on for some time, and a rented council house nearby. 'Won't be for too long, lad' he had told Charlie. 'Put yourself about and find out when the cash is taken out and what firm takes it to the bank'.

Charlie was on a high being out of prison and enjoyed the thought of getting back to doing what he did best. Knowing the best way to go about his work he soon got on friendly terms with Gill Saunders, a young blonde in the office. During his second week there, over bacon butties and coffee in the works canteen, he worked the conversation round to her love life and her eyes filled up.

'Wot's wrong, Gill? Didn't mean to upset you', he told her as he reached for her hand.

'John's been cruel', she said. 'I don't know why'.

' 'ow d'you mean cruel?'.

'Well..............'.

'Come on Gill. Tell me'.

'Well..........we used to go out Saturday evenings, Charlie. But now he tells me he wants to go out with his mates after football'.

'Wot you mean........he plays?'

'West Ham. He goes to all their matches. Always going on about Green Street and his mates an' what they do after matches'.

'Green Street? What's that about?'

'Plaistow railway station ....Green Street leads to West Ham's ground he reckons. After the matches he's taken to drinking with his mates in a pub in that street.. I don't get to see him at all weekends'.

' Aint right, Gill, that. Wot do your girl friends make of him?'

'Think he's cruel they do. Don't you Charlie?'.

Charlie did and told her so. 'Look', he said as he took one of her hands, 'fancy coming out wiv me this

Saturday?'

Gill brightened up and looked at our Charlie's concerned face and nodded. 'I'd like that'.

'Where shall I meet you?'

'Round my place if you like. Mum's away at the moment – her sister's taken ill'.

'Will your dad be there?'

'He left two years ago. Broke mum's heart he did. Some other woman, you know. Never seen her'.

'Seven do?' Charlie suggested.

Gill nodded and squeezed his hand and forgot about John as she looked at the new man about to enter her life.

Bang on 7pm a showered and spruced up Charlie was cuddling Gill, who had taken the trouble to dress for the occasion. In his eyes she was a right turn on. Like Janet favoured, only because he had kept on at her about it, she too had on a similar short tight skirt and a revealing blouse. They were on a settee and Charlie had forgotten about Janet and doing his best to keep his rising old man in check.

'Charlie.................'

He stopped nibbling her neck 'Wot, love?'

'Charlie...............shall we........you know....'

'Wot love' he whispered when his hand had worked it's way down her blouse.

'Charlie........' she pulled his hand away and sat up and looked deeply into his eyes 'Shall we go to my room?'

In a flash Charlie had her to her feet and kissed her passionately and caressed her body until she giggled. 'Wot's tickled your fancy, love?' he asked as he continued to caress her lovely body.

'That', she said as she touched his bulge.

' 'e wants you. Come on' he said firmly as he took

her hand. 'Let's go up'.

'Oh, Charlie. You're so nice. Not a bit like John'. She led him up the stairs to her room and let him wrap his arms around her and kiss her tenderly. 'Charlie', she said as she eased away to look at him 'Have you got a girlfriend?'

Charlie wasn't falling for that one. 'No, love. Got a sister, Janet. twentyone she is, your age I'll bet'. He started to pull down the zip of her skirt.

'What's she like, Charlie?. She was helping him get the skirt off, completely unaware that the sight of her beautiful body standing there in bra, knickers, stockings and suspenders had hoisted his libido to a nearly uncontrollable lust.

'Like you', he panted and hurriedly stripped and lifted her up and dropped her on the bed.

'Charlie............................?'

'Wot?' he said as he busied himself taking off her stockings, suspenders and her flimsy knickers and fondled the blonde hairs and vagina.

'You do like me don't you?'

'Like you!' he panted as he straddled her and removed her bra.. 'I love you!' he said hoarsely as he eyed her beautiful boobs, which he expertly fondled and kissed.

Gillian managed to sneak a hand between them and touch his engorged penis.

'Put it in, please', he begged

She did and Charlie went at it with gusto.

'Charlie.......' she whispered to get his attention as he drove home.

'Wot love?' he panted.

'It's alright.....you know.............you can ....you know.........I'm on the pill'.

Charlie's pace picked up at the news but, ever the gent, he waited until she was climaxing and then they became a single entity as their passion took over until, finally, after lying on top of her for some minutes to soak up the magic of their love making and get some strength back, Charlie eased off and propped on an elbow beside her to stroke her glistening body and marvel at her beauty and tell her, again, he loved her because, with the ecstasy of their love making in control of mind and body, he knew he did.

Gill lay still and turned her head to study him, thrilling at his touch on her body and knowing that she didn't want the magic to end. 'Do it again, Charlie.............please'.

This time around he was content to caress and stimulated her and guide her hand to his penis and wait until she urged him to make love again.......................

Charlie woke up first and looked at Gill's blonde stresses and momentarily thought it was Janet until the memory of their love making the evening before flooded in. He stroked Gill's hair and she turned to face him and stroked his face. He drew her to him and rested his head against her neck and told her he loved her.

'Do you really, Charlie? We've only known each other two weeks. Tell me again'.

Instead of answering he moved on top of her and propped himself on elbows to gaze at her lovely, smiling face and her gorgeous blue eyes. He bent down and kissed her tenderly. 'Shall we?' he asked

Gill wriggled her hand between them and found his erection, opened her legs and put it inside and experienced wonderful thrusting minutes of togetherness with our Charlie, Janet's sex God.

'Toast or cornflakes Charlie?'. Thirty or so minutes had passed by and Gill had the kettle on and had already prepared herself a bowl of cornflakes, her favourite, as Charlie walked into the room.

'Toast, love', he told her as he settled in a chair and then looked at her. 'Gill, you're gorgeous' he told her admiringly. Wearing a silky dressing gown tied at the waist and hair tousled from the night before's activity she was so naturally sexy that Charlie felt an urge to make love to her there and then.

'Thank you, Charlie' she said, looking lovingly at him. 'John never told me the things you say'.

'Well, it's true. Ta', he said with his old man slackening as she put the toast in front of him.

She made their coffee and sat down to look at Charlie and stirred her cornflakes, remembering their love making and aware of the surge of affection for this new man in her life who made her feel special.

'Sweetheart', Charlie began 'what do you do in the office?'.

'Boring really. Invoices, statements, that sort of thing'. She twirled the cornflakes again and pushed the bowl away because suddenly she wasn't hungry, content to sit and look at Charlie.

'What happens to the cash?'

'There's a safe in the office. Each evening the manager puts it in it'.

'Bit like you and me' he said mischievously.

'Oh. Charlie!'. She giggled and slapped his hand.

'He nibbled his toast and nodded. 'Where does it go?'

'What do you mean?'

'You can't keep stuffing cash in a safe. It must go somewhere'.

'I see what you meant. Every Friday afternoon a security firm takes the money to a bank or somewhere'.

Charlie pushed his empty plate away and took a swig of coffee. 'Are you in that office?'

'Yes, Charlie. I don't have anything to do with the money, though'.

'Much money, is it?'.

'Well, the manager sometimes says it's been a good week when he's got twenty thousand pounds in the safe'.

'Many in his office?'.

'Funny question, Charlie. Why do you want to know?'

'Young geezers who fancy you?' Charlie asked as he artfully dropped his gaze.

'You're jealous! Go on, admit it!'. She was thrilled at the thought, watching him lift his gaze back to her and away again, then move his head slightly in contrived embarrassment.

'Can't blame me can ya?' he asked as he leaned to take her hand and dig out a bit more information. 'Tell me: are they young blokes, Gill?'.

'No, Charlie. Stop worrying about men fancying me. There's three others during the week. Two women and Chris, and he's an old bloke. On Friday afternoon it's just me and the manager'.

'That's good that is. I don't want uvver blokes leering at you!'. Charlie got up. 'Let me do the washing up, love', he said. When they'd finished he suggested they went for a drive. 'Fancy anywhere?'.

'I'd like my best girl friend to meet you, Charlie. Her and her boyfriend and us, we could go somewhere, couldn't we?'

'Anywhere you like'.

*

Masters studied the floor plan and listened to Charlie's information in silence but, knowing how Charlie was with Janet, he had to know more about the young woman 'So what is it. Friends or what, Charlie?'

'It's or what, Don. She's a smasher, she really is.

You'll make sure she won't get hurt?'.

'What about Janet? Do I detect a hint you're involved with this young lady. Gill, is it?'.

For once in his life Charlie felt guilty. 'Don, Janet mustn't know about Gill. She's so lovely. So is Janet', he added hurriedly, 'I love them both'.

Masters patted his arm and smiled 'Trust me, Charlie. Would I do anything to hurt you. Do you want me to give Janet a look while you're away?'.

'Fanks, Don. You're a real mate. I'll give her a bell and say its alright. Take 'er out for a meal.......she'd like that'.

Don Masters smiled and patted Charlie's arm 'You can rely on me, Charlie. I'll make sure she's alright.

*

Janet stepped out of her skirt and pulled her top over her head and stood face to face with Masters, aching for his touch on her body. He pulled her close and reached round her back to release her bra and bent to kiss her breasts before gently easing her down on the edge of the bed. He knelt down and undid the suspenders and took them off before rolling her stockings down and wriggling them off her feet. Still on his knees, he placed fingers in the hem of her knickers and eased them down and off. He gazed at her inviting vagina and toughed it with a caressing hand. Janet's body gave an involuntary tremble at his touch. He stood and looked into her expectant face and undressed, watching her reaction as he did so. Both standing now, for some seconds they stood close, each holding the other and reliving the blissful moments they had shared and were about to share again.

'Come to bed' she whispered. She eased herself onto the bed and again raised inviting arms. She looked at his erection, experiencing the wondrous feeling of love she remembered from their previous times together, when yearning for Masters to be Charlie had become love for the detective. 'Make love to me' she whispered as she held his expectant penis in her hand, experiencing it's heat, and then caressed his face. She loved the sensation of his arm around her and his fingertips slowly walking down her body, over her tummy and then tickling her hairs, and his penis tickling her stomach. Head thrown back, she eased it between her legs and into her expectant, moist, vagina.

'Do it, Don' she whispered. Her eyes were closed as the moment came and they were together and he was slowly making love to her and kissing her tenderly and cupping her breasts and..........................'Oh Don. Ohhhhh! This is so..........*so..... **beautiful!***' she gasped as their orgasms joined in a climatic moment.

Masters rolled to lay beside her and study her rapt expression, realising as he did so that he was thinking less of Jean of late. Their love-making had dropped off some time back. She was a lovely woman who, he convinced himself, had settled for the companionship they shared and the life-style they had. He wondered at the various pills she was taking but thought it best to wait to be told why. Now, looking at Janet, who was gazing lovingly at him, he realised he needed sex much more now than when he was younger; and was glad his job gave him the advantage of getting the regular sex he craved.

Janet, like John's Sheila, was in a dream world of love. Two men truly loving her was the pinnacle of her desire. Until Don had come into her life she had accepted that Charlie's love for her fulfilled her youthful yearning, but now that yearning had expanded to encompass Don's more mature love for her. It thrilled and excited her and she pushed aside the occasional troubling thought for her future.

*

Having memorised the get away route Masters had insisted he completed twice, Len Spence had pulled the car into the car park of Charlie's warehouse and killed the engine. He watched Masters open a folded piece of paper and spread it. 'It's the floor plan of the warehouse office'. He broke off to indicate the target end of the building. 'My snout drew this so we can rely on it. Watch the toing and froing, Len. I've cased the place and it's like this every weekday and Saturday. Friday afternoon, just before 2pm the cash, already bagged, is taken out of the safe and handed over to one of the crew of a security wagon. Bear in mind that 2pm on Fridays it's as busy as it is now. Watch the activity'.

The several sets of rubber swing doors leading to the loading bays were in fairly constant use as loaded trolleys were wheeled out and the goods stacked into waiting vehicles. The nearest exit was around 15 yards from the entrance door to the offices.

'Like this all day, Don?'. Spence questioned, watching the activity carefully as he spoke.

'All day, from around 9am'.

'How's it to be done?. Spence was using binoculars to study the building and the on-going activity.

Masters told him his plan. 'The security crew are to be kept in their vehicle. You'll need a man with a gun to make sure that happens. Two go into the office and grab the cash'...............

'You said the money was kept in a safe, Don'.

'Its a question of timing, Len. The money is taken out already bagged, like I've told you. The wagon will arrive a few minutes before 2pm.

'Not a balaclava job this?'

Masters was shaking his head. .Definitely not, Len. Kit the firm out with facial disguises.....wigs, moustaches, beards......come up with something'.

'And the getaway?'.

'This is important, Len. You stay in the car with the engine running; one man is to make sure the crew stay in their wagon. That must be Downey. Two go in and grab the cash and sling it in your car and off you go. If you do include Ted on the job, wait for him to get on board but bear this in mind, Len, the sweeney will be there. Don't hang around waiting for Ted if something goes wrong. There may be cock ups but you're escape is guaranteed. If you want Ted in the car he'll have to be quick getting on board. My arrangement with the sweeney is your car gets away'.

'Can't see a problem so far, Don. What's the take?'.

'Varies. Could be twenty grand'.

'And Downey gets nicked, yes?'

'Definitely. This job is about two things: earning a few bob and putting that bastard away. He shot me and has to go. If we're to pull the job he must be the one with the gun'.

Spence stared at the DI and thought for a while. 'It'll mean staying in that Hinkley doss house for a while', he said, his mind made up. 'But I reckon he'll want in. Are we alright for time on this one?'.

Masters nodded and smiled, relishing the idea of more time with Janet and nailing Downey. 'No rush. Their cash is always on the move. Bell me when you're ready and we'll have another meet'.

Masters got out and held up a hand as Spence drove away. Watching until his car had left the car park Masters smiled his satisfaction that his plan was a goer. "Your time's nearly up Downey" he said with grim satisfaction.

*

Derek Lynham, the flying squad detective inspector who had previously acted on Masters' word and pulled Fletcher for a chat, belled Masters and dropped Fletcher's name and suggested they meet. 'Somewhere out of the way', he suggested.

On Masters' suggestion of his usual café they agreed the meet and the DI was the first there and was tucked up in his usual corner when Lynham arrived and brought his coffee over and dropped into a chair opposite, leaning forward to shake Masters hand.

'Nice to see you again, Don' he said as he picked up his mug to take a sip 'Christ! That was hot'.

Masters smiled at the other man's discomfort. 'So. What's so important about Fletcher?'.

'Probably nothing, but he's nicked a car and stashed it in a lock up. He's not your average car thief, Don, so we reckon he's got a job lined up'. After a minute or two Lynham told Masters how it had gone when his squad had pulled Fletcher. 'We found an automatic'. He stopped when he saw the other man's reaction.' Yeh, I know, but if you'd had an ident we'd have nicked him'.

'Why are you telling me this?'.

'We took a grand and the gun -can't leave arseholes with a shooter can we! The point is he's stashed a nicked car. Could he be coming after your witness?'.

'Wouldn't make sense. The man he hit wasn't a witness'. Masters' mind switched to the probable blag he'd lined up and changed the subject ' I've got something for your squad if you're interested'.

'Such as?'

'A blag. A four man firm, armed'.

'Names?'

Masters gave the other DI enough information to keep his interest. 'My snout will stay in the car. The one with a gun is your prime target, so be careful. His job is to make certain that the security crew stay in their cab while the job goes off. . If a second man manages to get in the car that's okay.

Lynham was interested. 'When and where?'.

Masters pulled out the floor plan of the warehouse office and indicated the room with the safe. 'At most there'll be two employees in that room on the day. One is a young bird. On the day I hope to have her replaced'.

'Reason?'

'She's tied in with one of my snouts'.

Lynham was studying the plan. 'How's it going off?'

Masters explained the plan he'd agreed with Len Spence.

'Sounds okay, Don. Run of the mill. Keep me posted. When you've got it sorted give me a bell in time and I'll bring the squad down and recce the area'.

Both detectives got up and for a moment looked at each other before Masters smiled and said 'Like old times, Derek'.

*

Now that her care order had been varied Anne was much happier. Living at home with mum was alright because she could slope off to be with Janet when she wasn't working at the hairdresser's. And Charlie was working away, Janet had told her, which made it smashing. She'd told her mum she was going to stay overnight with Janet whenever she wanted to, ignoring tears and pleading to mix with her local friends.

It was lovely tucked up naked in bed with Janet. They had become soul mates and the closeness of their ages mattered because Janet's mothering wasn't like mum's: more like lovers she told herself, thrilling at the thought. When they went out together they held hands, something Anne had always wondered about at school, but found natural with Janet. Some nights when they were in bed she kissed her and cuddled up to Janet's lovely, soft boobs and experienced the softness of her pubic hairs in her searching fingers. Janet had opener her legs at that moment, she remembered, and she had touched her vagina and Janet had moaned, arched her back and wriggled. Lovely that, she told herself. And in the mornings Janet's fussing wasn't a bit like mum's.. When Janet was close she would touch her hand and be amazed at the thrill she got; and kiss her again, and that was really lovely as well.

The next morning she was looking at Janet's naked, beautiful body, at her protruding breasts, and reliving their togetherness and wanting it to always be like that.

' Will I have breasts like yours' she asked Janet, cupping her own as she asked that.

Janet stood with her bra in her hand and smiled 'We're all different, Anne. Your boobs are alright. They'll develop a bit more, I suppose'.

'What's it feel like when a bloke holds them?'

'Come here and I'll show you' she said. She fondled Anne's breasts and smiled. 'Feel anything?' she asked.

'Is that what a man does?' Anne asked. 'Didn't feel much'.

'That's because I'm not a man. Hasn't your boyfriend done that?'.

'Yeh, not like wot you showed me. He squeezes them like'.

Anne watched Janet finish dressing and pop off to the kitchen and snuggled down again to relive their exquisite moments together......................

'I'm off, Anne. Be back around six' Janet called.

With Janet gone Anne hugged herself and touched her breasts and imagined Janet's hands on them. Lovely, really lovely she remembered, and Janet was so lovely too.

On the bus home she wondered why Janet talked so much about detective inspector Masters; and appeared....what?........excited?....yeh, that was it. Remembering, Anne was jealous. Janet was her best friend.. It wasn't right.

*

'Should ring Janet really'. Charlie was tucked up with Gill and all of a sudden thought about her.

Gill Saunders rolled towards him, puzzled. 'Why, Charlie?'.

'She'll wonder where I am' he answered, without realising what his remark might mean to Gill.

'She's not your mum, Charlie. Surely you can stay out without her say so!'.

Even while Gill was saying that he knew what a prat he'd been. 'I worry about her, love. She's had a bad time wiv a bloke recently, you know'.

'Charlie..........oh, Charlie. I wish I'd had a brother like you to care for me. We must go out so you can ring her'.

He pulled her closer and kissed her. 'Not right now though' he told her as he began caressing her body.

'Oh, Charlie...............0h Charlie..................*oooh!.* Her back was arched with the exquisite sensation of his searching hand and she looked lovingly at him. 'Oh, Charlie, she whispered.............'let's do it now!'.

Chapter thirty four

The deputy governor of Pentonville prison watched a police officer attaching a wired microphone to Jakeson's underclothing, and help him pull on a shirt to conceal the wires. 'Is that it?' he asked.
The A10 detective nodded.
'Very well. Leave us now'.

*

Detective inspector Brian Lindley wasn't unduly concerned when an associate of Jakeson got word to him that he wanted a meet. So far as he was concerned the arsehole was well and truly banged up and might, who knows, put up some villains for who knows what. His squad, in their car outside, passed the time sharing the bottle around and evaluating the birds in the squad's typing pool. Betty, as usual came out top.

Inside, guided by a screw to a side room in the prison, Lindley sat and waited and stared hard at Jakeson when he was brought in and pushed down into a chair on the other side of the table. He waited until the screw had left the room to casually observe ' I see you're an escape risk', when he took in the coloured top the man was wearing.

Jakeson had been advised to keep calm and lead the detective into his trap. He smiled at Lindley and started his unscripted endeavour. 'Still earning?', he chucked in for starters.

'Are you thick or what? Why am I here?'. Lindley was half out of his chair when Jakeson flapped his hands at him. He sat down and waited.

'The blagging, Brian. I thought we had a deal. I'm doing twenty frigging five here, know what I mean?'.

'So? You shot the finger. How was I supposed to help?'.

'You could've lost the gun for starters. The deal was the gun got lost so...........what the frigging hell happened? My bird got a tug, she gets two frigging years, and I get stitched up by that frigging Masters and you're sitting there with that poncy smile and you ask me how could you help me! You should have kept to our deal and lost the gun'. Jakeson had lost the plot and was shouting the accusation and Lindley was showing his concern.

'Keep it down' he hissed.

'You knew Bateman was on to our deal and you knew he got greedy. I told you. A grand he said would do for starters'. He stared at the detective 'Do you remember what you told me? No?' He watched the detective who sat and stared back. ' Then I'll remind you. 'What's a gun for? That's what you said'.

'You pulled the trigger. That's why you're in here so don't muck about with me. Try to involve me and I promise you'll regret it'.

'That's your last word is it?'

'You've wasted my time, Phil. You're a frigging loser'.

Jakeson half rose and leaned across the small table to stab a finger at the detective, forgetting why the meet was on in his anxiety to make his threatening point.' I'm not taking this on my own, you bastard. It was your career on the line, remember? You said that and don't forget it'.

Lindley stayed silent but his initial caution was giving way to anger at the way the slag was mouthing off at him.

He too rose and shoved *his* face close to the other man's.'You fucked up, you prat, when you left your prints in the car. You're only in here because of that'.

'Bollocks, it's the gun. And you gave it to my bird and she's banged up. I'm not having it. I want her out'.

Lindley had taken as much shit as he was prepared to take from Jakeson and stepped away from the table to stare down and say ' There's nothing you can do to me you arsehole. I meet your kind every day of every week and, believe me, you're all losers. That just about sums it. You and me know the script for that killing: I spell it out and you do the hit. Do your time, Phil, and stop squealing'.

'That's it is it?'

'That *is* it, Phil. Settle down and do the time'.

*

Charlie's information regarding the warehouse layout was detailed. Knowing customers would be in the building but at the rear of the offices when their goods were being checked, removed any possibility the robbery would go pear shaped from that direction. The rear door from the back office into the warehouse was kept locked during working hours. Access to the front office with the safe was via a door, unlocked during working hours, leading from the passageway; the other office was to the rear of it, accessed via a communicating lockable door The main entrance door, immediately in front of the passageway, was always unlocked.

Masters was parked away from the office with Lynham, watching the security van pull up close to the main entrance and the passenger climb out and enter the building, reappearing with one bag, just as Charlie had told them. The whole operation was over in three timed minutes, during which time customers had entered and left via the six rubber swing doors under a covered way almost continuously during that time, and loaded their backed-up vehicles.

'Got to be in the office', Lynham said as he took in the number of people in the vicinity of the security vehicle.

Masters agreed. 'That was what I had in mind. Two go in when the van enters the car park and do the business. Man three need only show his gun for around a minute. Any more than that and I reckon we'll have a war on our hands. He gestured at the people entering the warehouse 'Anyone could be a hero on the day. 'How many men are you bringing?'

'My squad can handle it'.

'Seen enough?'

Lynham nodded. 'Will you be around?'.

Masters was smiling 'Couldn't keep me away, Derek'.

*

'Call for you, guv'.

'Thanks, Dusty'. Masters took the handset and listened for a while. 'Thanks, might be useful' he said and listened again. 'Right, many thanks'.

'What was that about, guv?', Miller asked as Masters dropped the handset on its cradle.

'CID at Hinckley telling me that Downey has teamed up with two blokes with a London accent'. He smiled at Miller. 'Looks like the blag's a goer'.

'Got to hand it to Len', remarked Miller, admiringly.

*

The two A.10 CID officers sat and waited for commander Stewart to finish reading the transcript before detective inspector Keith Stannard, the senior of the two, asked, 'suspension, sir?'.

The commander sat back and closed his eyes, realising that Lindley had dug himself into a pit of shit out of which he might not get. Opening his eyes he stared directly at Stannard 'Your view is?'

DI Stannard shuffled his file into a tidy bundle before glancing at the commander 'Not relevant, sir. It's your decision'.

Stewart nodded and stood up. 'A shock this. I need time to think this through, inspector', he said as the other two stood. 'Inspector Lindley has a good record. Exemplary in fact. He may have an answer to this', he tapped the report. I'll send my response through the usual channels'.

'Thank you, sir. I'll leave the tape and transcript with you, shall I?'.

Stewart nodded and shook hands.

*

Two more weeks had slipped away blissfully for Gill and during their daily lunch break, she and Charlie left the warehouse and went to his car for a sandwich and a cuddle. It had been a long week for him. He'd phoned Janet each evening from a call box in the firm's car park, and told her how much he missed her. He was surprised how cheerful she sounded. Of course I do, she told him when he asked if she missed him. Yes, he has, she confirmed when he asked if Don had kept in touch. Don's a good bloke, he told her, glad that she had someone to turn to while he was away.

Each lunch break he'd told Gill about his sister's happiness and she was pleased for him, even saying, on this occasion, she was lucky to have a brother who thinks about her all the time. With a tinge of guilt Charlie's hug tightened when she said that. They finished their sandwiches and tidied up and Charlie, looking lovingly at her, asked about her mum's sister.

'She's not well, Charlie. Mum's going to spend the weekend with her'.

He saw the door edging open and pleaded, his testosterone alerting his balls that the start gun was on a hair trigger because a chance for a bit of leg over was in the offing. 'Sweetheart, I can't stand not being with you all week. Can we get together this weekend at least?'. He was looking into her eyes as he said that and quickly followed up with a pleaful, wide-eyed, stare.

Her answer was in her beautiful, inviting smile that sent tingles to his balls. 'Gill! Oh Gill!'. He was excited. ' You mean I can spend the weekend with you?' He took her hands and pulled her close and kissed her.

She pulled back. 'That hurt, Charlie!'.

'Wot did I do?'.

'Not you - the gear stick'. She inclined her head towards him, smiling at his excitement. 'We can have the whole weekend together, darling. Won't that be wonderful'.

Charlie was lost for words, until he remembered the planned robbery. .'Did the boss agree your afternoon off like I asked, love?'

'Not straight off, Charlie. Like you said to say I said my mum had her sister coming that weekend. Wanted to help mum get the house tidy.......... he agreed. But why, Charlie? You never said why did you?'.

He looked into her questioning blue eyes and made it up on the spot. 'Because, sweetheart, we're going to have the afternoon out together. Have a meal like'.

'Oh, Charlie. You're so thoughtful. I'd love that' she said as she pulled him back and gave him a kiss.

He checked his watch and opened the car door. 'Time to get back to work, sweetheart'.

*

On the day of the robbery the squad car arrived at 1.30pm and was parked close to the passing area in front of the warehouse office. Spence's stolen BMW arrived at 1.50pm and stopped directly in front of the passageway entrance to the offices, preventing the security van, which arrived on the dot at 1.55pm, from stopping where it usually did. The four plain clothed officers left their car and mingled with customers making their way to the warehouse entrances as Downey got out of the BMW and strolled to stand beside the passageway entrance door. Burke and Finley, the recruited fourth man, eased out of the rear seats, opened the passageway door and disappeared inside.

Precisely at 2pm the passenger in the security van opened his door and Downey moved to face him and raised his automatic, shouting to him to stay in the vehicle. Burke and Finley came out at that moment and ran the few paces to the waiting car. Two flying squad officers, shouting: 'armed police', had their handguns trained on Downey, and Burke, holding the bag, seized his chance and dived into the revving BMW as Spence gunned it away, leaving Finley stranded to be wrestled to the ground by two other squad officers.

Downey, his gun still trained on the security guard, was taken by surprise at the struggle with Finley and angled towards the officers holding him down, hearing again 'Armed police! Put it down!'. The armed officers, crouching now with two-handed grips on their automatics, waited for Downey's response but, in a surprised and fatal moment he turned his gun towards the officer who had called out and reeled backwards from the impact of two fatal shots, one to the head the other to the chest.

Masters had watched with satisfaction the unfolding drama from his car parked near the office. He left the car and stood over Downey. Blood was seeping down the side of his body, forming a small pool on the ground. Aware of a gathering crowd, he radioed for an ambulance and for back up officers to assist the squad officers secure the scene. The two officers who had fired at Downey were handing their guns to Lynham. Masters went into the office while a handcuffed Finley was being thrown into the back of the flying squad car and driven off.

The manager appeared to be in a state of shock and unable to concentrate on Masters questions. Gill's replacement for the afternoon, Steve Watts, a youngster, had been hit over the head with a gun and he too was apparently unable to concentrate on Masters questions while his gash was being attended to by the company's first aid woman.

'Are you up to answering a few questions, Steve?' Masters asked, again, this time watching the wound being dressed.

'Will it need stitches?' the youngster asked the woman, still not able to concentrate on Master's question.

'Probably', she told him. The ambulance shouldn't be long'.

'I've called for one' ,Masters told her

'I know. They told me when I phoned'.

The youngster swivelled to look at the detective 'Sorry officer. What d'you want to know?'.

'Descriptions. Can you help me?'

'Bit of a laugh really. They had those Mexican type droopy moustaches and I swear they were wearing wigs. I got this', he gingerly fingered his injury ' because I thought it was a bleeding joke and laughed at them. No joke was it!'.

*

Spence dumped the BMW half a mile away, leaving behind their wigs and false moustaches. The cash now safely in their own holdall, they strolled to the bus stop agreed with Masters and hopped on the next bus along.

Upstairs, with fags on the go, Len suggested to Ted, who wholeheartedly agreed, that the DI was in the wrong game.

*

Masters and Lynham, two days after the job, met in the café Masters favoured and tucked into fry ups, drank tea, and discussed the share out.

'My man gets ten grand', Masters said, explaining: 'He stood to lose most. We get five each'.

Lynham downed his fork and nodded. 'Nice one, Don. I enjoyed the fun and games'.

*

On the following Monday evening Masters and Charlie were sinking pints in a pub near the warehouse. 'It went well, Charlie', Masters told him, patting his hand. 'Your info was spot on. What's been said at your end?'

'Nuffink, Don. Gill says the boss has changed. He locks the office door now. Bit daft really now the money's been nicked'.

'Has she worked anything out?'

'Nah, Don. Why would she?'.

'Her afternoon off? She must have said something'.

'I fought that but she didn't'.

'Be careful, Charlie. Watch what you say. Here', he handed over three hundred pounds 'Treat Gill; and Janet if you get a chance'.

'I was going to talk to you about that, Don. The job aint bad, you know, I fink I'll stay for a while'.

Masters looked at Charlie and understood. 'Gill?'

'Yeh. We get on well, and I like being wiv her. I worry about Janet, Don. I aint got the heart to tell her about Gill'.

A relieved DI patted Charlie's arm.'Then don't tell her. See how things work out with Gill. Tell you what - I'll tell Janet you like the job. Bell her and give her some explanation she'll go for'.

Charlie was relieved. He loved being with Gill but not knowing how Janet was getting on had been worrying him. 'You're a good bloke, Don. A real mate'. He thrust out a hand. 'Fanks for looking after Janet for me'.

'The least I could do, Charlie'. Masters told him, already hardening at the thought of being with her.

*

The podgy Commander, ensconced in his plush chair, watched a smile spread across DI Lindley's face as the tape of the conversation with Jakeson came to an end. 'A10 want you suspended right away, Brian', he told the younger man. 'I may yet have to go down that route. Is anything else likely to crop up? Now would be the best time to tell me'.

'Not that I can think of, sir. The usual bastards are out there waiting a chance to have a go but no, no more than the usual risks we take'.

Stewart backed the tape. 'A10 are hanging their hat on this comment. Listen Jakeson's grating voice said "You and me know the script for that killing: I spell it out and you do the hit" '. He looked sympathetically at the inspector . 'Comment?'.

'Off the record, sir?'.

'Between you and me. What was the score back there?'.

'Bateman got greedy. Jakeson put himself up for the hit'.

There was a knock on the office door at that moment. The commander called out 'enter' and both officers waited silently while the female detective placed a tray with two mugs of coffee, milk and sugar and a plate of biscuits on the commander's desk and turned to smile at Lindley, before leaving and closing the door.

'Black, sir'.

Stewart pushed a mug and the biscuit plate across to the inspector and heaped two spoonfuls of sugar into his. 'Sweet tooth. Bad habit!' he said with a chuckle as he patted his girth.

Lindley smiled briefly and nibbled a biscuit and sipped his coffee, watching his boss do the same. He knew the interview was going well. He trusted Stewart. Each squad did. The man was a diamond who stood by his officers. 'Mind if I smoke, sir?'.

'Go ahead'. Stewart pushed an ashtray across the desk. He tapped the tape recorder. 'On the face of it you're in trouble. Is your squad involved?'.

Lindley shook his head.

'Good'. He nibbled another biscuit and leaned back in his chair to think. 'Right, Brian. He sat forward 'You got belled to have the meet. You admit to that. You firmly believed that Jakeson was going to put up villains for unsolved crimes. When he started on about the murder you went along with it to keep him on board until, of course, he finally pissed you off. Sound alright?'.

'Spot on, sir'.

'Right. Stay with that when A10 get to you. The Assistant Commissioner wants an expert to give the tape the once over'. He smiled. 'I think we know what that means, eh! Oh - I've arranged for new desk diaries to be issued to each detective. I want any reference to a meet with an informant on the run up to this matter omitted. Best be on safe ground, eh?. With A10 on the prowl we won't know if some bastard or other out there will seize the chance to stick a knife into any of my men'.

'When is the enquiry getting under way, sir?'.

'When I say. For now A10 have left it with me and I've stalled them. When I give the nod they'll have you in for the interview. It'll be under caution, Brian. Be cooperative but stick to our agreed line and you won't necessarily be suspended. When I get their final report I'll make that decision'.

Lindley was relieved. 'Thank you, sir'.

*

The internal formalities surrounding Downey's death dragged on but, with so many witnesses available from the scene, it became apparent that the flying squad officers who fired the fatal shots had no other choice. And Downey's gun, being proven to be the one that fired the bullet into Masters all those months before, took the sting out of Makepeace's usual tirade about blaggers having it on their toes with the cash from the job.

*

Chapter thirty five

'Are you sure this is the best way to go?'.

Jean Masters couldn't answer.

The doctor reached to touch her hand. 'Mrs. Masters. He should be told', he told her sympathetically.

'I know. Of course I know'. She looked at the doctor again and lowered her tear-stained face. 'You're right, but nothing can change what's happening to me'. Through moist eyes she stared mistily at the man who had just told her one of her lungs had to be removed. Fear shuddered her body.

'Mrs. Masters. He has to know the operation is next Tuesday. You'll have to be in here Monday morning'

*

Don Masters walked beside the trolleyed bed wheeling Jean to the anti room, where an anaesthetist was waiting to introduce the required intravenous drip. He saw her faint smile disappear and her face relax as she drifted into unconsciousness. As the staff ushered Don out of the room he watched her bed being pushed through swing doors into the operating theatre.

That evening, her bed adjusted for her to sit upright, Jean was wheeled into the ward and Don was able to hold her hand at last. She smiled weakly at her husband and Valerie Miller, and glanced around the six bed ward and back to them before she greeted them with a husky hello.

They moved away from the bed while a nurse fussed with the drip and drain, and got a nod from Jean when asked if she was comfortable. Smiling at them, the nurse left.

Don kissed Jean's forehead ' I love you so much, darling. You're going to be alright'.

He pulled a chair close to the bed while Valerie pulled a chair from beside the empty bed at the other side.

'How do you feel, sweetheart?', he asked, knowing as he spoke the words couldn't express his deep concern for her plight and the terror he was convinced she was consumed by. He felt her fingers tighten on his and her answer was a smile but her pale, exhausted, appearance told the real story.

*

It was ten days before Jean was cleared to go home. During that period an oncologist had explained to Don there was no certainty cancer wouldn't return. He explained that Jean's lung cancer had been advanced; and there was a possibility of cancer cells moving to her other lung. Her regime of chemotherapy was explained to him. 'It is important she keeps to the programme. At some point she will be required to return here to review the procedure'.

*

Jean's constant headache determined Don to get her back to the hospital. After what seemed ages to Jean she was taken to another part of the hospital for a brain scan. With her head marked, she was eased into the tunnelled machine that would determine whether the cancer has spread to her brain. An hour later Masters was told it had.

'My wife mustn't be told' said a distressed Masters. 'Please be careful when you speak with her'.

The radiologist understood what he was being asked and told his wife who, until then, had been waiting in another room, 'Keep to the prescribed medication, Mrs. Masters, and you'll be fine'

'What about the headache?' she asked anxiously

'Probably a side effect of the medication. We'll arrange an appointment for you to return here in six months for a further scan'.

*

Charlie was enjoying his job and his life with Gill. Janet was a fading memory and Gill noticed that he wasn't so concerned about his sister lately. She said so.

'Don't need to bell her sweetheart. Her new bloke seems okay'.

'Did Janet say that, Charlie?'

'Yeah................she's alright'.

'Oh, Charlie. I'd love to meet her. She seems a girl I could get on with, really she does'.

Which was the very last thing he wanted. 'I'll bell her soon and work something out', he said with a disarming smile. He drew her onto his lap and cuddled up to her. 'You're a smasher, Gill, you really are'. He ran his hands down her thighs and felt her shiver. 'Cold love?'

Gill smiled at him and shook her head. 'I love it when you caress me Charlie, that's all. Makes me feel......come on. Let's go up' she said impetuously.

*

What's wrong Don?'. Janet pulled herself onto an elbow and studied Masters face. 'What is it darling?'

For the best part of half an hour Masters and Janet had lain in bed. Janet had fondled his libido-affected penis from time to time and he had cuddled her but, when she had eased herself onto him and reached for his penis it remained slack. Now, looking at him, she knew something was seriously wrong. 'I've done something, haven't I? What is it Don?'.

He took her hand away and kissed it. 'You've done nothing, sweetheart. Truly. Nothing. It's me'.

'Don't you love me any more?'

I love you more and more each time we're together'.

Confused, Janet continued to search his face for a reason. He looked so sad. For weeks now, she realised suddenly, he had been getting sadder and sadder. 'Is it your job, darling?.

Don shook his head and knew she had to be told. 'It's Jean. She's dying, Janet. Bloody cancer'.

Horrified she whispered 'Oh, my God'.

'Both lungs and her brain'. Masters eased to sit on the edge of the bed and reached back for Janet's hands. 'None of this is your fault' he told her kindly. 'I can't seem to get it together. We've been married for so................'. He broke off when he saw Janet's tears. 'We can't change anything, sweetheart. It's not my fault and it's not your fault' He squeezed her hands tightly in his and pulled her close and kissed her cheek. 'Even if we hadn't fallen in love it would have happened'. He studied her anguished face and stood up, pulling her to her feet and drawing her close to nuzzle her hair, enjoying that brief moment of his love for her.

'How long before................? Janet broke off the whispered the question and stared into his anguished face, tears trickling down her face.

Seeing them he put a finger against them to brush them away.. 'I know, sweetheart, I know. Its so bloody unfair. 'Weeks. Months. The doctors cant say'.

*

Chapter thirty six

'What's he in for?'

Miller was looking from Ted Read to the blood smeared face of the burly man sitting opposite the detective constable in the interview room.

'Rape, sarg'.

'And the blood?'

'Got stroppy, sarge'.

'Who'd he rape?'.

'I haven't raped any frigging cow!' the prisoner said defiantly.

Miller pulled him out of his chair and recognised him when he was face to face. 'He's our knicker knocker!'..

'Dead right sarge. That's how I got onto him. There aren't two like him out there are there!'.

Miller shoved the man onto his chair and pointed at the detective constable. 'You heard what he told me. You've raped a bird. Not a frigging cow'. The emphasising punch that followed sent him sprawling off his chair to an untidy heap against a wall.

'Who's the woman, Ted?' Miller demanded as he stared down at Joe Swift.

' Daryl Browne. Works in Boots. I've seen her from time to time. Right tasty'.

Where'd he do it?'

'Her flat. Must have followed her home'.

'Where's that?'.

Read told him. 'Brazen bastard - anyone could have seen him on her first floor balcony'.

'Did they?'.

'So far, no sarg'.

'I didn't rape anyone!' came from the floor.

The sergeant crossed to the man and bent down to

stare at him. 'Shut your frigging mouth you arsehole!' He kicked at Joe's sprawled legs and turned his attention to Read. 'Tell me more'.

'Got a shout over the phone from her. Nickerless when I got there. SOCO have got his Y fronts bagged up, and a semen stained handkerchief'.

'How'd you get onto him?'.

Read smiled as he recalled. 'Her description was enough. Like you said, sarge, he's our knicker knocker. That's right isn't it?' he said to Swift.. ' Big bloke isn't he?'. he said as he turned to grin towards Miller 'Say hello to the sergeant, Joe'.

Swift nodded and looked from one man to the other. 'Where we going from here then?' he asked with a lack of confidence natural for his predicament, especially with Miller towering over him.

But the sergeant was fresh from a verbal bashing from Valerie: with the three women's death floating around his subconscious he had taken it out on her. His need for sex, coupled with his need to subjugate women when he was in the throes of sexual arousement had frightened her. He bent over and thumped Joe again before, scruffing him by the collar, he hauled him up and planted him in a chair.

Joe stared at Miller defiantly. 'Fuck you' he said.

'That's what you did to the bird'. He glanced at Read. 'Made a statement?'.

Read stared thoughtfully down at Swift. 'He will, sarge. He will'.

'The woman - got her statement yet?'.

'No, sarg. I'm nipping round this evening'.

Miller patted Read's arm. 'You've got enough on your plate with him. I'll get it for you'.

*

One by one the relatives and Master's colleagues drifted off and he looked down at the mass of flowers and cards and saw Jean, alive and happy and healthy and smiling as she always did until he was aware of Janet who had moved beside him. She squeezed his hand reassuringly but said nothing.

'Hard to take in, Janet', he said quietly.

'Nobody knows how you feel, darling. I just wish I'd met her'.

He nodded and said nothing. Jean had gone to her death not knowing about Janet but had been forgiving about Kay. 'She was a wonderful woman, Janet. Truly wonderful'.

'Darling, stay as long as you want. May I stay with you?'.

Don returned her squeeze but turned away from the emotive display which was heightening his guilt. 'Let's go, sweetheart'. We can't change anything'.

*

Masters and Miller looked at the woman in the bath whose head was barely clear of the water at the overflow level. Her eyes were wide open and she was clearly dead in the bloodied water that told its sad story. Her husband, who had made the call, stood in the door.

'Know her do we?' Miller queried.

Masters nodded. It was clear that the sergeant was untroubled by the sight: Sheila Walters' demise had been predicted at the nick following her break up from John Barton.. 'Wrist job Dusty', Masters observed needlessly from the blood-stained evidence.

"No doubt, Don. Stupid bitch. All alike aren't they: their terms or nothing. Your Kay was no exception...and she got what she deserved, just like the others'.

Masters glanced at the sergeant, the unstructured

thoughts that had floated in and out of his mind during the many weeks since the last woman had died taking on a disquieting reality. .He looked away. "it can't be" he told himself sternly.

'Something wrong, Don?'.

Masters shook his head and stared down at the dead woman. 'Mixed thoughts, Dusty' he said quietly. 'John'll have questions to answer at the inquest'. But as he spoke his thoughts had switched back to Miller again.................it had been his car...............his blanket......... the belt..........was it his? No, he told himself. That can't be.

'Can't be off it, Don', Miller was speaking cheerfully. 'He was a pratt to get so involved. Bloody obvious to me that's why she topped herself'.

*

Daryl Browne stood in the chained-doorway and stared fearfully at Miller, who was smiling and holding out his warrant card.

'Detective sergeant Miller, Miss Browne. May I come in?'.

'Would you hold it up, please', she said, her voice faint with worry.

'Oh. Sorry'. The sergeant thrust the card closer and smiled. 'Okay? I need to take a statement regarding the assault'.

Relieved but still anxious the young woman slid the chain out of it's groove. Opening the door wide she stood to one side and waited for Miller to enter the hallway. 'I told the other detective all about it', she told the sergeant, who had stopped in front of her and was clearly admiring her. 'Go through there', she pointed to an open doorway.

Miller dragged his eyes from her sexy curves and

inclined his head and pointed.

'Yes'. she confirmed. Uncomfortable under his searching gaze, she pulled her cardigan tightly around herself and followed him as far as the living room doorway and waited while he chose an armchair and dropped into it, smiling up at her.

'Officer', she began nervously, 'The other detective said a police woman would take my statement. I would be happier for a woman officer to be here'.

Miller saw she was biting her lip and hugging herself, and appeared ready to bolt from the room. He grinned. 'There's nothing to worry about, miss. You're safe with me'.

Something about Miller was frightening her. She was shaking her head and had moved to the far side of the doorway. 'I want you to go. Please go'. She pointed to the front door. 'Please go'.

He hauled himself up and stared, unaware his contempt for women was written across his face; but his anger was evident.

'Please go now. I'm not happy with you here'. She moved into the hall and stood back when he brushed against her.

He opened the front door and stared back at her, by now angrily frustrated to be dismissed. 'You're all alike you know', he told her. 'You probably got what you deserved'.

She closed the door and leaned against it, her heart thumping and her mouth suddenly dry. For perhaps a minute she stayed leaning against the door, reliving her nightmarish experience, the sergeant's face merging with the rapist's. She moved away from the door and picked up the phone.

*

John Barton and Gillian were enjoying their newly found happiness and Sheila was banished from conversation. Sitting across from her in the restaurant, John was a happy man again. He had carefully packaged and slotted away his guilt and had, naturally, he was a man after all, convinced himself he was innocent of any wrong doing.

'Sad about Sheila, John', Gillian ventured with her fork hovering above her plate. He hadn't said anything about her since she'd read the article to him about her death. His silence on that subject since then had troubled her. She reached across and squeezed his hand to get his attention .'Is it in the past, sweetheart?. Is it?'.

He squeezed back and smiled. 'Of course it is, darling', he answered brightly.

*

DCS Makepeace gestured for Masters to take a seat, and waited until he had done so and was looking him in the eye before leaning forward to put his concern bluntly. 'Detective sergeant Miller - tell me about him', he asked, staring intently at the DI.

Surprised at the unexpected question Masters smiled, and spread his hands. 'Dusty's a good officer, surely you know that?'.

'Leave out the crap, inspector. What do you really know about him?'.

'You've lost me, sir. What's this about?'.

'Women, inspector. Miller has overstepped the mark, frankly. Your raped woman... Browne. Why in God's name did you allow Miller to interview her in her home - alone, mark you. She's made a written complaint about his conduct'.

Mystified, Masters shook his head. 'I didn't allow it. This is the first I've heard of it'.

'"Got what she deserved", he apparently told her. 'Is she a prostitute?'.

Masters thoughts immediately scanned his half-buried concern regarding Miller and his attitude to women. Valerie had unburdened herself on Jean about his behaviour. Now the detective chief superintendent's statement fitted with what he had been told by Jean....... but surely not?. 'No, sir. Enquiries have established she has an unblemished character'.

Makepeace's anger was evident. 'Frankly, inspector, the man's a time bomb. I expect you to deal with this expeditiously'. He pushed the woman's statement across his desk. 'And make sure your report is on my desk by Monday'.

*

Daryl Browne had been positive an hour earlier, pointing to Swift on the identification parade. Now, nervously, she sat opposite Masters in an interview room. Woman police sergeant Alice Goldsmith sat beside him taking down her statement. Prompted by her, Daryl recounted how Swift had forced his way in when she answered the bell and dragged her to her bedroom. 'He pushed me onto the bed and dragged my knickers off. I was terrified. I couldn't move a muscle. I told him I was having a period............I wasn't, but I thought.........hoped........ he might stop. He took his trousers and underpants off and got on top of me and told me to..to..put it in'. She looked at the sergeant for support in her embarrassment with Masters there, listening unsmilingly to her details of the attack.

Alice touched her hand sympathetically. 'The inspector understands, you mustn't feel any embarrassment. But I need every detail, it's important'.

'When he'd been, you know, he got up. He

threatened me not to tell anyone. He knew where I worked he said and would get me. It was awful, just awful'.

'Did he hit you?'.

Daryl shook her head.

'Tell me what happened once he'd got off you?'.

'I remember he wiped his penis on a handkerchief - he took it from a trouser pocket. Then he put them on and left'.

'What happened to the handkerchief?'.

'He left it - and his underpants. The detectives who came here have them'.

'You've identified your attacker at the parade. Apart from recognising his face - was there anything else you can recall?'.

'Yes - tattoos on his forearms. Swirly things - might have been snakes'.

'Thank you, Daryl. Sign the caution at the top and each page, please............and here, where I've corrected my mistakes'.

She waited for her to do so and then, looking quickly at Masters before smiling at the young woman, added persuasively. 'The inspector wants you to relate exactly how detective sergeant Miller conducted himself at the interview'.

*

After DCS Makepeace read Miss Browne's statement he pushed it aside and picked up Masters brief report. Grunting, he put it down and looked intently at the DI. 'This skirts around the issue, inspector. Is Miller just a nasty bastard with women....or do we have something far more serious to deal with here?'.

'Meaning our murders?'.

'Frankly, yes'.

Masters saw that Makepeace was as concerned as himself at the innuendo floating about the division. He sat back and gave himself time to think clearly before saying. 'There's not a shred of evidence to suggest Miller as the killer. The jury believed the belt was Lakey's. If Miller planted it surely he did it to strengthen the case. We've all done that, it's what we have to do to get these bastards put away'.

'Yes, yes, I know that, but what about his car in that road where Flaxman's body was found, and the Watson woman? Then there's the blanket -forensic have matched the soil on it with the soil where the women were found'.

Masters rummaged through the file on his lap and pulled out Miller's statement. 'He covered that. He's been overside with a flying squad typist for some time. Takes her there.........it's a quiet road with a couple of handy lay-bys and grassy areas. According to her statement she won't have it off in a car - hence the blanket. That would explain the soil samples, I suppose. She can't put a date to any of their trysts'.

The DCS snorted. 'Convenient, inspector'.

'I suppose she's typed so many statements for the squad she knows when it's best to be vague'.

'Is she covering for him?'.

Masters spread his hands. 'No, is surely the answer to that, sir. She knew it was regarding murder when she was interviewed for an alibi statement'.

Makepeace leaned back and stared at the ceiling, clearly troubled at what he was hearing. Turning his beady gaze to Masters he said. 'The belt is the cruncher. We either have a copy cat murderer out there or, if Miller *is* the killer, you've locked up an innocent man. God! What a nightmare!'

'Copy cat, sir? the last one was strangled with rope'.

'For Christ's sake, inspector. 'Three women have

been strangled. If it is Miller who killed the first two, doesn't it follow that the third one was killed with a different belt or rope or whatever?'.

Four, Masters told himself grimly, visualising Kay Bruce's headlong fall. He shook his head. 'I can't see it, sir. He's a violent sod, always has been, but not a murderer. When we find Sheila Watson's killer we'll be able to get rid of these suspicions'.

'And on that front: any break through?'.

'No, sir'.

Makepeace shuffled the papers into a file. 'This lot goes no further, inspector, unless we get evidence pointing to him as our man. Agreed?'.

'I think that's the best way to go, sir'.

*

Janet was in the master bedroom for the first time. She stared silently at the bed he had shared with Jean and was overwhelmed with sadness. Don turned her to face him and held her face, gently wiping away her tears. He kissed and cuddled her and sat her on the bed Sitting now beside her and stroking her hair he knew as he spoke comforting words, they wouldn't banish her sadness.

Janet was aware of Jean's presence everywhere in the house. She had experienced it that first moment they had walked through the front door weeks before. Don had taken her into each room and said nothing while Janet saw Jean everywhere in the little things that a woman would understand. Even though the bedroom they used did not have Jean's presence, she had been unhappy.

'Can we really be happy here, Don? Can we?'.

'We can try, sweetheart. Give it time'.

'What about your family? And Jean's family?'

'Its our lives not their's, Janet. We never did live in each other's'.

'Will they accept me?'.

Don stood and pulled her up and took her hands. 'I love you my darling with every fibre of my body. Time heals. Once they get to know you they will accept you.. You've done nothing wrong so you must not worry what other people are thinking'.

'But it's so soon after Jean...............'. She broke off and tears welled up.

He pulled her to him and cuddled her tightly, stroking her hair as he whispered 'Darling, everything's going to be alright. If you find it too difficult to live here I'll sell up. Probably be for the best anyway'.

Janet pulled back to stare up at him 'Would you do that, darling. Really'.

'Certainly'.

*

Masters, his mind dwelling on Miller's possible involvement with murder and not on the road ahead, was overtaking a car at eighty miles per hour in the dual carriageway when it suddenly accelerated and swerved into the side of his Jaguar and pulled away, forcing him to slide and grind his car against the central barrier, throwing a stream of sparks into the night sky. His fight to control the car ceased when the car spun away from the barrier and bounced and rolled across the carriageways. Masters, the driver's door flung open, was catapulted into the air and lucky the car was airborne when he hit the concrete and rolled over and over until, with his clothes raggedly torn from his body, he lay still.

*

'How bad is it?' Makepeace asked Miller, who was sitting outside Masters' ward.

'Touch and go, sir. Be a while before we'll know how he'll come out of this'.

'Seen him?'.

'No, sir. One of the doctors told me head injuries like Don's could go either way'.

Makepeace, in spite of the suspicions he harboured told him firmly. 'Go home, sergeant'.

Miller shook his head. 'I'd sooner stay for a while'.

The DCS nodded and sat beside him. 'Bad business, sergeant', he said eventually. 'I've arranged for DI. Fountain to be transferred back to fill in for Don until I get a clearer picture. Bring him up to speed, sergeant. Work with him'.

Miller, nodding at the instruction, didn't spot the chief superintendent's quick side glance as he stood up that concealed concern he was suspected of murder.

*

Gloria Gardner was looking lovingly at her brother on a visit. 'Will he survive? The TV news reckons he's in a coma'.

'Doubt it. Should have seen it sis. His car careered across the carriageway -sparks flying everywhere. I pulled over to watch. He was lying on the road'. He grinned with pleasure at the memory. 'Looked dead to me'.

'Frigging good job, Adie. How'd you know he'd be on that road at that time?'.

'Easy, really. 'Belled his nick for a meet. Said I had info on a blagging coming up'.

'That easy?'

'That easy, sis. Coppers are all alike. Mention a blag and their aerials go rigid. Tagged along behind him, even overtook at one point and glanced across at him. After he overtook me I did the business'.

'Can the car be traced to you, Adie?'

'Stolen wasn't it. Dumped it didn't I'.

*

DI Brian Fountain quickly scanned the report he was holding and popped into sergeant Miller's office. He held it up 'We've had a break through, Dusty. SOCO have the car that hit Masters' Jag. Stolen from south London weeks before the incident. CRO have put up one Adrian Fletcher: his dabs are all over the bloody thing, and so is the Jag's paint'.

*

'Let me do it, guv'. Miller was staring hard at Fountain, who had just told him that Fletcher was in a cell below. ' I want it'.

Fountain nodded his agreement but warned the sergeant 'No blood, Dusty. And caution him first'.

Miller grinned back. 'Naturally, guv'.

Miller went down to the custody area and looked grimly at the uniformed constable on cell block duty. 'Leave us, son. Him and me are going to have a chat'

The constable grinned back. 'Be long will you?'.

'Go and have breakfast -it might get a bit noisy'.

'Right, sarg'. Unlocking a cell door and swinging it back he peeked at the expectant prisoner and grinned again 'Who's the lucky one then. You've got a very special visitor. Bell if you want assistance, sarge'.

Miller waited until the constable's footsteps told him he had closed and locked the cell passage grilled door before turning his attention to Fletcher who, by then, was on his feet staring at him, doing his best to keep fear under control.

'Adrian is it?'. Miller was by then standing directly in front of Fletcher and grinning disarmingly.

Fletcher nodded before the blow to his stomach doubled him up and the blow to the face sent him sprawling across the floor. Semi-conscious now, he didn't feel pain when he was kicked, nor when he was dragged to the open cell doorway and punched again and again.

Miller looked down with satisfaction at his handiwork and knew what he had to do.

*

'What are his chances? DCS Makepeace looked from the bandaged, unconscious detective inspector who was still in a coma, to the doctor who was studying the readout hooked over the end of the bed. 'It's been two weeks'.

The doctor shrugged. 'The operation has relieved the pressure on his brain but until............' he spread his hands 'well, until he's conscious and can speak we won't know if there has been brain damage'.

Makepeace gestured to the read out ' That doesn't tell you?'

'No, Too early'.

*

Fountain pushed the report away and glanced across at Miller's swollen face. 'Taken unawares?'. He prodded the report.

'Yeh. Jumped me. Like it says'. He pointed to the report.

'How is he?'.

'Belled the hospital this morning, guv. No change'.
'No change from what?'.
'Still bandaged up. Not saying much'.

The detective inspector knew the score but went along with it. 'A10'll have their dabs all over this one, Dusty. Who endorsed the charge sheet?'.

'Sergeant Tims'.

'Did he question you?'.

'No, guv. I gave him my report once Fletcher had been taken to hospital'.

'In line with this one?'.

Miller smiled. 'A copy,'.

'We wait, then. Rotating the officer at the hospital?'.

'Two hour shifts. We'll be the first to know when he's ready for a chat'.

*

Valerie Miller was alone when a brief evening report of the two murders was televised. The belt was displayed, with a close up of the buckle. A voice over reminded viewers that the belt was alleged to be the means by which the women had been strangled by Lakey. The camera cut to the stream beside the golf course at Walthamstead. The voice over asked viewers to contact the displayed telephone number if they recognised the belt, or had any information which might assist the enquiry. For some seconds she sat perfectly still in shock at what she had seen. He had always gone on about the plastic belts that came with trousers: The belt displayed was identical to the one she'd bought as a stocking-filler present the previous Christmas. "No bloody good. Don't last five minutes" he had said about the plastic ones.. It was good quality leather with a readily recognisable stainless steel embossed buckle which she immediately recognised. Experiencing a fear she had suppressed for many month, that one day his verbal violence would spill over into actual violence, and recalling he had been using his hated plastic belts for weeks, she galvanised herself and threw clothes into a holdall and ran downstairs, searching for her car keys. Finding them she left the house, slammed the door and dropped into her car. In gear now, she told herself to keep calm and concentrate on the traffic. She manoeuvred onto the road and picked up speed, thankful that her mother lived nearby. She would know what to do............

*

Makepeace sat in the leather armchair in the Commissioner's plush, spacious, office and stared in wide-eyed disbelief at what they had been told. 'I can't believe it', he muttered. Turning his worried gaze to Assistant Commissioner Smithery, he asked for his opinion. 'It can't be, Charlie, surely. Can it?'. Smithery was looking at Geoff Hinds, whose expression when he fixed his steely gaze on him said he believed it.

To emphasise his belief he thumped the desk angrily. 'I knew that frigging belt would bounce around the park. I was never convinced you know. Too pat. He took an almighty chance planting the bloody thing - if, that is, he did plant it', he added cautiously, looking from one to the other. 'Now we have his bloody wife of all people sticking the knife in'.

'The jury had no doubt, sir', Makepeace reminded him. But even as the words passed his lips he knew he was in a quandary. He had Daryl Browne's statement tucked in a file in his desk; and now this bombshell had gone off. How to go about it..........?.

'What is it, George? Face run out of blood?'.

The DCS cleared his throat and stared back at

Hinds, who had sat forward, his posture demanding an answer. 'There was another incident.......a young woman who was raped made a complaint against Miller. He took it upon himself to go alone to her flat - where she had been raped would you believe it - and behaved appallingly, suggesting nastily at one point she'd probably got what she deserved'.

Hinds looked questioningly at Smithery 'You know about this?'.

'No, Geoff'. He turned to Makepeace. 'What was done about that?'.

The DCS wriggled uncomfortably before offering a weak explanation. 'I discussed it with detective inspector Masters, naturally. Apparently the sergeant has been having a domestic of some sort with his wife. Could have been at the root of his behaviour. Between us we thought it best to let the dust settle. She hasn't raised the domestic issue'.

'She has now though, hasn't she', Hinds said sarcastically.

Makepeace shook his head. 'No, sir. Her concern is a missing belt - that's all. I'm sure the sergeant will have a rational explanation that'll put this thing to bed'.

The Commissioner flapped his hands at them. 'Let's stay with the bloody belt. She bought it at Marks and Sparks in Walthamstead on the run to the previous Christmas', right?. He pointed at Makepeace and demanded: 'Get somebody onto it. You know the drill: how many did they stock; how many did they sell. Then get onto the manufacturer: how many were made and, more particularly, how many were distributed in Walthamstead. And do not interview sergeant Miller. Couple this with detective inspector Lindley's behaviour - oh, that bloody tape! I should have ignored Commander Stewart's recommendation'. He sat back and stared at the two officers. 'If we can't see a way forward we have the makings of a bloody nightmare for the Met'.

Smithery, concerned to keep it at arm's length, nodded his agreement.

Makepeace's thoughts though had shifted to Masters who, his Martha had so many times agreed, was the one officer who could unsettle his steady ship. The man was a bloody time bomb. His thoughts raced over his escapades, most of which had been near the knuckle. If Miller's alleged misbehaviour - he couldn't put it higher because all he had done was to plant necessary evidence on a criminal, then, well, I ask you?, he told himself, if Masters gets dragged into the enquiry - where will it end?.

*

Lindley was fronted with two A10 detectives, one of whom, Stannard, had opened a paper file of documents that had filtered down from the Commissioner's office. 'The allegation, inspector Lindley', he stopped speaking to stare coldly at the DI before going on, shuffling his papers, 'is that you conspired with Jakeson to murder Philip Bateman. He has made a statement to that effect. I have it here'. He pointed down at the file.' You are not obliged to say anything but anything you say will be taken down in writing and may be given in evidence. Is that clear?'.

'Quite clear, and all this is a load of bollocks'. Lindley sat forward and stared hard at the two men. 'I understand you have a tape of my interrogation of Jakeson in prison. Put it in there', he pointed to a recorder on the desk. 'I want to hear it at first hand'.

The two detectives exchanged a worried glance and the one doing the talking shook his head and fingered the file before looking up at Lindley, explaining 'The tape is unreadable, I'm afraid. But I have a transcript here'.

Lindley smiled. The commander had kept his word.

'You're smiling, inspector?'.

'It's unreadable, yes? So how the bloody hell did you manage to get it transcribed?'. Staring at the other man's discomfiture, Lindley leaned forward and angrily pointed a finger at his interrogators. 'A villain makes an allegation and you go for it. And..........', he shook a fisted hand at them, 'your transcription is no use and you know it. Put the tape in that machine and let me hear it or stop this charade!'.

The two officers were hauling themselves up, knowing that the interrogation was at an end. But they shared a knowing glance before Stannard answered. 'This is not the end of it, inspector. 'The tape may yet prove to be, er, viable'.

Lindley stared back while he tried to untangle that remark from what had taken place. 'Viable?'.

Stannard let a rare smile flick across his otherwise stern face. 'That's for the future, inspector'. We have made notes of your remarks'.

'Is that it then?'

When neither spoke Lindley got up and went to the door, where he turned, looking from one to the other. 'If there's to be a next time do your job right. Check facts before you accuse. Don't believe the first thing you hear'. With that said he left the room and slammed the door.

'Frigging wankers', he muttered aloud as he walked down the corridor.. 'Wankers!', he said loudly.

Back in the office Stannard gathered his papers and smiled at his colleague. He and his boss knew someone high up at the Yard must have authorised it to be electronically spoiled. 'We may yet get that bastard', he said grimly. 'What can be rubbished can be sorted'.

*

Lindley was a very contented man. Commander Stewart had that morning assured him the enquiry was at an end, and now he and the commander were enjoying a celebratory meal in the usual flying squad watering hole.

His stomach gratefully filled with their chosen meal the DI held up his glass to his boss. 'Thanks boss', he toasted, smiling.

Stewart raised his glass and smiled back. 'You were lucky on this one, Brian'. He gestured with his glass. 'To smoother waters!'.

Lindley smiled and sipped his wine but Jakeson's angry face hovered, a reminder of a score he would settle one day. He changed the subject to the flavour of the month at the Yard. 'What's the score with Miller, guv?'

The commander shrugged. 'Cloak and dagger stuff - the usual A10 enquiry.

Lindley looked intently at his boss. 'Perverting the course of justice is doing the rounds, guv. What's he done: fitted him up?'.

'That's at the root of it'.

'But for the grace of God, eh!'.

*

Already slim, the weeks since the accident had caused Janet to lose weight and her thinness was obvious to the hospital staff, who had seen her so many times since Don was brought in. The doctors were pleased with his progress, confident, one told her, that he would recover.

Yet again, as the weeks had slipped by, Janet was resting a hand on his, sitting beside his bed, dabbing away her tears with the other, looking intently at the man she loved whose bandages had been removed, firstly from his legs and arms and now from his head and she saw his face for the first time in the long, agonising weeks of her watch. The nurse settled Masters head on the inclined pillow and turned to smile to Janet. As she made her way to the door she said kindly to her. 'Keep talking to him. 'I'm sure he'll hear you'.

Janet badly wanted to believe the nurse, but the agonising weeks had undermined her confidence. 'You'll get through this darling', she whispered, glad to be able to talk to his bruised face, trying to convince herself he would improve. 'Oh Don, darling, I miss you so much. And Charlie sends his best wishes. Did I tell you he's got a new girl friend? Gill, he says 'er name is. I've told him about us, Don, 'ad to didn't I? Pleased for us he says he is. Wanted to come in and see you but I said no. Did I do right, darling?'.

She sensed a movement in the hand she was touching. There it was again!

'Darling......can you hear me?' she reached under his hand and held his fingers. 'Squeeze my fingers darling, please'.

There it was a again!

'Don! You can hear me! Please..........do it again!'. Feeling his light pressure yet again she gently pulled her hand free and pressed the bell.

*

Kathy Peel was staring at Gloria Gardner's angry face, her threats of vengeance hanging in the air between them. 'What can you do for him, Gloria?', she spoke persuasively. ' He's bang to rights according to the grapevine'.

'But he's my brother, Kath. I've got to do somefink

for him'.

'Like what?'.

'Spring him, if I can'. She sat quietly for a few minutes while she untangled her mixed up thoughts. 'That's what I'll do', she said, her mind made up. 'On the trip to court, or on the way back. I'll put the word out for a firm to do it'.

'And that's how your husband was sprung - and look what happened to him. And then what: he's out – where's he going? You need to think it through. Passport, that sort of thing. He won't be safe in this country'.

Gloria saw the sense in her friend's words and nodded her agreement but was determined.. 'I'll find a firm that'll take care of everything. I'm not having my brother locked away for attempted murder; and that copper's not getting away either. I'll get a firm to finish the job -with no cock ups'.

*

Detective inspector Fountain cradled the receiver and popped across to the detective sergeants' office and scanned the three officers who were looking enquiringly back at him. . 'Don's going to be alright', he told them 'I've just had a call from the hospital. He's conscious'.

*

'You're a lucky bloke', Miller said feelingly as he touched Masters' arm and drew up a chair opposite Janet, who gave him a fleeting smile before returning her concerned gaze to the DI.

Masters offered a weak smile. 'I don't have any memory of the accident. I've seen the newspaper cuttings but they didn't ring any bells. You've got him, yes?'.

'He was in here, guv. Been remanded. The sweeney has given us a statement establishing he had the nicked car stashed in a garage long before he rammed you. His dabs are all over the bloody thing; and your Jag's paint is on it. He's got no chance'.

Masters was aware Janet was squeezing his hand and saw her tears well up. 'What is it, sweetheart?'.

She fumbled in her handbag for a tissue and dabbed her eyes, her anguish evident to both men. 'Must you stay in the police force, darling? It's too dangerous'. She broke off to regain composure and looked from one man to the other. 'Every day you mix with 'orrible people. Where is all this going to end?'.

Masters squeezed her hand. 'Look at me, darling', he said softly. When she did he said gently, 'I'll think about it. I will, I promise you. I'll be out of here soon. We'll go away somewhere. Abroad if you like. Anywhere you fancy'.

'Oh, Don, darling!'. Her face lit up at the promise. 'Can I book a holiday? Can I really?'.

'Look into it. And, sweetheart'. This time he held both her hands. 'Put our house on the market. Who knows, there might be a buyer out there'.

Miller, his thoughts elsewhere, touched Masters' arm briefly when he saw Janet's beaming expression, and got up. 'Look after him, Janet. Must be off'.

*

The next two weeks slipped away and Janet was in heaven. Don was home on sick leave and together they were poring over holiday literature. She preferred Italy.

Masters reached for her hand and squeezed it as he smiled lovingly at her radiant face. ' Let's get the new car out, and nip into town'.

As they settled in his new Jaguar and drove out of the driveway neither paid attention to a car a couple of hundred yards back from that exit.

'That's them'. The heavily set man sitting beside the lean long-haired driver pointed to Masters' car leaving the driveway. 'Follow it. Keep well back. Let's sus out where they're they're going. This has got to be done right'.

Masters kept his speed down and let his hand rest in Janet's and occasionally glance at her, smiling when he caught her eye.

Over and over Janet had re-lived the details of the attacks on him and her smile hid concern for his safety. On edge, she flicked her gaze to the door mirror and then to Masters. 'The car behind, Don. It's been there for a while now. Have you seen it?'.

Masters nodded. Like her he was on edge and had realised the car was pacing his varied speed. 'I have sweetheart. I won't take a chance', he said quietly. 'I'll do a left and see what it does'.

Masters, without indicating, swung left and Janet stared into the mirror.

'It's still behind us. I'm scared, darling. It's definitely following us'

'Pass the radio, sweetheart. I'll have it pulled over'.

Janet's fear for his safety heightened when she listened to him saying what he wanted done. 'What's going to happen, Don? you're scaring me'.

He handed back the radio and patted her hand. 'Taking no chances, that's all'. Choosing his words so as not to alarm her, he said 'I'm going to have a chat with them'.

He drove at a steady speed for about five minutes until he got back the answer he expected. Passing a T junction, he gestured to an unmarked police car whose lights were flashed, waiting to exit. 'Car number one', he told her as it dropped in behind them. 'There'll be a second one up the road. It'll drop behind the car following us'.

Two minute later it happened as he said and he slowed to a standstill at red traffic lights, the cars behind closing up. 'Stay in the car' he said quietly to Janet.

He got out quickly and joined the other officers surrounding the target car, guns trained on the two men in the front seats.

'Armed police! Get out! Do it now! Get down on the ground!' an officer barked, his handgun trained on the driver.

Bystanders froze and watched the two men being hauled from their car, spread-eagled on the road handcuffed, and dragged to one of the police cars.

*

'Who have we got?' Masters was scanning the charge sheets. 'Two automatics. I was right then'.

'Well spotted, guv' Tims told him. 'As of this moment they're Vincent Pullen and Frank Briggs. CRO checks are underway'.

Masters nodded his satisfaction. 'Janet's in the waiting room, skip', he told the sergeant. She's

worried sick about what could have happened. I'll run her home. The interrogations can wait until the morning'.

Masters arrived at the police station in the morning to be told by sergeant Tims that the DCS wanted to see him. He fingered the telephone log. 'His office at 11am. Wants an update on the prisoners'.

'Their CRO files arrived?'.

'They have'. Tims handed over two bulky dockets.

Masters had time to do it so he nipped up to his office and flipped quickly through them. Both men had been pulled by the flying squad eighteen months before for robbery and walked out of a charge.

He ran a finger down the list of Pullen's associates and stopped at Gardner. 'So'. he told himself with satisfaction. 'Now I know who set the arseholes onto me'.

He reached for the phone and was put through to Makepeace's office. 'Tell the boss', he told the secretary 'that I'm busy interviewing the prisoners'.

*

Vinnie Pullen, pushed down in a chair by Miller, stared dismissively across at Masters. 'Nothing to say so don't waste your time'.

'The automatic says ten years at least'.

'No comment'.

'Friend of Gloria?.

'No comment'.

Masters leaned forward and spoke quietly when he stared. 'I know who pulled your strings, Vinnie. You're not the first. Did she tell you about her brother? No?' He let a smile flick across his face. ' He tried and got himself banged up for his failed effort'. He studied Pullen's hard face for a while. 'Want to talk to me?'.

'No comment'.

Masters nodded and spread his hands 'I've got the message, Vinnie. Hard man. Bang him up, Dusty'.

Miller nodded to the constable leaning against the wall, and gestured for Pullen to stand. 'Hands behind your back, mate'. Pulled didn't resist the cuffs but at the door he turned and stared at Masters. 'It'll happen you know', he muttered.

Briggs took a similar line to Pullen. He didn't need telling prison gates were looming, but he knew if he kept the charge at unlawful possession of a gun, it was a hundred per cent better than possession with intent to murder. He took the fag offered and began the process of looking after number one. 'What's on offer here, then?', he asked, his smiling face shifting from Masters to Barton, who had brought him up from the cell block, fascinated by the tattoo of a naked woman on Briggs's bicep.

'Naming names', Masters suggested. 'Or do you fancy a twenty stretch?'.

'Had words with me mate?'.

Masters nodded

'Said nothing. Right?'.

Masters agreed with a nod.

'If I give you a name - what's in it for me?'.

'Experience tells me a few years less than your mate'.

'Can you guarantee that?'.

'I can'. The lie flowed easily.

Barton shifted beside Briggs and tapped the bicep 'What's that all about?'.

Briggs grinned. 'Watch'. He flexed his upper arm slowly and the tattooed woman spread her legs over the bulging muscle.

'Bugger me! Clever bastard whoever came up with that one', the sergeant said admiringly.

'Statement is it Frank?' Masters suggested

*

Valerie Miller was regretting making her statement. Her mum, Dorothy, Dot to her friends, had bided her time to get at the truth and had insisted. In dribs and drabs Valerie had explained how her love life had disappeared down the plug hole. Dusty was, she found out, a cruel man who became violent in bed. It depended on his mood when he was sexually worked up, which wasn't always when Valerie was aroused. When that occurred - Valerie had learned not to turn her back on him. She did once, mum learned from a tearful Valerie, and she was raped from behind - and he'd almost strangled her when he was coming.

'You did the right thing', she told her daughter firmly. 'He's a bad man'.

*

Makepeace gestured the DI to a seat opposite his desk and waited. 'Wanted to congratulate you, Don. Good bit of work collaring the blaggards. Well done', he said, constructing a smile that was gone as soon as it was fashioned.

Masters accepted the veiled congratulation with a nod and took out his cigarettes and held the packet up, questioningly.

'Carry on. I'll have one, thanks'.

Masters shook one out and lit his own, waiting for Makepeace to light up before enlarging on the arrest of Pullen and Briggs. 'Their CRO files link Gloria Gardner with Pullen. I'm in no doubt whatsoever that bitch put the fingers onto me'.

'Let me have their files', Makepeace demanded, his hand outstretched.

Masters pushed them across the desk and waited while Makepeace worked it out for himself. 'I see why you take that view, inspector', he said with an undertone that told Masters he was going down the devil's advocate route again.. 'You've upset so many people. ....I can think of at least a dozen who would have a go at you'. He pushed the files away and sat back, his expression challenging Masters to say differently.

Masters knew he was wasting time on that front.. 'Is there anything else you want me for, sir?'.

The DCS nodded and opened a file in front of him. Pointing down to it he said, by way of explanation 'A10 job on Miller'.

Masters showed his surprise. 'Miller, sir?'.

'The Lakey trial. It would seem it's gone pear shaped. We've got another appeal to contend with'.

It was common knowledge the rubber heels were prowling around after Dusty, but the DCS's words suggesting Miller was in serious trouble resurrected troubling thoughts. Kay Bruce's face hovered............. Could it be?. 'Where does Dusty figure in their enquiry sir', he asked

'It's been under wraps but I can tell you now. The belt Miller produced in evidence. Lakey still denies it was his, but guess what?'.

Masters stared at Makepeace, the 'guess what' adding to his worry. 'What sir?'.

Makepeace was making the most of his news. He'd astutely fingered Masters to agreeing to distance himself from Miller, agreeing that A10 carry out the enquiry. Now he let a concerned expression settle before he told Masters the news. 'Miller had an identical belt'.

'Had, sir?'

'Had. His wife has made a statement. His one has disappeared'

Masters hunched forward, searching the other man's expression for an explanation for the clearly pointed suggestion that Miller was up to his neck in....................what? 'I thought the belt business had been dealt with at the trial?' he said..

'Lakey denied it was his, as you will recall. His legal team have been informed about Miller's missing belt and have stuck in another appeal'.

As the DCS was speaking Masters was rapidly recalling the defence case at the trial, and seeing Lakey's angry face when Miller was giving his evidence. 'Smearing Miller - is that the name of the game Lakey's playing?

'Your words, inspector. Hopefully it'll be Lakey's last throw of the dice'.

*

For once his Viva was behaving itself. Charlie had given in to Gill's pressure and agreed to drive to Masters' home. He still loved Janet but was glad Don was her friend. From time to time on the journey, with Gill tucked up close beside him, his real worry was Gill still believing Janet was his sister. And he hadn't told her Masters was a detective inspector.

'Charlie sweetheart', Gill said lovingly as she held tightly to his hand. 'Are you sure your sister won't mind us dropping in like this?'.

He kept his eyes on the road and checked the fuel gauge ' 'ave a top up soon, love', he told her. 'Nah. Janet wants to see you. She reckons you from what I've said. And Don, you'll like him. He's older that my sis. She loves 'im though. You'll see'.

An hour later, they sat in the car and stared at Masters home 'Its lovely, Charlie. Does he know we're coming?'.

'Yeh. Been through the wars Don 'as. Aint been out of hospital long'.

Janet adjusted the interior mirror and studied her face and fluffed her hair. 'Will I do, Charlie', she asked anxiously while she stared critically at her reflection. She knew her outfit was alright because he had said so. She would have preferred slacks but he'd said no to that. "Short skirt, Gill. Stockings, the works. Janet always wears a skirt and looks lovely. I want you to look as lovely as 'er" he had said before they set out.

He was giving her a sideways look. ' You're a stunner darling, perfect. Come on, let's see if they're in'.

Don had seen the Viva pull up and had the door open and was waving to them, admiring Gill's slim body in her tight, short skirt.

Nervously, Gill held tightly to Charlie's hand, wondering if Janet was in the house.

'Charlie! Good to see you again. So this is Gill?'. Masters, who had walked down the drive to where Charlie has stopped the car, gave her a friendly smile and hugged her. 'Come in. Janet'll love to see you both'.

Hand in hand again they followed him inside and Charlie stopped dead to gaze at Janet, who was standing by the living room door, as beautiful as he remembered her. 'Gill, sweetheart, meet Janet', he said nervously.

Gill was smiling as she went quickly to Janet and hugged her. 'Charlie's told me so much about his love for you, Janet', she said when she broke away to gaze into her eyes. 'It's really lovely to meet you at last'.

Janet took Gill's hand. Come and sit down'. She led her to a settee and, once settled asked 'Tell me how you met Charlie'.

Charlie hadn't moved far into the room and looked nervously at the animated women and beckoned to Masters. 'She still thinks she's my sister, Don. ', he said quietly. ' I'm in shit 'ere aint I?'.

The detective put an arm round Charlie's shoulder and led him from the room. 'The truth, Charlie', he told him. 'It's for the best. Let the girls chat for a while. I'm sure once Janet and Gillian have got to know each other it'll be easy to explain why you told her that. Let's have a beer while they get to know each other'.

They were still in the kitchen when Gill and Janet came in, hand in hand , smiling the smile of a secret shared. Gill crossed to Charlie and tickled his nose mischievously 'Janet's told me everything. Sister indeed!'.

Charlie was relieved she was smiling and asked, nervously, 'You don't mind, Gill?. I didn't know how to tell you, honest I didn't'.

'But your love is real, Charlie. I saw that. And Janet has found love as well as us'.

Janet had crossed to Don and was cuddling up to him and looking at an embarrassed Charlie. 'It's alright, Charlie. It really is. I'm pleased for both of you'.

'Let's go out and celebrate'. Masters looked questioningly at Charlie and the girls. 'Agreed?'.

Don chose a carvery on the outskirts of town. After their meal, the wine and coffee, Don suggested they go back to his and Janet's place for a nightcap. Staying for the night was Janet's idea initially, but Don picked it up and urged Gill and Charlie to stay and have breakfast before heading home.

In the morning while they were in bed Charlie told Gill about Masters' job. 'Don's a detective inspector'.

She pulled back to look at him. 'How do you know that?'

'I've known Don for a long while, Gill'. He slid his arm from under her and sat up and placed his pillows against the head board. 'Move away, sweetheart. I'll do your pillows. We need to talk about my past. There're are fings you ought to know about me'. During the process of altering the pillow layout he worked out what to say. When the pillows were propped up and she was resting he took her hands and then lost courage to say what had to be said.

'What is it, Charlie?. There's more isn't there?'. She

stared at him, her worry making it harder for him to tell her the truth about his relationship with Masters.

He nodded and looked away while he still searched for the right words.

'Charlie.........what is it?'.

'I've been to prison, Gill'. He was staring at her when the words came out in a rush and her shocked expression scared him.

She eased her hands away from his and hunched round to face him. 'There's more, isn't there?', she said as colour drained from her face.

Charlie had lowered his head and was nodding. Looking up and staring into her worried eyes he pleaded 'Gill, sweetheart. I should have told you from the beginning but I didn't want to lose you'.

His crestfallen face was too much for Gill and she turned and kissed him. Smiling as she did so she stroked his face and whispered. 'I love you and always will. But it was a shock. I've never known anyone who's been to prison. What did you do?'.

He slid from the bed and donned the dressing gown Don had provided, searching for the words.

'You're frightening me, Charlie', Gill told him as she too got up and pulled on the dressing gown Janet had given her. 'Is it bad, Charlie. Is it?'.

He shook his head. 'Look, sweetheart. Let's go down and see if any coffee's on the go. I'd like Don to hear what I want to tell you'.

An hour later, sitting at the kitchen table with Janet and Don, she was told about his time in the various homes, his housebreakings, and his one term of imprisonment, and how Don had taken care of Janet while he was inside. Neither Don nor Charlie told her about their criminal relationship or their involvement in the armed robbery at the warehouse where she worked with Charlie. From time to time she looked at Masters and then at Janet and understood how their love for each other had grown, just as her love for Charlie had. She took Charlie's hand and kissed him. 'I'll always love you, darling' she whispered.

Janet had been holding Don's hand and at that moment squeezed it. She was happy but relieved. Seeing Charlie again with his new found love had worried her because she knew, deep in her heart, that he loved her just as she loved him. But their love had been overtaken by her deeper love for Don.

*

The ever increasing life blood of prison grapevine with its web of information, where friends of inmates chatted to each other and to prisoners at visiting times, getting the chit chat of nefarious daily doings out of the way, before getting to serious stuff of active villainy, was the raison d'etre of prison life.

'Kath', Gloria muttered to her friend angrily, having picked up the news on the aforesaid grapevine that Pullen and his mate had been captured, and meaning Masters, said, her eyes narrowed to slits. 'Has he got a charmed life or wot',

'I told you didn't I'. Kath told her earnestly............'keep it simple. All this creeping around won't work. Shoot the buggar in 'is 'ouse. Couldn't be easier'.

You reckon?'.

'Wot better way?, Gloria. Catch the bugger wiv 'is eyes shut'.

*

Chapter thirty seven

The appeal judge raised a hand and stopped Lakey's counsel in mid sentence. 'You have not produced new evidence here today', he said frostily. 'You will recall the jury had knowledge of your client's allegation that the belt had been planted by detective sergeant Miller. This court cannot draw the conclusion sought by you. That the sergeant no longer possesses a similar belt does not constitute evidence that detective Miller perverted the course of justice. The evidence of the manufacturer accepting the imperfection to which Mrs. Miller referred as a manufacturing blip does not corroborate her evidence. His belt therefore may not be the only belt with such an imperfection. Appeal dismissed'. With that said he rose and inclined his head to both counsel and left the court.

Makepeace and Smithery were relieved. In court keeping a watching brief their worst nightmare had been resolved.

'Well, George', Smithery said quietly to the other man on their walk to the car park 'That's one lid screwed down'.

'What about his wife, Charlie. Will she leave it there?'

They walked in silence, both men believing that only the machinations of the legal process had in all probability let Miller of the hook for murder. At the car Smithery turned to his colleague and spread his hands. 'God knows, George' he said quietly. 'But have we a serial murderer in the CID at Walthamstead, that's more to the point, isn't it?'.

'Want my opinion?'.

'I think I know it, George. What to do about it is the problem'.

'If he's the villain we believe him to be - how many more are sitting in the cupboard waiting to have a go at him?' Makepeace responded as he settled in the car.

'You've got a point. The problem is the one we've always had. Bring him down and who does he bring down? Think what he knows............the way we work.............shafting villains right and left. I mean, George, it could be a bloody nightmare. What does he know about what you've got up to. And me, for that matter?'.

'True, Charlie, true. So what do we do?'.

'We leave it where it is. If the silly bugger does it again, well, that's when we need to come up with a plan of sorts. Agreed?'.

"Agreed'.

*

Miller was relieved. His thoughts had festered during the elapsed time from the A.10 inquisition He'd faced them down, demanding they come up with evidence and stop insinuating. He'd skated over the car in the lay by; and Betty, God bless her, had stood by him and put that line of enquiry to bed. "Fuck you Lakey" he said to himself as he walked from his car to his mother-in-law's front door.

Now, standing on the doorstep and staring at the frumpy woman who was telling him his wife was asleep, his anger at the bitch boiled over. 'I want to speak to her, now', he demanded angrily.

'Haven't you done enough to her?'. She stared coldly at the man she had always disliked. 'Just go away. I've always said you were trouble - and you've proved me right'. Having said that she slammed the door in his face.

For a short time he stared at the solid mahogany

glass-paned door and hated the bitch. 'You're a frigging cow', he told the door as he turned away and walked back to his car.

*

For commander Bob Stewart the report lying on his desk spelt trouble. The report by A10 detective inspector Broughton made that very clear indeed. Angrily pushing the report to one side he picked up the statement made by Williams and slowly read it again, putting it down when he'd finished to lean back and consider the implications, his mind racing through a mixture of possible pit fall scenarios, the obvious one topping them all: detective inspector Brian Lindley was back in the frame for complicity to murder: The tape being rendered useless was destroyed by Williams' statement. He got up and started pacing, stopping to peer at the photo of himself when promoted to commander. Straightening the frame he resumed pacing and stopped at the window to stare out at the traffic along Victoria Street, unconsciously aware initially but consciously finally of the routine nature of civilian life below encompassed in the snarled up traffic and people-crowded pavements, a million miles apart from his which, if A10 were holding back information nailing him, would see him charged with accessory to murder and consign him to the imprisoned inner life the shell of which he was staring down at. Returning to his desk he picked up the phone.

'Get detective inspector Broughton here, he ordered.

The handset replaced he resumed pacing, his mind engaged in an attempt to resolve the implication for himself of the Jakeson tape; and Lindley knowing, with the approval of Deputy Commissioner Smithery, he had arranged for it to be electronically unreadable. An hour later he invited the suited and tied Broughton to sit, and did so himself, facing the man who could, if his worries were anywhere near right, have placed his toes on the first rung of his ladder to disaster.

'Coffee?', he asked the inspector with a forced smile.

'Thank you, sir. I'd appreciate one', was the calm reply as legs were crossed and unseen fluff swatted.

While Stewart was on the phone ordering coffee he studied Broughton's demeanour but got nothing back but his easy smile as he continued his glance around the office.

'Be a few minutes, inspector'. He held up Broughton's report. 'What's the background to this?'.

'My boss was told to get an officer to Williams' prison and take his statement under caution. That's what we did, sir'.

'The call went straight to A10?'.

Broughton shook his head. 'The commissioner's office set it up'. Gazing unblinkingly at the commander he gestured to the statement on the desk. 'No prompting, that's exactly how he said it. We taped the interview, sir. My boss has had copies made: might be needed at court he said- if it gets that far. The tape is with the Commissioner'.

The door was opened at that moment and Stewart's personal assistant came in with their coffees.

The commander meanwhile was still experiencing icy fingers which, he inwardly prayed, were not revealed in his expression. He waited until Broughton had taken a few sips before asking 'Has inspector Lindley been informed?'.

'No, sir. Being a flying squad DI, my report and Williams' statement has been forwarded secondly to you'.

'Secondly?'.

Broughton nodded. 'A copy is naturally in the

channel to the Commissioner, sir'.

Stewart got to his feet and leaned across the desk to shake Broughton's hand. 'Thank you, inspector', he said with assumed gravity. 'This allegation is very serious. Very serious indeed. I need time to think about it. I'll get my decision through channels to your department. Must work closely on this. No slip ups. If this is true then.......' he shook his head. 'Frankly I'll be appalled. Inspector Lindley's got an outstanding record'.

The A10 officer got to his feet. 'Is that all, sir?'.

Stewart nodded. 'Inform your commander I'll deal with this quickly'.

Once Broughton had gone the commander resumed his pacing. When a chilling thought occurred he looked at his telephone Was it tapped? If it was -when did it go on? Knowing how C11 and A10 worked the possibility was there. The phone at home? He dragged up Broughton's demeanour: calm; not a flicker; maintained eye contact all the time. What did he really know? His hand automatically reached for the phone but he stopped short of picking up the handset. What a nightmare! Lindley's probable fate went to the back of his mind, and then resurfaced when he recalled the damage to the tape. He started pacing again and tried to think clearly: nothing, he reminded himself, had been written down. He glanced at the phone and tried, desperately, to think back: had he used it? It was no use. His troubled mind couldn't get into gear. On impulse he decided to have words with Lindley, but using the internal phone was a non-starter. The official car was out as well. He locked the damning report and statement in a desk drawer and left. Best he used his own car.

An hour later his DI stared at him on the doorstep, What a surprise, sir'. Lindley stepped to one side and gestured his commander into the hall. 'Let me take your coat, it's soaked'.

Stewart shrugged the top coat off and handed it to the inspector. Looking down the hall he asked quietly. 'Where's Marion?'

Lindsey thumbed to the living room.'Watching the tele. Surprise this, sir. Something up?'.

Stewart nodded and ran his fingers through wet grey hair. 'We need to talk'.

The DI recognised the obvious change in his boss's demeanour and took his arm, nodding down the narrow hall to the dining room. 'I'll let the missus know you're here'.

The flying squad commander studied the man who had returned from the living room and was handing him a can of beer. 'We've got a serious problem, Brian', he told him when their cans were on the table between them. He offered his cigarette packet.

The DI took one and lit up. He flicked his lighter and offered it to his boss, watching and waiting while Stewart blew smoke at the ceiling. 'What's gone wrong, sir?, he asked quietly.

'Bateman.............his killing's gone pear shaped, Brian. I'll be frank, Williams has backed Jakeson's account and lumbered you'. He watched as the colour drained from Lindley's face. 'Yes, it's bloody serious but.............'. He stared hard at the other man. 'When push comes to shove it's their word against your's'.

Lindley held his boss's gaze while his mind raced back over the events leading up to Bateman's murder.

'Talk to me, Brian', Stewart urged when Lindley remained silent.

The DI looked down and then back at Stewart while he chose his words carefully. 'How detailed do you want this, sir?'.

'Everything, Brian. Because of the new William's

tape we're in the shit together'.

Lindley recognised Stewart's concern and held back while he stared at the man. He was being asked to do something he'd never done before and, if he was frank and told his boss precisely how his blag had been set up, he would be throwing his career away if Stewart was conning him.

'Brian?'.

'Comes down to trust, sir'.

The commander patted Lindley's arm. ' Trust? of course I trust you. And you can certainly trust me. I've always backed my men to the hilt. Brian, I trust you to be straight with me. I've never told my men to name a snout: golden rule that. But this time I must know everything or I can't help you'.

Lindley quickly made up his mind to trust Stewart and to relate how a simple blagging had gone wrong. 'Jakeson is, was it now turns out, a bloody good snout. I'd used him on three other blaggings. Then that frigging solicitor got greedy'.

'How did that come about?'.

Phil told him too much, about bail.............'.

'About me?'.

Lindley spread his hands. 'Not by name - but he worked something out and told Jakeson he wanted a cut from the twenty grand'.

'Why didn't you fill me in on this lot!'.

Lindley spread his hands again.

'Fair enough, Brian, but it's too late now. Tell me everything. It's important'.

The detective inspector told how he had found out via a reliable snout that twenty thousand pounds was up for grabs in the factory. 'Easy tickle, sir. The blag went off without a hitch'.

Stewart broke in impatiently. 'That much I know.

Who was the snout?'

'Tattooed Jimmy, guv. Up to then I thought things were going as sweet as a nut until, that is, he decided to tell Bateman - then that bastard got greedy'.

Stewart was nodding his head. 'Can't trust a snout, Brian. Don't we all know that. Go on: tell me what happened next'.

'I told Phil to settle it with the solicitor'.

The commander kept a steady gaze into the inspector's eyes. 'Settle it, Brian?'.

'Settle it, sir. It was down to him how'.

'You're forgetting I've heard the tape'.

Lindley smiled broadly. 'Tape? Rubber heels admitted the tape was no bloody use: thanks to you, sir', he added.

Stewart stared hard at the inscrutable expression that concealed, what? He picked up his can, and put it down again, thinking hard about his dilemma. That bloody tape! And A10 had a transcript. Who else? The Commissioner! He got back to his reason for being there. 'Bill Williams has made a statement corroborating Jakeson's account . Says he was present when you and Jakeson had your chat in the squad car. He's fingered you, Brian. Says you set up the killing'.

'He would wouldn't he'. The detective kept his steady gaze into his boss's eyes and added, persuasively, 'He's a liar. That the gist of it, sir?'.

Stewart nodded. 'Rubber heels are going to have you in again, Brian. Armed with Williams' corroborating statement you're in the shit. Can any man in your squad overturn Williams' evidence?'.

Lindley shook his head. 'I'm not lumbering any of them. When's it to be, sir?'.

Stewart got up and spread his hands. 'Out of my control now. This one has gone to the top. Now listen: for obvious reasons be careful what you say on any phone, here or at the Yard. Go about your work in the usual way but make no meets with informers. We know how A10 operate - by now somebody may have climbed on the bandwagon and knifed you'. He pushed out a hand and shook Lindley's. 'We didn't have this meeting'.

*

Charles Smithery had heard it all before. Miller's brush with the rubber heels was uppermost in his mind when he said firmly. 'It comes down to this, inspector.. Kick at a moral stone and the underclass climb out from under. Sums up your enquiry. Huh?'.

Broughton shrugged his apparent agreement, looked sideways at his departmental head, but kept quiet because this particular interview wasn't his first. Bent coppers figured highly on his nasal radar and Lindley was no exception to the informed smell. Biding his time he watched and waited for his reports and statement to be thoroughly read through.

'Is this it?'. Smithery, or slippery as he was generally known to the CID, peered over his spectacles, firstly at Broughton and then at his boss.

Both men knew that slippery had risen through the greasy ranks with the panache that would have attracted the admiration of seasoned villains. "Get out from under" Smithery was well respected by most current members of the CID. His various escapades were legend: pear-shaped robbery enquiries; cock-ups on murder investigations, villains on his payroll - the circulating stories went on and on. He was, his admirers reckoned, so bent he could bring a smile to a corpse. Now he was looking from one man to the other and offering his usual prove it to me smile.

Broughton tried. 'Open and shut, sir. Williams has

stated........'.

Smithery waved a dismissing hand. 'Evidence, my dear boy, evidence', he disclaimed haughtily, staring down his nose at the two underlings.'Give me irrefutable evidence'.

Nudged by his boss Broughton tried. 'You have it there, sir. In his statement, he states.........'

'My dear boy, please. Evidence. The man is lower life alleging that one of my officers is, what, I dislike using the word: dishonest!. Outrageous!'.

'But he was there, sir............'.

'Inspector. Let me explain my credo to you: each of my men is innocent of an alleged demeanour until irrefutable, you hear me, *irrefutable* evidence proves otherwise'.

'But sir........'.

'No buts, inspector. A lawyer will pull your villain's evidence to shreds. Now'. He stood up and glanced from one seated man to the other. ' Unless there is anything else?'.

Broughton stood and looked at his boss, who shrugged. 'Thank you, sir', he said as he. looked at the legend. 'Shall I inform detective inspector Lindley of your decision?'.

'Do that with my blessing, inspector'.

Once the officers had left Smithery nipped down the corridor and popped his head around commander Stewart's door. 'Got a minute, Bob?', he queried, giving that worried looking man a quick smile.

Stewart gestured to a chair. 'What's up, Charlie?'.

Smithery, settling in the chair and swivelling to face Stewart, cocked his head and demanded. 'I

want you to tell me everything detective inspector Lindley has been up to'.

*

'Slippery's not wearing the rubber heels' case against you, Brian'.

Betty, Miller's tasty bit, the belle of the flying squad's typing pool, sank her gin and it, nudged Lindley and held up her empty glass.

'Top her up, Bert', the DI told his squad sidekick. 'So tell me, Betty darling. Where's all this coming from?'.

She winked knowingly. 'Lucinda, slippery's bit on the side'.

'Hear that lads', Lindley called to his beer-swilling squad. 'Your guvnor's in the clear. Cheers'.

'Cheers, guv' they called back.

'Tell me more, love. Squashed the rubber heels did he?'.

'Bollocked them he did. Knight in bloody armour you are!'. With that said she sank her top up and held up her glass.

Lindley held up it up to the barman and jiggled it. Gesturing to one of his squad he pointed to Betty. 'When she's downed it take her home'.

*

Chapter thirty eight

55 years old Geoffrey Hinds had a year left of his five year tenure as Metropolitan Police Commissioner. The papers in front of him, which he had read through twice to be certain the contents were as bad as the covering report, might, he thought despairingly, ruin his chance of a knighthood on retirement. 'Fred Lampard will get it sorted', he told himself grimly as he checked his watch. 'Should be here soon'. His phone rang and he listened, giving a sigh of relief. 'Show him in', he told his personal assistant, 'and bring coffees through'.

Standing, he held out a hand to one of Her Majesty's Inspector of Constabulary: a plump, elderly man; who shook it warmly.

'Sit down, Fred. I'm glad to see you'.

Easing himself onto the chair Hinds had pointed at he wriggled to get comfortable and smiled across at his friend. 'What have you got for me, Geoff?', he asked, grimacing at the usual twinge.

'Something wrong down there Fred?.

Lampard gave a rueful smile. 'Hip playing up. Getting old -osteo-arthritis I've been advised'.

'Oh. I'm sorry to hear that. No more golf then!'.

'Packed that in a year back'.

Hinds nodded and moved on to the reason his friend was there. 'The Home Secretary wants you on this one. Allegations of corruption and possibly, I'll put it no stronger than that, of multiple murder. Might have got as far as my deputy commissioner for crime: you know Charlie Smithery, I believe?'.

'Yes. Ex chief constable of Wessex. Met him once'.

'Nasty smell about this one. My flying squad commander may be dragged in; and one of his DI's. And............', he paused to stare at his friend, 'detective inspector Masters, *again*!'.

Lambert raised an eyebrow at the mention of the detective inspector. 'Specifics?', he asked interestedly.

The Commissioner pushed a thickish file across his desk. 'Read that lot, Fred', he advised his friend. 'I won't try to minimise the seriousness of your enquiry. It goes beyond Masters and the various allegations that have surfaced. At his station there's a detective sergeant who might well be a multiple killer. He's part of your enquiry..................'.

Lambert broke into Hinds flow of words. 'Killer!.

'Killer, Fred. A10 have done their best but he's either a crafty bastard or completely innocent. Understand this, Fred. I'm jumping the gun here but once you've read that lot', he nudged the file, 'we'll need to get together to decide which way to go'.

Lampard studied his friend's expression and got the intended message.' The Met, Geoff?'.

'You've got in one, Fred'.

Lampard let the file stay on the desk while his thoughts ran back to his Leytonstone enquiry. ' Sneed was small fry on that enquiry. Masters got lucky'.

The door opened and his assistant brought in their refreshments, smiled, and left.

'Help yourself to the biscuits, Fred. Let's not fight over the chocolate ones!'.

Both men made their choice and sipped and Hinds, his cup back on the tray, looked intently at the other man. 'We're also looking at allegations of murder against DI Lindley. He's been put in the frame by a couple of villains - both doing time for the killing'. He smiled wearily and studied Lampard's concerned expression. 'No absolute proof, Fred, but the damage has been done. In there', he tapped the file, 'is all I have. You'll find statements by locked up villains Lindley and Masters had dealings with; and names of men on the fringe. Miller is an enigma. The word is he's a violent bastard but murder................sort it Fred. For Christ's sake put it to bed'.

Lampard looked at the file and then at Hinds. Pointing at it he suggested: 'The evidence in there must be strong, Geoff, or I wouldn't be sitting here. How strong?'.

Hinds spread his hands. 'Strong enough. At Masters' nick it was common knowledge he was having an affair with a Mrs Bruce. Her old man, by the way, died in an incident in a local park - he was wheel-chair bound and drowned in a lake. She was found dead a day later - the coroner accepted she fell down stairs and broke her neck'.

'And you don't believe that?'.

'Frankly I don't know what to believe. It might have been the accident he decided, it might have been suicide; but it might have been worse'.

Lampard sipped and waited.

Hinds hunched forward. 'Masters and detective sergeant Miller had interviewed her the day her husband drowned', he explained. 'With what has been filtered to me about Miller anything is possible'.

Lampard was intrigued. 'What has Miller been up to?'.

Hinds leaned forward and stared at the HMI. 'Let me be frank, Fred. On its own the Lindley enquiry is bad enough; but with Masters and Miller in the frame it could turn out to be the worst publicity the Met has had to live through. You'll know about the Lakey trial?'.

Lampard nodded. 'Alleged one if the investigating team framed him, as I recall. Lost the appeal?'.

'That's right, Fred. But............', he pushed Mrs. Miller's statement across the desk. 'Read that and you'll understand my worry. Anyway, I've laid on three detective sergeants and three detective constables to work with you. For security you'll be using Tintagel House on the south side as your base. None of the officers has any connection with this place. Hopefully', he held up crossed fingers and smiled, 'none has any connection with the officers or villains mentioned in there'. He tapped the file. 'I've authorised pool cars for you and your team. You can use the basement car park if you wish but I would advise against that. Use the one at Tintagel House. You'll be staying at the Burlingham Hotel round the back of the Yard: your team will have to make do with a section house billet. Have I covered everything?'.

Lampard mentioned an obvious obstacle. 'Divisional cooperation, Geoff. It simply won't be there. Last time I knocked my head against a wall of obstruction. How can you overcome it this time?'.

Hinds had been expecting the concern. 'Memos have already gone to each division. You are enquiring into efficiency from the beat up. My instructions are for your team to be given all the support needed'. Hinds stood and thrust out a hand. 'I know you'll be thorough, Fred. Good hunting!'.

*

Frederick Lampard, at 62, had aged fairly well. Hair had turned grey, but he still had it, which was a bonus for his life style. He'd served thirty years, the last five but one as a Chief Constable at the top of the greasy pole. Still in that role reality dawned when he was approached about retirement with a promise he would be considered for the post of one of Her Majesty's Inspector of Constabulary, a position when offered he accepted.

Fred preferred the slim type to cuddle up to; but Mavis, his wife of 25 years, blonde but now going grey, ensconced in their Yorkshire home with her cat, had let herself go a bit and bedroom activity, she made it very clear, was definitely off limits.

Still being up for it he frequently sought the company of well presented, slim, blonde, prostitutes. His pocket diary contained the phone numbers of those he had bedded and, sitting on the bed in his room at the Burlingham, he flicked pages, stopping from time to time to put lithe bodies to names and relish the experiences he'd had. He stopped flicking at Margaret, untiring Margaret he recalled with a satisfied smile and made a call. When she answered, memory flooded back of their exquisite times together when he was running the Leytonstone enquiry. His old man stirred. 'It's Fred, Margaret'.

'Fred?...........Oh, Mr. Lampard! How are you?'.

'Fine, just fine. And you?'.

She pulled her dressing gown over her bare knees and watched her client dressing. 'I'm well, Fred. Staying at the Burlingham again?'.

'Yes, Margaret. Can I pop over tonight?'.

'One moment Fred'....................she counted the notes the young man had placed on her bedside table and nodded to him, holding a finger to her lips while she flipped her diary. Cupping the receiver she waited until the door closed. 'Of course. What time?'.

'Eight o'clock?'.

'That will be fine, Fred. I 'm looking forward to seeing you again'.

*

Later that evening, pleasured by Margaret in the chair they favoured, showered and refreshed, it took half an hour to get to Tintagel House, via the Burlingham Hotel to pick up his briefcase, where the six detectives were waiting for him in the room set aside. 'Morning, gentlemen', Lampard said brusquely as he looked at each in turn. Let's get down to business. Firstly, are you clear on what we're to do?'. Their nods answered that. 'You are not to discuss what we're investigating to anyone, no matter how senior. Refer those that get nosey to me. I've had copies made of the information to hand. I want each of you to read them thoroughly. We've got officers in our sights: our task is to establish innocence or guilt. Can't be difficult can it!', he added with a grim smile.

'We in teams, sir?'.

'You are. We're digging into detective inspectors Masters and Lindley and sergeant Miller'. He laid file copies on his desk and tapped them 'Read them thoroughly. Come up with villains, in or out of prison, who can add to that information. They've put away many villains, but I want you to concentrate on what Masters been up since his present positing to Walthamstead. Sergeant Miller is in Masters team. Lindley's been in the flying squad for two years. When you've got names not mentioned in those files get back to me and I'll sort out who does what. Clear?'.

They nodded.

'That's it for now: get started'.

*

Len Spence dropped his holdall in the hall and saw from Jane's expression something was up. He took her by the shoulders and looked into her worried eyes . 'What is it, love? Come on...I can tell something's happened'.

She gripped his wrists and told him what had been on her mind since Betty Davenport dropped by that morning. 'Dave's been pulled in. From what she picked up earwigging at a door when the old bill was at her place early this morning, Jimmy and Brian have put him up for the blag you sorted'. She looked past him at the holdall. 'Don't tell me the gun's in it, Len'.

'No, love. In the lock up. There's fifteen grand in it though'. He was grinning broadly. 'Job went off sweet as a nut. Ted's got his share'.

'Len! For Gawd's sake! Get it out of here! The old bill could be lurking out there somewhere! I've told you before: nothing comes here'.

Spence had moved away and was hefting the bag, but inwardly he knew his missus was right. 'Keep calm, love', he said soothingly. 'I'll drop by the lock up again. But first I must make a call'.

'Len...........'. She pulled him close again. 'Who else knows about the lock-up?'.

'Only Ted'.

'Not Dave?'.

'No love............you think Ted might have let it slip?'. He was staring back at her but his thoughts had shifted to the possibility she had hinted at. 'No. He wouldn't. He's got his own lock-up to worry about'.

'How much is in it, Len?'. Her worried grip on his arm had tightened at the thought of losing a lot of dosh if the old bill came calling for a pay-off.

'Around thirtyfive grand, love - not including this', he raised the hold-all.

'Just be careful, Len. Can't trust no-one, you remember that. And the money'd be safer in our caravan at Yarmouth'.

'I'll see to it, love. You and me can nip there this weekend. But I must make that call: got to find out what's going on'.

*

Masters got the call and the following morning drove to the usual café. Spence was tucked in a corner scoffing a bacon sandwich with a steaming mug of tea beside him, staring at the approaching Masters as he chewed. Dropping into a chair opposite, Masters saw that Spence had troubles on his mind so asked the obvious: 'Fill me in, Len. What's up?'.

Swallowing the mouthful, Len picked up his mug and squirted tea around his closed mouth to clean his teeth before leaning forward to give the detective a suspicious stare. 'Why has Dave been nicked?'.

The news brought a worried expression to Masters' face. 'First I've heard of it, Len. Where's this coming from?'.

'His wife. Dave was nicked at his drum yesterday. From what Betty told Jane he's been tugged for the blag we sorted. Jimmy and Brian have put him in the frame. For all I know they might have fingered me an' all'. He kept his hard stare on Masters' face. 'Don't you lot work together?. You must have some idea what's going on?'.

'All this is news to me, Len. Did Betty say any more?'.

Shaking his head, Spence sat back and wiped his mouth with the back of a hand and lit a fag.

Masters saw from his expression he didn't believe what he was hearing. 'Believe me, Len. But I soon will. Be bloody careful who you meet and talk to until I find out what's going on'. He stood up. 'Don't bell me. I'll arrange a meet when I know more'. He stuck out a hand and Spence, who had also got to his feet and shook it. Still holding Masters' hand he stared into his eyes. 'I want to trust you, Don. Don't let me down'.

*

Word travelled fast to West End Central. Detective

inspector John Sayle got the tip off from his favourite tom that Lampard was back in town and staying at the Burlingham; and knocking off Margaret, again.

'When?'.

'Yesterday evening, John. Saw him come in. Stayed an hour'.

'Thanks Kim. You free this evening?'.

'Always free for you, John. Make it nine o'clock: busy up to then'.

'I'll be there'.

*

Daphne Jenkins, a lovely blonde was achingly missing Brian Winch. On yet another visit they'd chatted about the usual, but she knew he was excited about something else. 'Tell me, love. What is it?'. She dotted her fag and glanced across at the screw. ' He aint listening', she urged, 'tell me'.

'Had a visit, aint I'. He leaned closer. 'A copper'.

Daphne, Daff to Brian and his mates, nodded but a frown creased her forehead. 'Been in here a year Brian. Aint done nuffink have you?'.

'Don't frown like, Daff. Not me he's after. You know that copper wot nicked me.....Masters?'.

'Yea. Well, sort of'.

'It's him'.

'What d'you mean it's him?'.

'It's him he's after. Got the message straight off I did. Bent he is'.

'Did he say so?'.

'Didn't have to did he. Questioned me about the break ins he did. Wanted me to tell him all about that frigging detective and Charlie. Seen George, he had. Reckoned he stuck the knife in the copper and Charlie'.

'What did you tell him?'.

'Told him about Charlie an' all I did. Still pissed off about him'.

'Here love. Have some fags'. Daphne pushed her hand covering a packet across the table and Brian slid it from under, eye-balling the watching screw until the packet was out of sight.

'Ta, Daff. Do wiv 'em. You might get a visit from the dick. He knew about you'.

The expression on Daphne's beautiful face immediately shifted to concern and the frown was back. She and her mum still had nicked clothing and cosmetics in the garage. Most of their nicked gear had found new homes but times were hard out there: buyers were looking for bargains. 'Oh, Brian', she whispered fearfully. 'What did he say about me?'.

'Nuffin' much. Knew you an' me knocked about together. Knew about George's bird an' all. Like I told you - it aint you they want. It's that Masters bloke'.

'Mum'll go mad, love. She really will. Never been sussed and now this'. On edge with the worry of it all she gripped her lover's hand. 'Got to go, love. Never know do ya. Can't trust the old bill, my dad says they're filth'.

'True that, Daff. The screw's heading this way', he whispered, and spotted the other visitors were making their way to the exit. 'Give us a kiss....and don't worry'.

*

George Brothwell's bird, Judy Finnegan, studied Daphne's worried face and then the gear stacked from floor to ceiling at the back of the garage. 'I can't, Daph. Really I can't. Mum'll do her nut if I ask her'.

'But Judy............*please*. You dad's got a Tranny, he could shift that lot in no time. He could store it in his mate's garage. It wouldn't be for long', she urged her friend.

'Maybe the copper won't come here?'.

'And maybe he will! Brian told me he knew I was his girlfriend. Mum don't know about the copper.............she'll go mad if I tell her'.

'She'll ask why my dad's moving the stuff. What then?'.

'Got some buyers lined up aint he. I'll tell her that'.

'I'll ask him this evening'. She watched her friend lower the door and took her hand and walked with her back to her house. 'Dad's got to be careful, Daph. Him an' his mates have pulled jobs lately....no it's alright', she said quickly when Daphne let her concern show. 'Dad does money not stuff. Stacks of room in the garage'.

'The old bill don't know about the garage do they?'.

'No, Daff. Dad's got a deal going with the local dicks. Your stuff'll be safe enough'.

*

Detective sergeant Browning, leader of a Lampard team, shrewdly reckoned that uncovering relationships was the key to success. Once Winch and Brothwell had seen the light and come across, he and his mate had housed Charlie Hobbs in the house he shared with Gillian; and a search at CRO turned up Ray Jenkins, father of Daphne, Brian's bird. Jenkins was on record for housebreaking as a youngster; a bit of GBH - on two occasions; and a not guilty on an armed robbery charge the previous year. His accomplice, also found not guilty of that charge, was Judy's father, Kirk Finnegan. Their CRO files appended detective inspector John Sayle at West End Central as the unsuccessful officer running the case. With Charlie Hobbs in his sights he soon got to Masters, and

Makepeace, his chief superintendent. Reading the arrest files and court papers he filled in the missing pieces and recognised which way Masters' wind had blown at those times.

'I agree'. Lampard told him when he'd read through the report. 'A bit of the softly softly approach might work with Hobbs. From his background I'd hazard a guess he's a thicko'.

'You alright, sir?', the sergeant asked when his boss slid his arse about on the hard chair.

'Fine, sergeant. Just fine. Hip - you know'.

'Oh. I see'. Remembering what he had originally had in mind he asked 'What do you want done about Jenkins and Finnegan? They got away with their blag because the officer running the job cocked up'.

'How?'.

'Failing to follow procedure at the ID parades. The judge stopped the trial and instructed the jury to bring in a not guilty verdict'.

'Sweetener?'

'Smells of it, sir'.

'I agree. Put that to oneside for the minute: Len Spence..........'., he gestured to a thickish file of papers, 'according to Cooke and Burke he was on the job as well. Now Davenport', he flicked through his papers before peering at the other officers, 'he states that Spence not Fred put him up to driving a car for the job. So much for friendship!'. He sat back and thought. 'Makepeace now. He stated to you'..............he pointed to one of the detective constable...............'that detective sergeant Fountain had alleged that a detective constable Barton had admitted giving false evidence relating to an identification parade. How much weight should we attach to that?'.

'It's hearsay, sir, but believable. Masters may have got him to give that evidence'.

'And promotion followed for both of them. Strange way to handle the allegation!'. Lampard leaned back and studied the ceiling for a few seconds, which stretched to a couple of minutes, squirming when his hip gave him gyp, before suddenly he brought the floating chair legs down and said, decision made, 'Bring in Hobbs'.

*

The blag back then had been a doddle. Detective inspector Sayle admitted at the time they'd played a blinder. It was right up there with the best. His guvnor had congratulated him with a "well done, John" in the West End central canteen. His percentage from the blag had been a fairish earner. But the phone call worried him: Jenkins, he heard, was a worried man. Now, in a café he heard it again. 'One of your lot's put my daughter in the frame. And no', he said when he saw the puzzled look on the detective's face, 'I haven't a frigging clue. Sort it. She's a a good girl so leave her out of this'.

'Ray', Sayle leaned forward to make his point. 'I've no idea what you're going on about. Leave her out of what? Daphne's not on my radar'.

'That's not what she's picked up from prison. Her boyfriend's told her your lot have her in their sights. It aint right. Like I said: leave her out'.

'Are you going off half cocked or what? I'm still in the dark', the detective said, spreading his hands and demanding, 'Just what's been going on?'.

Jenkins stared hard at the officer. 'Sort it. If she gets grief from your lot you'll get grief from me. I mean it', he added ominously to the worried detective.

*

Having belled Masters for a meet, Sayle looked across the café table and unburdened his concern about Lampard nosing around. 'I've no real idea what he's after, that's what worries me, Don. I'm getting it in dribs and drabs. Did you know he's shagging a tom? The mind boggles, I mean he's in his sixties, must be'.

Masters was intrigued at the news. 'Got a name for her?'.

Sayle nodded. 'Margaret Bland. Works my manor'.

'Know where?'.

'Oh, yes. Same house as my snout'.

'That's interesting, John. It gives us something to work with down the road. This Margaret bird : young, old?'.

'Tasty bit in her thirties at a guess. My snout reckons Lampard used her services the last time he was in town - that's the Sneed enquiry'. He grinned across at Masters. 'Rocked your boat back then didn't he!'.

Masters nodded but he was deep in thought. The rumours flying around had the bastard questioning villains he'd put away and that spelled real trouble. Spence was sure he'd been put in the frame by Burke and Cook. And Davenport was giving Spence a wide berth. And then there was Charlie, who had belled him that a mate in the same nick as Brian Winch had got word to him he'd been put up for a burglary.

Seeing Masters expression change he asked 'What is it?'.

'He's got to be stopped, John', the DI told him. 'Fancy another cuppa?'. When his friend nodded he stood and stared hard at Sayle. 'Give it serious thought, John. I've got too much at stake to let Lampard run loose on my manor'. He turned away and walked to the counter. When he got back with their mugs Sayle told him he agreed.

With his mind on what Charlie had told him Masters explained his thinking: 'I know his team have sussed the girl friends of two youngsters I put away. They're the daughters of your two blaggers, Jenkins and Finnegan'.

Sayle had already made that connection, remembering Jenkins threat. 'Where d'you get it from, Don?'.

'Word from a very reliable snout, John. He's got a friend doing bird with my scallywags. Lampard and his crew'll do what we do, he'll get to your blaggers, and then to you'.

'Christ! It never occurred to me'.

'Well think about it now. If he and his team question them, what are they going to say? Your snout'll get drawn in, and then it'll be your turn. I'm in that boat, John'.

Sayle sipped his coffee and stared unseeingly at Masters, trying to see through the misted confusion to the end game. 'You got anything in mind?'.

'The tom's the best way. I can't see how to do it at the moment but she's the key'.

'Makes sense', Sayle muttered while his thoughts jumped about a bit.. 'My snout could help there. Alright, I agree'. He looked at Masters grim face and understood his friend was very serious. 'Leave it to me for a few days, Don. I'll work something out and get back to you'.

Both men clambered to their feet and shook hands. Masters, still holding the other man's hand held it tighter when he said 'I mean it, John. He's got to be stopped. Stop him and the snooping around stops with him. Agreed?'.

'Definitely'.

On their walk to their cars Masters told his friend

he'd arrange a meeting with commander Stewart. 'He'll want to keep tabs on anything Lampard turns up'.

'Want me there?'.

Masters, leaning against his car by then, thought before shaking his head.. 'Stay on the side lines, John. I'll keep you posted'.

Sayle dropped into his car. nodded, and was gone.

*

Stewart and Masters had polished off the last of their Indian meals and were on brandy, mulling over the various solutions they'd toyed with. Stewart wiggled his glass as a pointer when he said the obvious, again: 'We've got to catch the bastard with his trousers down'.

Masters had already been down that route and said so. 'I agree. Point is keeping our noses clean when its done. Who can we trust to join the firm?'.

'What about DI. Sayle's snout? Tom is she?'.

'She is', Masters confirmed.

'Sound out Sayle. Find out if he's up for using her'.

*

Chapter thirty nine

With six months gone since the robbery, Charlie and Gillian were more deeply in love and still living in the the two up and down council house Masters had found for them

Now, sitting in the sparse windowless room in Tintagel House he was facing detectives who, hopefully he prayed inwardly, didn't have a clue about his criminal relationship with Masters; but the way the interrogation was going it seemed it was definitely Masters they wanted to nail.

Charlie had been detained as he and Gillian, enveloped in Charlie's cuddle, approached the front door of their house. Gillian, pushed to oneside in the kerfuffle on the footpath when he was being handcuffed, had demanded unsuccessfully to know why her man was being taken away.

Now, vividly remembering how the detective had rudely shoved her away when he was being hustled into their car he stared at detective sergeant Blade, unable to prevent his intense dislike showing.

The interrogation had been ongoing for an hour and Charlie's composure had been nudged a bit, his worried expression let that much slip, but the two detectives quizzing him missed the significance of Charlie's discomfort when they dragged detective inspector Masters name into their chat up line.

'Got on well with him by all accounts', Blade suggested, watching for a reaction.

Charlie got the drift and kept a steady gaze on the detective he despised. He hadn't been told why he'd been pulled in, but mention of Don's name clued him up. "So that's their game", he thought as he smiled back. 'Don't know 'im that well do I', he said, trying to appear casual.

Knowing Charlie's answer was miles from the truth, Detective sergeant Blade remained patient. 'Tell you what Hobbs', he said, changing tack, let's have a cuppa. Fancy one?'.

Hearing that Charlie shrugged and nodded and stared around the interview room. Lampard, his hip giving him gyp again, was standing on his good leg by a wall and smiled at Charlie, who let a flickering smile cross his face in acknowledgement.

'Ta', Charlie told the constable who'd come in with a tray and pushed a cup across the table at him. Blade sipped and studied Charlie and shot a glance at Lampard, remembering his assessment of Hobbs as a thicko. "You're not that, me old lad" he told himself. Brightening, he suggested to Charlie 'Let's get back to Brian Winch and George Brothwell. Not best pleased with you, Hobbs. Brian says you set up the break in'.

'Wot break in?'

'Charlie, lad. We're not idiots. The job you did a runner from'.

Charlie shrugged.

'Is that a yes?'.

Charlie played it safe and shrugged again.

'Tell me about detective inspector Masters'.

'What's to tell'.

Nice bloke?'.

'Nice enough, I suppose'.

'What...even though he got you three years?'.

'Bang to rights wasn't I'.

Blade changes the subject abruptly. 'Tell me about Janet'.

'Meaning?'. Charlie was suddenly very attentive.

'Well...........my enquiries tell me she was your bit of stuff. Now she's Masters' bit of stuff. You alright with that?'.

'Have you talked to her?'.

'No, Hobbs, I haven't. But I'll get round to it'. He let time drift, meanwhile lighting a cigarette and offering Charlie one which he took with a 'Ta'.

Blade's colleague detective constable Pear, shaped like one with his wide hips and big belly, was maintaining his silent role, spotted what he thought was a chink in Charlie's armour when Janet was mentioned. He nudged Razor, as he was known, and whispered something in his ear.

Blade looked thoughtfully at Charlie. 'Still got something going for Janet?'.

'Leave her out...........just leave her out', Charlie said angrily.

Blade changed tack. 'What about Bill?'.

Charlie was puzzled. 'Bill?'.

'Gore. Bill Gore. He's put you in the frame for the burglary he went down for. Not best pleased with you, either, Hobbs. Doing a runner again. Your speciality that'.

The questioning was getting heavy and Charlie wished Masters was in the room.

'Well?'.

'Well what?'.

'Your speciality - setting up fellow villains'.

Charlie fashioned an indignant expression. 'Dunno wot you're going on about', he said. 'Yeh, I knew 'im. Worked wiv 'im once'.

Razor and his side kick gazed at each other, clearly believing they were getting somewhere with Charlie who, ignoring them, had leaned back in his hard chair and was staring at the ceiling.

His defiance was not lost on Lampard, who suggested to him 'Arrest Janet do we?'.

Charlie swung his gaze to him, and then at detective sergeant Blade. His anger showing he demanded, thumbing towards Lampard, 'Who's 'e?'.

'Our boss, Hobbs. He's why you're in here. And depending on how our chat ends up she stays in the clear or gets nicked'.

Making that implied threat indicated how little they understood Charlie, who loved Janet and Gill equally. He sat listening to their crap which, in the normal course of events would have sailed over his head and been completely ignored, but not this time. He was angry, and it showed. 'Leave Janet out of this, you arseholes', he told them.

Lampard hopped across the room on his good leg and squeezed Blade's shoulder. 'Bang him up. We'll start afresh in the morning'.

*

Jane Spence's natural worry that the filth were out there somewhere faded when Len eased his car beside their mobile home on the caravan park in Yarmouth. The first one out she opened the caravan door and beamed at her man. 'Thank Gawd' she declared, breathing in the stale air wafting out. ' It's nice to be here'.

Len got out and gazed around at the other brick-skirted mobile homes, and nodded his agreement as he lugged his holdall up the steps and handed it to Jane.

"I'll stash the cash wiv the uvver', she declared. 'Where's the screwdriver?'.

'Kitchen drawer, love'.

*

Don Masters, with the phone receiver at his right ear, held up a hand to Miller, who had just entered his office. 'Who? Right. Try not to worry, Gill......... yes.......yes..........leave it with me. Yes, of course. When

I've got something I'll get back to you'. He replaced the receiver and looked at the sergeant, who had settled in the chair opposite his desk. 'It seems that Lampard's done his homework', he told him quietly. He sat back he stared at Miller's questioning face. 'He's pulled Charlie in', he explained.

'Who's Gill?'.

'Charlie's woman. If he's got any sense he's told her sod all'.

'Rely on that can we?'.

'No option. I think it's time for John Sayle's tom to come up with something to put a spanner in his works'. He lifted the handset and dialled West End Central. 'DI Sayle, please', he told the woman who answered. While he waited to be put through he eyed Miller, who was frowning. 'John's alright, Dusty. He's our best bet, believe me'.

*

The West End Central detective inspector nipped away from his station to spruce himself up for his assignation. Unlike most of his colleagues, Sayle was still a bachelor. The very last thing he wanted was a permanent relationship; and enjoying sex with Kim, his present bedmate, provided for all his desires; and her being a prostitute made his enjoyment of their dalliances even better. Eyelid fluttering birds were not for him. In his twenties he'd learned all about security-seeking women who professed love but were really out for a lasting relationship. When it became obvious to the various maidens he'd bedded that it was all he wanted and good bye, they drifted to his mates and the silly sods married them.

At her apartment door he rang the bell and stood in front of the glass peep-hole. It was something he knew she wanted: being sure who was out there was essential in her game.

The door swung open and there she was, Beautiful Kim in the slinky dress she always wore for him. She stood to oneside for him to pass and patted his bum. 'Go through, John. I've got an hour, that's all', she explained.

Sayle thought he understood. 'An hour for me - or until your next client'. he queried as he shook off his coat.

'For you of course'. She went straight to the bedroom and left the door wide open. Turning, she did as she always did for him, seductively beckon.

John, waiting for the gesture, went in and, as always while she stood still, he slid off her dress and took his time tweaking and removing silky underclothes, kissing boobs and hoisting her into his strong arms and, kissing her on the way, lowered her onto the silk sheets of the King sized bed.

Laying there she was a picture so alluring that, unusually for him, this time he stripped slowly, content to soak up the magic of her presence. Finally, naked, he slipped beside her and began his practised routine which they each enjoyed. His eventual penetration, and her faked orgasmic cries when his passion erupted were, for him, the raison d'etre of his existence.

Cigarette time came and went and Sayle got round to what Masters wanted. 'So what do you think, Kim?', he asked. He didn't expect her to do it but by the look on her face she might.

'I dunno, John. Bit risky. Fancy a cuppa?'.

'Could do with one. I'm serious, Kim. At least ask her'. The detective climbed out and turned on the shower, quickly rinsing himself down and donning his clothes. Joining her in her kitchen he dropped into a chair and picked up his mug and sipped, watching for a reaction.

'Margaret's a good friend, John. I dunno, really I don't'. Kim placed a mirror on the table between them and carefully applied her working face..

'Got many this evening?'.

'Three regulars'.

'You'll at least think about it.......yes?'.

Face on she looked across and smiled. 'How do I look?'.

'Lovely, Kim. You always do'.

'Alright.............I'll think about it. Now you really must go. I've got half an hour to tidy up the place'.

*

Her Majesty's Inspector of Constabulary spent his usual time preparing to meet her for the second time that week. He studied his reflection in the long mirror and patted his stomach. Remembering her comment he told himself ruefully, "Should get it down, Fred". On the whole though - not too bad for an old'n. He checked his watch. Time to be off again.. Because Margaret's place was a walking distance away and the evening was mild and not raining, he decided to walk. Excited at what awaited him, he stepped out in Margaret's direction, singing under his breathe and telling himself how good life was to be free of the missus's nagging.

Margaret had bade her last customer farewell and was spending luxurious minutes under her shower. Removing the shower head from it's parking slot she directed the hot stream of water between her legs and, satisfied with the result there, turned the jet against her belly and boobs. It was important they were clean because Fred was particular about her boobs. Job over she towelled and sprayed and donned the dressing gown he had bought her the last time he was in town.

She glanced at the wall clock: thirty minutes to go.

He was early when he pressed the bell but Margaret didn't know that. She opened the door a crack and smiled with relief. 'Come in Fred. I thought I'd overbooked'. Taking his hand she led him to the settee and helped him out of his top coat. 'There. That's better, isn't it?'. Once he'd settled himself on the settee, wriggling to get his dodgy leg comfortable, she poured and handed him a glass of his favourite white wine. Chinking her glass with his she said 'Bottoms up'.

Lampard smiled at the possibility it was a joke. 'Later, Marge. I'll down this first'.

Margaret smiled and sat beside him and brushed a speck from his trousers. Smiling, she asked: 'Tell me why you're really in town'.

He squeezed her fingers and told her frankly. 'Chasing dishonest coppers, Marge. Too many about'. He handed her his glass. 'Help me up, Marge. It's this bloody hip'.

Once he was on his feet he tweaked her dressing gown cord and gazed with even more admiration at her perfect body. 'Help me out of my clothes. You know what I like'.

Margaret took time doing it because it was the way he liked it. With him naked she slipped off her dressing gown and moved close in front of him, reaching for his engorged penis and, using fingertips, stroked it, staring into his half-closed eyes, and feeling the sharpness of his fingernails digging into her waist.

'Stop!', he whispered urgently. 'I mustn't go yet'.

She led him to his favourite reclining chair and held his hands while he settled back and stared up at her, expectantly. 'Now, Marge. Now!', he urged.

They always started this way because of her concern for his dodgy hip, and Fred Lampard was, as ever, grateful. He sat starkers on the special chair Margaret acquired after his first trip to town, and Margaret expertly straddled him and located his penis straight off. Holding her bare bum as she pushed against his rigid old man he whispered into the boobs that were slapping his face, 'Lovely, Marge, lovely'. He licked a nipple and screwed his head to look up at her. 'Alright up there?', he gasped as he fired both barrels.

Easing off his slackening manhood she stood up, smiled down into his half-closed eyes, nodded, and reached for a small towel she kept handy. Wiping off his sticky stuff she patted his head and reached for her dressing gown. 'Works every time, Fred. Nice for you was it?'.

'Lovely, Marge. I needed that'.

'It's a shower and off, Fred. I've got a busy evening'.

Already heading for the shower he raised a fluttering hand. 'Fifteen minutes, Marge, and I'll be gone'.

*

Quentin Lacey was curious. Sitting in the snug of their usual boozer he sipped his wine and waited for John Sayle to put in an appearance. The phone call hadn't let much slip, except there was a chance of a scoop. He was sipping when Sayle sauntered in and waved as he went to the bar. Glasses in hand the detective inspector dropped into a chair opposite the reporter, pushing a glass across. 'Cheers', he said, holding up his glass.

'Cheers'.

Both men sipped and Quentin, an investigative reporter for the Daily News, waited for Sayle to tell him what the meet was about.

'Fred Lampard', Sayle said out of the blue.

'Who's he?'.

'One of Her Majesty's Inspectors of Constabulary,

Quentin. Might be the scoop of the year for you. Fancy catching him with his cock hanging out?'.

The reporter stared hard at Sayle. 'You are serious aren't you?'. he said, his voice tinged with hope.

'Deadly serious. He's having it off with a tom. Can't get better than that, surely!'.

With the prospect of a scoop Quentin queried: 'Where, when, and how much, John?'.

'The where is here'. Sayle pushed a piece of paper across. 'Second floor. I can provide keys to get you in to do the business. A grand'll cover it'.

'Up front?'.

'When you get the keys will do. Still interested?'.

'Definitely, John'.

'Fair enough. Leave it with me for a few days. I'll sort the time and the day one hundred per cent. I must have the keys back. Fair enough?'.

Quentin looked over his glass rim.'What's it really about?'.

Sayle sat back and studied his friend. 'Trust you - yes?'.

'Definitely'.

'Right. He's on a fishing expedition. He's trying to nail friends of mine'.

'Point made, John'. He raised his glass and smiled his cheeky smile. 'Can't have that can we!'.

Sayle pointed to their glasses. 'Another one?'.

'Thanks, John, but I've got to get back'.

*

The unintended consequences of Lampard's sniffing in divisions and the Yard had spread widely. Bent officers were peering nervously over shoulders; and villains doing bird who'd cooperated with Lampard's teams were salivating at the enjoyable prospect of beating up convicted detectives. Masters, who Hinds had instructed was not to be interrogated without irrefutable evidence, had sailed on regardless with lovely Janet; and Charlie, who loved Gill even more, had relished fronting the bastards who'd been trying to stitch up his mate Don.

Spence had been pulled in but had successfully no-commented the allegations of his fellow blaggers; and Dave Davenport had a memory recall when Masters got word to him via Len to remember it was Fred in a pub.

The intended consequences were far from achieved. Lampard's files had grown thick with anecdotal evidence; but real evidence, the stuff coppers were ever hopeful of unearthing to earn a few bob, was thin on the ground. The totality of what was discovered came down to whom to believe.

Lampard was confident his teams could at least get enough on Masters, Lindley and Miller to put an end to their careers.

Janet had not been pulled in: Hinds had stepped in on that one as well. Because she was co-habiting with Masters, his insistence that suspicion was not sufficient to humiliate her even, as Lampard had insisted, if it could open the door to bringing Masters down. Lampard was angry, as he told his team of detectives, but he had no other option.

Villains were up for doing coppers down; but word in prison was: where would it all end? Charlie's housebreaking mates, their girl friends and the reprobates that Master had locked up, one by one saw the sense of silence when word got to them: prison life does that to villains. They had to face their fellow inmates daily, and many had good reason not to dish the dirt on their CID conspirators.

Lampard was in the hotel dining room and studying the

synopsis of what his men had gleaned, and realised, finally, he had sod all on Masters. That's twice you bastard, he told himself Lindley maybe. But Miller? Betty of the flying squad sin bin had remained useless as a witness. Clever girl, he reckoned. But the doubt remained, frothing Lakey was a constant reminder of that.

Lampard pushed away his soup bowl and raised a hand. The eagle-eyed waiter, pushing his laden trolley, weaved between tables and stopped at his and slid Fred's main meal in front of him. Receiving the expected nod he moved on and Fred tucked into his roast beef and veg and thought ahead to Margaret………………………………

*

When it flashed, Margaret was, as usual, faking but Fred Lampard was in the throes of a ball-emptying climax; and the wondrous sexual exhilaration and fulfilment Fred was experiencing was captured and etched forever into the film of the smirking photographer.

Fred and Margaret, peering in astonishment at the two men, one of whom was snapping away, and still clinging together in sweaty endeavour, were late to realise the significance of what had just been recorded for posterity.

Quentin tip-toed to the recliner and dropped his card between the perspiring couple. 'See you on the front page', he said with a disarming chuckle.

Margaret was the first to regain her self respect. She eased herself from Fred's shrinking penis and, still straddling and heedless of her naked state, stared up and demanded 'Who are you?'.

'Press, love', Quentin responded. 'Anything you'd

like to tell me about him?'.

Fred Lampard saw his longed for knighthood disappearing down the swanny. He looked down over his protruding belly at his naked state and recognised, as any sensible copper would when the chips have fallen badly, that his exposed cock, and naked Margaret, who was still straddling him, had done for him. 'Which newspaper do you work for?', he managed to say while he was doing his best to help Margaret up. Succeeding in that he struggled out of the recliner, his train of thought definitely chaotic but slowly getting into gear.

"Not the point is it', Quentin told him. 'You're news. The media will go into overdrive once they get what we've got on you'.

By now clear of Fred's legs and clad in her dressing gown Margaret asked, a hoped for persuasiveness in her tone. 'Can we settle this here and now?'.

'Why not', Quentin told her. 'We can agree a fee if you tell me all'. He sat on an armchair and watched Lampard dress. 'Something wrong down there?', he queried when Fred stumbled trying to pull on his trousers.

Dodgy hip', Lampard told him automatically. He carried on dressing, his thoughts a million miles from the flat. His wife's accusing face looming large, he turned to study the men who had him by the short and curlies. 'What happens now?'.

'Use your loaf - front page tomorrow'.

'Do you have to go that far? Can't we come to an arrangement?'.

'What have you got in mind?'.

'A thousand pounds perhaps?'.

Quentin shook his head and looked across to Margaret 'I think we need to talk'.

She looked at Fred, who was staring pleadingly at

her, and then back at Lacey. 'Keep your tape recorder on and fire away'.

*

Commissioner Hinds, seated behind his resplendent desk, pushed a newspaper to one side and picked up the next one in the pile. With a slight deviation from the Daily News coverage it told the same story. He pulled the Daily News back in front of him and stabbed it and glared across at Lampard, who was slumped in a chair, head in hands.

'You stupid bastard', he said to him. 'This has finished you, you must know that'.

Lampard was beyond consolation and could only nod.

Hinds leaned forward to make a point, 'This bloody woman set you up. She will have been paid a mint for her story. My God, Fred. What made you do it! And offering the reporter a thousand pounds! Where was your brain'.

Lampard lifted his head briefly and then stared down at the carpet. 'I thought I could trust them. It's as simple as that'.

'Trust!'. Hinds said coldly as he continued to stare at Lampard.'Trust a prostitute! Trust a reporter!Are you mad! You realise this puts your enquiry to bed. How can I convince CPS, let alone the Director of Public Prosecutions, your enquiries are faultless? How. Tell me that? Where was your judgement?'.

Lampard couldn't face Hinds. He was thinking way ahead to the nagging he was going to get; and the ridicule at The Home Office.

'You are well and truly tainted, Fred. Nobody will believe a word you say. And this................' he pulled Lampard's file in front of him, 'is useless. If your investigation were to get to court you'd be ripped to pieces. God knows how I can explain what's gone wrong to the Home Secretary'. He stood up and peered down at the crestfallen, broken man. 'You'll be fired, you must know that. My view is it would be better all round if you were to resign forthwith. Go home, Fred'.

*

Word of Lampard's demise quickly slid down the greasy, corrupt pole at New Scotland Yard, and fanned out to the divisions, relieving the minds of the many bent detectives who, knowing what they had been getting up to on a daily basis, had temporarily accepted the necessary resolve to go straight while his campaign was on-going. Gladly they returned to the corrupt CID life that was a necessary adjunct to the way things should be done. Solicitors and their villainous clients gladly returned to paying their dues to the CID; and Metropolitan CID life returned to the normality of quick earners.

*

Masters was naturally relieved. His scheme had worked better than he could have hoped.. Murdering Kay Bruce had, from time to time naturally, concerned him. He was only too aware that all it would take was for an apparent insignificant piece of evidence to add to circumstantial evidence to bring him down. Somebody out there with a good memory for times and dates could have done it. The old biddy so far was the only one who had mentioned his Jaguar being in its usual spot, but..............and he recognised it was a big but, with Lampard out of the picture he felt reasonably sure no other witness had been unearthed: but what if one *had* been found, and that evidence lay on Lampard's file waiting to be picked up, recognised it for what it was by an ambitious detective, and nailed him?

He decided to stop thinking about Kay's tumble and get back to work. He nipped into the sergeant's office and beckoned to Miller, with a tipped-cup gesture, to follow him to the canteen and there, over coffee, because it had surfaced again, relived her demise to a dismissive Miller, who was his usual truculent self. '

I don't give a fuck, Don. She's ashes and it's over. Period'.

Masters held his mug to his lips and studied the sergeant. He sipped and put it down and put the question that needed an answer. 'Did you do it?'.

Miller stared questioningly at the DI.'What's this - the confessional?'

Masters stared back. 'No........we're friends. Friend to friend...........did you do it?'.

'It ends here?'.

Masters nodded.

'Then yes'.

'Want to tell me why?'.

Miller sat back and stared at the ceiling and appeared to be thinking. 'Don', he said, sitting forward and staring at Masters, 'Women piss me off. Tits and fanny that's all they've got'. Warming to his explanation he went on 'Why the frigging hell won't they settle for a shag? But no.............they want a relationship. It's always the same'.

'Is that how you understand Val?'.

'I don't want to get into that one'.

'She still at her mother's?'.

Miller nodded.

'Over is it?'.

Miller nodded.

'What are you going to do?'.

Miller grinned. 'Women need a good fucking........there's plenty of 'em out there'.

*

Len Spence's admiration for Masters' plan was written across his weather-beaten face. Can't see any problem'. He reached across the café table and shook Masters' hand. 'Me and Ted'll do it'. Devouring a chunk of his thick bacon sandwich he looked at Masters and grinned. 'You're in the wrong game, Don', he told him admiringly.

*

'Darling', Janet called out to her lover when he climbed out of the Jaguar and turned to wave. 'How has your day been?'.

She stood impatiently in the open doorway, adoring him as he crunched across the shingle. He took her hand and guided her into the hall. ' Just another routine day at the nick', he said softly as he placed his arms around her and nuzzled her neck. 'We really must pick up that postponed holiday. Sun and sand.........Italy wasn't it?'.

Janet turned within his arms to gaze up at his smiling face and then buried her head on his chest and shivered involuntarily when his strong arms closed more tightly around her. 'Oh, Don', she whispered. 'My beautiful man'.

*